NOW YOU DON'T

Now You Don't

Fiona Townsend

Northshore Noir Press

Northshore Noir Press
Toronto, Canada
www.northshorenoir.com

ISBN: 978-1-998648-47-4
eBook ISBN: 978-1-998648-48-1

For more information visit: northshorenoir.com or fionatownsend.com

Contents

Chapter 1

Cal Dempsey clicked through the evidence database. Case number 2438-19. Three-year-old strangulation case. Prostitute in the park. Every detective before her had missed it. The fiber match was right there in the supplemental analysis. Blue polyester with traces of motor oil. Same as Zamora's work gloves. She'd found it last night at 2 AM. Hadn't gone home.

The bullpen hummed with morning activity. Desk phones chirped. Keyboards clicked. Coffee cups steamed. Dempsey hunched over the warrant request form, pen scratching as she filled in the boxes by hand. Her back ached. Her eyes burned. Worth it.

Two female detectives from Robbery hung gold tinsel along the edges of their desks. December first. Christmas. Dempsey barely registered the date as she wrote it on the form.

"Suspect: Darius Zamora." She printed the letters in careful block capitals.

Knight's voice boomed across the room. "Bet Dempsey's idea of a hot date is a fresh corpse."

Polla's laugh followed, high and nervous. "Better conversation than you, Knight."

"At least I have conversations." Knight leaned back in his chair until it creaked. "When's the last time you had a life outside this place, Dempsey?"

Dempsey didn't look up. The form required her full concentration. Address. DOB. Prior arrests. The evidence chain that connected Zamora to the dead woman. It needed to be perfect. No technicalities. No loopholes. No way out.

She flipped through her case notes. Highlighted the fiber analysis. Made copies. Stapled them to the warrant application.

The case had gone cold under two previous detectives. Hussain had worked it first, then Miller before he retired. Both good detectives. Both had missed the fiber evidence. Not their fault. The original crime scene tech hadn't labeled it properly.

Dempsey had found it by accident. Looking for something else entirely when the mislabeled evidence bag caught her eye. A hunch made her send it to the lab. The results came back yesterday afternoon. Perfect match to Zamora's work gloves. Gloves he'd been wearing when they first questioned him three years ago. She'd seen them in the interview video.

The detectives with the tinsel laughed as they taped it up. One dropped a length that sparkled on the floor. Neither noticed.

"What do you think, RB?" Knight kicked his desk, sending his chair rolling toward Polla's desk. "Think Dempsey talks to her reflection just to hear a human voice?"

Polla adjusted his glasses. Smiled weakly. Looked away.

Dempsey printed her name and badge number on the last page. Signed and dated it. Put everything in order. Three years waiting for justice. The dead woman had a name. Carla Mendez. Twenty-six. A daughter in foster care. A mother in Phoenix. Dempsey had their numbers ready for when they made the arrest.

She carried the completed warrant request to the copier. Added the final lab report to the packet. The fiber wasn't just similar to Zamora's gloves. It was a perfect match down to the specific type of motor oil. Venneroil 10W-48. Same as in Zamora's garage. Proof he'd been there. Proof he'd lied.

Her desk phone rang. She crossed back and picked up.

"Dempsey."

"My office. Now." Chief Brandt's voice. Clipped. Pissed?

Dempsey hung up. Glanced at the warrant request in her hand. She wanted to get this to the DA immediately. Zamora worked nights. Slept during the day. Best time to arrest him would be afternoon. She wanted the warrant by noon.

"Chief wants me," she told Knight as she passed his desk.

"Better you than me." Knight spun his chair. "Probably wants to know why you're still wearing yesterday's clothes."

Dempsey ignored him. The chief's call couldn't have come at a worse time. She needed to move on Zamora today. Before he could run. Before the evidence could get contaminated or lost again.

She tucked the warrant request into a folder. Carried it with her. She'd go to the DA right after meeting Brandt. Whatever the chief wanted could wait.

The hallway to Brandt's office stretched long and quiet. Mint green walls. Polished floor. Budget meeting notices tacked to a bulletin board. Dempsey passed an office where detectives watched surveillance footage, their faces lit blue by the screens.

She rehearsed what she would tell Brandt. In and out. Fifteen minutes tops. She had a case to close. A killer to catch. A family to call with news they'd been waiting three years to hear.

Brandt's door was closed. Dempsey knocked twice. Heard "Enter" from the other side. Turned the handle.

Chief Brandt's office smelled like lemon cleaner. A water stain spread across the ceiling in the far corner. Brown. Old. Dempsey had been watching it grow for months. Brandt sat behind her desk, reading glasses perched on her nose, reviewing a document that she set aside when Dempsey entered.

"Close the door."

Dempsey did. Stood with the Zamora file pressed against her leg. Waited.

Brandt removed her glasses. Folded them carefully. Set them on a stack of personnel reports.

"I hear you broke the Mendez case."

"The fiber evidence matched. Zamora's work gloves. I need to get the warrant to the DA."

Brandt nodded. "Good work. Cold cases are the hardest."

"Three years. But we've got him now."

"You're going to make the family very happy."

Dempsey shifted her weight. The conversation felt wrong. Too much praise. Too much small talk. Brandt didn't do small talk.

"I need to catch the DA before noon if we want to make the arrest today."

"About that." Brandt leaned back. Her chair creaked. "I have another assignment for you."

Dempsey's grip tightened on the file. "I'm in the middle of three active cases."

"Knight can handle the Zamora arrest."

"It can wait until tomorrow."

"Your call. The warrant request has your name on it. Your case, your collar."

Dempsey didn't move. The Zamora case had consumed her for weeks. Every night. Every weekend. She'd reviewed every report. Every photo. Every interview. What was one more day, except everything.

"What's the assignment?" Her voice stayed flat.

"Mara Snowden hasn't shown up for work in two days."

"The photographer?"

"Yes. She missed a scene yesterday morning. Another today. Not answering calls or texts."

Dempsey's eyebrows drew together. "That's a welfare check. Patrol can handle it."

"I want you to do it."

"Why?"

Brandt tapped her fingers on the desk. Once. Twice. "She was scheduled to testify in the Parsons case next week. Key witness."

The Parsons case. Drug dealer with three bodies on him. One of them a cop. The trial had been all over the news.

"You think something happened to her?"

"I think our best crime scene photographer missing work right before a major trial warrants attention."

Dempsey thought of the warrant request in her hand. The DA expecting her. Zamora sleeping, unaware they finally had him. The tidy arrangement of evidence she'd constructed that someone else would present.

"I can get the warrant, then check on Snowden."

"No."

"The family deserves—"

"They deserve to know we caught him. And they will." Brandt leaned forward. "This is important, Dempsey."

Dempsey knew that tone. No arguments. No negotiation.

"You have Snowden's address?"

"Brownstone on Fourth and Pine. Apartment 3B." Brandt handed over a slip of paper with the details. "She lives alone. Department tried calling but got voicemail."

"Who's the emergency contact?"

"A little early for that, hmm?"

Dempsey took the paper. Folded it. Slipped it into her pocket.

"If it's just the flu, I'm coming back to get my warrant."

"Fair enough." Brandt picked up her glasses. Put them back on. Reached for the document she'd been reading. "Call me when you know something."

Dempsey turned to leave.

"And Dempsey?"

She paused at the door.

"Keep this quiet. Just a routine welfare check as far as anyone needs to know."

Dempsey nodded. Stepped out into the hallway. Let the door close behind her.

She stood there a moment. Stared at the Zamora file in her hand. Three years of work. Three years of dead ends and false starts. Three years of a killer walking free. And now she was doing a welfare check instead of arresting him.

Knight was at his desk when she returned to the bullpen. Feet up. Phone to his ear. Laughing at something.

She walked past, went to her desk, put the file in the drawer. Collected her coat, gun, badge. Checked her watch. 11:30. If Snowden was just sick, she could still make it back. No she couldn't.

Dempsey sat down and quickly sent an email: *Request meeting tomorrow, 6:00PM, to get run through evidence, get warrant. ~ Dempsey.*

The female detectives had finished with their tinsel. It sparkled under the fluorescent lights. Christmas music played faintly from someone's computer. Dempsey felt a thousand miles removed from all of it. She hit send, locked up her desk, and left.

She took the stairs down to the parking garage. Cold air hit her face when she stepped outside. Her unmarked car waited in its spot, frost on the windshield. She scraped it quickly. Started the engine. Let it run while she checked the address Brandt had given her. Fourth and Pine. Fifteen minutes in midday traffic.

As she pulled out of the garage, her phone rang. The DA's office. She let it go to voicemail. Nothing she could say would change anything now. Hoped for the best.

She turned toward Fourth and Pine. Snow began to fall in fine, dry flakes. Perfect weather for staying home sick. Maybe that's all it was. She'd check the apartment. Find Snowden with a fever. Be back in time to salvage something of the case she'd solved.

But as she drove, Brandt's words echoed. Key witness. Major trial. Keep it quiet. Something didn't add up. Dempsey's detective instincts, dormant since leaving the bullpen, began to wake up.

The brownstone at Fourth and Pine looked expensive. Five stories. Red sandstone. Black iron fire escape zigzagging up the facade. Snow fell against it, melting on contact, making the stone slick and dark. Dempsey parked across the street. Checked the address against Brandt's note. Right place. Wrong assignment.

Dempsey crossed the street. Snow caught in her hair. Melted down her neck. The cold felt good after too many hours in the precinct's dry heat. She hadn't showered since yesterday morning. Hadn't changed clothes. Hadn't slept more than twenty minutes at her desk.

The building entrance had an intercom system. Brass plate with apartment numbers. 3B. Snowden, M. Dempsey pressed the button. Waited. Pressed again. No answer.

She pulled out her phone. Dialed the number Brandt had given her. Let it ring until voicemail picked up. A woman's voice, professional and clipped: "This is Mara Snowden. Leave a message."

Dempsey didn't. Slipped the phone back into her pocket.

A man with a dog exited the building. Held the door open with his elbow. Looked Dempsey up and down.

"Thanks," she said, moving past him.

The lobby smelled musty. Marble floor. Old mailboxes with tarnished brass doors. A potted plant drooping in the corner. The elevator had an "Out of Order" sign taped to it. Dempsey took the stairs.

Third floor hallway. Faded carpet runner down the center. Sconce lights with yellow bulbs. The kind of building that had been fancy once. Still tried to look it.

Apartment 3B at the end of the hall. Heavy wooden door. Brass numbers. Dempsey raised her fist to knock.

Stopped.

The door wasn't fully closed. Open about an inch. No splintered wood around the lock. No tool marks on the frame. No forced entry.

Dempsey's hand moved to her gun. Didn't draw it yet. She leaned close to the gap.

"Ms. Snowden? Police."

Silence from inside.

"Mara Snowden? Detective Dempsey, Metro PD."

Nothing.

Dempsey considered her options. Call for backup. Standard procedure for an open door. But this wasn't a crime scene. Not yet. Just a welfare check on a photographer who'd missed work. Probably left her door unlocked by accident. Gone to the doctor. Visiting a friend.

Except people don't leave their doors open in the city. Especially not people who live alone. Especially not people scheduled to testify against a drug dealer with three bodies on him.

Brandt's words echoed. Key witness. Major trial. Keep it quiet.

Dempsey drew her weapon. Held it low at her side. Used her left hand to push the door open wider.

"Police. Anyone home?"

The door swung inward without resistance. No chain or deadbolt engaged. Just the door left slightly open. Like someone had intended to close it but hadn't quite managed. Or hadn't cared.

Dempsey took a breath. Felt the familiar focus settling over her. This wasn't the Zamora case. But it was something. Her instincts rarely lied.

She stepped back. Called Brandt. Got voicemail. Left a message.

"Chief, Dempsey here. At Snowden's apartment. Door's open, no signs of forced entry. No response inside. I'm going in."

She ended the call. Checked her email. Nothing from the DA. Put the phone away.

Traffic sounds filtered up from the street below. A horn. Brakes squealing. Normal city noise. Nothing to match the twist in her gut that said this wasn't normal at all.

Dempsey positioned herself to the side of the doorway. Drew her weapon properly now. Held it in both hands, pointed down.

"Police. Entering the premises."

She used her foot to push the door all the way open. Stood listening for any sound from inside. Heard nothing.

The smell hit her first. Jasmine. Strong but not overwhelming. Like a candle had been burning recently. Or perfume.

Dempsey took a step into the apartment. Paused. Listened again. Still nothing.

She glanced back at the hallway. Empty. No neighbors peeking out to see what was happening. No witnesses if this went bad.

Dempsey adjusted her grip on the gun. Stepped fully into the apartment. Kept her back to the wall. Eyes scanning for movement. Ears straining for any sound.

The entryway opened into what looked like a living room, though she couldn't see much from her position. No obvious signs of struggle or disturbance. No broken furniture. No blood spatters on the visible walls.

Her phone vibrated in her pocket. She ignored it. Focus on the scene. Deal with Knight later.

Dempsey moved forward another step. Checked corners. Checked shadows. The apartment felt empty but she couldn't be sure. Not yet.

She took another breath of jasmine-scented air. Thought of Zamora, who should be in handcuffs by now. Thought of Mara Snowden, who should have been at work yesterday.

Thought of the door, left open just enough to be noticed by someone at this end of the hall.

Her hand steady on the gun, Dempsey prepared to clear the apartment room by room.

Dempsey swept the apartment in a pattern. Living room clear. Kitchen clear. Bathroom empty. Closets checked. Nobody home. No Mara Snowden. No signs of struggle. No blood. Just a tidy apartment with the scent of jasmine hanging in the air and a desk with items arranged too perfectly to be coincidence.

"Mara?" Her voice sounded loud in the silence. No answer.

She holstered her weapon. The immediate danger had passed. Now it was time to observe. To see what the apartment told her.

The place was neat. Orderly. Bookshelf with photography books and crime novels. Couch with a throw blanket folded over one arm. Kitchen with clean counters. Single mug in the dish rack. A woman who lived alone but kept her space ready for company.

Dempsey checked the bedroom again. Queen bed made with military precision. Corners tucked. Pillows arranged. Closet with clothes hung by type and color. No sign anyone had slept here recently.

She returned to the living room. The desk sat against the wall opposite the couch. Oak surface. Clean. Three items placed in the center. A closed laptop. A spiral notebook. A printed photograph face up.

Dempsey approached slowly. The items hadn't been left randomly. Someone had arranged them deliberately. A message. For whoever found them. For her.

The laptop was closed. Silver. No visible fingerprints on its surface. The notebook beside it, spiral-bound, green cover. Closed as well.

The photograph drew her eye. Color. High quality. Professionally printed on glossy paper.

A dead man in an alley.

Dempsey recognized crime scene photos. Had seen hundreds. This was different. This wasn't documentation. This was composition.

The photographer had crouched at the feet of the corpse. Shot upward along the body. The angle made the dead man look larger than life. Important. Like a fallen statue. Sodium streetlights cast everything in amber and shadow. No flash had been used.

The victim lay on his back. White male. Twenties maybe. Death metal t-shirt now ruined with blood. One arm flung outward. The other across his chest. His legs bent at odd angles. The way bodies lay when they collapse, not when they're arranged.

Dempsey leaned closer. Three wounds visible. A bloody mess at the crotch where denim and flesh became indistinguishable. A neat bullet hole in the center of the chest. And the head... part of the skull missing. Execution style.

This wasn't a random mugging. This was professional. Multiple wounds. Multiple messages. Emasculation. Heart shot. Head shot. Someone wanted this man very dead.

The photograph made it look like a Renaissance painting. The lighting. The composition. The careful framing that captured the stillness of death and the violence that caused it. Beautiful and terrible at once.

No police evidence markers visible. No measurement tools or case numbers. This photo wasn't from the official crime scene documentation. This was taken before the police arrived. Or by someone who knew how to work a scene without disturbing the evidence.

Someone like Mara Snowden. Crime scene photographer.

Dempsey didn't touch the photo. Didn't move any of the items. She paused, looking again at the dead man's face. Familiar, but incomplete. She needed an ID on the victim and the scene location. And she needed to know what case Snowden was testifying on. This doesn't look like a simple missing person anymore.

Studied the photo again. Someone had wanted him dead in a specific, message-sending way.

Dempsey took out her own phone camera. Photographed the desk arrangement exactly as she'd found it. The laptop. The notebook. The printed photo. Evidence of evidence.

Traffic sounds continued from the street below. A siren wailed in the distance, growing fainter. The jasmine scent seemed stronger now, or maybe she was just more aware of it. The smell of someone who should be here but wasn't.

She looked again at the photo. The dead man in the alley. The artistic composition. The professional eye that had captured death as a moment of terrible beauty. Mara Snowden's eye.

A key expert in a major trial who had missed work for two days. A door left open. A photograph carefully placed for someone to find. None of it was coincidence.

Stood in the silent apartment. Waited for Brandt to call back. The dead man in the photo stared up at nothing, his secrets as carefully arranged as the items on the desk.

Chapter 2

Dempsey leaned closer to the photograph. The dead man's face nagged at her memory. Familiar despite the missing portion of skull. She'd seen him before, not in person but in a case file. The Tapani homicide from July. Outside The Dump nightclub.

Stefan Tapani. That was the name. She remembered the details now. Shot multiple times on July eighth. The case had landed on Detective Harris's desk. Harris was decent but overworked. The case went cold after two weeks of dead ends. No witnesses willing to talk. No surveillance footage. No shell casings left behind.

Dempsey straightened. Stepped back from the desk. Considered what she was looking at. A professionally printed photograph of a murder victim. Arranged deliberately in the apartment of a missing crime scene photographer. A photographer who was supposed to testify in a major trial next week.

The photograph wasn't standard police documentation. It was art. The composition too perfect. The lighting too deliberate. Snowden hadn't just happened upon the scene. She'd positioned herself. Calculated the angle. Captured the exact moment when violent death became still beauty.

Dempsey reached for her pocket. Pulled out a pen. Used the plastic end to gently lift the edge of the photograph. The desktop beneath was clean. No markings. No additional photographs. She raised the edge higher. A glimpse of handwriting on the back.

She tilted the photograph more. Black ink. Neat lettering. Three words visible.

"For U Callisto"

Dempsey's hands went cold. The pen nearly slipped from her fingers. The apartment's warmth suddenly felt oppressive rather than comfortable. She moved the pen down carefully, not touching the photograph directly.

Callisto. Her given name. Not the one on her badge or driver's license or any official paperwork. Only her birth certificate carried that name. The name her mother had chosen before abandoning her to the system. The name Dempsey had rejected at fourteen and legally changed at eighteen.

Nobody called her Callisto. Nobody knew to call her that.

Yet here it was, written on the back of a photograph showing a man murdered in an alley. A photograph displayed in the apartment of a missing police photographer.

Dempsey stepped back from the desk. Breathed deeply. Tried to process what she was seeing. The jasmine scent felt heavier now. Invasive. Like it was filling her lungs, crowding out the oxygen.

She pulled out her phone. Opened the camera app. Took multiple photos of the desk arrangement exactly as she'd found it. The laptop. The notebook. The photograph of Tapani's corpse. She moved closer. Took detail shots of the photograph itself. Tried different angles to capture the glossy surface without glare.

Her hands steadied as she worked. The shock receded, replaced by professional focus. Document everything. Preserve the scene. Follow procedure. The familiar mental checklist gave her something to hold onto.

She moved to the side of the desk. Angled her phone to photograph the writing on the back of the print without disturbing it further. "For U Callisto." Clear in the viewfinder. She took three shots to ensure at least one would be perfectly focused.

Dempsey lowered her phone. Stared at the photograph again. The dead man in the alley. The artful composition. The personal message.

The corpse stared at nothing through dead eyes. The bullet hole in his chest a perfect black circle against the pale skin visible through his torn shirt. The missing portion of skull creating a shadow on the pavement behind his head. The bloody mess at his groin speaking of specific rage.

Someone had wanted Stefan Tapani dead in particular ways. Emasculated. Heart shot. Head shot. A message killing. And now his photographed corpse had become another message. One addressed directly to Dempsey by a name she'd discarded decades ago.

She checked her watch. Almost an hour since she'd entered the apartment. The welfare check had transformed into something else entirely. Not quite an investigation yet, but no longer routine. She needed to report what she'd found. Needed to find out why Brandt had sent her specifically to Snowden's apartment. Needed to understand what connection existed between a missing photographer, a months-old unsolved homicide, and her own carefully guarded past.

The photograph lay on the desk exactly as she'd found it. Perfectly centered. The dead man captured in a moment of terrible beauty. The message on the back a riddle Dempsey didn't yet have the context to solve.

She took one final photo of the entire desk. Stepped back to get a wider shot of the room. Snowden was a photographer. She'd understand the importance of composition, of documenting a scene properly. Dempsey found herself taking extra care with her phone camera. Trying to frame each shot the way a professional might. As if being observed. As if being judged.

The thought sent another chill through her. She lowered the phone. Put it back in her pocket.

Dempsey stood at the desk for another moment. Considered the laptop. Closed. Silver. Pristine. She reached into her pocket. Retrieved her pen again. Used the plastic end to lift the lid, tap a key. The screen lit up instantly. No password prompt. Just a desktop with folders labeled by date.

She turned away. Should not have done that. Standard protocol: don't examine electronic devices without a warrant. Don't access personal data without authorization. The rules scrolled through her mind automatically. She wasn't supposed to be snooping through a missing person's computer.

A siren wailed outside. Drew closer, then faded as it passed the building. The normal rhythm of the city continuing while Dempsey stood in a stranger's apartment, staring at a dead man's photograph addressed to her by a name no one should know.

This wasn't standard protocol anyway. Just a welfare check. Not a crime scene. Not yet. No signs of struggle. No blood. No body. Just a missing photographer and some peculiar items left on a desk.

She tapped the laptop closed with her pen. Put the pen back in her pocket. Looked at the spiral notebook. Green cover. College-ruled. The kind sold in every convenience store and stationery shop in the city. She picked it up. No need for the pen this time. This wasn't digital evidence. This was paper. Tangible. Old school. Plain view.

The notebook opened easily. Not new. The spine cracked from use. The first page contained a single list. Four names. Four notations. Neat handwriting. Black ink.

TAPANI - paid in full

BONNER - paid in full

DUKE - paid in full

PASS - paid in full

Dempsey read the list twice. Recognized only one name. Tapani. The dead man in the photograph. The murder victim from July.

The other names meant nothing to her. Bonner. Duke. Pass. Common enough names. Could be anyone. The notation beside each one caught her attention more. Paid in full. The same phrase repeated four times.

She flipped through the remaining pages. All blank. Just the single list on the first page. Four names. Four payments. One notebook otherwise empty.

Dempsey closed the notebook. Set it back on the desk exactly as she'd found it. Stepped back. Considered the implications. Paid in full. Like a debt settled. Like accounts balanced.

Was Snowden running some kind of side business? Loan shark? Bookie? Didn't fit the profile of a police department photographer. The job didn't pay enough to have capital for loans. Or this apartment. Bookies needed connections, networks, enforcers. Snowden worked alone. Came to crime scenes. Took photographs. Left. Professional. Friendly. Friends with every goddamn cop in the city.

Dempsey walked away from the desk. Moved through the apartment again. Checked the kitchen more thoroughly this time. Clean counters. Empty sink except for the single mug in the dish rack. Refrigerator with basic essentials. Milk. Eggs. Takeout containers. The food of someone who lived alone and didn't cook much. Nothing expired.

She moved to the bedroom. Stood in the doorway. Took in the scene again. Queen bed made with military precision. Nightstand with a lamp and a book. Dresser with nothing on its surface. Closet door closed.

Standard protocol said don't go through personal items without cause. Don't invade privacy without justification. Don't exceed the parameters of the assignment.

But this wasn't standard protocol. This was a welfare check on a missing photographer. A photographer who had left a murder victim's photograph with Dempsey's birth name written on the back. A photographer who had left a notebook with the victim's name and the phrase "paid in full" beside it.

This was something else. Something that required further investigation.

Dempsey entered the bedroom. The jasmine scent was stronger here. Source not visible. No candles. No incense burners. No perfume bottles left open. Just the persistent sweet smell filling the space.

The bed remained perfect. Undisturbed. No body had slept there last night. No rush to leave had caused wrinkles in the comforter. Just the methodical, precise arrangement of someone who made their bed each morning without fail.

She approached the dresser. Six drawers. Three on each side. The only place in the bedroom where personal items might be stored out of sight. She glanced back toward the apartment door. Still open as she'd left it. No sounds from the hallway. No indication anyone else had entered.

This wasn't breaking and entering. This was a welfare check. She had legitimate reasons to be here. Chief Brandt had sent her specifically. That meant something.

Dempsey reached for the top drawer. Pulled it open slowly. Carefully. The drawer slid smoothly on well-maintained tracks. No sound. No resistance.

Inside: neatly folded undergarments. Some basic, some more than basic. Nothing scandalous. The drawer of someone who valued function sometimes and appearance at other times.

But there was something else. Not clothing. Something that didn't belong with the panties and folded socks. A book. No, not a book. A journal.

Black leather. Expensive looking. The kind sold in specialty shops rather than convenience stores. A serious journal for someone who took their writing seriously.

Dempsey looked at it. Didn't touch it. Yet. Considered the implications of its placement. Not on the desk with the other items. Not displayed openly. Hidden among personal items. Private. Secret.

Another siren wailed outside. Louder this time. Emergency vehicles headed somewhere nearby. The sound peaked as it passed the building, then faded gradually as it continued down the street.

Dempsey looked back at the journal. Black leather against white cotton. A stark contrast. Deliberate. Everything in this apartment felt deliberate. Arranged. Staged. Like one of Snowden's crime scene photographs. Composition. Lighting. Perspective. All calculated for maximum effect.

She reached for the journal. Hesitated. This wasn't standard protocol. This was crossing a line.

But the photograph on the desk had been addressed to her. Her real name. Her birth name. That made it personal. That changed the parameters.

Dempsey picked up the journal. Held it in her hands. Felt the weight of it. The texture of the leather. Smooth. Expensive. Well-used. The spine creased from opening and closing many times.

The jasmine scent clung to it. As if the journal had absorbed the smell from long exposure. As if it had been held by hands that carried the scent. Snowden's hands. Sat on her lap as she wrote.

She opened the journal. And sat on the edge of Mara's bed. The mattress barely gave beneath her weight. Firm. Expensive. The first page wasn't text. It was a photograph. Black and white. Professional quality. Dempsey's own face in profile, caught in a moment of concentration at her desk in the precinct.

She turned the page. Another photograph. Dempsey walking to her car in the department parking garage. Then another. Dempsey at a coffee shop counter. Her standing at a crime scene, badge visible on her belt. Her profile illuminated by streetlight as she examined evidence.

All black and white. All beautifully composed. All taken without her knowledge or consent.

Her pulse quickened. Water dripped steadily from the eaves outside the window. The snow had stopped but left its mark. Like Snowden had left her mark on Dempsey's privacy.

She turned another page. Text now. Handwritten. The same neat script as the note on the photograph and the list in the spiral notebook.

"Callisto at her desk today. The light caught her profile perfectly. The strength in her jaw. The focus in her eyes. I wonder what she sees when she looks at crime scene photographs. Does she see the artistry or just the evidence? Does she understand what the composition reveals about the photographer?"

Dempsey's mouth went dry. She turned another page.

"I watched Callisto at the Richardson scene today. She noticed details no one else saw. The pattern in the blood spatter. The void where something had been removed. She thinks differently. Sees differently. I want to know how she sees me."

More photographs followed. Dempsey entering her apartment building. Dempsey at the grocery store. Dempsey jogging in the park near her home. All candid. All taken from a distance with a telephoto lens. All showing moments when she believed herself alone or anonymous in the crowd.

The journal was thick. Dozens of pages filled. Months of observation. Documentation of Dempsey's movements, habits, routines. Stalking disguised as art.

She skipped ahead. Found pages that made her breath catch. Not just observations now. Fantasies. Explicit descriptions of what Snowden imagined Dempsey looked like beneath her clothes. What sounds she might make when aroused. How she might taste. How she might respond to touch.

Drawings accompanied the text. Skillful renderings of Dempsey's body in positions and states of undress she'd never allowed anyone to see. Intimate details guessed at but rendered with conviction. A fantasy version of Dempsey exposed on the page.

Her hands trembled. The journal felt hot against her fingers. Her pulse hammered in her ears.

She'd never been the object of such attention. Never been desired this intensely. Never been kissed. At forty-eight, she'd built walls so high that no one had scaled them. She'd told herself it was by choice. That the job required her full focus. That personal entanglements would only complicate her work.

But the truth was simpler and harder. She believed herself unworthy of desire. Unattractive. Unwanted. Her body an ugly vessel for carrying her mind to crime scenes. Not something to be admired. Not something to inspire fantasies.

Yet here were pages of evidence to the contrary. A woman had watched her. Wanted her. Imagined her naked and willing. Had seen beauty where Dempsey saw only functionality.

It was invasive. Disturbing. Unethical. A violation of her privacy and professional boundaries.

It was also the first time she'd felt seen as a woman rather than just a detective.

Dempsey closed the journal. Her face felt hot. Her throat tight. She stood from the bed. The water continued to drip outside. Steady. Rhythmic.

She looked down at the journal in her hand. Evidence of stalking. Evidence of obsession. Evidence that should be logged, documented, submitted to the investigation into Snowden's disappearance.

Evidence that would become part of the official record. Available to Brandt. To Knight. To everyone in the department. Her private body exposed through another's imagination. Her routines mapped for anyone to follow.

Dempsey made a decision.

She slipped the black leather journal into her jacket pocket. The weight of it against her side immediately familiar. Like her gun. Like her badge. An object that changed who she was by its mere presence.

She returned to the living room. To the desk with its arranged items. The laptop. The spiral notebook. The photograph of Stefan Tapani murdered in an alley.

That photograph had been left for her specifically. "For U Callisto" written on the back. Her name. Her birth name. That made it hers. Made it personal rather than professional.

She picked up the photograph. Slipped it into her inside pocket alongside the journal. The evidence of Snowden's obsession with her safely hidden from view. From scrutiny. From official documentation.

Dempsey pulled out her phone. Called Brandt. The chief answered on the second ring.

"Dempsey. What did you find?"

"Apartment's empty." Dempsey's voice remained steady. Professional. Revealing nothing of what she'd discovered. "No signs of struggle. Everything neat. Organized. Bed made. Dishes clean. Looks like she left voluntarily."

"No indication where she went?"

"Nothing obvious." The lie came easier than expected. Slipped out without hesitation. Without the telltale signs of deception that she'd been trained to detect in suspects. "No notes. No packed bags. Just an empty apartment."

"Damn." Brandt's sigh carried through the phone. "The Parsons trial starts Monday. We need her testimony."

"Want me to keep looking? Check with neighbors? Friends?"

"No. Come back to the precinct. We'll put out a BOLO. See if patrol can locate her."

"I'll be there in thirty."

Dempsey ended the call. Stood in the silent apartment. The lie to Brandt settling between her shoulders like a new weight. The first deliberate omission in a career built on finding and reporting truth.

She did a final walkthrough. Kitchen clear. Bathroom clear. Living room clear. Bedroom clear. Everything as she'd found it except for the two items now in her pockets. The journal heavy against her side. The photograph a stiff presence against her chest.

Dempsey left the apartment. Closed the door behind her. Couldn't lock it without a key. Made a mental note to mention that to Brandt. Another small detail in a report that would omit the largest discoveries.

She took the stairs down to the lobby. Passed the drooping plant. The tarnished mailboxes. The marble floor worn by decades of footsteps. Pushed through the front door into the cold afternoon air.

The sky had darkened toward evening. The brief snowfall melted on the sidewalk. Water dripped from awnings and eaves. The sound following her as she walked to her car. Steady. Persistent. Like the weight of what she'd found. Like the secrets she'd decided to keep.

Dempsey sat in her car outside Mara's building. The Tapani photograph lay flat on the steering wheel. Dusk crept across the street. The quiet broken only by distant traffic. She studied the image with her investigator's eye, separating aesthetic from evidence, composition from crime scene.

Beautiful in an ugly way.

Dempsey started the car. The engine rumbled to life, breaking the silence. She adjusted the heater. The cold had seeped into the car. Cold like the realization that Snowden wasn't just missing. She was involved in something darker. Something connected to murder. Something connected to Dempsey herself.

She pulled away from the curb. Merged into the light evening traffic. Streetlights flickered on as she drove. The city transitioning from day to night. From the visible to the hidden. From what could be seen to what had to be discovered.

The journal seemed to burn against her side. Not with shame or guilt but with possibility. With the unexpected validation of being wanted. Of being seen. Of being the focus of someone's attention in a way she'd never experienced before.

It was wrong to feel flattered by obsession. By invasion of privacy. By stalking. She knew this intellectually. Understood the psychological dynamics at play. Recognized the danger signs.

But knowledge didn't stop feeling. Didn't prevent the small bloom of warmth that came with being desired after so many years of solitude. Of isolation. Of believing herself unworthy of attention.

Dempsey drove through increasingly busy streets. Past restaurants filling with dinner crowds. Past bars starting to draw evening patrons. Past the normal rhythms of a city moving from work to pleasure. From obligation to choice.

She had choices to make now. Report what she'd found. Turn in the evidence she'd taken. Face the consequences of her deception.

Or continue alone. Follow the thread that connected Tapani to Snowden to herself. Unravel the mystery without the constraints of official procedure. Without the eyes of the department watching. Without Knight's mockery or Brandt's judgment.

The photograph in her pocket. The journal beside her. The weight of secrets already kept. The decision seemed already made.

Dempsey smiled again. Brief. Determined. A decision cemented. She would find Mara Snowden. Would understand the connection between them. Would discover what "paid in full" meant.

And she would do it her way. Alone. Outside the rules. Like the maverick detective she'd never allowed herself to become.

The traffic light ahead turned red. Dempsey stopped. Waited. The journal beside her. The photograph against her chest. The path ahead uncertain but compelling.

The light turned green. She drove forward. Into the city. Into the night. Into whatever waited for her beyond the rules she'd spent a career upholding.

Chapter 3

Dempsey arrived at the precinct before seven. The bullpen sat empty. Just her and the fluorescent lights and the hum of the air conditioning. Perfect. She needed privacy for what came next.

She'd barely slept. The journal and photograph had kept her awake, their presence in her apartment a physical weight. She'd locked them in her desk drawer at home rather than risk carrying them back to the precinct.

Evidence of her own compromised ethics.

Dempsey logged onto her computer. Typed her password. Navigated to the case database. The system moved slower than usual. Or maybe her impatience made it seem that way.

She typed "Tapani, Stefan" in the search field. Hit enter. Waited while the system churned through records. The cursor blinked. Once. Twice. Three times.

The file appeared. Case number 07-2438. Homicide. July 8th. Status: inactive. Detective assigned: Harris, W.

Dempsey clicked to open it. The digital case file expanded across her screen. Tabs for scene documentation, witness statements, forensic reports, follow-up investigation. Standard structure. Familiar territory.

Coffee smells drifted from the break room. Someone had arrived early and started the first pot. Dempsey ignored the aroma. Ignored the hunger in her stomach. Focused only on the screen.

The first page of the file contained basic information. Victim: Stefan Tapani, 23. Male. Caucasian. Found deceased in alley behind The Dump nightclub. Apparent homicide. Multiple gunshot wounds. Time of death estimated between midnight and 2 AM on July 8th.

Next-of-kin notification to Rebecca Tapani, ex-wife. Body released to Glenwood Funeral Home after autopsy.

Dempsey scrolled through crime scene documentation. First responding officers: Maxwell and Smith. Crime scene processing team: Bryant, Peterson, Petrov. Photographer: Lincoln, A.

Not Snowden.

Dempsey stopped scrolling. Read the name again. Photographer: Lincoln, A. Not Mara Snowden. The official department photographer at the Tapani crime scene had been Andy Lincoln.

She checked the report time stamps. Lincoln had arrived at 2:42 AM. Processed the scene until 4:15 AM. Standard procedure. Standard documentation. No mention of Snowden being present.

Yet Mara had a professional photo of the scene. A photo taken before police arrived or from angles they didn't document. A photo left specifically for Dempsey to find.

She clicked on the crime scene photo tab. Twenty-six images uploaded by Lincoln, A. All time-stamped, numbered, logged according to protocol. She opened the first one.

Wide shot of the alley behind The Dump. Flash photography. Harsh white light illuminating brick walls, dumpsters, the body splayed on the ground. Evidence markers placed around shell casings, blood spatter, a discarded cigarette butt. Clinical. Procedural. Documentation rather than art.

Nothing like Mara's photograph.

Dempsey moved to the next image. Close-up of Tapani's face. Eyes open. Vacant. Part of his skull missing where the exit wound had blown it apart. The flash made his skin look waxy. Unreal.

She clicked through each photo methodically. Lincoln had done his job well. Every angle covered. Every piece of evidence documented. Every standard procedure followed.

The precinct began to fill with morning sounds. A door opening. Footsteps in the hall. Someone laughing near the break room. Dempsey tuned it all out. Stayed focused on the screen.

The official crime scene photos showed blood spatter patterns consistent with close-range gunshots. No shell casings. Blood pooled beneath the body. Signs that Tapani had died where he fell rather than being moved post-mortem. Two guns, two shooters.

All textbook. All by the book. All nothing like what Mara had captured.

Dempsey scrolled back to the case summary. Three gunshot wounds. One to the groin. One to the chest. One to the head. Unable to determine the order. No defensive wounds.

Tox screen showed low levels of cocaine. Ballistics indicated two different .22 caliber weapons used. No matches in the database.

The case had gone cold quickly. Attributed to gang violence or drug-related crime. Harris had worked it for two weeks before hitting dead ends. No witnesses willing to talk. No surveillance footage. No significant leads.

Dempsey double-checked the personnel list. Lincoln had been the only photographer listed. No mention of Snowden anywhere in the file. Not as primary photographer. Not as backup. Not as observing. Nothing.

She pulled out her phone. Navigated to the photos she'd taken at Snowden's apartment. Found the image of the Tapani photograph on the desk. Zoomed in.

The difference was stark. Lincoln's photos showed a crime scene. Mara's showed a fallen man. Lincoln's documented evidence. Mara's created emotion. Lincoln's served investigation. Mara's served... what? Art? Message? Confession?

The angle in Mara's photo was low, at the victim's feet, looking up along the body toward the face and the destroyed skull. No flash. Just ambient sodium street lighting giving everything an amber glow. No evidence markers. No scale references. Nothing to indicate police presence.

The photo could only have been taken before the police arrived. Before Lincoln. Before Maxwell and Chen. Before anyone officially documented the scene.

But was it even Mara's? Or one she had come by. One taken by someone else, trying to get the evidence in the back door.

Dempsey zoomed in further. The composition was deliberate. Perfect. The body positioned to create lines leading the eye from the bloody groin to the chest wound to the destroyed head. A progression of violence captured with an artist's eye.

And on the back, those three words: "For U Callisto."

The precinct noise grew louder. More detectives arriving. Phones ringing. Keyboards clicking. Normal morning activity building around her while she stared at evidence of something abnormal. Something that didn't fit the official narrative.

Dempsey locked her phone. Set it face-down on her desk. Sat back in her chair.

Someone, likely Mara, it must have been Mara, had photographed a murder victim before police arrived. Had kept that photograph rather than submitting it as evidence. Had left it specifically for Dempsey with a message using a name no one should know.

The connections refused to align. The pattern remained incomplete.

She turned back to the computer screen. To the official crime scene photos taken by Lincoln. To the documented evidence that told one story while Mara's photograph suggested another.

What had Mara seen that night in the alley? What had she done? And why had she wanted Dempsey, specifically, to find that photograph three months later?

Dempsey closed the image viewer. Returned to the case file. Perhaps the witness statements would provide the missing link. Perhaps something in the follow-up investigation would explain Mara's connection.

Coffee smell grew stronger as the break room filled with early arrivals. Dempsey ignored it. Ignored the voices and laughter drifting across the bullpen. Focused only on the screen and the mystery it contained. The mystery Mara had left specifically for her to solve.

Dempsey clicked on the witness statements tab. Four interviews conducted on scene. Four people who happened to be in the alley when police arrived. Four people who claimed to see nothing. Standard procedure would have included follow-up interviews. There weren't any.

The bullpen had filled completely now. Detectives at their desks. Phones ringing. Keyboards clicking. The normal rhythm of police work building around her while she remained isolated in her focus.

She opened the first statement. Witness: Bonner, Deirdre. Female, 35. Address and contact information recorded. Statement given to Officer Goode at 3:17 AM, July 8th.

Bonner claimed she'd been cutting through the alley after leaving The Dump when she discovered the body. Didn't see the shooting. Didn't hear gunshots. Didn't see anyone running from the scene. Just stumbled upon the corpse and immediately called 911 from a burner phone she carried for emergencies.

Dempsey frowned. People didn't typically call emergency services from burner phones. That detail should have flagged follow-up.

The statement continued. Bonner had waited for police to arrive. Had been cooperative but insisted she knew nothing valuable. Had no connection to the victim. Had never seen him before. Just wrong place, wrong time.

Dempsey moved to the next statement. Witness: Duke, Barney. Male, 42. Statement given to Officer Veard at 3:22 AM, July 8th.

Duke also claimed to have been cutting through the alley after leaving the nightclub. Also claimed to have discovered the body after the shooting. Also claimed to have seen and heard nothing. Also claimed no connection to the victim.

The pattern continued. Third witness: Pass, Turner. Male, 29. Same story. Cutting through the alley. Found the body. Saw nothing. Heard nothing. Knew nothing.

Someone at a nearby desk unwrapped a tuna sandwich. The smell drifted across the bullpen. Sharp. Intrusive. Dempsey's stomach growled. She ignored it. Kept reading.

Fourth witness: Yes, Erin. Female, no age listed. No address provided. Statement given to Detective Harris at 3:45 AM, July 8th.

Yes had been inside The Dump. Had left. Had discovered the body after she noticed other people in the alley. Had seen and heard nothing. But Yes added one detail the others hadn't mentioned. She insisted they all stay to talk to police. Said it was the right thing to do.

Dempsey leaned back in her chair. Something felt wrong. Four witnesses all discovering a body at almost the same time, but only one calling? All seeing nothing. All hearing nothing. All just happening to be in that particular alley at that particular moment.

Too convenient. Too neat. Too unlikely.

She read the names again. Bonner. Duke. Pass. Yes.

Dempsey sat up straight. Her hands went still on the keyboard.

Bonner, Duke, Pass.

The names in Mara's notebook. The list with "paid in full" written beside each one. The same names as three of the four witnesses at the Tapani murder scene.

She pulled out her phone. Found the photo she'd taken of the notebook page. Stared at it.

TAPANI - paid in full
BONNER - paid in full
DUKE - paid in full
PASS - paid in full

The victim and three witnesses. All marked "paid in full" in Mara's handwriting. All connected to the same crime scene. Only Erin Yes missing from the notebook list.

Dempsey set her phone down. Looked back at the witness statements. Read each one again with new attention. Looked for details she'd missed. Connections. Contradictions. Anything that might explain what "paid in full" meant in this context.

Nothing stood out. Just four brief statements from four people who claimed to see nothing. Four people who, by coincidence too perfect to be coincidence, had all been together when they discovered Tapani's body.

Dempsey rubbed her eyes. Tried to make sense of the pattern.

Tapani had been involved with drugs. His record showed multiple arrests. Possession. Intent to distribute. Maybe Mara had been supplying him. Maybe she'd supplied the others too. Bonner. Duke. Pass. Maybe "paid in full" meant settled accounts. Debts cleared. Business concluded.

But why mark Tapani himself as "paid in full"? He was the victim. The dead man in the alley. How had he paid anything to anyone?

And why wasn't Yes on the list? She'd been there too. Had given a statement. Had insisted the others stay at the scene. But her name wasn't in the notebook. She hadn't "paid" whatever the others had paid.

Dempsey leaned in again, looked closer at the photo of Yes's witness statement. Short. Vague. Little personal information provided. No age. No address. Just a name, a gender, and a generic description: "Short young person wearing sunglasses at night and a medical mask."

Sunglasses at night. Medical mask. Face concealed. Identity hidden.

What if Mara had been there that night? What if she'd witnessed the murder? Or more than witnessed?

Dempsey's mind raced through possibilities. Drug deal gone wrong. Money due. Blackmail. Any number of scenarios that might connect a police photographer to a dead drug dealer and three witnesses who saw nothing.

But none of them explained the photograph left for her. None explained "For U Callisto" written on the back. None explained why Mara had been watching her, following her, documenting her movements in that journal.

The tuna smell grew stronger. Someone laughed nearby. A printer whirred to life at the far end of the bullpen. Normal workday sounds that felt increasingly distant as Dempsey's focus narrowed to the connection she'd found.

Dempsey sat back. Let the pattern form in her mind. Incomplete. Unsatisfying. But a pattern nonetheless.

Mara had been at the murder scene. Had taken the photograph before police arrived. Had disappeared before police arrived. No one mentioned a woman on her hands and knees taking a photo, who left the scene.

Had Mara paid them to keep her name out of it?

The simplest explanation: Mara had been dealing drugs. Tapani was a customer who'd crossed her. Maybe tried to steal from her. Maybe threatened to expose her. She'd killed him or had him killed. The other four—Bonner, Duke, Yes, Pass—had been there. Had seen it happen. She'd bought their silence. Had paid them to tell police they saw nothing.

But Erin Yes. The missing piece. The witness not marked "paid in full." The person in sunglasses and a mask who insisted everyone stay to talk to police.

Dempsey closed the witness statement files. Stared at her computer screen without seeing it. The drug theory made sense on the surface. Explained some connections. But left too many questions unanswered.

Why document the murder in a photograph? Why keep it? Why leave it for Dempsey specifically? Why use a name no one should know?

And why disappear now, three months after the murder, just before testifying in an unrelated case?

None of it fit together cleanly. None of it satisfied the detective's need for logical connection. For cause and effect. For motive and opportunity.

But it was a start. A thread to pull. A path to follow.

She needed to find these people. Needed to re-interview the witnesses. Needed to understand what had really happened that night. And what it had to do with her.

Dempsey sat back, tossing her pen on to her desk. She reached into her drawer and pulled out her lunch. Plain cucumber sandwich in a plastic baggie. She'd made it last night between reading Mara's journal entries and staring at the Tapani photograph. Food as fuel. Nothing more.

She unwrapped it while turning back to her computer. Started with Turner Pass. The youngest of the three witnesses besides the mysterious Erin Yes. If anyone might talk, might break the apparent conspiracy of silence, a twenty-nine-year-old seemed the best bet.

Dempsey took a bite. The cucumber crunched between her teeth. Cool. Bland. She barely tasted it as she typed Pass's name into the department database. Criminal records. Traffic violations. Incident reports. Any official contact with law enforcement.

The search returned nothing. No arrests. No tickets. No warnings. Not even a parking violation. Turner Pass had lived twenty-nine years without leaving a mark on police records. Unusual but not impossible. Some people just stayed out of trouble.

She tried another approach. Social media. Not her standard for routine investigations, too unreliable, but this wasn't routine anymore. This was personal. This connected to Mara. To the photograph. To "Callisto."

Pass's social media page appeared immediately. Profile photo of a smiling young man with sandy hair and glasses. Outdoor setting. Hiking trail. Mountains in the background. Normal. Ordinary. Nothing suggesting connection to drug deals or murders.

Dempsey scrolled through recent posts. Or rather, posts about Pass rather than by him. Messages of condolence. Memories shared. Photos posted as tributes.

Turner Pass was dead.

She stopped chewing. Set the sandwich down. Leaned closer to the screen.

"Rest in peace, brother. Gone too soon."

"Still can't believe you're not here anymore. Miss you every day."

"Heaven gained another angel. We're all devastated by your sudden passing."

The most recent post dated November 29th. Just days ago.

Dempsey swallowed her bite without tasting it. Clicked through to find an obituary link someone had shared. Standard format. Turner Alexander Pass, 29, died unexpectedly on November 28th. Survived by parents John and Martha Pass. Memorial service held at Glenview Chapel. Donations in lieu of flowers to American Heart Association.

No cause of death listed. Just "unexpectedly." That could mean anything. Accident. Suicide. Murder. Heart attack. The donation suggestion hinted at the latter, but obituaries often obscured uncomfortable truths about how someone died.

Dempsey needed facts. Not social media sympathy. Not vague obituary language.

She opened a new tab. Logged into the Medical Examiner's Case Management system using her department credentials. Searched for Pass, Turner. The system churned for a moment before returning a single result. Case file 11-4872. November 28th. Pass, Turner Alexander.

Dempsey opened it. Scanned the preliminary information. Physical description matching the social media photos. Address: 83 Azalea Lane. Emergency services called at 6:17 PM by neighbor who found Pass collapsed beside his bicycle in his front yard.

She continued reading. Paramedics arrived at 6:23 PM. Subject already without pulse. Attempted resuscitation unsuccessful. Pronounced at the scene at 6:45 PM. Body transported to the medical examiner's office for autopsy.

The break room coffee maker hissed as someone brewed a fresh pot. The smell drifted across the bullpen. Dempsey ignored it. Focused on the screen. On the details of how Turner Pass had died four days ago.

Autopsy findings: no sign of disease or pre-existing condition. Toxicology clean. No drugs. No alcohol. Healthy twenty-nine-year-old male in good physical condition.

Cause of death: commotio cordis. Cardiac arrest resulting from a precise blow to the chest during a specific moment in the heart's electrical cycle. Rare but documented. Most common in young athletes hit by baseballs or hockey pucks.

In Pass's case, the M.E. had determined he fell on his bicycle. The handlebar grip struck his chest at precisely the wrong moment. A freak accident. One in a million. The heart simply stopped.

Dempsey scrolled further. Found additional notes from the examination. A fresh scratch or light slash on Pass's palm. Appeared to have occurred immediately prior to death. Consistent with falling and catching himself on something sharp. Possibly the edge of the bicycle frame or a nearby bush.

The M.E. had ruled the death accidental. Police never investigated further. Case closed.

Dempsey sat back. Took another bite of her sandwich without thinking about it. Chewed mechanically while processing what she'd learned.

Turner Pass, witness to Stefan Tapani's murder in July, had died in a freak accident on November 28th. His name in Mara's notebook marked "paid in full." His death coming just days before Mara herself disappeared.

Coincidence seemed increasingly unlikely.

Dempsey pulled up her phone again. Found the photo of Mara's notebook page. Stared at the four names. Tapani. Bonner. Duke. Pass. All marked "paid in full."

Tapani murdered in July. Pass dead from a freak accident in November. Two down. Two to go.

Dempsey opened the Tapani case file again. Found Yes's witness statement. Read it carefully. Looking for details she'd missed. For clues to identity. For anything that might lead her forward rather than to another dead end.

Short young person. Sunglasses at night. Medical mask. Generic description that could fit dozens of people. Hundreds. No useful identifying information.

But one detail stood out on re-reading. Yes had been the one to insist they all stay. Had convinced Bonner, Duke, and Pass to wait for police. Had made sure they all gave statements. Had made sure they all entered the official record as witnesses who saw nothing.

Why? What purpose did that serve?

Dempsey closed the file. Wrapped the remains of her sandwich. Put it back in the drawer. She wouldn't be hungry again today. Not with what she'd discovered.

Dempsey needed to find Erin Yes.

Chapter 4

Dempsey's computer screen blurred. Her eyes burned from staring at it too long. She blinked, refocused. The search for Erin Yes had yielded nothing useful in three hours. No address. No record. No trace beyond that witness statement from the Tapani murder scene. A ghost who'd insisted the other witnesses stay and talk to police.

The precinct had emptied around her. Day shift gone. Evening shift out. Just her and the night cleaning crew. A janitor pushed his cart past her desk, wheels squeaking on linoleum. The sharp smell of industrial bleach followed him.

She rubbed her eyes. Checked her watch. 6:48 PM. The fluorescent lights hummed overhead. Constant. Irritating. She'd been at her desk since morning, forgetting to eat after that half-finished cucumber sandwich from lunch.

Her cell phone rang. The vibration rattled against her desktop. She glanced at the screen. Gzowski. The District Attorney. She felt a cold shock in her stomach.

"Dempsey," she answered, professional tone masking sudden dread.

"Where the hell are you?" Gzowski's voice tight with anger. "Everyone's been waiting for forty-five minutes."

Dempsey's mind raced. Meeting. Zamora case. The cold-case strangler she'd wrapped yesterday. The meeting she'd requested. The meeting scheduled for 6:00.

"Caught in traffic," she lied. "Accident on Franklin."

"You confirmed this morning. We've been calling the precinct."

She glanced at her desk phone. The message light blinked red. Four, five, six times. She'd been so focused on finding Erin Yes she'd tuned everything out.

"I'll squeeze through an alley." She stood, knocking her chair backward. "Twenty minutes."

"Make it fifteen. I've got the judge waiting to sign your warrant."

Dempsey hung up. Cursed under her breath. Zamora. How had she forgotten Zamora? The case she'd spent so long building. The cold case she'd solved just yesterday. The strangler who'd killed a prostitute in the park and left blue heat resistant polyester fibers that matched his work gloves.

Because of Mara Snowden. Because of a black leather journal filled with erotic writings. Because of a photograph signed "For U Callisto."

The Zamora file still sat in her drawer where she'd put it. She yanked it out. Flipped it open to confirm all the paperwork was there. Evidence chain. Lab reports. Witness statements. Three years of work by three different detectives condensed into forty-eight pages.

She snapped it closed. Grabbed her coat from the back of her chair. Her phone and keys from the desk. Shoved everything into her pockets.

The cleaning cart blocked the aisle. The janitor bent over, picking up a wastebasket.

"Excuse me," she said, voice clipped with urgency.

He straightened. Moved the cart three inches.

Dempsey squeezed past. Her hip caught the edge. Bottles of cleaning solution rattled. One tipped over. She ignored it. Kept moving.

Knight sat at his desk near the exit. Polla beside him. Both still working despite the hour. Or pretending to. Knight's computer screen showed a football game. Polla doing the crossword in yesterday's newspaper.

Knight looked up as she approached, coat half-on, file clutched against her chest.

"Where's the fire, Dempsey?"

She didn't slow down. Didn't respond. Fifteen minutes to reach the DA's office downtown. Rush hour traffic. No way to make it in time.

"Must be some hot date to rush out like that," Knight called after her.

Polla snickered. Pushed his glasses up with one finger.

"Too late for the early bird special," Knight continued. "Senior discount ends at six."

Dempsey hit the elevator button. Jabbed it three times in succession. The doors opened immediately. She stepped inside. Turned. Saw Knight and Polla still watching her. Knight said something else. The doors closed before she could hear it.

The elevator descended. Her reflection stared back from the brushed metal doors. Hair disheveled. Eyes tired. She hadn't slept properly in two days. Not since finding Mara's journal. Not since seeing those photos of herself through someone else's eyes.

The elevator reached the garage level. The doors opened. Dempsey strode to her car, keys already in hand. So much effort building the Zamora case. One distraction nearly derailing it. She couldn't let that happen.

She unlocked the car. Tossed the Zamora file onto the passenger seat. Started the engine. The dashboard clock read 6:54. No way to make it downtown in fifteen minutes. Not even with the light bar she kept in her glove compartment but wasn't supposed to use for administrative meetings.

Dempsey pulled out of the garage. Hit the main road and immediately encountered stopped traffic. Red taillights stretched ahead for blocks. Rush hour gridlock.

She thought of Gzowski waiting. The judge ready to sign the warrant. The chance to finally arrest Zamora slipping away because she'd spent the day obsessing over a missing photographer and a three-year-old murder case that wasn't even hers.

Dempsey pulled into the turning lane. Made a hard right at the next intersection. She knew a shortcut through the warehouse district. Less traffic. More potholes. Worth the risk to her suspension.

The streets darkened as she left the main roads. Fewer streetlights here. Fewer cars. She pushed the speedometer higher. The Zamora file slid on the seat beside her with each turn.

Dempsey couldn't let Tapani distract her. Couldn't let Mara's disappearance derail what she'd built. The warrant had to be signed tonight. The arrest made before Zamora could run.

She checked her watch. 7:02. Still no way to make it in fifteen minutes. But maybe twenty. Maybe the judge would wait. Maybe Gzowski would stall. Maybe the work wouldn't be wasted because of one day's distraction.

Dempsey pressed the accelerator harder. The car jumped forward. She'd deal with Tapani later. With Mara and her journal and her photograph later. With "For U Callisto" later.

Right now, she had a killer to catch. The one she'd been hunting. Not the photographer who'd just appeared in her life yesterday.

Zamora first.

* * *

Dempsey stood outside the DA's office, warrant in hand. Twenty-three minutes late. Gzowski had been furious. The judge irritated. But they'd signed it anyway. The evidence was solid. The fiber match undeniable. The warrant giving her the legal right to arrest Darius Zamora for murder of Carla Mendez now rested in a manila envelope against her side.

Rush hour crowds pushed past on the sidewalk. Office workers heading home. Restaurant staff arriving for evening shifts. A hot dog vendor three storefronts down filled the air with the smell of grilled onions and sauerkraut.

Dempsey stared at the warrant. The culmination of diligent work. Nearly derailed because she'd let herself get distracted by Mara Snowden's disappearance. By a photograph of a dead man. By her own name written on the back. By words of lust wrapped in black leather.

Callisto. The name she'd abandoned at fourteen and legally buried at eighteen.

She tucked the warrant into her inside jacket pocket. Protected. Secure. Pressed the button for the crosswalk. Waited while traffic crawled past. Evening commuters with empty eyes. The light changed. She crossed.

Her car sat in a fifteen-minute loading zone. No ticket yet. Small mercies. She unlocked it. Slid behind the wheel. Started the engine. The digital clock on the dashboard read 7:48 PM. Zamora worked nights. Slept during the day. Best time to arrest him would be now, before his shift started at midnight.

She pulled her phone from her pocket. Found Velasquez's number in her contacts. Officer Tomás Velasquez. Rapid Arrest Squad. The department's specialists in warrant service. In taking down potentially dangerous suspects with minimal drama. She pressed call.

He answered on the second ring. "Velasquez."

"It's Dempsey. I've got the warrant for Zamora."

"The strangler from the park?" His voice crackled through the car speaker. Reception spotty between downtown buildings.

"Yeah. Judge just signed it. I'm heading back to the precinct now."

A horn blared behind her. She checked the rearview mirror. A delivery truck needed her parking space. She put the car in drive. Pulled out into traffic.

"What's the situation?" Velasquez asked.

"Suspect works nights at Allied Chemical. Lives alone. No known weapons, but three priors for assault. Warrant's for the murder of Carla Mendez three years ago."

"The fiber match case?"

Word traveled fast in the department. Knight must have been talking. Taking credit probably.

"Yeah. He'll be getting ready for work soon. Best window to grab him is in the next hour."

"Text me the address. I'll get a team together. Meet you at the precinct in thirty."

"I'll be there." Dempsey ended the call.

She navigated through downtown traffic. Slow. Congested. Headlights and taillights reflecting off glass storefronts. The warrant secure in her jacket pocket. She'd hand it to Velasquez. Let Rapid Arrest do their job. Three months of solving the case. She could wait one more hour to see it close.

Her phone buzzed. Velasquez confirming the team. Four officers. Standard approach. Knock first. Force entry if necessary. Zamora's apartment was a second-floor walkup in Riverdale. No rear exit. Low risk of escape.

The traffic light ahead turned red. Dempsey stopped. Checked the cross traffic. Pedestrians hurried through the intersection. A woman in a dark coat stood on the far corner. Short. Brown hair falling just past her shoulders.

Mara?

Dempsey's heart skipped. She leaned forward. Gripped the steering wheel tighter. The woman turned. Her profile visible under the streetlight. The same cheekbones. The same posture. Camera bag over one shoulder.

The light turned green. Dempsey hesitated. The car behind her honked. She pressed the accelerator. Moved forward. Kept her eyes on the woman as she passed through the intersection.

Not Mara.

The woman's face was rounder. Her hair lighter. The bag over her shoulder not a camera case but a laptop carrier. Just someone who looked similar from a distance. In bad light. To eyes that had been staring at Mara's journal for two days.

Dempsey shook her head. Cursed under her breath. The obsession was getting worse. Seeing Mara everywhere. Thinking about the journal. The photographs. The explicit fantasies written in that neat handwriting.

For U Callisto.

She pressed the accelerator harder. Focused on what mattered. The warrant. The arrest. Closing the Mendez case after three years. Justice for a woman strangled in a park. Justice for a family that had been waiting too long.

Not Mara Snowden's disappearance. Not Stefan Tapani's unsolved murder. Not the mystery of who knew her birth name. Those were distractions. Side quests. Rabbit holes that had already cost her time and focus.

Dempsey made the turn toward the precinct. The street less congested here. Faster. She'd be there in ten minutes. Would meet Velasquez. Would hand over the warrant. Would see this through to completion.

Zamora would sleep in a cell tonight. Would face charges tomorrow. Would stand trial for what he'd done to Carla Mendez three years ago.

Then, only then, would she return to the other mystery. The one that had arrived unexpectedly in her life. The one with her name—her real name—written on the back of a dead man's photograph.

For now, Dempsey needed to finish what she'd started. Needed to close the case she'd been building for three years. Needed to be the detective she'd trained to be. Professional. Methodical. Focused.

Not the woman who kept seeing Mara Snowden on street corners. Not the woman who kept thinking about a black leather journal filled with explicit fantasies about her. Not the woman who'd felt a strange flutter in her chest when she realized someone desired her.

She needed to be Detective Cal Dempsey. Not Callisto. Not the object of Mara's obsession.

The precinct came into view ahead. Lights on in scattered windows. The parking garage entrance open. Dempsey signaled. Turned. The warrant solid against her chest. The case ready to close.

Three years of work. Almost derailed by one day's distraction. Never again.

* * *

Dempsey poured another inch of red wine into her glass. The bottle was cheap but drinkable. A saxophone played from her stereo. Something old. Davis maybe. She didn't know jazz well enough to identify it. Just knew it filled the silence of her apartment better than the television.

Her phone sat on the coffee table. Screen dark. She'd silenced it after the last call. Velasquez confirming the arrest. Zamora in custody. No resistance. Asked for a lawyer immediately. Smart. They always did that in the old cases. They'd had time to think about what might come for them.

Three years hunting him. Three months on her desk. Case closed. She should feel satisfied. Completed. Instead she felt hollow. Empty. The conclusion was less dramatic than the chase.

She could have gone back to the station. Watched the booking. Started the paperwork. Instead she'd come home. Opened a bottle of wine she'd been saving for no particular occasion. Put on music she rarely listened to. Created the appearance of celebration without the feeling.

The wine tasted bitter on her tongue. She set the glass down. Untied her shoes. Kicked them off. Her apartment was small. Clean. Functional. A couch. A coffee table. A bookshelf with procedure manuals and travelogues. Nothing personal on display. No photographs. No mementos. No evidence of a life outside the job.

Mara would be disappointed.

The thought came unbidden. Unwanted. But persistent. Mara Snowden with her artist's eye. Her attention to composition. To lighting. To the small details that revealed larger truths. What would she see in this apartment? In this life Dempsey had built?

The journal. Hidden in her desk drawer. The book where Mara had recorded her observations. Her fantasies. Her desires.

Dempsey went to the desk. Unlocked the drawer. The black leather journal sat where she'd left it. Expensive. Well-used. The creases in its spine evidence of frequent opening. Frequent writing. Frequent thinking about her.

She carried it back to the couch. Held it in her hands. Felt its weight. The texture of the leather. Smooth beneath her fingers. She opened it.

The photographs came first. Her face in profile at her desk. Her walking to her car. Her buying coffee. Candid shots taken without her knowledge. Without her consent. Private moments captured by a stranger's lens.

She turned the pages. Found the passages she'd been thinking about since first reading them yesterday. Mara's neat handwriting. Black ink on cream paper.

"What would her skin taste like? The curve of her neck. Her collarbone. Breasts. The inside of her. I think about this constantly."

Dempsey's face warmed. Her pulse quickened. She read the passage again. Slowly. Each word deliberate. Each image forming in her mind.

"I imagine her voice changing when touched properly. Low. Throaty. The sound she'd make if I pressed my mouth between her legs. If I ran my tongue along her. If I slipped my fingers inside her while staring into her eyes."

Her hands trembled. The journal heavy against her palms. Sweat formed at her hairline. Between her breasts. Behind her knees. Places she rarely noticed. Rarely acknowledged as part of herself.

At forty-eight, Dempsey had never been kissed. Had never felt another's hands on her body in desire rather than violence or medical necessity. Had never experienced what Mara described so vividly in these pages.

She'd told herself it was by choice. That the job required her full attention. That relationships created vulnerabilities she couldn't afford. That she didn't need the complication.

Lies told for so long they'd calcified into truth.

The real reason simpler. More painful. She believed herself undesirable. Untouchable. A body built for function rather than pleasure. A face meant for intimidation rather than attraction.

Yet here was evidence to the contrary. Pages of it. A woman who'd watched her. Wanted her. Imagined her naked and willing. Had seen beauty where Dempsey saw only utility.

She turned another page. Found a drawing. Skillfully rendered. Her face in closeup. Eyes half-closed. Lips parted. The image of pleasure. Of abandon. Of a woman experiencing what Dempsey never had.

Her skin felt too tight. Too warm. The wine in her blood. The words on the page. The jazz still playing from the stereo. All contributing to a state she rarely allowed herself to enter. Desire. Want. Need.

Dempsey closed the journal. Set it beside her on the couch. Picked up her wine glass. Drank what remained in a single swallow. The alcohol spread warmth through her center. Temporary. Artificial.

She thought of Mara. Where was she now? Why had she disappeared? What connection did she have to Stefan Tapani's murder? To the names in her notebook marked "paid in full"? To the message written on the photograph?

For U Callisto.

Questions without answers. Mysteries without solutions. Yet.

Dempsey stood. Carried her empty glass to the kitchen. Washed it in the sink. Left it in the rack to dry. Returned to the living room. Picked up the journal from the couch. Held it against her chest for a moment.

The jasmine scent still clung to its pages. Faint now. Just a trace. But present. A reminder that this object had been held by other hands. Had rested on another's lap. Contained another's most private thoughts.

Thoughts about her.

Dempsey went to her bedroom. Small. Plain. A queen bed with navy sheets. A nightstand with a lamp and alarm clock. A dresser with nothing on its surface. No photographs. No decorations. Just function. Just necessity.

She undressed methodically. Hung her jacket in the closet. Folded her pants and shirt. Set them on the dresser. Removed her underwear. Placed it in the hamper. Stood naked in the center of the room.

Her body reflected in the dresser mirror. Tall. Lean. Strong shoulders from years at the shooting range. A scar on her right thigh from a knife fight her rookie year. Another on her abdomen from an appendectomy at sixteen. The geography of a life lived in physical spaces. In confrontation with physical dangers.

Not the body of desire. Not the body Mara had imagined pressed against her own. Not the skin Mara had wondered about tasting.

Yet it was. It must be. The evidence was there in black ink on cream paper.

Dempsey turned away from the mirror. Put on a t-shirt. Cotton. Worn. Functional for sleep. Nothing like the lingerie Mara had drawn her wearing in one of the journal's later pages.

She picked up the journal from the dresser where she'd set it. Carried it to the bed. Pulled back the covers. Slid between cool sheets. Placed the journal beneath her pillow.

The book's weight registered through the thin pillow. Present. Undeniable. Like the want that had bloomed in her while reading it. Like the questions still unanswered about its author. Like the name written on a dead man's photograph.

For U Callisto.

Dempsey reached for the lamp. Turned it off. Lay in darkness. The journal beneath her head. The taste of wine still on her tongue. The image of herself as desired rather than merely useful settling into her bones.

Tomorrow she would return to the mystery. Would try again to find Erin Yes. Would look deeper into the connection between Mara and Tapani. Would follow the thread that led from "paid in full" to murder to her own abandoned name.

But tonight, just tonight, she would allow herself to wonder. To want. To imagine what it might feel like to be kissed for the first time at forty-eight. To be touched by hands that had already touched her through a camera lens. Through black ink on cream paper.

To be Callisto rather than Dempsey, just once before sleep claimed her.

Chapter 5

Dempsey typed "Bonner, Deirdre" into the search field. Hit enter. Waited for the system to respond. The database churned. Ancient hardware struggling with basic requests. The air conditioning clanked as it shut off, the sudden silence more noticeable than the previous noise. Heat would build soon. Already she could smell the off-gassing from old carpet, desk laminate, decades of trapped air.

Three days hunting for Mara. Three days since finding the photograph. The journal. The list with names marked "paid in full."

The cursor blinked on her screen. Once. Twice. Three times. No results found.

She tried again. "Bonner, D." More waiting. Same result.

Dempsey leaned back in her chair. Stared at the monitor. Deirdre Bonner had been at the Tapani murder scene. Had given a statement. Had claimed to see nothing. Had been one of four witnesses who just happened to be in that alley at the exact moment a man was shot three times.

And now her name was nowhere in the system.

She tried a different approach. NCIC database. National records rather than local. Typed the name again. Waited.

Polla appeared at the edge of her desk. Coffee mug in hand. Tie loosened. He rocked back on his heels like a man with nowhere better to be.

"Knights says you've been glued to that screen for days." He sipped his coffee. Set it on her desk without a coaster. "Working the Zamora case?"

Dempsey kept typing. Didn't look up. "Zamora's done. In custody."

"So what's got you burning through database access time?" He leaned closer. Tried to see her screen. "Some new body drop?"

"Old case." She kept her answers minimal. Didn't want conversation. Didn't want his coffee leaving rings on her desk. Didn't want anything but results from this search.

"Old like last month or old like last year?" Polla shifted his weight. Moved his coffee mug a fraction closer to her keyboard. A small provocation. A test to see if she'd react.

She didn't. "July."

"That was cold fast." He laughed at his own joke. Waited for her to join in. When she didn't, he continued. "What's so special about a July case in December? Christmas spirit making you nostalgic?"

The NCIC search returned nothing. No Deirdre Bonner. No criminal record. No wants or warrants. No fingerprints on file. No DNA in the system. Nothing.

Dempsey started a new search. DMV records. Vehicle registrations. Driver's licenses. If Bonner had ever driven a car legally in this state, there would be a record.

Polla was still talking. Words that filled space without adding value. Background noise less interesting than the air conditioning.

"...so Knight's got a pool going. How long before you crack and take a day off. I've got twenty on never."

The DMV search crawled. Their system even slower than the department's. Dempsey watched the status bar creep forward pixel by pixel.

"You could at least pretend to listen." Polla's voice sharper now. The friendly facade cracking. "Professional courtesy and all that."

"Busy." One word. All she had time for. The search still running. Nothing yet.

"Always busy. Always working. Always the perfect detective." He picked up his mug. Sloshed coffee deliberately close to her keyboard. "You know what your problem is, Dempsey?"

She didn't answer. Didn't care what he thought her problem was. Cared only about finding Deirdre Bonner. About understanding why her name was in Mara's notebook. Why she'd been marked "paid in full." Why she'd been at the Tapani murder scene claiming to see nothing.

"Your problem," he continued, voice rising, "is you think you're better than the rest of us. Above normal human interaction. Above taking a joke. Above having a goddamn conversation when someone's trying to be friendly."

The DMV search completed. No results. Bonner either didn't drive or used a different name for her license.

Dempsey finally looked up at him. "You done?"

Polla's face flushed. "Yeah. I'm done." He picked up his coffee. "Enjoy your screen. Only friend you've got, looks like."

He walked away. Back to his desk across the bullpen. Back to Knight and the others who thought they were funny. Who thought they understood her.

Dempsey returned to her search. Tried the tax database. Property records. Utility companies. Court filings. Birth records. Each search met the same wall of silence. No Deirdre Bonner.

A person without paper trails. Without official existence. A ghost who materialized only long enough to give a witness statement at a murder scene and then vanished back into whatever shadow realm she inhabited.

Like Mara had vanished. Like Erin Yes had never been more than a name and a vague description.

Dempsey went back to the Tapani case file. Reread Bonner's statement. Female, 35. Blonde. No address provided. Just a cell phone number. She picked up her desk phone. Dialed the number.

"The number you have reached is not in service."

She hung up. Tried again, adding *67 to block her caller ID. Same response.

Disconnected. Like Bonner herself.

She pulled up her photo of Mara's notebook page. The four names. Tapani. Bonner. Duke. Pass. All marked "paid in full." Tapani dead in an alley. Pass dead from a freak accident with his bicycle. And Bonner... what had happened to her?

Dempsey switched to social media. Official databases had nothing. Maybe Bonner's digital footprint would reveal something the government had missed. She created a dummy account. Standard procedure for investigating civilians. No trace back to the department. She typed "Deirdre Bonner" into the search field. Hit enter. Waited. Light snow began falling outside the window. Small flakes that disappeared on contact with the glass.

The search returned multiple results. Common enough name. She scrolled through profiles. Eliminated based on location. Age. Appearance. None matched the blonde, 35-year-old woman from the witness statement.

She adjusted the search. Added "Weller County" to narrow results. The system churned. Offered fewer options. Still no obvious match.

Dempsey tried a different angle. News archives. Local papers. TV stations. Anything that might have mentioned Bonner. She typed the name into the news search. Added the date range from July to present.

Three results. She clicked on the first one. A community theater review from August. Wrong Deirdre.

The second result. A real estate listing from September. Agent named Deirdre Bonner. Photo showed a woman in her fifties. Wrong age. Wrong Deirdre.

The third result. Dated November 8th. Local newspaper. "Woman Dies After Car Plunges Into Weller Lake." Dempsey clicked. The article loaded.

"Deirdre Bonner, 35, was found dead early Tuesday morning after her vehicle entered Weller Lake. A passing motorist spotted the car partially submerged near the boat launch. Emergency responders pronounced Bonner dead at the scene."

Dempsey read it twice. November 8th. Mara's notebook said "Paid in full." And now Bonner was dead.

Like Turner Pass. Another witness from the Tapani murder scene. Another name in Mara's notebook. Another debt "paid in full."

She logged out of the news site. Opened the Traffic Services Database. Typed her credentials. Waited while the system authenticated her. The bullpen had emptied for lunch. Just her and the humming computers and the light snow falling beyond the windows.

Dempsey entered the date. November 7th. Filtered for fatal accidents. Three results appeared. She clicked on the second one. "Vehicle in Water, Fatality, Weller Lake, 4:30 AM."

The case file loaded slowly. Piece by piece. First the header information. Case number. Reporting officer. Then the initial narrative. Then attached photos.

Investigating officer: Daniels, T. Patrol responded to 911 call from Sienna Warren, who was driving to early work shift and noticed vehicle lights in the water at Weller Lake boat launch. Upon arrival, officers found a 2018 red hatchback partially submerged. Driver still in vehicle. No signs of life. Medical Examiner called to scene.

Dempsey scrolled through the photos. The car half-underwater. Headlights still on beneath the surface. Driver's side window intact. Driver's door closed. No skid marks on the boat ramp. No barrier damage. Just a car that had driven straight into the lake in the pre-dawn darkness.

The snow fell harder outside. Flakes that stuck now before melting on the window glass. Small white patterns that dissolved into streaks. The day darkening even though it was barely noon.

She returned to the report. Scrolled down. Found the incident reconstruction section. "No evidence of second vehicle involvement. No tire marks indicating sudden braking. Scene consistent with deliberate or accidental entry into water at moderate speed. Vehicle examined after recovery. No mechanical defects found that would explain loss of control."

Dempsey scrolled further. Victim identification section. "Deirdre Boner, 35, identified through driver's license found in purse on passenger seat. Next of kin notification attempted. No contacts found."

Bonner's name was misspelled in the system. Dempsey fired off an email to the supervisor to have the record corrected.

The Traffic Services report ended with a conclusion. "Accidental death due to drowning after vehicle entry into water. Contributing factors may include darkness, unfamiliarity with boat launch area, possible distraction or medical event. Case referred to Medical Examiner for final determination."

Dempsey closed the Traffic database. Opened the Medical Examiner's Case Management system. Entered her credentials again. Searched for Bonner, Deirdre. November 7th. The system returned a single result. She clicked to open the file.

Standard autopsy report. External examination. Internal examination. Toxicology results. Cause and manner of death determination.

Dempsey scanned the external examination section. Found what she was looking for halfway down the page. "Horizontal laceration across forehead, 2.3 inches in length, moderate depth. Atypical for vehicle impact. No corresponding damage to vehicle interior surfaces. Possibly sustained during water entry or from contact with external object prior to incident."

The M.E. had noted the wound was unusual but attributed it to the crash. The next line confirmed it. "No other traumatic injuries observed. No defensive wounds. No signs of struggle or restraint."

Dempsey continued reading. Toxicology negative for drugs and alcohol. Lungs contained lake water confirming drowning as immediate cause of death. Internal organs unremarkable. No evidence of pre-existing conditions that might have caused sudden unconsciousness.

The conclusion was brief. "Manner of death: Accidental. Cause of death: Drowning. Decedent appears to have driven vehicle into lake for unknown reasons and was unable to escape before vehicle submerged."

Dempsey closed the file. Stared at her blank screen. Thought about the pattern forming in front of her.

Stefan Tapani. Murdered in July outside The Dump. Marked "paid in full."

Turner Pass. Dead from a freak accident with his bicycle in late November. Marked "paid in full."

Deirdre Bonner. Drowned after driving into a lake on November 7th. Marked "paid in full."

Three names from Mara's notebook. Three deaths. And a fourth name still unaccounted for. Barney Duke.

The snow continued falling outside. Heavier now. Sticking to the ledge outside the window. Building a thin white line that would melt when the sun returned.

Dempsey opened a new browser window. Prepared to search for the last name on Mara's list. The last witness who had stood in that alley claiming to see nothing while a man lay dead with three bullets in him.

The last person who might still be alive to tell her what had really happened that night. What connected them all to Mara. What "paid in full" really meant.

The Medical Examiner's system was still open on her screen. She typed "Duke, Barney" into the search field. Hit enter. Waited for the confirmation she already expected.

One result appeared. November 13th. Six days after Bonner. Almost two weeks ago.

Dempsey clicked on the file. Read the summary first. Male, 42. Found deceased in vehicle in closed garage at his residence. Address: 34 Parrish Road. Carbon monoxide poisoning. Manner of death: suicide.

Her jaw tightened. Her neck muscles tensed. Three witnesses. Three deaths. Three names marked "paid in full."

She scrolled to the full report. The external examination showed no signs of trauma or struggle. No defensive wounds. No bruising consistent with restraint. Just the cherry-red coloration of skin typical in carbon monoxide deaths.

Dempsey continued reading. Found the toxicology section. Paused at a detail that stood out. "Blood analysis shows supratherapeutic levels of Zolpidem (10.2 mg/L). Consistent with oral ingestion approximately 1-3 hours prior to death. Concentration indicates consumption of multiple tablets."

Zolpidem. Sleep medication. Potent sedative. Enough in his system to render him unconscious or at minimum severely impaired.

The M.E.'s report continued. "Carbon monoxide saturation of hemoglobin measured at 74%, consistent with exposure of approximately 1-2 hours in enclosed space with running vehicle. Death would have occurred while subject was in severely impaired or unconscious state from combined effects of carbon monoxide and Zolpidem."

Dempsey read further. Found the investigative summary section. "Vehicle discovered in closed garage by landlord conducting welfare check after subject failed to respond to multiple calls. Engine no longer running (out of fuel). Keys in ignition."

She moved to the scene photographs. Duke slumped in the driver's seat of a Toyota sedan. Head tilted back. Eyes closed. Almost peaceful looking.

Classic suicide setup. Clean. Efficient. Painless once unconsciousness set in from either the pills or the carbon monoxide. Whichever came first.

Except for one detail. In the notes section at the end of the report: "No prescription for Zolpidem found among decedent's medications. Source of sedative unknown."

No prescription. A man with no history of sleep disorders or insomnia suddenly taking a massive dose of sleeping pills before sitting in his car in a closed garage.

Dempsey's mouth went dry. She reached for the water bottle on her desk. Found it empty. Kept reading.

The M.E. had ruled it suicide despite the inconsistencies. The report conclusion stated: "Subject appears to have ingested sedative medication, entered vehicle in garage, closed garage door, and started engine with intention of ending life via carbon monoxide poisoning."

Simple. Straightforward. Case closed without further investigation.

Like Bonner's drowning. Like Pass's bicycle accident. Deaths that raised questions but not enough for official suspicion. Not enough for anyone to look deeper.

Anyone except her.

Dempsey leaned back in her chair. Let her eyes unfocus on the screen. Three witnesses to Tapani's murder. Three deaths in November. Three names in Mara's notebook marked "paid in full."

And Mara herself missing. Just before she was scheduled to testify in the Parsons case. Just after the last witness died.

The conclusion formed itself with cold clarity in Dempsey's mind. Mara had marked their names in her notebook. Had tracked them down one by one. Had arranged their deaths to look like accident or suicide. Had paid the debt she believed they owed.

But what debt? What had these three witnesses done to deserve death in Mara's eyes?

Dempsey returned to the Tapani file. Reviewed the witness statements again. Four people in that alley claiming to see nothing. Four people who just happened to be there when a man was shot three times. Four people who gave vague statements and then disappeared back into their lives.

Until those lives ended. One by one. In November.

The snow had left a thin white line on the window ledge outside. Melting now in the weak winter sun. Disappearing evidence of what had fallen earlier.

Dempsey opened her notebook. Wrote the dates.

Tapani - July 8

Bonner - November 7

Duke - November 13

Pass - November 28

A progression. A timeline. A methodical elimination of witnesses.

She looked again at the photo of Mara's notebook page. Four names. Four notations of "paid in full."

But the fourth witness remained unaccounted for. Erin Yes. The one who had insisted they all stay to talk to police. The one who had worn sunglasses at night and a medical mask. The one whose name wasn't in Mara's notebook.

Someone who had slipped notice.

Erin Yes.

Chapter 6

Dempsey typed "Erin Yes" into the search field. Hit enter. The database hummed. No results. She tried again with quotation marks. Still nothing. The fourth witness from Tapani's murder scene didn't exist in any official record. Just like she'd suspected.

She switched databases. Criminal Records. DMV. Tax filings. Property ownership. Nothing. No Erin Yes anywhere in the system. The cursor blinked on the empty results page. Mocking her.

Burned milk smell drifted from the break room. Two detectives arguing over football. Someone slamming a cabinet door. Normal precinct sounds that barely registered as Dempsey kept searching.

She widened the parameters. State records instead of local. Birth certificates. Death certificates. Marriage licenses. The system churned, slower with the expanded search.

One result appeared. Erin Yes. Female. 61. Residence in Cedar Mills, three hours upstate. Driver's license photo showed an African American woman with gray-streaked hair and rectangular glasses.

Not the witness from the alley. Not the person in sunglasses and a medical mask who had insisted the others stay to talk to police.

Dempsey clicked back to the search page. Tried alternative spellings. Ehrin. Aaron. Yess. Yezz. Nothing that matched. No official trace of the fourth witness.

She pulled up the original witness statement again. "Short young person wearing sunglasses at night and a medical mask." Generic. Deliberately generic. A description designed to be forgotten.

A shadow fell across her desk. Knight leaned against the partition, coffee mug in hand. He smelled like cheap aftershave and cigarettes he wasn't supposed to be smoking in the stairwell.

"Hunting ghosts, Dempsey?" He nodded toward her screen.

She minimized the window. Too late. "Working a case."

"Which case?" Knight sipped his coffee. Set the mug on her desk without a coaster. "Zamora's wrapped. What's got you searching state records on a Tuesday afternoon?"

"Nothing that concerns you." She moved his mug to a stack of Post-its.

He didn't take the hint. Kept standing there. Watching her. "Chief know you're reopening old files?"

Dempsey looked up at him. Direct eye contact. No blinking. "Don't you have reports to file? Or are you caught up for the first time in your career?"

The argument in the break room got louder. Something about point spreads and bad calls. The burned milk smell intensified as someone microwaved yesterday's coffee.

"Just trying to be collegial." Knight picked up his mug. "But I forgot. You don't do collegial. You do cold and unapproachable."

"And you do intrusive and unhelpful."

He laughed. A sharp bark with no humor in it. "See you at the Christmas party, Dempsey. Oh wait, you never come to those either."

Knight walked away. Back to his desk across the bullpen. Back to pretending to work while streaming sports on his department laptop.

Dempsey returned to her search. Social Security records. Restricted access. She entered her credentials. Searched the name again.

No Erin Yes. No one with that name receiving benefits, paying taxes, or having a social security number issued to them. The witness had given a false name. Had created a paper trail just long enough to enter the official record before disappearing.

Like Bonner, Duke, and Pass had disappeared. Permanently.

The burned milk smell faded. Replaced by someone's fish sandwich from the deli down the street. Dempsey pulled her notebook from her drawer. Wrote in neat block letters:

IS SOMEONE KILLING ALL ASSOCIATED?

She underlined "all" twice. Tapped her pen against the page. Added:

WHY THESE PEOPLE? WHY TAPANI?

No answers presented themselves. Just more questions. More connections she couldn't quite grasp. More threads in a pattern still taking shape.

Dempsey reached for her desk phone. Dialed Brandt's extension. Three rings before the chief picked up.

"Brandt."

"It's Dempsey. Need to discuss a few things with you."

"About?" Brandt's voice clipped. Busy. Distracted.

"The missing person." Dempsey kept it vague. Didn't mention Mara's name. Tapani's name. The journal. The photograph. The list of names marked "paid in full."

Papers shuffling on Brandt's end. A muffled conversation with someone in her office.

"I've got meetings back-to-back today. Put it in an email."

"Rather discuss in person."

"Tough, Dempsey. Flag it urgent if you need to."

Brandt hung up before Dempsey could argue. The dial tone hummed in her ear for three seconds before she set the receiver down.

Email it. Type out her suspicions about a police photographer being connected to multiple deaths. About the evidence she'd taken from Snowden's apartment. About her own name, her birth name, written on the back of a murder victim's photograph.

No. Some conversations couldn't happen over department servers. Some theories couldn't be committed to writing without more proof.

She turned back to her computer. Tried one more search. Hospital records. Restricted to law enforcement for specific cases. She entered her badge number. Typed "Erin Yes" in the patient search field.

The system processed her request. Checked her credentials. Granted access.

No results found. No emergency room visits. No admissions. No outpatient procedures. No prescriptions filled. Nothing under that name in any medical facility in the county.

She closed all the database windows on her screen. Cleared her search history. Erased her digital footprints through the system.

This wasn't going in an email to Brandt. This wasn't going in any official report. Not yet. Not until she understood what connected them all. What made Mara choose her specifically.

Not until she knew what "For U Callisto" really meant.

Dempsey switched tactics. Typed "Mara Snowden" into a search engine. Public records might not tell her much, but social media could. People revealed themselves online in ways they never intended. Posted things they shouldn't. Created digital footprints they couldn't erase.

The search returned several results. Metro Police employee listing. Inactive Glitter-Jitter account. Department staff directory. She clicked through each one. Nothing revealing.

Just the professional facade. The carefully maintained public image of a police department photographer.

Then she saw it. SnipSnapCity account. Photography portfolio site. She clicked the link.

The page loaded. Clean white background. Black text. Profile photo of a camera lens rather than a face. Username: M_Snowden_Lens. Bio: "I see what others miss."

Dempsey scrolled down. The first images appeared. Black and white photographs of the city. Professional quality. Sharp contrasts. Deep shadows. The urban landscape transformed through Mara's lens.

A skyscraper reflected in the puddle of a back alley. Morning light slicing between buildings, creating geometric patterns across a brick wall. Steam rising from a street grate, ghostly in the darkness.

Dempsey clicked to the next page. More cityscapes. A homeless man sleeping on a bench, his face obscured, only weathered hands visible. Children playing in a fountain, frozen in mid-splash. An old woman feeding pigeons, her smile revealing missing teeth.

Each image precisely composed. Each telling a story without words. Each showing Mara's eye for detail. For the moments between moments. For what most people walked past without seeing.

Dempsey clicked again. Next page. More photographs. More moments captured. More evidence of a mind that observed constantly. That noticed everything.

She clicked again. Stopped scrolling. Her own face stared back at her from the screen.

The photograph had been taken outside the courthouse. Dempsey standing on the steps after testifying in the Paxton case last spring. She wore her navy suit. Hair pulled back. Expression intense. Focused on something beyond the frame.

But it wasn't just a snapshot. Mara had captured something else. Something Dempsey hadn't known was visible on her face. Determination, yes. But also isolation. Loneliness. A woman standing apart even in a crowded place.

The composition emphasized this. Dempsey centered in the frame but separated from the people around her by negative space. By subtle differences in focus that made others slightly blurred. By lighting that seemed to find her alone among many.

The caption was a single word: "Her."

Comments from Mara's followers appeared below the image.

"Stunning composition."

"The isolation is palpable."

"Who is she? The expression tells a story."

"Your best portrait yet."

No responses from Mara to any of them. No explanation of who Dempsey was. Just the photograph speaking for itself. Just "Her." As if no other identification was necessary. As if Mara's followers would understand the significance from that one word.

Dempsey's cheeks burned. She closed the browser tab. Sat back in her chair. The precinct continued its afternoon routine around her. Phones ringing. Keyboards clicking. Conversations about cases and lunch orders and weekend plans.

None of it registered. Just the image of herself seen through Mara's eyes. Seen in ways she hadn't known she could be seen. Professional, yes. Competent. But also human. Vulnerable. Alone.

And beautiful. The word came unbidden. Unwanted. She pushed it away.

Still open on her screen were the department databases. The Medical Examiner's Case Management system. The Police Case Management system. The tools of her investigation. The official channels she'd been using to search for answers.

For Erin Yes. For witnesses who were now dead. For connections between Mara and Tapani and herself.

Dempsey stared at the M.E. system search page. The cursor blinking in the empty field. Waiting. Suddenly a new possibility presented itself. One she hadn't considered before.

What if Mara wasn't missing? What if Mara wasn't hiding?

What if Mara was dead too?

The thought sent a chill through her that had nothing to do with the precinct's overactive air conditioning. Nothing to do with professional concern for a colleague. Something deeper. More personal. More connected to that single word caption. "Her."

Dempsey's fingers hovered over the keyboard. Typed slowly, deliberately.

"Snowden, Mara"

Her hand moved to the mouse. Cursor hovering over the search button. The database waiting to tell her if the photographer was among the dead. If the journal and photograph had been left as a final message rather than a breadcrumb trail.

Dempsey hesitated. Then clicked. The system churned. Searching records. Comparing names. Looking for matches in the database of the dead.

The precinct sounds faded. The afternoon light through the windows dimmed. Everything narrowed to the loading icon spinning on her screen. To the answer she both needed and dreaded.

The search returned zero results. Dempsey's shoulders eased. The tension she hadn't acknowledged draining away. Mara wasn't dead. Wasn't a name in the Medical Examiner's database. Wasn't a case number and a cause of death and a body waiting for someone to claim it.

She stared at the empty results page. Relief. Determination. If Mara wasn't dead, she was out there somewhere. Hiding. Watching. Waiting. The question was: for what?

"Everybody have a good night. Be safe out there." Knight's voice carried across the bullpen as he shrugged into his coat. Others responded with various goodnights. Routine end-of-shift exchanges.

Dempsey checked her watch. 6:45. Later than she'd realized. The precinct had emptied while she followed digital breadcrumbs. While she searched for ghosts named Erin Yes and stared at her own face through Mara's lens.

She closed the database windows. Cleared the search history. Logged out of the system. Standard procedure. Leave no traces. No evidence of where she'd been looking or what she'd found.

The computer shut down. Screen going dark. Dempsey gathered her coat from the back of her chair. Her phone from the desk. Her gun and badge from the drawer. Essential pieces of herself. The tools and symbols that defined her professional existence.

She took the stairs instead of waiting for the elevator. Two flights down to the lobby. Quiet this time of evening. Just the night desk sergeant behind bullet-proof glass. The cleaning crew starting their rounds.

Outside, the temperature had dropped ten degrees since lunch. December air slicing through her coat. Car exhaust mingling with the metallic smell of coming snow. The city preparing for night. For cold. For winter properly settling in.

Dempsey walked toward the parking garage where she'd left her car. One block east. She could have exited directly into the garage from the precinct basement, but needed the air. The space. The distance between her work and her thoughts.

Her mind circled back to the photograph. To seeing herself through Mara's camera. Through Mara's eyes. The image capturing something she hadn't known was visible. Hadn't known was there to be seen.

And that caption. "Her." Simple. Direct. Intimate. As if Dempsey was someone Mara's followers should already know. Should recognize from previous appearances. From previous discussions.

Had there been other photographs that Mara had posted? That people had commented on? That had been out in the world without her knowledge or consent?

A bus passed. Brakes hissing as it stopped at the corner. Passengers disembarking. Others waiting to board. Normal city rhythm continuing while Dempsey's thoughts spun in directions neither normal nor rhythmic.

She passed a department store. Large display windows facing the street. Three workers visible inside, assembling a Christmas scene. Mechanical elves. Animatronic reindeer. A Santa that would presumably move and speak once they finished connecting all the wiring.

Dempsey slowed. Stopped. Watched their efficiency. Their coordinated movements. One holding pieces in place. Another fastening them together. The third consulting a diagram, directing the others.

Christmas displays. The annual tradition of crafting fantasy worlds behind glass. Of creating scenes meant to draw families. Couples. People who had people to shop for. To celebrate with. To stand beside while watching mechanical elves and animatronic reindeer perform their programmed routines.

Dempsey had no such people. Had never had them. Had told herself she preferred it that way. That the job was enough. That the work filled whatever spaces might have contained relationships. Connections. The messy, complicated tangles of human interaction outside the clean lines of investigation.

One of the workers inside the window looked up. Noticed her watching. Smiled briefly before returning to the task. A moment of acknowledgment between strangers. Of seeing and being seen.

Like Mara had seen her. Had captured her image without her knowledge. Had posted it publicly with that single-word caption that somehow said everything without explaining anything.

"Her."

The first snow of the evening began to fall. Small flakes drifting down. Melting on contact with the sidewalk. With car hoods. With Dempsey's hair. Her shoulders. Her upturned face as she continued watching the Christmas display take shape.

Light from the store window spilled onto her face. Warm yellow against the blue-black evening. Against the white snow falling more steadily now. Against the solitude she wore as comfortably as her coat. Her gun. Her badge.

She'd never minded December before. Had treated it as just another month. Colder. Darker. But fundamentally the same as the eleven preceding it. A time for work. For cases. For the routine that structured her days and defined her purpose.

This December felt different. Felt weighted. With Mara's disappearance. With dead witnesses. With photographs taken without knowledge and journals written without consent. With her birth name on the back of a murdered man's picture.

With "Her" as the only identification needed.

Dempsey watched the Christmas display workers for another minute. Then turned away. Continued toward the parking garage. Toward her car. Toward the empty apartment waiting for her at the end of this day that had yielded more questions than answers.

The snow fell harder. The lights from the store window faded behind her. The cold settled deeper into her bones with each step.

Chapter 7

Dempsey paced her apartment. Three steps from the couch to the window. Five steps back to the kitchen doorway. Repeat. The clock on the microwave showed 12:43 AM. She hadn't slept. Hadn't tried.

Her socks made no sound on the hardwood. Just the occasional creak of floorboards. A television murmured through the wall from the next apartment. The muffled voices of a late-night talk show. Laughter that sounded canned. Distant.

She stopped at the window. Looked down at the empty street. Three stories below, a taxi cruised past. Yellow against black asphalt. No passengers. No purpose. Just circling for fares that wouldn't come at this hour in this neighborhood.

City smells drifted through the window frame. Exhaust. Garbage from the alley behind the building. The sharp tang of coming snow. All familiar. All part of the background noise of her life. Tonight it felt intrusive. Wrong.

Dempsey moved to the bathroom. Flipped on the light. Squinted against the sudden brightness. The white tiles gleamed. The chrome fixtures reflected her face. Tired eyes. Tight jaw. Hair disheveled from running her hands through it for hours.

She opened the medicine cabinet. Small orange bottle on the middle shelf. Sleeping pills her doctor had prescribed last year after the Keller case. "For occasional use only." She'd used them twice. Hated how they made her feel. Cotton-headed. Sluggish. Vulnerable.

Her fingers touched the bottle. Turned it. The pills rattled inside. White tablets that promised oblivion for six hours. Maybe eight. Long enough to reset. To face tomorrow with something resembling clarity.

She put the bottle back. Closed the cabinet. Her reflection stared back. Hollow-eyed. Drawn. The face of a woman who'd made a decision that couldn't be unmade.

Dempsey returned to the living room. The television next door had gone silent. The street outside empty now. No taxis. No pedestrians. Just pools of light from streetlamps on wet pavement.

The dining table sat against the far wall. Small. Functional. Just enough room for two people if she ever had guests. She never did.

The photograph and journal lay in the center. Evidence of theft. Of rules broken. Of lines crossed.

Dempsey stood over them. Looked down at the black leather journal. At the glossy photograph beside it.

Dempsey pulled out a chair. Sat. The wood creaked beneath her. The sound too loud in the silent apartment.

She opened the journal. The leather cover smooth beneath her fingers. Worn from handling. From Mara's hands opening it. Closing it. Running fingers over it while she wrote about Dempsey.

About Callisto.

The pages fell open to a passage she'd read a dozen times since taking the journal. Mara's handwriting neat. Controlled. Black ink on cream paper.

"I watched her at the Richardson scene today. The way she moved. Precise. Economical. No wasted motion. No hesitation. I stayed back, used the telephoto lens. Caught her profile as she kneeled beside the body. The concentration in her eyes. The set of her mouth. I wonder what that mouth would feel like against mine. Against my neck. Against my breasts. I dream about this at night."

Dempsey's breath caught. Her heart beat faster. She licked her lips. Dry. Chapped from winter air and nervous habit.

She turned the page. Found another passage. More explicit. More detailed. Mara's fantasies about Dempsey's body. About what she wanted to do to it. With it. The sounds she imagined Dempsey making when touched in specific ways. Places. Rhythms.

Her face warmed. Her skin prickled. Sweat formed along her hairline despite the chill in the apartment.

Mara had wanted more from her. Had written it all down in passages that burned against Dempsey's fingertips as she traced the words.

Her own breathing seemed too loud. In. Out. The sound of it filling the apartment. Mixing with the faint hiss of the radiator. The distant rumble of a garbage truck on the next block.

Dempsey closed the journal. Set her palm flat against the cover. Felt the heat of it. The weight. The evidence of obsession.

She looked at the photograph. Tapani's dead body. The artistic composition. The skilled eye that had captured violent death as a moment of terrible beauty.

The same eye that had captured Dempsey. That had seen past her carefully constructed walls. That had found something worth wanting. Worth documenting. Worth obsessing over.

It disturbed her. It should only disturb her.

But it didn't.

She reached for the photograph. Turned it over. Read those three words again. "For U Callisto." Her past and present colliding in a way she couldn't yet understand. Couldn't yet trace to its source.

Mara was out there somewhere. Hiding. Watching. Waiting. The question was: for what? In hiding from Tapani's killer? Someone working for Parsons, hoping to derail the trial?

And why had she left these breadcrumbs specifically for Dempsey to follow?

She put the photograph down. Closed the journal. Sat in the silence of her apartment with the evidence of someone else's obsession spread before her. With the unanswered questions multiplying in her mind.

With the uncomfortable knowledge that part of her, a part she'd denied for decades, wanted to be found. Wanted to be seen. Wanted to be Callisto rather than Dempsey, just once.

If only to understand what it meant to be wanted by someone who saw beyond the badge. Beyond the gun. Beyond the walls she'd built so carefully around herself.

Dempsey stood abruptly from the table. Pushed the journal and photograph aside. This wasn't getting her anywhere. She needed to organize her thoughts. Map the connections. See the pattern that was eluding her.

She walked to the hallway closet. Pulled out the roll of butcher paper she kept for case work. White. Wide. Perfect for spreading out complex investigations where digital notes became too confined, too linear.

The kitchen clock read 1:17 AM. Late enough that her neighbors wouldn't hear her moving furniture. She returned to the dining area. Cleared the table. The journal and photograph went into the drawer of the side table. Out of sight but not out of mind.

Dempsey unrolled the butcher paper across the table surface. Cut a sheet with kitchen scissors. The paper curled at the edges. She weighted the corners with whatever was handy. A coffee mug. A paperback. Her badge. A box of ammunition.

She stood over the blank expanse. Reached for the markers she kept in the drawer. Black for main concepts. Blue for connections. Green for dates and events. Red for warnings and dangers. The tools of visual thinking she rarely shared with colleagues.

Dempsey uncapped the blue marker. The chemical smell sharp in her nostrils. She wrote in the center of the paper, letters precise despite the hour: "Detective Dempsey's Investigations (Dec 1-3)."

She drew a circle around it. Added lines radiating outward like spokes. Four main branches. Four aspects of a case that was becoming more personal by the hour.

First branch: "Initial Assignments & Police Setting." She switched to green. Added the date range. December 1st to 3rd. Added "Precinct" with a brief note about finishing the Zamora case. Added "Brandt's assignment" with a question mark beside it.

Why had the chief sent her specifically to check on Mara? Had Brandt known something? Or had it been random chance that put Dempsey on this path?

She switched markers again. Blue for the second branch: "Mara Snowden Welfare Check." She pressed harder on this one, the felt tip squeaking against the paper.

Under this header she wrote: "Reported missing two days." Added: "Door ajar, no signs of struggle." Added: "Photograph found, related to Tapani murder." Added: "Journal documenting observations of me."

Dempsey paused. Drew a line connecting this branch back to "Brandt's assignment." There was something there. Something in the timing. The chief had sent her specifically to check on Mara right after the three witnesses had died. Right after Mara had disappeared.

She moved to the third branch. "The Tapani Murder Cold Case." Her hand moved faster now. The connections multiplying.

"Victim: Stefan Tapani, 23, drug dealer." She added what she knew about the July murder. The three shots. The messages those shots sent. The four witnesses who claimed to see nothing. The four names in Mara's notebook marked "paid in full."

She connected each witness to their manner of death. Pass: bicycle accident, November 28. Bonner: drowning, November 7. Duke: carbon monoxide, November 13.

Dempsey drew a question mark beside each one. She added another note: "Is someone killing everyone associated?" Then underlined it twice.

Was that someone Mara?

She moved to the final branch. "Mara's Obsession & Personal Impact." Her hand slowed. This was harder to map. Harder to quantify in the neat categories of investigation.

"Photographer. Works for department." Basic facts. Impersonal. Safe.

"Journal content – detailed observations." Still safe.

"Sexual fantasies about me." Not safe at all.

She added: "My birth name on photo: 'For U Callisto'." Then stopped. Stared at what she'd written. The most disturbing connection of all.

How had Mara known that name? Who had told her? Where had she found information that Dempsey had buried decades ago?

She added one final note, circled it in red: "WHY M.E.?"

Dempsey stepped back. Capped the marker. The map sprawled across her dining table. A web of connections. Of deaths. Of mysteries within mysteries. And at the center, her own name. Not just "Detective Dempsey's Investigations" but Dempsey herself. The target around which everything else orbited.

She took her phone from her pocket. Photographed the mind map from above. Checked that the image was clear, legible. Evidence of her thinking. Documentation of connections that might not be coincidence.

The kitchen clock read 2:03 AM. Nearly an hour spent mapping, connecting, questioning. An hour closer to dawn without being closer to answers.

Dempsey sat down. Stared at the pattern she'd created. Looked for what she'd missed. For the gaps in logic. For the leaps of assumption. For the places where evidence gave way to speculation.

The connections were there. The pattern visible. But the meaning remained obscure. The purpose hidden. The why unanswerable with the information she had.

Dempsey left the mind map on the table. Nothing more to add tonight. Her eyes burned. Her neck ached. The kitchen clock showed 2:47 AM. She'd been awake for twenty-two hours straight. The human mind wasn't designed to solve puzzles after that long without rest. Even hers.

She switched off the living room lights. Walked the familiar path to her bedroom in darkness. The floorboards creaked beneath her feet. The sound too loud in the empty apartment.

Dempsey didn't bother with the bedroom light. Undressed mechanically. Folded her clothes. Set them on the dresser. Pulled an oversized NYPD t-shirt from the drawer. Cotton worn soft from years of washing. Pulled it over her head.

The bed waited. Cold sheets. Firm mattress. The clock on the nightstand glowed 2:53 in red digits. She sat on the edge. Considered the sleeping pills again. Rejected the idea again. Needed to wake clearheaded. Needed to function tomorrow.

She lay down. Pulled the blanket to her chin. Stared at the ceiling. The streetlight outside cast shadows through the blinds. Thin bars across white paint. Like a jail cell. Like the cage of questions surrounding her.

Tapani. The witnesses. Mara. The photograph. The journal. Callisto.

Her eyes closed despite her racing thoughts. Exhaustion winning over anxiety. Sleep approaching despite resistance.

Dempsey drifted. Fell. Surrendered.

She stood in an alley. Night. Sodium lights casting everything in amber and shadow. A body on the ground before her. Male. White. Twenties. Three wounds. Groin. Chest. Head. Tapani. Just as in the photograph.

She kneeled beside him. Pulled gloves from her pocket. Snapped them on. Began examining the body methodically. The chest wound. Clean entry. Professional. The head mostly gone. Execution style. The groin a mess of blood and denim.

A camera shutter clicked from the shadows. Then another. Dempsey looked up. Couldn't see the photographer. Just darkness beyond the crime scene. Just the sounds of someone documenting her work. Click. Click. Click.

She returned to the body. Checked the hands. No defensive wounds. Checked the pockets. Empty. Wallet gone. Phone gone. ID gone.

Another click. Closer this time. The distinct whir of a camera advancing film. Old school. Not digital. The kind serious photographers still used for art rather than evidence.

Dempsey felt eyes on her. Watching from the darkness. Documenting her movements. Her expressions. Her focus on the dead man at her feet.

A flash went off. Bright. White. Blinding in the dim alley. She blinked away the afterimage. Returned to her examination.

The chest wound had no powder burns. Shot from distance. The head wound had stippling. Close range. The groin wound jagged. Personal. Message-sending.

Another flash. Brighter. She looked up. Saw nothing but darkness beyond the circle of light where she worked.

"Who's there?" Her voice echoed against brick walls. No answer came. Just another flash.

Dempsey stood. Reached for her weapon. Not there. Gun missing from its holster. Badge missing from her belt. She was defenseless. Exposed.

Another flash. So bright it seemed to change the scene. The alley wider now. Cleaner. The body still there but different somehow. Arranged rather than fallen. Posed rather than collapsed. A scene rather than a crime.

Flash. Brighter still. The shadows retreating further. The photographer still hidden but closer. She could feel the presence now. Just beyond the light. Just outside her vision.

"Mara?" She called the name without meaning to. Without deciding to.

Flash. The light lingered this time. Didn't fade immediately. Grew brighter. Took on direction. Two points of light now. Side by side. Moving. Approaching.

Not camera flashes.

Headlights.

A car engine roared. Tires squealed on asphalt. The vehicle accelerated toward her. Toward the body. Toward the evidence she'd been examining.

Dempsey tried to move. Legs slow to respond. Muscles refusing commands. The car closer now. Headlights blinding. Engine deafening. Death approaching at sixty miles per hour in slow motion.

She forced her body to obey. Dove to the side. Felt the rush of air as the vehicle passed inches from her. Heard the impact as it struck something behind her. Felt heat at her back.

Dempsey's eyes snapped open. Her body jerked upright in bed. Sweat soaked her t-shirt. Her heart hammered against her ribs. The bedroom dark but familiar. Real.

The clock read 3:27 AM. Thirty minutes of sleep. Thirty minutes of nightmare.

She pushed tangled hair from her face. Felt her pulse gradually slow. The dream images fading but not disappearing. The alley. The body. The photographer in shadows. The car transformed from camera flashes.

The warning her subconscious had tried to deliver.

Dempsey lay back. Stared at the ceiling again. Sleep wouldn't return now. Not after that. Not with the adrenaline still coursing through her veins. Not with the message still echoing in her mind.

She was missing something. Something important. Something dangerous. Something that connected Tapani's murder to Mara's disappearance to her own abandoned name.

Something worth killing for. Worth dying for. Worth dreaming about in the darkest hours before dawn.

Dempsey watched the shadows from the streetlight shift across her ceiling. Waited for morning. For clarity. For the next step in an investigation that had become more than professional.

That had become personal in ways she was only beginning to understand. That had awakened something in her that had slept far longer than she had tonight.

Something with her old name. Something called Callisto.

Chapter 8

Harris entered the bullpen at 10:30. He carried a small plastic Christmas tree with a cartoon face painted on the base. Three detectives glanced up, then returned to their screens. Harris set the tree at the corner of his desk, adjusted it twice, then sat down.

Dempsey watched from her desk. Waited. Let Harris settle in. Turn on his computer. Check his messages. She'd planned this approach since 5 AM when sleep had finally given up on her.

Harris took a thermos from his bag. Unscrewed the cap. Steam rose in a thin column. He sipped, winced, set it down. Routine completed.

Dempsey stood. Crossed the bullpen with her notebook tucked against her side. Stopped at the edge of Harris's desk. The Christmas tree looked worse up close. Plastic needles already shedding onto case files. The cartoon face was Santa, faded from years of storage.

"Morning, Harris."

He looked up. Lines deepened around his eyes. "What can I do for you, Dempsey?"

"Need to talk about the Tapani homicide."

Harris's posture changed. Shoulders squared. Jaw tightened. A case he'd worked and couldn't solve. A case now cold.

"What about it?" His voice flattened.

"I'm looking into it."

"Since when?" Harris leaned forward. His breath hit her. Coffee mixed with something sour. Last night's dinner. This morning's neglected toothbrush.

"Since yesterday."

Harris's eyes narrowed. The Christmas tree tilted as his elbow bumped the desk. "That's my case."

"Was your case." Dempsey kept her voice neutral. Facts, not challenge. "It's inactive now."

"Doesn't mean you can just pick it up." His breath got worse when he was angry. "We have protocols. Case assignments. Chain of command."

"Brandt told me to look into it."

The information landed. Harris blinked. His mouth opened, then closed. The chief hadn't told him she was pulling his case, giving it to someone else. The professional insult registered across his features in stages. Surprise. Confusion. Anger. Resignation.

"Brandt," he repeated. Not a question.

"Yesterday." Dempsey didn't elaborate. Didn't mention the welfare check on Mara. The photograph. The journal. The list of names marked "paid in full." Those were hers alone.

Harris studied her face. Looked for signs of deception. Found none because there were none. His shoulders dropped. The territory-marking anger replaced by something closer to curiosity.

"Sit down." He gestured to the chair beside his desk.

Dempsey hesitated. The chair looked too close to Harris and his breath. Too far from her own desk. Too much like accepting an invitation she hadn't sought. But the case mattered more than comfort.

She sat. Slowly. Kept her back straight. Her feet flat on the floor. Ready to stand if needed.

Harris turned his monitor so she couldn't see it. Old habit. Protect the investigation. Protect the notes. Protect the theories no one else had validated.

"Why's Brandt interested in Tapani now?" He kept his voice low. Private conversation in a public space.

"Didn't say." Another truth that wasn't the whole truth.

Harris studied her again. His eyes sharper than his rumpled appearance suggested. Twenty years of detective work showed in the way he watched her. Cataloged her responses. Looked for what wasn't being said.

"What do you know about Tapani?" He picked up his thermos. Sipped. Set it down again. A thinking gesture, not thirst.

"Shot three times. Alley behind The Dump. July 8th. Drug dealer with priors." Dempsey kept it basic. Let him fill in what she already knew. Standard interview technique.

"That's the file. What else?"

"Four witnesses. All claimed to see nothing. No leads developed. Case went cold after two weeks."

Harris nodded. Once. The minimum acknowledgment. He reached for his keyboard. Typed a password. The screen brightened with whatever he'd been protecting earlier.

"Why would Brandt pull you off active cases for this?" His question directed at the screen, not her. "You closed Zamora yesterday. Big win. Department's been after him for three years."

"Brandt didn't explain." Third partial truth. The chief had wanted her to check on Mara, not investigate Tapani. That connection she'd made herself.

Harris turned back to her. His eyes different now. Still professional but with an added layer. Suspicion. Not of her lying, but of something larger. Something he'd begun to piece together.

"You find something new? Something that wasn't in my investigation?"

"Maybe." Dempsey didn't elaborate. Couldn't without revealing what she'd taken from Mara's apartment. What she'd kept from official reports.

"You going to share?"

"That's why I'm here."

Harris leaned back. His chair squeaked under the shift in weight. The Christmas tree tilted again, then righted itself. The Santa face grinned vacantly at both of them.

"What do you want to know?"

Dempsey took out her notebook. Opened to a blank page. Clicked her pen. The ritual of documentation. Of official inquiry. Of investigation proceeding by the book even when it wasn't.

"Everything you remember that didn't make it into the reports."

Harris rubbed his palm over his face. The Christmas tree wobbled as his elbow hit the desk again. "Brandt was all over that case from day one. Kept asking for updates. Daily. Never seen her push like that on a standard homicide."

Dempsey made a note. Kept her face neutral. "Standard homicide?"

"Drug dealer shot in an alley. We get three or four of those a year." Harris shrugged. "Usually they're straightforward. Rival dealer. Bad debt. Territory dispute."

"But not Tapani."

"Couldn't establish motive. Couldn't find witnesses who'd talk." He sipped his coffee. His breath had improved. Mint gum hidden in his cheek. Courtesy for conversation.

"The four who gave statements," Dempsey said. "They all claimed to see nothing."

Harris nodded. "Too clean. Too consistent. Four strangers who just happened to be in the same alley at 2 AM. All with the exact same story."

"They knew each other."

"Had to. But none would admit it." Harris leaned forward. Lowered his voice. "I pushed. Got nowhere. Then Brandt told me to move on. Said it wasn't worth departmental resources. Too many active cases needing attention."

"How long did you work it?"

"Two weeks. Should have been two months minimum."

Dempsey wrote that down. Added a question mark. Strange for the chief to pull a detective off a case that quickly. Stranger still to assign another one to look into it months later.

"Tell me about the witnesses."

Harris pulled his keyboard closer. Typed briefly. "Bonner, Deirdre. Duke, Barney. Pass, Turner. Yes, Erin. All claimed to be at The Dump earlier. All claimed to be cutting through the alley afterward. All claimed to discover the body together."

"All claimed to see nothing."

"Nothing before the shooting. Nobody running away. No cars speeding off. No suspicious activity." Harris's tone flat with remembered frustration. "Four people with identical blind spots."

Dempsey turned to a new page in her notebook. "Tell me about Erin Yes."

"Why her specifically?" Harris's eyes narrowed.

"Just start at the top of the list."

He paused. Studied her. Decided to answer anyway. "Young. Short. That's all I got on physical description. Wore sunglasses at midnight. Had on one of those blue medical masks. COVID precaution, she said."

Dempsey looked up from her notes. "Masks. In the crime scene photos, none of the witnesses are wearing masks."

Harris frowned. Checked his screen. "You're right."

"Or maybe she was the only one wearing a mask in July when restrictions had ended."

"Possible." He shrugged again. "When uniforms responded to the 911 call, they secured the scene, separated the witnesses. Standard procedure. I interviewed them one by one. Yes was last."

"The crime scene photographer arrived at 2:42 AM."

"Lincoln. Yeah. He documented everything. Bodies. Evidence. Scene overview."

"Were the witnesses still there when Lincoln arrived?"

Harris thought for a moment. "Bonner, Duke, and Pass were. Yes had left by then."

"Left a murder investigation?"

"Gave her statement. Signed it. No legal reason to hold her."

Dempsey tapped her pen against the notebook. Once. Twice. Thinking. "Did you ask her to remove the sunglasses? The mask?"

"What?"

"During the interview. Did you ask to see her face?"

Harris's expression shifted. Defensive. "It was a witness interview, not an interrogation. She wasn't a suspect."

"But sunglasses at night. A mask when others weren't wearing them." Dempsey kept her tone neutral. Just facts. Not accusation. "That didn't strike you as unusual?"

"Course it did." Harris's voice hardened. "But she was a witness who probably did a shit ton of coke in the bar. She was a cooperative witness who called 911. Who convinced the others to stay at the scene. Who gave a statement. Who signed her name."

"A fake name."

Harris's eyes widened. Then narrowed. "You sure?"

"No Erin Yes in any database. Not DMV. Not Social Security. Not tax records." Dempsey didn't mention how long she'd searched. How many systems she'd accessed. "Ghost witness."

"Shit." He rubbed his face again. The Christmas tree trembled. "I should have pushed harder."

"What did she say in her statement? Exactly."

Harris turned to his computer. Typed. Read silently. "Same as the others. At The Dump earlier. Left around 1:30. Cut through the alley. Found the body with the other three. Saw nothing suspicious before or after."

"That's it?"

"She mentioned insisting they all stay. Said it was the right thing to do." He scrolled further. "That's the only detail that differs from the other statements."

"Why didn't you ask her to remove the mask and sunglasses?" She returned to the point Harris had dodged.

His face flushed. Jaw tightened. "Because she was a damned witness who had nothing useful to say. Because I had a dead drug dealer and three other witnesses telling the same story. Because it was 4 AM and I'd been on shift for fourteen hours."

His voice had risen. Two detectives at nearby desks glanced over, then away. Pretending not to listen.

"You didn't find it suspicious."

"I found it weird, not suspicious." Harris's anger receded as quickly as it had flared. "Look, if she'd been the only witness, sure, I'd have pushed harder. Asked for ID. Made her take off the glasses and mask. But with three others confirming the same story? It didn't seem worth the hassle."

Dempsey nodded. Wrote something down without looking at the page. A technique to make interview subjects fill silence.

"I screwed up." Harris's admission came quietly. "Should have been more thorough."

"Brandt was rushing you."

"Still my case. My responsibility." He adjusted the Christmas tree. Straightened it. Santa's faded face restored to the proper angle. "Why the interest in Yes specifically? There something about her I should know?"

He leaned forward, elbows on knees. "What's going on, Dempsey?"

She paused. Stood at the edge of his desk. Calculating how much to reveal.

"The other witnesses are dead."

Harris stared at her. Blinked twice. "What?"

"Bonner, Duke, Pass. All dead."

"Since when?" His voice dropped to a near whisper. The bullpen continued its normal activity around them. Phones ringing. Keyboards clicking. No one paying attention to their conversation.

"November. Within weeks of each other." Dempsey watched his face carefully. Looking for recognition. Guilt. Any sign he already knew. Found only surprise.

"How?"

"Pass died from a bicycle accident on the 28th. Medical Examiner ruled it commotio cordis. Heart stopped from impact." She kept her voice flat. Just facts. "Duke was found in his garage on the 13th. Carbon monoxide. Ruled a suicide."

Harris's mouth opened. Closed. "And Bonner?"

"Drowned. Car in Weller Lake on the 7th. No signs of struggle. No witnesses."

"Jesus." He ran a hand through his thinning hair. The Christmas tree tilted as his elbow bumped the desk again. He didn't notice. "Three witnesses. Three deaths."

"All in November."

"That's not coincidence." Harris's detective instincts overrode his initial shock. "That's a pattern."

"Yes."

"And now you're looking for the fourth witness." He made the connection quickly. "Erin Yes."

"Yes."

"You and I both know it's more than circumstance."

"But we can't prove it. Not yet."

Harris stood, paced. His shoes squeaked on the linoleum. "So what's your play? Why come to me?"

"Need background on Tapani. Need to understand why someone would kill him. And then the witnesses."

"Tapani was a piece of crap who deserved to die." Harris said it with sudden vehemence. Stopped pacing. Planted his hands on his desk. Leaned forward. "Drug dealer. Assault record. Multiple arrests. City's better without him."

Dempsey studied him. The outburst seemed genuine. Not calculated. Not covering something else. Just frustration from a detective who'd seen too many Tapanis. Too many repeat offenders. Too many cases that ended without justice.

"But why are the witnesses dying?"

"That's the question." Harris sank back into his chair. Energy draining as quickly as it had flared. "What's the connection? What did they see that night? What's worth killing for three months later?"

"That's what I need to find out."

Harris nodded. Turned to his computer again. Typed briefly. "Take a look at Tapani's criminal record. His associates. See who might have wanted him dead."

"Already tried." Dempsey didn't mention the hours she'd spent searching databases. Following digital trails. Looking for connections. "Most of his recent arrest records are sealed."

"Sealed?" Harris frowned. Typed again. "You're right. Last three arrests. All restricted access."

"Why would a small-time dealer's records be sealed?"

"Witness in a bigger case?" Harris scrolled through his screen. "Or he was connected to someone with pull."

Dempsey took out her notebook again. Opened to a new page. "Which arrests specifically?"

"Drug possession January three years ago. That one's open. Six months served." Harris continued reading. "Trafficking with intent June same year. Charges dropped. File restricted."

"Dropped why?"

"Doesn't say. That's the problem with sealed records." He scrolled further. "Sexual assault April two years ago. Charges dropped. Case restricted. Domestic violence May this year. Charges dropped. Case restricted."

Dempsey wrote each date. Each charge. Each restriction. "Victim names?"

"Not listed in the summary. You'd need the full files." Harris looked up at her. "Which means you need Brandt."

"Brandt."

"Chief's signature required for sealed files. Department policy." He shrugged. "She sent you down this rabbit hole. Make her give you the tools to navigate it."

Dempsey closed her notebook. Tucked it away. Harris was right. The next step led through Brandt. Through official channels she'd been avoiding. Through conversations that would require explaining how she'd connected Tapani to the dead witnesses in the first place.

"Appreciate the help." She turned to leave.

"Dempsey." Harris's voice stopped her. She looked back. His expression had changed. Concern replacing the earlier frustration. "Three dead witnesses means someone's cleaning house. Be careful where you step."

She nodded once. Acknowledgment without promise. Then walked away. Back to her desk. Back to the investigation that had become more complex with each new piece.

Three witnesses dead. One missing. Mara Snowden somewhere in the shadows. And Brandt at the center, pushing Harris off the case too quickly. Sending Dempsey specifically to check on Mara. Controlling access to the files that might explain it all.

The connections were there. The pattern visible but incomplete. Like a photograph with key elements deliberately left outside the frame.

Dempsey reached her desk. Sat down. Stared at her blank computer screen. The next move was clear. Unavoidable. She needed Brandt. Needed access to those sealed files. Needed official sanction for an investigation she'd been conducting off the books.

Which meant decisions about what to reveal. What to conceal. What to admit taking from Mara's apartment. What to keep hidden. Decisions that would determine not just the course of the investigation but potentially her career.

Dempsey reached for her phone. Three witnesses dead. A fourth missing. No more time for hesitation.

Chapter 9

Dempsey typed Tapani's name into the database. Hit enter. Waited for the system to respond. The search results appeared, a chronological list of encounters with law enforcement spanning five years. She scrolled through the entries, looking for the pattern that would explain why a dead drug dealer connected to Mara Snowden.

The assault case from five years ago came up first. Bar fight. Tapani had broken a pool cue over another man's head. Suspended sentence. Probation that he'd violated twice with missed check-ins. Standard stuff for a violent offender with poor impulse control.

Dempsey clicked on the next entry. Trafficking with intent, four years ago. Three ounces of heroin found during a buy-and-bust operation. Felony-level charges. She scanned the summary page. Charges dropped before trial. The case file contained photographs of the drugs, witness statements from undercover officers.

Solid evidence. Solid case. No reason for it to collapse.

She clicked deeper into the file. Found a notation buried in the prosecutorial summary: "Subject cooperation with ongoing investigation." A single line that explained everything. Tapani had cut a deal.

Dempsey leaned back in her chair. The afternoon sun slanted through the blinds, casting thin bars of light across her keyboard. The bullpen hummed with the usual sounds. Phones ringing. Keys clicking. Conversations half-heard.

She returned to the search results. Three years ago, Tapani was arrested twice. Once for sexual assault. Once for simple assault. Both times, prosecution declined to press charges despite sufficient evidence. The same pattern. The same implicit arrangement.

Two years ago, another sexual assault. No charges filed.

Then Tapani's last arrest before his death: drug possession. Small amount. Personal use. Prosecution declined again.

Dempsey opened the possession file. Read the arresting officer's report. Standard traffic stop for a broken taillight. Vehicle search based on "odor of marijuana." Eight grams of pot found under the passenger seat. Tapani claimed it wasn't his. Standard denial. No one believed him, but the charges disappeared anyway.

The clock on the wall ticked steadily. Each second marking time in an investigation that kept circling back to the same conclusion.

Tapani had been a confidential informant. A snitch. Someone feeding information to the department in exchange for leniency. For freedom despite his crimes. For permission to keep dealing, keep hurting, keep moving through the world with impunity.

She returned to the sexual assault from three years ago. Prosecution declined. The officer's notes indicated "insufficient evidence to proceed." But the medical examination had documented bruising consistent with forced intercourse. The victim's statement was locked.

Dempsey scrolled through the digital file. Looking for what wasn't there. For the gap in documentation that would explain why a case with solid evidence had been abandoned. Found it in a supplementary note: "Case suspended pending subject's cooperation in Operation Downtown."

The department had let a rapist walk to protect their drug informant. Had made that calculation deliberately. Had decided Tapani's information was worth more than his victim's justice.

She checked the simple assault from the same year. Bar fight again. Broken nose. Fractured orbital socket. Prosecution declined. Same reason. Same Operation Downtown.

Dempsey pulled a notepad from her desk drawer. Made notes in tight, precise handwriting. Dates. Case numbers. The pattern of escalation. The consistent protection from consequences. The transaction between Tapani and the department made explicit in the code language of police bureaucracy.

Now she understood Harris's frustration. The detective had inherited a murder case where the victim had been shielded by the department for years. Where potential suspects had ample motive but were difficult to identify because the records were sealed. Where the normal investigative pathways were blocked by administrative barriers designed to protect confidential informants even after death.

She opened the sexual assault case from two years ago. No charges filed despite, again, solid evidence. Physical examination consistent with assault. Witness and victim statements locked. Prosecution declined.

This time the supplementary note referenced "Operation Crossroads." A different investigation. A different exchange. Tapani's freedom for someone else's incarceration.

Dempsey made another note. Drew a line connecting the operations. Downtown. Crossroads. Major drug investigations where Tapani had been valuable enough to overlook his increasingly violent behavior.

The clock ticked louder. The office sounds faded as her focus narrowed to the screen. To the evidence of a system that made deals with devils. That accepted collateral damage in service of larger objectives. That created informants like Tapani, then couldn't protect them when those deals caught up.

Dempsey closed the final case file. Sat back in her chair. The investigation had taken a turn she hadn't expected. Had revealed layers of complexity that went beyond Mara and her photograph and her journal. That implicated the department itself in the chain of events that had led to Tapani's death.

And possibly to the deaths of the witnesses. To Mara's disappearance.

She needed those sealed files. Needed to know who Tapani had informed on. Who his victims had been. Who might have wanted revenge badly enough to execute him in an alley. To murder three witnesses months later. To vanish into the night leaving only a photograph signed with a name no one should have known.

For U Callisto.

Dempsey closed the database. Picked up her phone.

Dempsey dialed Brandt's extension. Let it ring four times. No answer. She tried the front desk. Asked for the chief. Was told Brandt wasn't taking calls. Dempsey hung up without responding. Looked at the clock on her computer. 4:45. Still time to catch Brandt before she left for the day.

She stood. Grabbed her notebook and phone. Took the stairs instead of waiting for the elevator. One flight up to the administrative level where the offices had actual doors and windows with blinds. Where the carpet didn't show decades of coffee stains. Where decisions got made about cases like Tapani's.

The hallway was quiet. No phones ringing. No conversations. Just the soft hum of the ventilation system and the muted sounds of keyboards from behind closed doors.

Brandt's office sat at the end. Corner position. Two windows. Glass door with her name and title etched in gold-colored letters. The blinds were open. Brandt visible at her desk, head bent over paperwork. Reading glasses perched on the end of her nose.

Dempsey approached. Knocked twice. Sharp. Professional. Not tentative but not aggressive either. Brandt looked up. No smile. No frown. Just the neutral expression she wore for subordinates interrupting her work.

She gestured Dempsey in with two fingers. A small movement that conveyed both permission and impatience.

Dempsey entered. Closed the door behind her. Remained standing. No invitation to sit had been offered.

"What is it, Detective?" Brandt removed her glasses. Set them on top of the file she'd been reviewing. Her desk was organized with precision. Files stacked at right angles. Pens aligned. Computer screen angled for privacy.

"Need authorization to formally investigate the Tapani homicide."

"The cold case from July?" Brandt's eyebrows rose. "Why?"

"New evidence."

"What new evidence?"

Dempsey hesitated. Calculated how much to reveal. How much to hold back. "It's connected to Snowden's disappearance."

"What?" Brandt's expression didn't change, but something shifted in her posture. A slight tensing. Almost imperceptible. "How?"

"When I checked Snowden's apartment, I found photographs she'd taken of The Dump nightclub. Multiple shots. Different angles. That's where Stefan Tapani was murdered in July." It disturbed Dempsey that the lie came so easily.

Brandt's expression didn't change. "She photographs abandoned buildings. It's part of her portfolio work. You've seen her public gallery. Haven't you?"

"Why that building specifically?" Dempsey asked, diverting attention from the fact that she had not seen Mara's public gallery of photos.

"Why not? It's visually interesting. Graffiti, decay, urban blight. That's her aesthetic." Brandt leans back. "You're connecting dots that aren't there, Detective."

"Maybe. But I need to rule it out. I need access to all of Tapani's files."

Brandt's expression changed. A crack in the professional mask. Surprise. Then something else. Concern. Calculation. Her eyes narrowed.

"Give me your theory."

Dempsey cleared her throat. "It's possible she saw or photographed something of concern. Maybe the Tapani killer saw her snooping around, scared her off. Maybe—"

"Enough. What has that got to do with his previous crimes?"

"That's what I need to find out." Dempsey shrugged. "But to do that, I need access to Tapani's sealed case files. Need to know who his victims were. Who might have wanted him dead."

Dempsey started to explain. Got three words in. "I found a—"

Brandt held up her hand. Palm out. The universal signal for silence. Dempsey stopped talking.

The office fell quiet. The ventilation system hummed. A clock on the wall made no sound, its second hand moving in silent sweeps. Brandt stared at her desk. At nothing. At something only she could see.

When she spoke again, her voice had changed. Softened. Lost its edge of authority.

"Mara is my niece."

Dempsey didn't respond. Couldn't. The words didn't make sense at first. Didn't connect to reality as she understood it.

"My sister's daughter." Brandt continued into the silence.

Dempsey's mind raced through the implications. The chief of police was related to the missing photographer. To the woman who'd been stalking Dempsey. Who'd been taking pictures without consent. Who'd written explicit fantasies in a journal Dempsey had stolen from her apartment.

"Why didn't you tell me this when you sent me to check on her?"

"Would it have changed how you handled the welfare check?" Brandt's professional tone returned. Her back straightened. "I kept it separate for the same reason she does. Professional boundaries."

Dempsey didn't answer. The question was a deflection. Of course it would have changed things. Would have contextualized the assignment. Would have explained Brandt's concern about a missed court appearance.

"I'll unseal the Tapani files." Brandt reached for her keyboard. Typed briefly. "You'll have access within the hour."

"Thank you." Dempsey waited for more. For explanation. For context. For anything that would make sense of this new connection.

"But I need your word that this stays absolutely private." Brandt looked up from her screen. "Whatever you find. Whatever connection exists between Mara and Tapani and you. It stays between us until we understand what's happening."

"I can't promise that."

"You can and you will." Brandt's voice hardened. "This is my family, Detective. My niece. I need to know what's happening before it becomes official. Before reports are filed. Before cases are opened that can't be closed."

Dempsey considered her options. Refusal meant no access to the sealed files. Meant professional suicide. Meant never understanding why Mara had written "For U Callisto" on a dead man's photograph.

"I'll keep it contained." Not a promise of silence. Not a guarantee of privacy. Just an acknowledgment of discretion. The most she could offer while maintaining her integrity.

Brandt seemed to understand the distinction. Nodded once. Returned to her keyboard. Typed again. The matter settled as far as she was concerned.

"I've authorized temporary access to the restricted files." She didn't look up. "I expect updates. Direct to me. No one else."

"Understood."

Brandt said nothing more. Just gestured toward the door with the same two fingers she'd used to invite Dempsey in. Dismissal as efficient as welcome.

Dempsey turned to leave. Had her hand on the doorknob when Brandt spoke again.

"Shut the door on your way out."

Dempsey complied. Closed the door firmly behind her. Stood in the quiet hallway processing what she'd learned. The chief of police was Mara Snowden's aunt. Had sent Dempsey specifically to check on her niece. Had kept that connection hidden until confronted with evidence she couldn't ignore.

Another piece in the puzzle. Another connection in the pattern. Another reason to keep digging until she understood what linked them all. Tapani. Mara. Brandt. Callisto.

And the three dead witnesses who had seen nothing.

She took the elevator down one flight. Give her a chance to think.

Dempsey glanced at the wall clock as she sat down at her computer. 7:31. Time to go home. The cleaning crew had already started their rounds. A vacuum whirred somewhere down the hall. The faint scent of industrial cleaner drifted through the empty bullpen.

Her email notification dinged. One new message. From I.T. Department. Subject: "Clearance Granted - Case Files #78102, #79144, #83921, #84001, #86772."

Dempsey clicked the message. Standard boilerplate about temporary access authorization. Restricted case files now available through her login credentials. Reminder about confidentiality protocols. Warning about unauthorized distribution of sensitive information.

She closed the email. Opened the department's case management system. Typed in her credentials. Navigated to the search function. Entered Tapani's name again.

The same search results appeared, but with no restrictions. No sealed files. No blocked access. Everything open for her review. She started with the oldest assault case.

Luis Hamilton, 38. Bar manager at The Rail. Tapani had been ejected for harassment of female patrons. Returned an hour later. Struck Hamilton from behind with a pool cue when the manager refused to let him re-enter. Fractured skull. Three days in hospital. Solid case with multiple witnesses. Tapani pled guilty for reduced sentence.

Dempsey made a note of Hamilton's name. Address. Current employment. Potential interview subject. Someone with reason to hate Tapani.

She moved to the trafficking case. The one where Tapani had first become an informant. The deal that had started his protected status. Three ounces of heroin. Enough for felony charges. Enough for serious prison time. The case had been solid until Tapani offered information on his supplier.

The supplier's name was redacted even in the unsealed file. An ongoing investigation apparently. But the details of Tapani's cooperation were clear. He'd worn a wire. Had recorded three transactions. Had testified before a grand jury. His reward: freedom. Charges dropped. Record sealed.

Dempsey continued through the files. The sexual assault from three years ago. Victim: Nola Middleton, 28. Waitress at The Dump. Tapani had followed her after her shift. Had forced her into his car. Had driven to a remote location. Had raped her for hours before letting her go.

Medical evidence had been solid. Rape kit positive for Tapani's DNA. Victim's statement detailed and consistent. Prosecution had prepared charges. Then Operation Downtown needed Tapani. The case suspended. The charges never filed.

Dempsey wrote down Middleton's information. Another potential interview subject. Another person with reason to hate Tapani. Another victim sacrificed for the greater good of a drug investigation.

The simple assault from the same year. Victim: Graham Cano, 42. Bartender at The Dump. Tapani had been cut off for excessive intoxication. Had thrown a punch. Had broken Cano's nose. Had been arrested on scene. Had walked free when the charges were dropped in exchange for his continued cooperation.

Another name. Another potential interview. Another pattern of violence centered around The Dump. The nightclub behind which Tapani had eventually been killed.

The drug possession case was straightforward. Traffic stop for broken taillight. Eight grams of pot found under the passenger seat. Tapani claimed it wasn't his. Standard denial. But the charges had disappeared anyway. His final protected act before someone put three bullets in him.

Dempsey sat back. Rubbed her eyes. The vacuum cleaner had moved closer. Now in the hallway outside the bullpen. The cleaner smell stronger. The clock showed 8:10. She'd been reading for over thirty minutes. Piecing together the history of a violent man who'd been protected by the very system designed to stop him.

Something nagged at her. A gap in her notes. A file she'd skipped.

She scrolled back through the search results. Found it. The sexual assault from two years ago. No charges filed. She'd been interrupted in reviewing it earlier. Had moved on without noting the details.

Dempsey clicked on the file. Standard format. Date. Time. Location. Responding officers. Victim information. She scrolled to the victim's name.

Mara Snowden, 34.

Dempsey's hands went still on the keyboard. Her breath caught. The vacuum in the hallway faded from her awareness. The clock stopped ticking. The world narrowed to those two words on her screen.

Mara Snowden.

She read further. The crime location: alley behind The Dump nightclub. The same alley where Tapani would be murdered a year later. The same alley where four witnesses would claim to see nothing. The same alley captured in the photograph signed "For U Callisto."

The details of the assault were clinical. Professional. Detective language describing violent personal violation. Snowden had been photographing the nightclub for a personal project. Tapani had approached. Had offered to show her a better angle from the alley. Had attacked her once they were out of sight. Had raped her against the brick wall. Had stolen her camera before fleeing.

Physical evidence had been collected. Rape kit positive for Tapani's DNA. Victim's statement detailed and consistent. Prosecution had prepared charges. Then the case had stalled. No explanation in the file. No reference to another operation. No justification for why Tapani had walked free again.

Just a case that disappeared. A rapist who escaped consequences. A victim left without justice. A photographer who kept taking pictures. Who kept working for the department. Who kept showing up at crime scenes where Dempsey worked.

Who started following Dempsey. Watching her. Photographing her without consent. Writing about her in a journal. Fantasizing about her in explicit detail.

And then leaving a photograph of her rapist's murder scene with Dempsey's birth name written on the back.

The vacuum cleaner stopped. The sudden silence jarring. Dempsey blinked. Looked at the clock again. 8:22. She'd been staring at the screen for minutes without moving. Without breathing properly. Without processing what she'd discovered.

Mara Snowden had been raped by Stefan Tapani in the same alley where he would later be killed. Had been denied justice by the same system that had protected him. Had been sent to photograph crime scenes despite her own victimization. Had been expected to continue functioning professionally in a world that had failed her completely.

And then had disappeared just after the witnesses to Tapani's murder started dying. Just after a list of names had been marked "paid in full" in her notebook. Just after she'd left evidence specifically for Dempsey to find.

The vacuum started again. Further away now. Moving down the hall. The cleaning staff continued their routine while Dempsey sat motionless at her desk. The pieces falling into place. The connections clarifying. The pattern taking shape.

Mara. Tapani. The photograph. The journal. Callisto.

And at the center, a single question Dempsey still couldn't answer:

Why me?

Chapter 10

Dempsey sat alone in the bullpen. The case file on her screen cast blue light across her face. Stefan Tapani's name at the top. Sexual assault. Victim: Mara Snowden. Case status: closed. No charges filed. She clicked through the documents with mechanical precision. Each tap of the keyboard echoed in the empty room.

The building had emptied hours ago. Just Dempsey and the night cleaning crew remained. A vacuum started somewhere distant, then stopped. The air conditioning had shut off at eight. The air felt stale. Heavy. She could hear her own heartbeat in her ears.

She opened the next document. The initial report. Officer Calhoun responding to Memorial Hospital. Female victim, 34, reporting sexual assault. Location: alley behind The Dump nightclub. Dempsey's eyes moved mechanically across the page. Reading but not absorbing. Not yet. Just collecting data.

She clicked again. The victim's statement. Mara's own words describing the attack. Dempsey forced herself to read each line. Each detail. Each moment of violation recorded in the flat, impersonal language of police documentation.

Her stomach tightened. Her jaw clenched. She kept reading.

Tapani had offered to show Mara a better angle for photographs. Had led her into the alley. Had been charming until they were alone. Had changed in an instant. Had pushed her against the wall. Had ignored her protests. Had taken what he wanted. Had laughed afterward. Had stolen her camera before leaving her bleeding on the ground.

Dempsey clicked to the next file. Medical examination photographs. She paused with her finger on the mouse. Inhaled once. Opened them.

The first image filled her screen. Mara's face. Left eye swollen shut. Purple-black bruising spreading across her cheekbone. Lower lip split, three stitches closing the wound. Right jaw discolored from impact.

She clicked to the next image. Neck bruises. Finger marks. A clear pattern of a strangulation attempt. Next image. Bilateral wrist bruising. Restraint marks. Upper arms showing distinct finger impressions where she'd been held down.

Dempsey kept clicking. Each image more damning than the last. Ribs. Back. Thighs. A methodical catalog of brutality inflicted by a man who had never faced consequences. Who had been protected by the same system that had sent Mara back to photograph more crime scenes. More bodies. More violence.

The final photograph showed Mara's right knee. Significant abrasion. Gravel embedded in the wound. The concrete of the alley ground into her skin.

Dempsey closed the file. Sat back. Stared at her screen. The vacuum started again, closer now. The cleaning crew making their rounds. Moving toward her. She barely heard it.

Brandt had sent her to check on Mara. Had acted concerned but not panicked when told her niece was missing. Had shown shock only when Dempsey mentioned finding the Tapani photograph.

Now it made sense. The chief had known about the assault. Had known her niece had been brutalized by a man who walked free. Had known and done what? Nothing. Nothing that showed in any record. Nothing that had kept Tapani from attacking others. From moving through the world unrestrained by consequence or conscience.

Had Brandt intervened for her niece? Had she tried to push charges against a protected informant? Or had she accepted the decision, telling Mara it was complicated, telling herself it was for the greater good of ongoing operations?

Had Brandt killed Tapani? Had him killed?

The questions circled without answers. The vacuum moved down the hallway outside the bullpen. The cleaner pushing it whistled tunelessly. The sound penetrated Dempsey's consciousness. Ordinary. Normal. Discordant against what she'd just seen.

Acid rose in her throat. Sharp. Sudden. She swallowed it back. The taste bitter on her tongue. Her stomach contracted again. More insistent.

Dempsey stood. Moved away from her desk. From the images still lingering on her screen. From the evidence of brutality documented with professional detachment.

She walked toward the door. Toward the cleaning cart visible in the hallway. Yellow vinyl bag attached to its side. Industrial cleaners stacked on the bottom shelf. Mop handles extending upward like prison bars.

The cleaner looked up as she approached. Mid-fifties. Balding. Bored eyes that widened as he registered her expression.

Dempsey reached the cart. Bent over the yellow bag. Vomited with sudden violence. Her body rejecting what her mind had absorbed. The sour smell of stomach acid mixed with the chemical scent of floor cleaner.

The cleaner stepped back. Said nothing. Just watched as she heaved again. As her shoulders convulsed. As everything inside her fought to escape.

When it stopped, Dempsey straightened. Wiped her mouth with the back of her hand. Felt sweat cold on her forehead. The cleaner still staring. Still silent.

"Sorry," she managed.

He shrugged. "Seen worse." His eyes moved from her face to her badge clipped on her belt. "Bad one, huh?"

She nodded. Didn't elaborate. Knew what made this case different from the hundreds of others she'd seen. The thousands of photographs of victims she'd studied. This one had broken through her professional armor. This one had reached past detachment and found something raw beneath.

The cleaner looked at his ruined bag. "That's why it's vinyl. You never know."

"Sorry," she said again. Meaningless repetition. Empty word.

He shrugged again. Returned to his work. Problem identified. Solution obvious. No need for further discussion.

Dempsey walked back to her desk. Her legs steadier than she expected. Her mind clearer. As if the physical purge had created space for what came next. For the connections she still needed to make. For the evidence she still needed to find.

She sat down. Wiped sweat from her upper lip. Took a breath. Clicked to close the medical examination photos. Moved to the next tab in the case file. The doctor's report waited. More details. More evidence of what Tapani had done. More professional documentation of Mara's pain.

She had seen enough. Understood enough. Would read the clinical description later when her stomach had settled. When the taste of bile was gone from her mouth. When she could process it as evidence rather than atrocity.

For now, she needed to keep moving. Keep looking. Keep following the breadcrumbs that had led her here. That would lead her to Mara. To understanding. To the truth behind a photograph signed with a name she'd abandoned decades ago.

For U Callisto.

Dempsey clicked the doctor's report tab closed. Too much detail. Too much damage cataloged in medical terminology. She moved to the next tab. Witnesses. Three names appeared on her screen. She stared at them. Recognized them immediately. Barney Duke. Turner Pass. Deirdre Bonner.

Fuck.

Her mind raced to connect these new dots. Not coincidence. Not possible. The same three people had witnessed both Mara's assault and Tapani's murder. Had given statements both times. Had been present for both crimes in the same alley.

Dempsey leaned closer to the screen. Clicked on Duke's statement first. Her eyes moved methodically across the text. Each sentence more damning than the last.

"I was at The Dump having drinks. Saw the female photographer talking with Tapani at the bar. She was flirting with him pretty hard. Touching his arm. Laughing at his jokes. Around midnight they left together. She was leading him toward the back door. Looked consensual to me. I didn't see them again until I left around 1:30 and heard someone crying in the alley. Looked like they'd had rough sex and she regretted it after. Didn't seem like my business."

Dempsey's jaw tightened. Teeth pressed against teeth. Pressure building. She'd seen the injuries. Had looked at the photographs. Had read the hospital report. Nothing about it suggested consent. Nothing about it supported "rough sex" as an explanation. Every physical detail screamed violence. Assault. Rape.

Yet Duke had seen flirting. Had seen consent. Had chosen to interpret a woman crying in an alley as regret rather than trauma.

She clicked on Pass's statement next. Different perspective. Same implication.

"I went outside to take a leak in the alley around midnight. Saw Tapani and the photographer going at it against the wall. Didn't look forced to me. I watched for a minute then went back inside. Not my fault if she changed her mind afterward."

Dempsey's hands clenched into fists. The statement contradicted both Duke's timeline and the physical evidence. Mara's injuries weren't consistent with consensual sex. The abrasions on her back didn't match being held willingly against a wall. The defensive bruising on her arms told a different story than the one Pass had witnessed or claimed to witness.

He'd watched. Had seen a woman being assaulted and had interpreted it as consent. Had done nothing to help. Had returned to his drink inside. Had left her there.

The vacuum cleaner had moved on to another floor. The bullpen silent now. Just the sound of Dempsey's breathing. Sharp. Controlled. Growing faster as she clicked on Bonner's statement.

"I left The Dump around 1 AM. Walked past the alley and saw a woman lying on the ground crying. Figured she was drunk. It happens a lot outside that place. Didn't stop to check on her. Just kept walking. Didn't seem serious at the time."

Three witnesses. Three versions. Three people who had seen pieces of what happened to Mara and had chosen to interpret them in ways that absolved Tapani. That absolved themselves of responsibility. That left a woman bleeding on concrete without help or justice.

And later, these same three had stood in the same alley beside Tapani's body. Had given statements claiming to see nothing. Had protected someone again. Not Tapani this time. His killer.

Brandt? Mara?

The realization hit Dempsey with physical force. A pressure behind her sternum. A tightness in her throat. The three witnesses had lied twice. First to protect Tapani from rape charges. Then to protect Mara from murder charges.

Why? Guilt over their earlier inaction? Payment? Threats? The files offered no explanation for the shift in loyalty. Just the evidence of two crimes connected by location, participants, and lies.

Heat rose in Dempsey's face. Spread across her chest. Down her arms. Her right hand opened. Closed. Opened again. The small muscles of her fingers twitching with suppressed energy.

The lies had cost Mara everything. Her sense of safety. Her trust in the system. Her belief that truth mattered. That evidence would bring justice. That her pain meant something to the world beyond herself.

These three had seen her victimized and had chosen to look away. Had chosen interpretation over observation. Had chosen to protect a man who had brutalized her. Had chosen comfort over courage.

And the system had accepted their statements. Had weighed them against physical evidence. Had decided three witnesses outweighed one victim's testimony. Had closed the case. No charges filed.

The same system that had protected Tapani as an informant. That had looked the other way as he continued dealing drugs, assaulting women, breaking bodies and laws with impunity. The same system that Dempsey served. That she believed in. That had failed Mara so completely.

The vacuum started again on another floor. Distant. Rhythmic. Ordinary sound against extraordinary revelation.

Dempsey's rage built with each passing second. Not the hot flash of momentary anger but something deeper. Colder. More absolute. The certainty that something fundamental had been broken. That justice wasn't just blind but corrupt at its core.

Her right hand formed a fist again. Tighter than before. Knuckles white beneath the skin. She stared at the screen. At Bonner's statement still displayed. At the words that dismissed a woman's trauma as drunken regret.

The rage peaked. Found focus. Found target.

Dempsey's fist connected with the screen before she realized she'd moved. The impact jarred her arm to the shoulder. The monitor rocked backward but didn't fall. Didn't break. Just displayed a smear of blood where her knuckle had split on contact.

She pulled her hand back. Looked at it with detached curiosity. Blood welled from the small cut. Bright red against pale skin. Minor damage. Nothing compared to what Mara had endured. Nothing compared to the wounds that had been documented in those photographs.

The pain registered distantly. Unimportant data. Secondary to the information she'd uncovered. To the pattern now clear before her.

Mara had been raped. The witnesses had lied to protect her attacker. The system had failed her. Then Mara had killed Tapani. The same witnesses had lied again, this time to protect her. And now all of them were dead. She was taking her vengeance.

Mara had marked them "paid in full" in her notebook. Had systematically eliminated everyone connected to her assault. Everyone who had failed her that night. Everyone except Dempsey. Everyone except Callisto.

Dempsey stared at the names on her screen. Bonner. Duke. Pass. And the fourth witness. The one Harris had interviewed last. The one wearing sunglasses at midnight and a mask when no one else was. The one who had convinced the others to stay at the scene. Who had ensured they all gave statements. The one not in the notebook.

Erin Yes.

Dempsey's pen stopped moving. Her breath caught.

Erin. Yes.

Not a name. A word broken in two. A clue left in plain sight for anyone who knew how to read it. For anyone who understood mythology the way Mara did. The way she had understood Callisto.

Erinyes.

The Greek goddesses of vengeance. The Furies who hunted those who escaped justice. Who punished crimes the courts couldn't touch. Who drove the guilty to madness and death.

"Jesus Christ." Dempsey's whisper barely disturbed the air.

Mara hadn't witnessed Tapani's murder. She had orchestrated the entire scene. Had stood there with three witnesses who had failed her. Had made them watch as she executed the man who had raped her. Had forced them to finally see what they should have seen the first time. Had made them complicit in justice administered when the system refused.

And then she had signed the witness statement. Had left her calling card for anyone smart enough to decode it. Erin Yes. Erinyes. The goddess of vengeance marking her work.

Dempsey stood abruptly. The chair scraped against hardwood. Her hands shook as she picked up the case file. Harris's notes about the witness who wore sunglasses and a mask. Who had no record in any database. Who had vanished after giving her statement.

Because she had never existed. Just a persona. A performance. Mara hiding in plain sight while documenting her own crime scene. Taking her revenge while ensuring the witnesses understood their role. Their guilt. Their debt.

Paid in full.

Dempsey's question remained: why her? Why leave the evidence specifically for someone who hadn't been involved? Who hadn't failed her? Who hadn't known her then or now?

Dempsey flexed her injured hand. The blood had already stopped flowing. The pain faded. She looked back at the screen. At the three witness statements from three now-dead witnesses. At the evidence of a system that protected the wrong people. That valued the wrong truths.

She understood Mara's rage. Understood her need for justice when the system offered none. Understood the path that had led from victim to vigilante.

What she didn't understand yet was her own place in that path. Her own role in a story that had begun long before she entered it. A story that had led to her door with three words written on the back of a dead man's photograph.

For U Callisto.

Dempsey left the precinct through the side door. Cold air hit her face. Her breath clouded in front of her. The cut on her knuckle stung in the night air. She walked toward the parking garage two blocks away. Street nearly empty at this hour. Just the occasional car passing. Headlights sweeping across wet pavement. The city quiet but never silent.

A delivery truck idled at the curb. Exhaust rising in white plumes. The driver leaned against the hood, smoking. His cigarette a pinpoint of orange in the darkness. He watched her pass without interest. Just another cop working late. Nothing special.

Her mind replayed the nightmare from the previous night. The alley. The body. The headlights coming at her. The sense of danger approaching too fast to avoid. Her subconscious had tried to warn her. Had processed the connections before her waking mind could assemble them. Had recognized the pattern hidden in plain sight.

She crossed at the corner. Waited for the light even with no cars coming. Old habit. Rules followed automatically. Her thoughts elsewhere. On Mara.

The pieces aligned with terrible clarity now. Not Brandt. Brandt would never have asked Dempsey to find Mara if she was complicit in Tapani's murder.

It had to be Mara.

Her Mara.

Mara had killed Tapani. That much was certain. Had shot him three times in specific, symbolic places. Groin. Heart. Head. The rapist. The abuser. The liar. Each bullet a sentence carried out. Each wound a judgment rendered.

Not revenge. Justice. The justice the system had denied her. The consequence Tapani had escaped through his connections. Through his value as an informant. Through the protection of a department that weighed his information against her violation and found her wanting.

Dempsey passed a bar. Music leaked through closed doors. Bass notes felt more than heard. Three people smoking outside glanced at her, then away. The badge visible on her belt marking her as authority. As other. As someone to be wary of rather than welcome.

She kept walking. Her pace steady. Unhurried despite the revelations spinning through her mind. Despite the knowledge building with each step.

Mara had killed Tapani. Had taken a photograph worth framing. Beauty from pain.

Then had vanished. Had disappeared from a life that no longer fit. From a role that had become intolerable. From a system that had failed her so completely that her only recourse was to work outside it. Beyond it. Against it.

But the witnesses remained. The three who had seen her assault and looked away. Cruel. Heartless. Reprehensible. But not criminal.

Dempsey stopped walking. Stood motionless on the sidewalk. A new understanding forming with such suddenness that it halted her physical momentum.

"Paid in full."

The words from Mara's notebook. Written beside four names. Tapani. Bonner. Duke. Pass. Not a record of debt settled but of judgment executed. Of accounts balanced through death. Of justice administered when the system refused.

Mara had killed them all.

The drowning wasn't an accident. Bonner hadn't simply driven into the lake at 4 AM. The strange wound on her forehead suddenly explained. Blunt force. Incapacitation before being sent into the water. Before drowning while unconscious.

The suicide wasn't suicide. Duke hadn't taken pills he didn't have a prescription for. Hadn't started his car in a closed garage by choice. Had been drugged first. Positioned. Arranged to look like suicide. The evidence there in the medical examiner's report. The inconsistencies noted but not investigated.

Even Pass. The bicycle accident. The "freak" occurrence of commotio cordis. The precise blow to the chest that stopped his heart. Not chance. Not misfortune. Calculation. Planning. Execution.

None of it was coincidence. All of it was judgment.

Dempsey started walking again. Faster now. The garage just ahead. Her car waiting on the third level. Her mind racing ahead of her feet. Connecting final dots. Completing the pattern.

Mara had killed four people. Had executed judgment on those who had harmed her. Had marked them paid in full in her notebook. Had documented their deaths with the same professional detachment she brought to all her work.

Then had left the evidence for Dempsey to find. Had wanted her specifically to see the pattern. To understand what had happened. To read the message signed "For U Callisto."

But why? What connection existed between her and Mara? What shared history could explain Mara's fixation on her? Why leave breadcrumbs for a detective who hadn't known her before? Who hadn't been involved in her case? Who hadn't failed her as the others had?

Dempsey reached the garage entrance. Swiped her card at the reader. The gate lifted. She walked through. Her footsteps echoed in the concrete structure. The smell of exhaust and oil and damp concrete filled her nostrils. Familiar. Ordinary. At odds with the extraordinary knowledge she now carried.

She took the stairs. One flight. Two. Three. Emerged on the level where her car waited. Walked toward it. Keys already in hand. Mind already moving to what came next. To the conversation she couldn't avoid. To the truth she couldn't conceal.

Dempsey stopped beside her car. Stood with her hand on the door handle. The metal cold against her palm. The cut on her knuckle a dull throb. A reminder of rage expressed. Of control temporarily lost. Of the human beneath the detective.

She had to tell Brandt. Had to report what she'd discovered. Had to explain that the chief's niece was a serial killer. That Mara had murdered four people in calculated succession. That the missing photographer wasn't a victim but a perpetrator. That the evidence led nowhere but to this conclusion.

The truth would destroy Brandt. Would end her career. Would tear apart whatever relationship existed between aunt and niece. Would transform concern into horror. Worry into disgust.

But the truth couldn't be buried. Not by Dempsey. Not after what she'd seen in those files. Not after what she'd learned about a system that protected the wrong people. That valued the wrong things. That had driven a victim to become an executioner when all other paths to justice were closed.

Dempsey unlocked her car. The beep unnaturally loud in the quiet garage. She stood a moment longer, hand still on the door handle. The weight of knowledge heavy across her shoulders. The burden of what came next pressing down with physical force.

Tomorrow she would tell Brandt. Would explain what she'd found. Would lay out the evidence step by step. Would watch understanding dawn in the chief's eyes. Would see the moment when concern for a missing niece transformed into something else entirely.

But tonight, she would carry the knowledge alone. Would drive home with it. Would sit with it in her empty apartment. Would try to understand her own place in a story that had begun long before she entered it. That had led to her door with three words written on the back of a dead man's photograph.

For U Callisto.

Chapter 11

Dempsey parked across from The Dump at midnight. The building stood dark against darker sky. Boarded windows. Peeling paint. Graffiti tags marking territory nobody wanted anymore. The place where it had all started. Where Mara had been attacked. Where Tapani had later died.

Snow began falling. Small flakes drifting down. Catching in her hair as she stepped out of the car. She pulled her collar up against the cold. Stood on the sidewalk studying the building. The Dump had been closed for months. Business license revoked after too many fights. Too many overdoses. Too many nights requiring police presence.

The marquee still hung above the entrance. Letters missing from whatever message had last been displayed. Just empty tracks where neon had once glowed. The front doors chained shut. Padlock rusted from recent rains.

Dempsey's anger built as she approached. Heat in her chest despite the cold. This was where Tapani had cornered Mara. Had offered to show her a better angle for photographs. Had led her into the alley. Had changed in an instant.

She touched the cold metal of the door chain. Tested its strength. Solid. Unmoved since the club's closure. She stepped back. Looked up at the facade. Second floor windows broken. Jagged glass teeth in vicious smiles.

Garbage from the street had collected against the building's edge. Fast food wrappers. Cigarette butts. Used condoms. The residue of city life coated every surface. Cars passed behind her. Occasional headlights sweeping across the abandoned nightclub. Illuminating then abandoning it again.

Dempsey circled the building. Stayed close to the wall. The side street was narrower. Darker. The smell of rancid grease from a restaurant dumpster. Urine from makeshift toilets in building corners. Discarded needles glinted in the streetlight.

She counted doorways. Two emergency exits. Both secured with chains similar to the front. No way in without bolt cutters or a key. She made a mental note. Kept moving.

The back of the building faced the alley. The alley where it had happened. Both crimes. Separated by a year but connected by location. By participants. By violence that bred more violence.

Dempsey stood at the alley entrance. Let her eyes adjust to the deeper darkness. Sodium lights from the main street barely penetrated here. Just enough to cast long shadows. To create pockets of black where anything might hide.

She stepped into the alley. The smell changed. Garbage more concentrated. Exhaust from the street trapped between buildings. Something dead in one of the dumpsters. Rat maybe. Or pigeon. Nothing larger.

The back door to the club was solid metal. No window. Just a keypad lock that would require a code to open. Staff entrance. Delivery entrance. The door Mara had been led through on the pretense of a better photograph.

Dempsey moved further into the alley. Noted the dumpster locations. Two large bins against the opposite wall. Spaced about thirty feet apart. Enough room between them and the club's back wall for a car to pass. For someone to be pinned against brick with no escape.

The case file photos came back to her. Mara's injuries. The bruising. The defensive wounds. The knee torn open on concrete. It had happened right here. In this space. Against this wall.

Her hand touched the brick. Cold. Rough. Unyielding. Like the system that had failed Mara after. That had taken her statement then dismissed it. That had weighed her trauma against Tapani's value as an informant and found her wanting.

Dempsey's jaw clenched. Teeth pressed against teeth. She forced her hand away from the wall. Continued her examination of the scene.

The alley opened to the street at both ends. Exits that offered the illusion of escape. But the dumpsters created blind spots. Places hidden from anyone passing by. Someone could be attacked here while people walked not thirty feet away. Could struggle while traffic continued normally.

Dempsey walked the length of the alley. Measured distances with her stride. From the club's back door to where Tapani had been found was eighteen steps. Just far enough from the street to be invisible to casual observation. Just close enough to the door for staff to find the scene when taking out trash.

She looked up. Second floor windows overlooked the alley. All broken now. No cameras mounted on any wall. No electronic eyes to record what happened here. Just brick and concrete and metal witnessing without judgment or memory.

Had Mara stood in this exact spot when she shot Tapani? Had she thought about her own attack as she pulled the trigger? Had she felt anything at all? Or had it been cold calculation? Justice administered when the system refused.

The snow fell harder. The flakes larger. Already beginning to stick to the ground. To cover blood long washed away. To hide evidence of crimes no one had properly investigated.

Dempsey returned to the alley entrance. Studied the sight lines from there. Anyone entering from the street would see only what the alley's geography allowed. Only what the lighting revealed. Only what they were looking for.

The witnesses had all claimed to see nothing. Had all protected Mara after failing to protect her a year earlier. Had all paid for that protection with their lives.

Dempsey walked back to her car. Snow crunched beneath her boots. Already accumulating. Already transforming the urban landscape into something cleaner. Purer. A deception of white over persistent grime.

She sat behind the wheel. Didn't start the engine immediately. Just stared at The Dump through falling snow. At the building where everything had started. Where Mara had been changed from victim to perpetrator. From photographer to executioner.

The anger in Dempsey's chest hadn't faded. Hadn't cooled with exposure to December air. If anything, standing in that alley had intensified it. Had made Mara's pain more real. More immediate. Had made the system's failure more absolute.

Dempsey started the car. Checked the time. 12:43 AM. December 5th now. The day she would tell Brandt that her niece was a murderer. That Mara had killed four people in calculated succession. That the evidence led nowhere but to this conclusion.

She pulled away from the curb. Left The Dump behind in darkness and accumulating snow. The place had witnessed enough. Had held enough secrets.

Dempsey pulled off to the side of the road at Weller Lake. Cut the headlights but left the engine running. The heater fought against December cold. Snow fell harder now, white flakes visible in the dashboard glow. This was where Deirdre Bonner had died. Where her car had entered the water. Where she'd drowned while unconscious from a blow to the forehead.

She checked her watch. 1:06 AM. The lake stretched black beyond her windshield. Water invisible except where snow hit the surface. Small specks dying in the melt, circles in darkness.

Dempsey opened her door. Stepped out into accumulating snow. Already an inch on the ground. Her boots left clear prints as she walked toward the water's edge. The boat launch was a concrete ramp disappearing into the lake. No barrier. No gate. Nothing to prevent a vehicle from continuing straight into the water.

She studied the approach. The road curved gently toward the launch. Nothing sudden. No sharp turn that might cause an accident. Just a gradual descent toward the water. Designed for boats on trailers. Not for cars without them.

The Medical Examiner had noted no skid marks. No evidence of sudden braking. Just a car that entered the water at moderate speed. A woman unconscious behind the wheel. A drowning ruled accidental despite inconsistencies.

Headlights appeared around the curve behind her. A car approached slowly through the snow. Dempsey turned. Raised her hand to shield her eyes as the vehicle passed. The light blinded her momentarily. Left spots dancing across her vision when it was gone.

That moment of blindness triggered something. A theory forming. The M.E. report had mentioned a horizontal laceration across Bonner's forehead. Unusual for a crash. No corresponding damage to the vehicle interior.

Dempsey walked to the edge of the boat ramp. Looked down at where it disappeared into black water. How had Mara done it? How had she gotten Bonner here? How had she ensured the drowning would look accidental?

She had two scenarios. First: Mara incapacitated Bonner elsewhere. Brought her here unconscious. Placed her in the driver's seat. Set the car moving down the ramp. Let physics and water do the rest.

Second: Mara met Bonner here. Perhaps under pretense of discussion. Conversation. Confrontation. Struck her across the forehead with something heavy. Something narrow enough to cause a laceration rather than blunt trauma. Put her unconscious in the car. Same result.

Both required strength. Planning. Determination. Both required the cold calculation Dempsey had seen in the notebook with names marked "paid in full."

The snow fell in her hair. On her shoulders. The lake water lapped at the concrete edge of the ramp. Regular rhythm like breathing. Patient. Endless.

She tried to picture the scene as the M.E. would have found it. Car partially submerged. Headlights still on beneath the surface. Driver's side window intact. Driver's door closed. Bonner inside, unconscious then drowned.

Something about that detail nagged at her. The windows. The doors. Had they been open or closed when recovered? The Traffic Division's report hadn't specified. An oversight that might matter.

If Bonner had been conscious when the car entered the water, survival instinct would have kicked in. She would have tried to escape. Would have opened a window or door. Would have fought to live.

But if she'd been unconscious first, those details would reveal Mara's method. A closed window meant the car had filled slowly. The water rising around unconscious Bonner until it covered her completely. A crueler death. More certain.

An open window or door meant faster filling. Faster drowning. Less time for something to go wrong. For Bonner to regain consciousness. For a passing motorist to notice.

Dempsey reached for her notebook. Flipped to a clean page. Wrote with precise letters despite the falling snow: "Check: was Bonner window open? Was passenger door open?"

She underlined it twice. Added: "Check car recovery photos. Water line on interior. Flow pattern."

The lake water kept its rhythm against the boat ramp. Regular. Hypnotic. Dempsey stared at the spot where Bonner's car had entered. Where it had gradually sunk while water replaced air inside. Where a woman had died unable to fight for her life.

Another car passed on the road behind her. Slower this time. Cautious in the accumulating snow. Dempsey didn't turn. Didn't raise her hand. Just let the headlights sweep across her back. Create her shadow on the water's edge. Stretch it long then shorter then gone.

She thought about Mara. About what it took to kill this way. To plan so meticulously. To execute judgment on those who had failed her. Those who had seen her suffering and looked away.

Not heat-of-the-moment violence. Not passionate revenge. Something colder. More deliberate. Justice administered when the system refused. Punishment carried out when courts would not.

Dempsey closed her notebook. Tucked it back into her jacket pocket. The snow was falling harder now. The flakes larger. Wetter. The temperature dropping further. Her breath visible in clouds before her face.

She walked back to her car. Left footprints that were already filling with fresh snow. Erasing her presence as she retreated. Removing evidence of her investigation.

Inside the car, she brushed snow from her hair. From her shoulders. Let the heater warm her hands. Her face. Not her thoughts. Those remained cold. Clinical. Professional.

Bonner had lied to protect Tapani. Or keep herself out of it. Had seen Mara bleeding in an alley and kept walking. Had interpreted trauma as drunkenness. As something that "happens a lot" outside nightclubs. As someone else's problem.

Then had lied again to protect Mara. Had given a statement claiming to see nothing when Tapani was shot. Had entered the official record as a witness who witnessed nothing.

Had tried, perhaps, to balance accounts. To make amends. Too late. Too little. The debt marked paid in full with drowning while unconscious.

Dempsey started the car. Checked her watch again. 1:32 AM. She had two more scenes to visit. Two more deaths to reconstruct. Two more debts paid in full to understand.

She pulled back onto the road. Left Weller Lake and its black water behind. The snow continued falling. Covering the boat ramp. The shore. The spot where she had stood examining a murder disguised as accident.

Covering everything in white that would melt by morning. That would reveal again what lay beneath. What had always been there waiting to be seen by anyone who looked closely enough.

Dempsey drove slowly down Azalea Lane. The wipers struggled against the snow. Houses dark at 2 AM. Mailboxes reflected her headlights. Numbers gradually increasing. 77. 79. 81. Then 83. Turner Pass's house. Where he'd died from what the Medical Examiner called commotio cordis. Heart stopped by impact. A freak accident with his bicycle. Except for the knife wound on his palm.

She pulled to the curb. Angled her car so the headlights illuminated the front yard. Cut the engine but left the lights on. The house sat back from the street. Single-story. Neglected since Pass's death three weeks ago. No porch light. No lights at all.

The snow fell steadily now. Already covering the lawn. The driveway. The scattered toys never collected after Pass's death. A plastic tricycle. A soccer ball. A Frisbee half-buried in white. Children's possessions abandoned like their owner.

Dempsey knew she would find nothing conclusive here. No evidence missed by the initial investigation. No proof that Mara had killed Pass. Just a location to see. To stand where it happened.

She got out of the car. The cold hit her immediately. Sharper now than earlier. The temperature still dropping. Her breath clouded before her face as she walked up the driveway where Pass had died.

The Medical Examiner's report came back to her. Pass found near his bicycle in this driveway. No witnesses. No signs of struggle beyond a small cut on his palm. Heart stopped from a precise blow to the chest. One-in-a-million occurrence. Freak accident. Case closed without investigation.

Except it wasn't random. Wasn't chance. Was Mara continuing her methodical elimination of witnesses. Of those who had seen her assault and done nothing. Who had interpreted rape as consent. Who had watched "for a minute then went back inside."

Dempsey's anger rekindled thinking about Pass's statement. His casual admission of voyeurism. His dismissal of Mara's trauma as regret for consensual sex. His utter failure as a human being when witnessing another's pain.

The driveway had a slight slope toward the garage. Nothing steep. Just enough for a bicycle to gain momentum if released without a rider. For a fall to have some force behind it. For a precise blow to the chest to stop a heart.

A basketball hoop stood at the edge of the concrete. Backboard weathered. Net tattered. The driveway beneath it worn from years of play. Of children bouncing balls. Of a father teaching jump shots. Of normal life continuing after witnessing assault and doing nothing.

This bothered Dempsey most. The normality. The compartmentalization that allowed Pass to watch a rape, walk away, then return home to children. To family. To the routines of ordinary existence untroubled by what he'd seen. What he'd failed to do.

She moved to where the body had been found. Just there, near the garage door. Where the bicycle had allegedly fallen with Pass. Where his heart had stopped from a precise blow. Where his palm had been cut by something sharp.

That detail had always been wrong. Didn't fit the accident narrative. A cut on the palm suggested defense. Suggested resistance. Suggested Pass had seen something coming. Had tried to block it. Had failed.

Dempsey pulled out her notebook. Made notes in the headlight glow from her car. "Knife wound inconsistent with bicycle fall. Defensive. Saw attacker?"

She pictured how it might have happened. Mara approaching Pass at his home. Confronting him about what he'd seen in that alley. About his lies afterward. About the debt still unpaid.

Pass responding with dismissal. With continued denial. With the same callous disregard he'd shown that night. Mara producing a knife. Pass seeing it. Raising his hand in defense. The blade catching his palm before she switched tactics. Before she struck his chest with something else. Something precise. Something that stopped his heart instantly.

Then staging the scene. The bicycle placed just so. The body positioned to suggest accident. The knife wound minimized, obscured. Just enough to pass cursory examination by a Medical Examiner not looking for murder.

Dempsey wrote again in her notebook. "Mara knew about commotio cordis? Medical knowledge or research?"

She looked back at the house. Dark windows staring at her like empty eye sockets. Children's toys scattered across the yard. Evidence of life interrupted. Of consequences finally catching up to a man who thought he could watch suffering without being touched by it.

Snow continued falling. Covering the driveway. The yard. The spot where Pass had died. Where his heart had stopped from a blow too precise to be accidental. Where he had paid in full for what he'd seen and failed to do.

Dempsey returned to her car. Brushed snow from her coat. Her hair. Sat behind the wheel with her notebook open. Added one more line: "All three witnesses saw assault, did nothing, then protected murderer. Why protect Mara after failing her?"

The question had no immediate answer. Just theories. Guilt maybe. Belated conscience. Or something more direct. Threats. Blackmail. Coercion. Mara compelling their silence through methods not yet clear.

Whatever the reason, their protection hadn't saved them. Their second chance to do right hadn't balanced the scales. Their debt had been marked paid in full with deaths disguised as accident, suicide, misfortune.

Dempsey started the car. The heater blew cold air at first, then gradually warmed. She took one last look at Pass's house. At the basketball hoop. At the toys now becoming white mounds under accumulating snow.

Dempsey drove away from 83 Azalea Lane. Left Pass and his abandoned home behind. The snow kept falling. Covering everything. Transforming the scene into something pristine. Something untouched. Something that hid the ugliness beneath a temporary blanket of white.

One more stop. One more death to understand. One more debt paid in full to witness before dawn came with its obligation to tell Brandt what her niece had done. What Mara had become when the system failed her. When justice refused her. When those who saw her pain looked away.

The For Sale sign in front of 34 Parrish Road leaned at an awkward angle. Dempsey pulled to the curb. The snow had stopped. The air cleared. Moonlight reflected off new white covering lawns and rooftops. The house where Barney Duke had died sat dark behind bare trees. Garage door closed. Windows blank. A home waiting for new life after death had visited.

Three AM. The neighborhood silent. Dempsey got out of her car. Her movements slower now. Four hours of investigation in December cold taking its toll. She approached the crooked sign. Straightened it without thinking. Professional tidiness extending even to this.

Her boots left prints in the fresh snow. Clean impressions leading from street to house. Evidence of her presence that would remain until morning sun melted it away. Until rain washed it clean. Until the world continued its cycle of revealing and concealing.

She stood before the garage door. Studied its blank surface. The Medical Examiner's report replayed in her mind. Duke found in his car inside this garage. Engine no longer running. Fuel exhausted. Body slumped in the driver's seat. Death from carbon monoxide. Classic suicide setup.

Except for the Zolpidem. No prescription found. Bottle mislabeled as aspirin. Dosage high enough to render him unconscious or severely impaired. High enough that he couldn't have driven himself anywhere. Couldn't have arranged his own death.

Dempsey pictured how it happened. Mara gaining Duke's trust somehow. Meeting him. Talking with him. Slipping crushed pills into his drink. Waiting for them to take effect. For his eyes to droop. His speech to slur. His coordination to fail.

Then guiding him to the car. Helping him inside. Placing him in the driver's seat. Starting the engine. Closing the garage door. Leaving him to die slowly as carbon monoxide replaced oxygen in his bloodstream. In his tissues. In his brain.

Cold. Methodical. Certain.

Had Duke recognized her? Had he made the connection between the photographer he'd seen "flirting" with Tapani and the woman now in his home? Had he realized too late who she was? What she represented? What debt had come due?

Dempsey touched the garage door. Cold metal beneath her fingers. Inside was where it happened. Where the third witness had paid in full for seeing assault and interpreting it as consent. For hearing crying and thinking "regret." For deciding another's trauma wasn't "his business."

She moved away from the door. Walked around the side of the house. Looked at windows all dark. Curtains drawn. No way to see inside without breaking glass. No reason to try. Nothing left to find that would change what she already knew.

Dempsey pulled out her notebook. Made another note in moonlight bright enough to read by. "Check: Mara medical records for Zolpidem prescription?"

She doubted Mara had obtained the drugs legally. More likely bought on the street. Easy enough to find if you knew where to look. If your job took you to crime scenes across the city. If you photographed the aftermath of drug deals gone wrong. Drug houses raided. Dealers arrested with their merchandise still on them.

Mara would have known where to get what she needed. How much to use. How to ensure Duke couldn't resist or escape once the drugs took effect.

Knowledge gained through professional exposure. Through years documenting the city's darkest corners. Through access granted by a badge and a camera and a role within the system that had failed her.

A dog barked somewhere down the street. Sharp. Sudden. Dempsey's head snapped toward the sound. The noise continued. Grew louder. A neighbor's pet disturbed by her presence perhaps. By the unfamiliar scent of stranger in the night.

The barking snapped her back to present reality. To the cold seeping through her coat. To the late hour and the job still to be done. The conversation waiting with morning. With Brandt. With the truth that couldn't be buried.

Dempsey returned to her car. Sat behind the wheel without starting the engine. Looked at the house where Duke had died. At the garage where carbon monoxide had filled his lungs while he sat unconscious from drugs he hadn't knowingly taken.

She had visited all four scenes now. The alley behind The Dump where Mara was assaulted and Tapani later killed. The boat ramp at Weller Lake where Bonner drowned unconscious. The driveway on Azalea Lane where Pass's heart stopped from precise impact. And now the garage on Parrish Road where Duke died breathing poisoned air.

Four locations. Four deaths. Four debts marked paid in full in a notebook left for her to find. A pattern of retribution carried out with cold precision. With planning. With certainty.

Not the actions of someone damaged beyond reason. Not crimes of passion or desperation. Something more deliberate. More absolute. Justice administered when the system refused.

The same system Dempsey served. That she believed in despite its flaws. That she worked to improve from within rather than condemn from without. That had failed Mara so completely she saw no option but to become judge, jury, and executioner.

Dempsey started her car. The dashboard clock read 3:17 AM. Hours still before dawn. Before the conversation that would change everything. That would transform Mara from missing person to murder suspect. That would end Brandt's career. That would reveal truths no one wanted to face.

She pulled away from the curb. Left Duke's house behind. Left the crooked sign she had straightened. Left the fourth location in a pattern of retribution she now understood completely.

Chapter 12

Dempsey sat at her kitchen table. The butcher paper spread before her, covered in her own handwriting. Four AM and she hadn't slept. Couldn't sleep. Not with Mara's puzzle pieces scattered across her life.

The street outside her window was quiet. No cars. No voices. Just the occasional click of the radiator fighting December cold. The rest of the city slept while she traced connections between the dead.

She picked up her phone. Pulled up the photo she'd taken of Tapani's murder scene. The one Mara had left for her to find. The one signed "For U Callisto." The image glowed blue in the dim apartment. Tapani's body in the alley behind The Dump, posed like artwork under sodium lights. Three wounds. Three messages. Three bullets fired with surgical precision.

Dempsey zoomed in on the composition. Studied the angle. The lighting. The deliberate framing that transformed violent death into something almost beautiful. Not a crime scene photograph but an artistic statement. A signature piece.

She set the phone down. Picked up Mara's spiral notebook. Flipped through pages of observations, notes, details about cases she'd photographed. Normal. Professional. Then the list of names. Tapani. Bonner. Duke. Pass. Each marked "paid in full" in that precise handwriting.

The notebook fell open to a page she'd read a dozen times since finding it. A page about her. About Callisto.

"She doesn't know I exist yet. Doesn't see me watching. Doesn't understand what connects us. But she will. When it's time. When everything is paid. When justice has been served. She'll understand why it had to be her. Why it couldn't be anyone else."

Dempsey's hand tightened on the notebook. The cryptic words revealed nothing new no matter how many times she read them. Did Mara expect Dempsey to understand? To hide the evidence? To protect her?

She turned back to the butcher paper timeline. The four deaths mapped in chronological order. Tapani first in July. Then the three witnesses in November. Bonner on the 7th. Duke on the 13th. Pass on the 28th. Three weeks of methodical elimination disguised as accident, suicide, misfortune.

But why had the witnesses protected Mara at Tapani's murder scene? Why claim to see nothing when they must have seen everything? What had Mara done or said to ensure their silence?

Dempsey stared at their names written on the butcher paper. The same three who had seen Mara's assault and done nothing. Who had interpreted violence as consent. Who had looked away when looking would have cost them nothing.

Then they had protected her. Had lied for her. Had entered the official record as witnesses who witnessed nothing.

Guilt, maybe. Belated conscience. The second chance to do right what they'd done wrong the first time. Or something more direct. Threats. Blackmail. Coercion.

Dempsey's pen tapped against the table. Rapid. Irritated. The sound too loud in the silent apartment. She wrote on the butcher paper: "WHY PROTECT MARA?"

No answer presented itself. Just theories without evidence. Possibilities without proof. Questions without resolution.

She knew what Mara had done. Had reconstructed each death. Had visited each scene. Had traced the path from victim to vigilante with professional detachment. With cold calculation. With understanding that grew with each discovery.

But motive remained unclear. Not for killing Tapani, that was obvious. Revenge for assault. Justice when the system refused it. But why leave the evidence for Dempsey specifically? Why sign the photograph with a name no one should have known?

"For U Callisto."

The pen snapped in her hand. Plastic cracking under pressure she hadn't realized she was applying. Ink leaked onto her palm. Onto the butcher paper. A black stain spreading across Duke's name. Partially hiding it.

Dempsey threw the broken pen across the room. It hit the wall with a sharp crack. Left a mark on the white paint. Evidence of frustration finally expressed. Of control temporarily abandoned.

She wiped her hand on her pants. Stood up. The chair scraped against hardwood. The sound harsh in the pre-dawn silence. She paced the small living room. Three steps one way. Three steps back. Movement without purpose except to burn the energy building inside her.

It wasn't adding up. Something was missing. Some connection she couldn't see. Some link between Mara and herself that explained everything but remained hidden.

She needed more. More information. More evidence. More pieces to complete the puzzle Mara had created specifically for her to solve.

Dempsey stopped pacing. Looked at the clock. 4:23 AM. Too early to do anything official. Too early to knock on doors or make calls or file reports.

But not too early to keep looking. To follow leads that existed outside official channels. To continue an investigation that had become more than professional. More than procedural.

Personal. Private. Between her and Mara now.

Dempsey went to the hall closet. Grabbed her coat. Her keys. Her gun and badge from the table by the door. Essential pieces of herself. The tools and symbols that defined her professional existence.

She left the apartment without looking back at the butcher paper timeline. At the evidence spread across her dining table. At the broken pen on the floor leaking the last of its ink.

The answers weren't there. They were out in the city somewhere. In places she hadn't yet looked. In connections she hadn't yet made. In the space between Mara Snowden and Callisto Dempsey that still remained undefined.

She took the stairs down to the street. Pushed through the building's front door into cold December air. Her breath clouded before her face as she walked to her car parked at the curb.

The city still slept. Still dark. Still quiet except for the occasional distant siren marking trouble somewhere beyond her reach. But answers waited. Mara had ensured that. Had left enough breadcrumbs to be followed if Dempsey was smart enough. Determined enough. Connected enough to see the pattern hidden in plain sight.

She got in her car. Started the engine. Sat for a moment with her hands on the wheel. Direction formed in her mind. Next steps clarified. The investigation continuing despite the hour. Despite the rules broken. Despite the lines crossed.

Time to move forward.

Dempsey parked across from Mara's building. Light fog hung between streetlamps. The city was just waking up. Delivery trucks rumbled two blocks over. A newspaper carrier's bicycle chain squeaked as he passed.

She crossed the street. Checked the building's front entrance. Still slightly ajar, just as she'd left it days ago. No crime scene tape. No police presence. Just an apartment building with one missing resident and a door that wouldn't close properly.

Dempsey slipped inside. The lobby smelled like old carpet and someone's burned toast. She took the stairs to the third floor. Her footsteps echoed in the stairwell. No need for stealth. No need to hide.

Mara's apartment door stood unlocked. The landlord hadn't secured it after Dempsey's first visit. Hadn't changed the locks. Hadn't done anything to protect the space of someone who might never return.

She entered without hesitation. The apartment felt different in early morning light. Less mysterious. More ordinary. Just a place where someone had lived. Had worked. Had planned four deaths with methodical precision.

Dempsey moved directly to the desk. To the laptop sitting closed but not packed away. Not hidden. Just waiting, like everything else Mara had left behind. Waiting to be found by someone who knew where to look. She'd already violated the welfare check, contaminated the scene, kept evidence from her chief. What was one more felony between a detective and a serial killer?

She sat in the chair. Opened the laptop lid. The screen lit up immediately. No password prompt. No security measure. Just the desktop appearing with standard icons arranged in neat rows.

Too easy. Too accessible. Like the journal and photograph left in plain view. Mara wanted these things found. Wanted them examined. Wanted them understood by the right person.

Dempsey moved the cursor to the file explorer icon. Clicked once. The window opened to the main directory. She navigated to Downloads without hesitation. The folder where most people kept files they'd acquired but hadn't yet organized. Where digital breadcrumbs accumulated unintentionally.

Nothing at all. Very intentional. Mara was enjoying the game, making Dempsey work for her. Next, the Recycle Bin. Also empty.

Dempsey sat back in the chair. Let her eyes move around the apartment. The orderly space. The precise arrangement of furniture. The lack of dust despite Mara's absence.

A place maintained with the same attention to detail shown in her murders. In her photography. In her justice administered when the system refused.

The city outside the window had fully awakened now. Traffic sounds filtered through glass. Car horns. Bus brakes. The rhythm of people moving through their ordinary lives while Dempsey sat in the apartment of someone who had abandoned ordinary forever.

She turned back to the computer. The laptop was too clean. Too sparse. Like a stage set rather than a working tool.

What else had Mara wanted her to find? What breadcrumbs waited on this machine? What connections between four deaths and a detective named Callisto remained hidden in plain sight?

Dempsey clicked on the browser icon. The window opened immediately. History tab right there on the toolbar. No attempt to hide digital footprints. No effort to conceal what Mara had been researching before she disappeared.

The browser history loaded. Three main categories of sites appeared. Travel pages about Denmark. Online stores selling camera equipment. Chat sessions with an AI conversation bot.

Dempsey scrolled through the travel pages first. Copenhagen hotels. Danish visa requirements. Winter weather patterns in Scandinavia. Practical research for someone planning to leave the country. Someone looking for somewhere far from New York. From four deaths. From a system that had failed her.

The camera equipment searches came next. High-end lenses. Professional-grade bodies. Accessories for low-light photography. The tools of Mara's profession. The instruments she had used to document crime scenes. To capture her own crime with artistic precision.

Nothing incriminating in either search pattern. Nothing that explicitly connected to Tapani or the witnesses. Just the normal online activity of someone planning travel and considering work upgrades.

The AI chat sessions were different. More personal. More revealing. Conversations with a machine designed to respond without judgment. To answer questions without asking why they were being asked. To engage without the human complications of suspicion or concern.

Dempsey clicked on the most recent chat. The log opened. Timestamp showed it occurred three days before Mara disappeared.

MARA: I'm thinking about traveling somewhere. Where would you recommend?

AI: That depends on what kind of experience you're looking for. Do you prefer cities, nature, warm climate, cold climate?

MARA: Somewhere far from here. Somewhere people don't ask too many questions.

AI: Many countries could fit that description. Denmark might be a good option. It offers privacy, excellent infrastructure, and people tend to respect personal boundaries.

MARA: Tell me more about Denmark.

AI: Denmark is known for its high quality of life, social stability, and low crime rates. Copenhagen, its capital, offers rich culture while maintaining a relaxed atmosphere. Danish people generally respect privacy and don't tend to be overly inquisitive with strangers.

MARA: That sounds perfect. Thank you.

Simple. Straightforward. A conversation about travel possibilities that had apparently influenced Mara's subsequent research.

Dempsey scrolled to the next chat session. Dated one day later. The content shifted dramatically.

MARA: Tell me about the goddess Callisto.

AI: Callisto was a nymph in Greek mythology who was a follower of the goddess Artemis. She took a vow of chastity as part of Artemis's hunt retinue. Zeus became enamored with her beauty and seduced her (in some versions by disguising himself as Artemis). When Callisto became pregnant, breaking her vow, Artemis cast her out. Later, Zeus's jealous wife Hera transformed Callisto into a bear. Eventually, Zeus placed her in the sky as the constellation Ursa Major (the Great Bear).

MARA: What would have happened if Callisto had not been seduced by Zeus?

AI: If Callisto had not been seduced by Zeus, her life would have remained stable and tragic-free, defined by the hunt and her loyalty to Artemis, but she would have been an insignificant figure in mythology rather than the subject of a major celestial myth.

MARA: So she needed the tragedy to become significant?

AI: In terms of mythological importance, yes. Without the Zeus episode and subsequent transformation, Callisto would likely be a minor footnote in Artemis's story rather than a figure remembered through one of the most prominent constellations in the night sky. Her suffering and transformation gave her lasting significance.

MARA: Thank you. That helps me understand something important.

Dempsey stared at the screen. Read the exchange again. The connection between mythology and murder clarifying with each word. Callisto. The name Dempsey had abandoned decades ago. The name Mara had written on the back of a dead man's photograph. The name that connected them in ways still not fully understood.

The traffic outside the window grew louder. Morning rush hour building. The sun had fully risen now, burning away the last of the fog. Light filled the apartment, casting the laptop screen into sharp relief.

Dempsey thought about the myth. About Callisto transformed by violence. About suffering that led to significance rather than destruction. About a name abandoned that still defined her in someone else's eyes.

Was Mara setting herself up to be hunted? Creating a mythological narrative where Dempsey—where Callisto—pursued her across time and space? Establishing herself as significant through deliberate tragedy?

Or was Mara the hunter? The one transforming others through violence? The one creating her own myth with four carefully executed deaths and a detective left to piece together the pattern?

The answer remained elusive. Hidden in the spaces between what Mara had left behind and what she had taken with her. Between the crimes documented and the messages implied. Between the myth of Callisto and the reality of Dempsey sitting in an empty apartment reading the digital breadcrumbs of a killer.

The browser history showed one more AI chat session. Dated the day before Mara disappeared. Dempsey clicked it open. Read the single exchange.

MARA: How do you know when justice has been served?

AI: That's a profound philosophical question. Justice is often considered served when appropriate consequences have been delivered for wrongdoing, when victims feel their suffering has been acknowledged, when balance has been restored, or when society's values have been upheld through proper procedure. Different philosophical and legal traditions define justice differently.

MARA: And when the proper procedure fails?

AI: When established procedures fail to deliver justice, societies often face significant moral and ethical challenges. Some philosophical traditions argue that justice must sometimes exist outside formal systems. However, vigilante justice raises serious ethical concerns about due process, proportionality, and the potential for error or abuse.

MARA: Thank you. That's all I needed to know.

Dempsey closed the browser. The conversation echoed in her mind. When proper procedure fails. When established systems break down. When justice must exist outside formal structures.

Mara had answered her own question through action rather than philosophy. Had administered justice when the system refused. Had marked debts paid in full with precision and certainty.

And had left the evidence for Dempsey specifically to find. For Callisto. For the detective who understood procedure but hadn't yet decided what justice truly meant when the system itself was corrupted.

The myth and the murder investigation merged in Dempsey's mind. Callisto transformed by violence. Significance born from tragedy. Justice existing outside established order when that order failed its most vulnerable.

Dempsey wondered if Mara wanted to be hunted, to become part of a significant criminal myth. Or if Mara was the hunter, creating her own mythology with four deaths and a detective left following breadcrumbs to an ending not yet written.

Chapter 13

Dempsey shrugged off her coat. Let it fall on Mara's couch. If she was going to search properly, she needed to get comfortable. The apartment had grown warm with morning sun streaming through the east-facing windows. Too warm for December. For a detective who'd been up all night tracing a path of methodical murder.

She slipped off her shoes. Left them by the couch. Padded in sock feet to the kitchen. The refrigerator hummed in the corner, a steady domestic sound at odds with the absent photographer's nighttime activities.

Dempsey pulled open the refrigerator door. Cold air hit her face. The contents were sparse but orderly. Yogurt. Cheese. Vegetables in clear containers. A half-empty bottle of white wine. Three pears in the crisper drawer, still firm. She took one. Closed the door.

The pear was cool against her palm. Heavy. She carried it to the sink, ran water over it. Watched the droplets bead on the green skin. Something so normal in an apartment filled with evidence of calculated revenge.

She dried the pear on a kitchen towel hanging from the oven handle. Returned to the living room. To the laptop still open on the desk. To the next step in understanding Mara Snowden.

Dempsey sat in Mara's chair. The cushion still held the impression of its owner. She took a bite of the pear. Crisp. Sweet. Juice on her tongue while she opened the word processor application with her free hand.

Recent files appeared in a neat column. Five documents. Three titled "Resume" with different dates. One called "Holiday Recipes." One labeled "Shopping List." Nothing suspicious. Nothing revealing. Nothing connected to four murders or a message signed "For U Callisto."

She opened each file. Scanned the contents quickly. The resumes showed Mara's professional progression. Freelance work. Department contract. Awards for crime scene photography. Technical proficiency described in bullet points.

The recipes were for Christmas cookies. Gingerbread. Sugar cutouts. Chocolate drops. Instructions copied from websites. Measurements in precise fractions.

The shopping list contained ordinary items. Milk. Bread. Coffee. Things Mara would never use again. Things left behind when she disappeared into whatever new life she had planned. Perhaps in Denmark. Perhaps elsewhere.

Dempsey closed the word processor. Took another bite of pear. The sweetness almost cloying now. She swallowed. Opened the email application next. The program loaded quickly. Mara's inbox appeared. Hundreds of messages organized into folders. Professional communications separated from personal. Newsletters sorted by topic. Everything in its place.

She clicked on the "Sent" folder. Scrolled through recent messages. Department correspondence about scheduling. Responses to family emails. Confirmation of online purchases.

Then.

Four emails sent on the same day, July 1st. One week before Tapani's murder.

The recipient names jumped out immediately. Duke, Barney. Bonner, Deirdre. Pass, Turner. The three witnesses. The three who had seen Mara's assault and looked away. The three who had later protected her after Tapani's murder. The three who were now dead.

Dempsey clicked on Duke's email first. The subject line read only "July 8." The message itself was brief. Direct. Chilling in its simplicity.

"Two years ago, you watched. $250 to watch again. The Dump. July 8. 2AM. Do not reply, just be there."

Acid rose in Dempsey's throat. Sharp. Bitter. She swallowed it back. Her hand tightened around the pear. Juice ran between her fingers, down her wrist.

She clicked on Bonner's email. The exact same message. Word for word. Then Pass's. Identical. All sent within minutes of each other on July 1st.

The picture cleared with terrible precision. Mara had lured them back. Had offered payment for the same behavior they'd exhibited during her assault. Had appealed to the same voyeuristic impulse that had led them to watch rather than intervene. Had known they would come.

And they had. All three. Had shown up at the appointed time. At the appointed place. Had expected to witness another assault. Had expected to earn $250 for their silence afterward.

Instead, they had witnessed Tapani's execution. Had become accomplices through their presence. Had tied themselves to Mara through their expectations. Through their willingness to watch suffering for profit.

Dempsey set the half-eaten pear on the desk. Wiped her hand on her pants. The sweet smell now turned her stomach. Food had no place beside such calculated darkness.

Mara's plan unfolded in her mind with crystalline clarity. Lure the witnesses back with the promise of money. Ensure they arrived expecting to see a repeat of her assault. Force them into complicity by making them present for Tapani's murder. Guarantee their silence afterward with the threat of exposing their intentions. Accessory after the fact. Obstruction of justice. Conspiracy to commit murder.

Brilliant. Terrible. Perfect.

So they had to lie. Had claimed to see nothing. Had protected her out of self-preservation rather than belated conscience. Had entered the official record as witnesses who witnessed nothing because the truth would damn them as surely as it would damn her.

Dempsey leaned back in the chair. The apartment air felt suddenly stale. Heavy with the weight of what she'd discovered. With the evidence of how thoroughly Mara had planned not just revenge but the protection of that revenge. Had ensured silence before the first shot was fired.

She looked again at the emails. The timestamps. The identical wording. The certainty behind them that these three people would respond exactly as predicted. That they would return to the scene of their moral failure for another chance to profit from someone else's pain.

Mara had known them. Had understood the darkness that allowed them to watch assault without intervention. Had recognized something in them that would respond to her invitation despite its obvious wrongness.

The plan had worked perfectly. All three had come. All three had witnessed. All three had lied to protect themselves. And later, all three had died.

Dempsey checked the date stamps on the emails. All sent July 1st. One week before Tapani's murder. One week for the witnesses to consider the offer. To wrestle with whatever passed for conscience in people who watched assault without intervening. To decide if $250 was worth returning to the scene of someone else's trauma.

They had all decided yes.

She took another bite of pear. The sweetness no longer repulsed her. Just fuel now. Sustenance for a brain that had been working non-stop since yesterday morning.

Her eyes moved from the screen to the window and back. Morning traffic sounds filtered through glass. A siren somewhere distant. The city continuing its rhythm while she pieced together a murder four months cold.

Dempsey clicked back to the sent folder. Scrolled through every email from June and July. Looked for Tapani's name. Found nothing. No messages to the man who had assaulted Mara. No electronic breadcrumbs leading to the main target of her revenge.

It made sense. Tapani wouldn't need the same bait as the witnesses. Wouldn't respond to an offer to watch someone else's assault. His motivation had been different. More direct. More personal.

Mara had set him up some other way.

Dempsey returned to the inbox. Searched for Tapani's name. No results. No communication from him to her. No digital record of contact between rapist and victim in the days or weeks before his execution.

She swallowed the bite of pear. Juice ran down her chin. She wiped it with the back of her hand, leaving a sticky residue on her skin. The fruit was nearly gone now. Just core and stem remaining.

Dempsey scanned the desktop for other communication apps. Found none. No messaging platforms. No social media shortcuts. No dating applications where Mara might have created a false profile to lure Tapani back to the scene of his crime.

Whatever method she had used to arrange his presence at The Dump on July 8th, it hadn't left traces on this laptop.

Which meant what? Phone contact most likely. Text messages. Voice calls. Communications that would be stored on a device Mara had taken with her when she disappeared.

Dempsey opened the browser again. Checked the history more thoroughly. No dating sites. No encrypted communication platforms. No evidence of online personas created to entrap a rapist.

She returned to the emails. Re-read the messages to the witnesses. Simple. Direct. Effective. The same approach would have worked on Tapani but with different bait. Not money. Something else he wanted. Something only Mara could provide.

What had she offered him? What could compel a man to meet his victim at the same location where he had assaulted her?

Forgiveness, perhaps. The chance to apologize. To clear his conscience without legal consequences. Of course not. It had to be more aligned with his original crime. The opportunity to repeat it. To dominate again. To take what he wanted from someone he'd already broken.

Dempsey would never know for certain without Mara's phone. Without the communications that had lured Tapani to his death at precisely the right moment for three witnesses to observe his execution.

But she knew enough. Had enough to take to Brandt. To explain what Mara had done. How she had killed Tapani. How she had ensured the witnesses' silence. How she had later hunted them down one by one. How she had marked their debts paid in full.

Enough to explain everything except why "For U Callisto" had been written on the back of a dead man's photograph.

Dempsey clicked each open program closed. The emails disappeared from the screen. The browser history vanished. The word processor shut down. She left the laptop as she'd found it. Open. Accessible. A deliberate trail for the right person to follow.

She stood. The chair rolled back. Her legs stiff from sitting. From hours of investigation that had started yesterday morning and continued through the night. Through crime scenes revisited. Through death reconstructed. Through a killer's methodology revealed step by step.

The pear was down to its core now. Seeds visible in the white flesh. She carried it to the kitchen. Tore a paper towel from the roll mounted under a cabinet. Wrapped the remnants carefully. Tucked the small package into her pocket rather than leave evidence of her presence in Mara's trash.

The kitchen looked exactly as she'd found it. Clean counters. Organized space. Nothing out of place except the absent owner who had planned and executed four deaths with the same precision she brought to her home. To her photography. To her life before it transformed into something darker.

Dempsey returned to the living room. To her shoes left by the couch. To her coat thrown across cushions. She put them on mechanically. Mind already moving to what came next. To the conversation with Brandt that couldn't be avoided. To the truth that had to be told despite its consequences.

Dempsey closed Mara's apartment door. She walked toward the building's entrance, footsteps echoing in the empty hallway. Morning light spilled through the lobby's glass door, harsh against the dim interior.

The front door was still ajar. Just as she'd left it days ago. She pushed it open, stepped into December morning. The temperature had risen with the sun. Snow from last night melted on sidewalks, creating dark patches on concrete. Steam rose from sewer grates. From car exhaust. From coffee cups clutched by pedestrians moving with Monday purpose.

A garbage truck groaned at the corner. The hydraulic arm lifting bins with mechanical precision. The smell of rotting food briefly overwhelmed the usual city odors of exhaust and wet pavement.

Dempsey walked to her car. Unlocked it with the key fob. The beep too loud in the morning air. She slid behind the wheel. Closed the door. Sat without starting the engine.

Her phone was in her pocket. Brandt's number in her contacts. The conversation waiting to happen. The truth waiting to be told. A niece who had murdered four people. A chief whose career would end when that truth became official.

She took out her phone. Held it. Stared at the dark screen.

What if Brandt was involved? What if the chief had known about Mara's plans? Had facilitated them somehow? Had ensured her niece could execute justice when the system refused?

It made a certain sense. Brandt had known about Mara's assault. Had known Tapani walked free. Had pushed Harris off the murder case after just two weeks. Had told him it wasn't worth departmental resources when any homicide would normally get months of investigation.

Had Brandt helped Mara escape afterward? Arranged her disappearance? Provided resources for a new life somewhere beyond reach?

Then why send Dempsey to check on her? Why create the possibility that someone would connect these dots? Would find evidence leading back to Brandt herself?

It didn't track. Unless Brandt hadn't known about the three witness murders. Had believed Mara responsible only for Tapani's death. Had thought the case safely cold until the witnesses started dying.

Brandt had nothing to do with any of it. Was simply a concerned aunt who wanted someone to check on her missing niece. Who had no idea what that niece had done. Who would be devastated when she learned the truth.

Dempsey's phone vibrated in her hand. The screen lit up with an incoming call. Brandt's name displayed in white letters against black background. The coincidence sent a chill across her shoulders despite the warming car interior.

She answered. Put the phone to her ear. Said nothing.

"Dempsey." Brandt's voice came through clearly. Professional. Controlled. "I need you in my office in an hour. Full update on the Snowden welfare check."

Dempsey's throat tightened. Her free hand gripped the steering wheel. The leather warm beneath her palm.

"I'll be there."

"Good." A pause. The sound of papers shuffling. "Have you found anything connecting her disappearance to the Tapani murder?"

The question hung in the space between them. Loaded. Dangerous. Impossible to answer truthfully without revealing everything she knew.

"I'll bring you up to speed when I see you." Neutral. Noncommittal.

Another pause. Longer this time. Brandt weighing the response. Finding it insufficient but accepting it for now.

"One hour, Dempsey. My office." The line went dead. No goodbye. No pleasantry. Just directive and disconnection.

Dempsey lowered the phone. Set it on the passenger seat. Leaned back against the headrest. Closed her eyes briefly.

One hour to decide what to tell Brandt. What to reveal. What to conceal. How to explain that her niece had killed four people in calculated succession. That the evidence led nowhere but to this conclusion.

That Mara had left it all for Dempsey specifically to find.

Dempsey opened her eyes. Started the car. The engine caught immediately. Heat began flowing from vents still set to maximum from her drive to Mara's apartment in pre-dawn cold.

She pulled away from the curb. Left Mara's building behind. The secret emails. The detailed planning. The calculated path from victim to vigilante when all other roads to justice were blocked.

Ahead lay Brandt's office. The conversation that would change everything. The truth that couldn't be buried no matter how much damage it would cause. No matter how many careers it would end. No matter how many lives it would destroy beyond those already lost.

Chapter 14

Dempsey arrived inside twenty minutes. She hung her coat over the back of her chair. Set her coffee on the desk. The bullpen buzzed with unusual energy for a Monday morning. Detectives clustered around Knight's desk. Backs slapped. Voices raised. Something about a high-profile arrest. She opened her laptop without looking up.

"Three shots center mass!" Knight's voice carried across the room. "Perp didn't know what hit him."

Laughter rippled through the group. Five detectives. Two uniformed officers. All focused on Knight's story. None glanced toward Dempsey's corner.

She logged into the system. Entered her password deliberately. One letter at a time. Forty minutes until her meeting with Brandt. Forty minutes to decide how much truth to tell.

"The bodega guy couldn't believe it," Knight continued. "Said I moved like something from an action movie."

More laughter. Someone whistled. Hussein offered a fist bump that Knight accepted with exaggerated humility.

Dempsey opened her email. Nothing new from Brandt. Nothing related to Mara. The Zamora file was marked closed. Her strangulation case. Weeks of work on a cold case that confounded two other detectives. Sleepless nights. Evidence she found that everyone else missed. Her suspect was still alive.

Nobody had clustered around her desk afterward. Nobody had offered fist bumps or bought her drinks.

The coffee tasted bitter. She set it down. Opened a blank document. Started typing notes for her meeting with Brandt. Facts only. Mara Snowden. Missing photographer. Department contractor. Chief's niece. Rapist's killer.

She deleted the last line.

Knight's voice rose again. "So I tell the guy, drop it or I drop you." He paused for effect. "Guy thinks I'm bluffing."

The gathered officers leaned closer. Hushed anticipation. Knight knew how to work a room.

Dempsey's fingers hovered over the keyboard. She needed to decide what Brandt could hear. What had to remain unsaid. The evidence she'd collected illegally. The search of Mara's apartment. The pattern of retribution carried out in calculated succession.

She typed: "No signs of struggle in apartment. No indications of kidnapping or harm."

True but incomplete.

"Then the guy pulls a second gun," Knight's story continued. "From his ankle holster. Can you believe that?"

Collective groans from his audience. They'd all encountered hidden weapons. All faced that moment when a supposedly disarmed suspect revealed a backup.

Dempsey added to her notes: "Personal items appear untouched except for specific items apparently left for the investigator to find."

Her fingers paused over the keys. How much to write about the photograph? The journal? The list of names marked "paid in full"? Once on paper, she could not deny it. Each revelation would lead to questions she couldn't answer without admitting her own violations. Her unauthorized investigation. Her concealment of evidence.

Knight slammed his palm on his desk. The sound echoed through the bullpen. "So I dive right. Roll behind the counter. Come up shooting."

Applause now. Genuine admiration for quick thinking. For reflexes that had kept Knight alive in a situation that could have ended differently.

Dempsey deleted her note about items left for the investigator. Rewrote it: "Personal items appear untouched. No indication of planned absence."

The half-truth sat on her screen. A compromise between professional obligation and personal certainty. Between what she could prove and what she knew.

Knight stood up. Spread his arms wide. Reenacting his confrontation with the suspect. His audience widened the circle to give him space. Their backs to Dempsey. Their attention entirely captured.

She added: "Victim had previous connection to Stefan Tapani homicide."

Brandt had asked for secrecy. Let her decide who else would read the report.

"Guy didn't stand a chance," Knight declared. He made finger guns with both hands. Pointed them at his imaginary opponent. "Bam. Bam. Bam."

A detective whose name Dempsey couldn't recall whistled again. Made a comment about Knight's shooting range scores. About his department record for qualification.

Dempsey sipped her coffee. Cold now. She swallowed anyway. Fuel for the conversation ahead. For the meeting that would determine Mara's fate. And possibly her own career.

She typed: "Recommend expanded search parameters. Consider possibility victim left voluntarily."

The word "victim" stuck in her mind. Inaccurate in so many ways. Mara was victim, perpetrator, vigilante, executioner. Was photographer, planner, hunter, prey. Was missing, fleeing, hiding, waiting.

Waiting for what? For Dempsey to find her? To understand her? To join her?

"For U Callisto."

Knight roared suddenly. Pounded his chest with closed fists. An ape gesture. Primal. Territorial. His audience laughed. Clapped. One mimicked the movement back at him. Male bonding through mock aggression.

Dempsey closed her laptop. The noise was too much. The contrast too stark. Her isolation too complete in a room full of colleagues celebrating someone else's victory while her own remained unmarked.

She checked her watch. Thirty minutes until the meeting. Not enough time to visit Records for the additional files she wanted. Not enough time to properly prepare for the questions Brandt would ask. For the truths she would have to tell. For the lies she would have to construct around those truths.

Knight's celebration continued. A coffee cup knocked over in the enthusiasm. Brown liquid spreading across his desk. Someone grabbing paper towels. Laughter redoubling at the minor crisis.

Dempsey gathered her notes. Her phone. Left the cold coffee on her desk. Stood up. No one noticed. No one called her name as she walked toward the door. No one interrupted their celebration to acknowledge her departure.

She took the stairs instead of the elevator. One flight up to Brandt's office. The stairwell was quiet. Cold. Her footsteps echoed against concrete. The sound reminded her of the parking garage. Of standing beside her car the night before. Of making the decision that had led her here. To this moment. To this choice about what to reveal and what to conceal.

The stairwell door closed behind her with a metallic click. Final. Certain. Like a trigger being pulled. Like a decision that couldn't be unmade once taken. Like truth that couldn't be unlearned once known.

Like justice that couldn't be undone once administered.

Dempsey reached the administrative level. Carpet instead of linoleum. Actual doors instead of cubicle dividers. Brandt's assistant looked up from her computer. Made eye contact. Pointed to the chief's door without speaking. The gesture clear: go in, she's waiting.

She knocked once. Entered without waiting for a response. Brandt sat behind her desk. Reading glasses perched low on her nose. A file open before her. She didn't look up immediately.

"Close the door."

Dempsey did. The latch clicked into place. The sound of the assistant's typing muffled but still audible. A steady rhythm of keys that would mask their conversation from anyone passing by.

"Sit."

She took the chair opposite Brandt. Leather. Comfortable. Positioned to be lower than Brandt's own seat. A subtle power dynamic built into the furniture arrangement.

Brandt closed the file. Removed her glasses. Folded them precisely. Set them on the desk with the earpieces facing away. Every movement controlled. Deliberate. The actions of someone who organized her world down to the smallest detail.

"Update me on my niece."

Dempsey met her eyes. Steady. Professional. "No sign of Mara. No indication of forced entry at her apartment. No evidence of struggle."

"And?"

"Her personal items appear untouched. Her laptop was there. Clothing in closets. Nothing that suggests a hasty exit." The half-truth again. Practiced in the bullpen. Delivered now with the confidence of rehearsal.

"What about her camera equipment?"

A detail Dempsey hadn't considered. "Some present. I'm not familiar enough with her inventory to know if anything is missing."

Brandt's jaw tightened. A small tell from a woman who rarely revealed anything unintentionally. "Her Nikon D850 would be there. Black body. Professional grade. Expensive. Did you see it?"

"No. But I wasn't looking for specific equipment."

"It would be in a hard case. Black with red interior padding. Custom cut for the camera and three lenses."

Dempsey thought back to her searches of Mara's apartment. Remembered no such case. "I didn't see it."

Brandt leaned back. "She wouldn't leave without that camera. It's her primary work equipment."

"Is it possible she's on assignment? Maybe out of town on a job?"

"I would know about it." The words carried absolute certainty. "Is there anything else you found? Anything unusual?"

Dempsey hesitated.

"Do you think she left the country?" Brandt asked the question directly. Eyes never leaving Dempsey's face.

The intensity of her gaze made Dempsey's skin prickle. Too focused. Too searching. Looking for something specific in Dempsey's response.

"Is there reason to think she might have?"

"I asked you first, Detective."

Dempsey made a decision in that moment. The evidence in her possession couldn't be revealed without admitting her own violations. Her unauthorized investigation. Her concealment of evidence. But there was more to it. Something in Brandt's manner raised warning flags. The specificity of her questions. The intensity of her focus.

"I have no evidence suggesting she left the country." Truth again. The browser history on Mara's laptop showing Danish travel research wasn't evidence. Wasn't something Dempsey could claim to have found legally.

Brandt studied her. Looked for the lie hidden within the truth. For the evasion concealed by technical accuracy.

"Do you need additional resources? Another detective to assist?"

The question came from nowhere. Blindsided Dempsey completely.

"For a welfare check?"

"For finding my niece." Brandt's voice hardened. "If this is beyond your capabilities, I can reassign it."

"That won't be necessary." Dempsey kept her tone neutral despite the implied criticism. "I'm pursuing several leads."

"Such as?"

"Her professional contacts. Places she frequented. People who might know her plans." All things she should have been doing if this were a normal missing persons case. All actions she hadn't taken because the evidence pointed elsewhere. Toward murder. Toward revenge. Toward debts marked paid in full.

"Detective Hussein has experience with missing persons cases. He could work with you."

Dempsey leaned forward. "Is there something specific you're concerned about? Something about Mara's safety you haven't shared with me?"

The question hung between them. A challenge wrapped in professional courtesy. A probe disguised as cooperation.

Brandt's expression didn't change. "I'm concerned about my niece's whereabouts. About the fact that she missed a court appearance. About the unusual nature of her disappearance."

"What court appearance?"

"Traffic violation. Nothing serious. But Mara is responsible. She doesn't miss obligations."

Another detail Brandt hadn't mentioned before. Another piece that didn't align with the chief's apparent concern.

"I don't need assistance." Dempsey kept her voice level. "But I do need clarity. Are you concerned that Mara is in danger? Or that she's running from something?"

Brandt's eyes narrowed fractionally. "I could ask you the same question, Detective."

The subtext was clear. Both holding back. Both sensing the other's reticence. Both circling around truths neither was ready to speak aloud.

"I have no evidence suggesting either scenario," Dempsey said finally. The statement technically true but fundamentally dishonest.

Brandt watched her for another moment. Searching for the crack in her professional facade. For the tell that would reveal what Dempsey knew about Mara. About her crimes. About her connection to a detective who had once been called Callisto.

"Find her, Dempsey. That's all I'm asking. Find my niece and tell me she's safe."

The simplicity of the request belied its complexity. The impossibility of fulfilling it without revealing everything. Without exposing Mara's actions. Without ending Brandt's career along with her niece's freedom.

"I'll do my job." The only promise Dempsey could make with integrity intact.

Brandt nodded once. Picked up her glasses but didn't put them on. Just held them. A gesture that suggested the conversation wasn't finished despite the apparent conclusion.

"Is there something else I should know?"

Dempsey considered the question. All its possible meanings. All the truths that could answer it.

"No." The lie came easily. Professionally delivered. Necessary in this moment before she understood more about Brandt's own knowledge. About her potential involvement. About whether aunt had helped niece escape after justice had been administered when the system refused.

Dempsey fought the urge to fidget under Brandt's stare. Her hands stayed flat on her thighs. Her breathing remained even. Professional stillness practiced through hundreds of interrogations. She decided to change tactics.

"Has Detective Harris spoken with you recently?"

Brandt's eyebrows lifted. The question had caught her off-guard. "No. Why would he?"

"I consulted him about the Tapani homicide. Found some oddities in the case."

The temperature in the room seemed to drop. Brandt's posture changed. Shoulders squaring. Jaw tightening. The glasses in her hand now gripped with white knuckles.

"What does Tapani have to do with finding my niece?"

"Potentially nothing." Dempsey kept her voice neutral. "But I was exploring all connections."

"You must know what that bastard did to my niece." The words came through clenched teeth. Raw emotion breaking through Brandt's professional exterior.

Dempsey nodded once. "I saw the file."

The glasses in Brandt's hand creaked under pressure. Plastic frame bending. She set them down before they could snap. Her hand trembled. Just once. Then steadied.

"Then you understand why his murder isn't my primary concern." A statement that bordered on admission. On acknowledgment that justice administered outside the system might be acceptable when the system itself failed.

"I'm just following leads, Chief." Dempsey kept her face neutral. "The witnesses in the Tapani case are—"

"What witnesses?" Brandt's voice sharpened. Focus returning. The momentary emotional breach sealed over with professional inquiry.

"Three individuals who claimed to be present when Tapani's body was discovered. All gave statements saying they saw nothing."

"And?"

"They're all dead."

Brandt didn't blink. Didn't react. Showed no surprise at information that should have shocked any law enforcement professional. Any chief of police. Any aunt whose niece might be connected to multiple homicides.

"What do these witnesses have to do with Mara?"

The question demanded a decision. Truth or lie. Revelation or concealment. Dempsey chose the path that kept her investigation alive. That kept Mara's trail open for her to follow. That kept Brandt's involvement, whatever it might be, still unclear.

"Nothing, as far as I know." The lie felt heavy on her tongue. "But the photograph in Mara's apartment was concerning."

"*The* photograph?"

"A crime scene photo of Tapani. One that shouldn't have left evidence storage."

Brandt's eyes narrowed. "You didn't mention this before."

"I'm mentioning it now." Dempsey met her gaze steadily. "It was on her desk. In plain view."

"And you're just telling me this now?" Brandt's voice rose. Control slipping again.

"It was one of many," she lied. "I needed to establish context before sharing details."

"What was in the photograph? Exactly."

Dempsey hesitated. The truth would reveal too much. Would show she knew about the handwritten message on the back. About "For U Callisto" inscribed in Mara's precise handwriting. About a connection that shouldn't exist between detective and photographer.

"Tapani's body in the alley. Standard crime scene documentation."

"Nothing unusual about it?"

"Just that it was in her personal possession. Department protocol—"

"Stay out of the Tapani case." Brandt cut her off. Voice hard. Final. "It belongs to Harris. Your only job right now is finding Mara. Nothing else. Not witnesses. Not photographs. Not department protocols. Just my niece."

"Chief—"

"This isn't a debate, Detective." Brandt stood up. Her height an advantage. Her position absolute. "Find Mara. That's an order. Leave Tapani to Harris."

Dempsey remained seated. Let the power imbalance stand. Sometimes appearing to yield created space for later movement.

"Understood."

"Is it?" Brandt leaned forward. Hands planted on the desk. "Because I'm not convinced you grasp the priority here. My niece is missing. Everything else is secondary."

"I'll find her." Dempsey made the statement with quiet certainty. A promise she would keep, though not in the way Brandt expected. Not with the outcome the chief wanted.

"Good." Brandt straightened. Collected herself visibly. Professional mask sliding back into place. "Report directly to me. Daily updates. No one else needs to be involved."

"Yes, Chief."

"You're dismissed."

Dempsey stood. Moved toward the door with unhurried steps. No sign of the urgency building inside her. Of the connections forming in her mind. Of the certainties clarifying with each new piece of information.

Brandt knew more than she was saying. Had reacted to the witness deaths with suspicious lack of surprise. Had ordered Dempsey away from the Tapani case with unusual vehemence. Had isolated the investigation to just the two of them.

Protection. Of Mara. Of herself. Of something neither was ready to name aloud.

Dempsey opened the door. Stepped through. Closed it behind her with a soft click. The assistant still typed. Steady rhythm unchanged. Unaware of the currents shifting beneath the surface of ordinary police business.

The hallway stretched before her. Empty. Quiet. The path forward was unclear but the direction was certain.

Find Mara. Understand the connection. Follow the trail of bread crumbs left specifically for a detective once called Callisto. For a woman who understood justice when the system failed. Who recognized revenge wrapped in procedure. Who saw patterns others missed.

Dempsey walked toward the stairs. Away from Brandt and her orders. Away from limitations placed on an investigation already beyond conventional boundaries. Away from a chief protecting her niece from consequences already set in motion.

Toward whatever waited at the end of Mara's trail. Whatever revelation had been prepared specifically for her. Whatever truth lay hidden behind four deaths marked "paid in full" and a photograph signed with a name that should have been forgotten.

For U Callisto.

Chapter 15

Dempsey reached her brownstone at 11:43 PM, exhausted. Her eyes burned from staring at screens all day. State databases, federal systems, ALPR networks, airport manifests, border crossing records. Looking for any trace of Mara Snowden. Finding nothing.

The street was empty. A single streetlight cast long shadows across the pavement. Birds chirped from somewhere in the dark. A cold wind pushed dead leaves along the curb.

She climbed the five steps to her building's entrance. Her key scraped against the lock, too loud in the quiet. She pushed the door open and started up the interior stairs.

Something felt wrong.

Dempsey stopped on the second-floor landing. Listened. The building held its usual sounds: a television murmuring behind someone's door, the hum of old plumbing, the creak of settling wood. Nothing out of place. But her instincts insisted otherwise.

She continued to the third floor. Her apartment was twenty feet down the hallway. The overhead light flickered, making the shadows pulse.

A white rectangle stood out against her dark door.

Paper. Taped there.

Her hand went to her weapon. She drew it, held it low against her thigh. Moved down the hallway pressed against the wall, minimizing her profile. Ten feet. Five. Close enough now to see it was a folded note secured with clear tape.

Dempsey stopped. Scanned the hallway in both directions. The stairwell behind her. The emergency exit at the far end. No movement. No sound except her own breath.

She reached out with her left hand. Peeled the note free. The tape came away cleanly. She pocketed the note without reading it, keeping her weapon up.

Her apartment lock clicked open. She turned the knob and pushed the door inward with her foot, staying to the side of the frame. Darkness inside. She listened for breathing, movement, the shift of weight on old floorboards.

Nothing.

"Police," she announced to the empty apartment.

Dempsey entered fast and low, weapon tracking her eyeline. Kicked the door shut behind her with her heel. Left the lights off. The faint glow from streetlights through her blinds gave her enough to work with.

The entryway was clear. She moved to the living room. Checked behind the couch, the armchair. The kitchen was empty, just the dirty coffee mug still in the sink where she'd left it that morning. The refrigerator hummed its usual rhythm.

Down the hallway. Bathroom first. She reached around the doorframe and flipped the light switch. Empty. Shower curtain pulled back. No one in the tub.

The bedroom was last. Door ajar. She nudged it fully open with the barrel of her gun. Scanned the corners. Under the bed. The closet door was closed.

Dempsey stood to the side and yanked it open. Hangers rattled. Her clothes hung undisturbed. Stack of old shoes on the floor. Spare blanket on the shelf above.

She flipped on the bedroom light. Holstered her weapon. Moved back through the apartment turning on lights room by room. Everything exactly as she'd left it. Nothing disturbed. Nothing taken. No signs of forced entry beyond the note on her door.

Someone had been here. Had watched long enough to know she wasn't home. Had touched her door. Left a message.

For her specifically.

Dempsey went back to the hallway. Looked both directions one last time. Empty. Silent. She pulled the door shut, turned the deadbolt, slid the chain into place. The metallic scrape echoed in her quiet apartment.

She stood with her back against the door for a moment. The note in her pocket felt heavier than paper should.

The kitchen table sat under a single overhead light. She sat down, positioned the lamp to shine directly on the surface. Pulled out the note. Unfolded it carefully.

Standard white copy paper. Folded neatly into thirds. The handwriting was neat, unhurried. Blue ink.

"Wilmington Warehouse, 1789 Cizer Street, 3 AM tonight ~ M"

Dempsey read it three times. Simple. Direct. A location, a time, an initial.

Her hands trembled. She pressed them flat against the table.

M for Mara.

She checked her watch. 11:51 PM. Just over three hours until the meeting time.

Dempsey pulled out her phone. Typed "Wilmington Warehouse 1789 Cizer Street" into the search bar. The results loaded immediately. An abandoned storage facility on the city's industrial outskirts. Scheduled for demolition in six months. Owned by a property development company based in Delaware.

She pulled up street view. A brick building with boarded windows. Chain-link fence. No businesses operating nearby. Isolated.

Perfect for an ambush.

She switched to satellite view. The warehouse sat on a large empty lot. One road in, one road out. A loading dock in the back faced dense trees. No other structures within a quarter mile.

Dempsey set her phone down. Stared at the note again.

Three AM. The dead hour. When the city slept and even patrol cars ran on skeleton crew.

The method was familiar. Too familiar.

She stood abruptly. Carried the note to her bedroom. The black leather journal lay in her nightstand drawer where she'd hidden it days ago. Mara's journal. Full of photographs of her. Full of explicit fantasies about someone named Callisto.

Stolen evidence. Her career would end if anyone knew she had it.

Dempsey unlocked the drawer. Took out the journal. Brought it back to the kitchen table and set it beside the note under the bright light.

She opened the journal to one of the handwritten pages. The neat script filled the cream-colored paper. Detailed observations about Dempsey's routines, her habits, her body language. Fantasies that made Dempsey's face flush even now.

She positioned the note directly beside the open journal. Studied both under the lamp.

The handwriting matched. The distinctive way the lowercase 'g' looped. The slight rightward slant. The pressure points where the pen dug deeper into the paper. The spacing between words.

No question. The same hand wrote both.

Dempsey sat back in her chair. The note was real. Mara was alive. Mara had been here. Had stood outside her door. Had touched the paper now sitting on her kitchen table.

Had invited her to an abandoned warehouse at 3 AM.

The same way Mara had invited three witnesses to watch Tapani die. The same careful, minimal approach. Location. Time. Initial. No explanation. No context. Just an invitation that was really a summons.

Dempsey closed the journal. Left both items on the table. Stared at them under the harsh kitchen light.

Three hours to decide if she was walking into a trap.

Dempsey stood at her bedroom window. Pushed the blinds aside with two fingers. The street below remained empty. No movement. No cars. She let the blinds fall back into place.

Twelve seventeen AM. Two hours and forty-three minutes.

She paced. Living room to bedroom. Bedroom to kitchen. Her apartment had never felt smaller. Four rooms that suddenly couldn't contain what she needed to think through.

The journal sat on the kitchen table beside the note. Both under the lamp's harsh light. Evidence of two different crimes. Mara's stalking, Dempsey's theft. Evidence of obsession on both sides, if she was honest.

She opened the refrigerator. Found the half-empty bottle of red wine. Poured a couple of ounces into a glass. Set it on the counter. Stared at it. Didn't drink.

The radio sat on the bookshelf. She turned it on. Late-night jazz filled the silence. Saxophone notes that hung in the air like smoke. She turned it off after thirty seconds. The silence rushed back, louder than before.

Twelve twenty-four AM.

Dempsey returned to the kitchen table. Sat down. Picked up the journal. Opened it to a random page.

"I watch her move through the world like she's the only solid thing in it. Everything else just arrangements around her gravity. I want to know what her skin tastes like. The hollow of her throat. The inside of her wrists. I want to hear the sounds she makes when—"

She closed the journal. Her face felt hot.

Forty-eight years old. Never been kissed. Never desired.

Until Mara.

A serial killer who had executed four people with methodical precision. Who had stalked Dempsey for months, maybe years. Who had photographed her without consent, written explicit fantasies about her, learned her routines down to which coffee shop she visited on Tuesday mornings.

Who had somehow seen something in her that no one else had ever seen.

Dempsey stood. Paced again. Poured the wine down the sink without tasting it.

She should call Brandt. Report the note. Get a tactical team assembled. Do this by the book. That's what a good detective would do. What a good cop would do.

But if Dempsey called it in now, Brandt would take over. Would have to. This was her niece. The chief couldn't let a subordinate handle something this personal. And Dempsey would have to explain the stolen journal, the contaminated evidence, all the rules she'd already broken. Her career would be over either way. The only question was whether she'd learn the truth first.

Twelve forty-one AM.

The rational part of her, the trained investigator who'd spent twenty years following evidence, building cases, respecting procedure, knew the warehouse was a trap. Knew going alone was suicide. Knew this invitation was designed to isolate her, to put her somewhere no backup could reach in time.

But something deeper, something she'd kept locked away for decades, wanted to see Mara alive. Wanted to hear her voice without the filter of official statements and department politics. Wanted to understand why Mara had chosen *her*. Why her birth name. Why the photographs. Why the journal left where she'd find it.

Why "For U Callisto" on the back of a dead rapist's photograph.

Dempsey stopped pacing. Stood in the center of her living room. Looked around at the evidence of her life. Furniture but no personality. Books about procedure and law. An unread book on the coffee table. No photographs on the walls. No mementos from travel she'd never taken. No gifts from lovers she'd never had.

Nothing that said anyone had ever been here besides her. Nothing that said she'd ever let anyone in.

Until the journal. Until Mara had forced her way into Dempsey's awareness, into her thoughts, into the empty spaces of her apartment where desire had never been allowed to exist.

One seventeen AM.

Dempsey went to her bedroom. Opened her closet. Found her backup weapon in its lockbox. Loaded it. Tucked it into an ankle holster. Her service weapon went into its usual holster at her hip.

She found her tactical flashlight. Checked the batteries. Put it in her jacket pocket along with extra ammunition.

She turned off all the lights except the bedside lamp. Stood in the dim room, looking at the locked drawer where the journal had been hidden. Where it would stay hidden if she didn't come back.

If she went to the warehouse, she was walking into whatever Mara had planned. If she didn't go, she'd spend the rest of her life wondering. Wondering if Mara had wanted to explain. Or confess. Or something else entirely.

Wondering if this had been her only chance.

The rational investigator in her screamed *trap*. Screamed *procedure*. Screamed *call for backup*.

But the woman who'd read that journal every night for a week, who'd traced the photographs with her fingertips, who'd felt something unfamiliar bloom in her chest when she understood that someone had watched her, wanted her, desired her, that woman was already reaching for her keys.

Dempsey made her decision.

She grabbed her keys and headed for the door. Locked it behind her. The note and journal remained on the kitchen table under the lamp's light. Evidence of what she'd chosen. Evidence of why.

The stairwell was empty. The building silent. The street outside dark and cold.

She got in her car and started the engine. Programmed the GPS even though she didn't need it. Standard procedure when walking into the unknown. Leave a trail for whoever came looking.

One fifty-eight AM.

Sixty-two minutes until three AM. Until she found out if Mara wanted to explain herself or bury her.

Until she found out if desire could survive meeting its object. Or if obsession only worked from a distance, through camera lenses and stolen moments and fantasies written in neat blue ink.

Dempsey pulled away from the curb. The city was quiet at this hour. Empty streets. Traffic lights cycling for no one. She drove west toward the industrial district. Toward an abandoned warehouse. Toward the first person who'd ever wanted her.

Toward Mara.

Chapter 16

Dempsey drove west on Hanover Street at 2:43 AM. No traffic. The GPS mounted on her dash recited turns she already knew. If she disappeared tonight, investigators would have her route.

She checked her rearview. Empty. Sideview. Empty. The intersection ahead cycled through red to green for no one. Her headlights caught the reflective paint on the empty bus stop. The twenty-four-hour diner was dark despite its neon promise.

The GPS told her to turn right in five hundred feet.

She slowed at a red light, checking all directions. A lone pickup cruised through the intersection perpendicular to her. Late model, blue with a white cap, couldn't make out the plates. Not following her. The light changed. She accelerated.

The streets narrowed as she left downtown. Fewer streetlights. More shadows. Industrial zone. Warehouses and loading docks lined both sides now. Most properties had security lights, cyclone fencing. The Wilmington building stood darker than the others when she turned onto Cizer Street. No exterior lights. Chain-link fence with gaps.

She killed her headlights a block away. Drove the final stretch in darkness, using only ambient light from distant streetlamps. She rolled to a stop across from the warehouse, engine idling.

The tactical assessment came automatically. Twenty years of police work had trained her eyes to see trouble before it happened.

No vehicles visible. No lights inside the structure. One entry point visible from street, a loading bay door standing partially open. The gap a rectangle of deeper black against the dark exterior. Wide enough for a person to enter. No movement. The building sat silent, dead-looking.

She killed the engine. Listened. City sounds carried here. Distant traffic, the hum of the industrial zone's electrical grid. Nothing from the warehouse. She drew her weapon, checked it. Holstered it again.

The chain-link fence caught plastic bags and fast-food wrappers, urban tumbleweeds trapped mid-flight. The asphalt of the lot was cracked, weeds pushing through like desperate fingers. Good ground for tracking if she needed to. Bad for silent approach.

She got out of the car. The door closed with a muffled thunk. She stood motionless, letting her eyes adjust fully to the darkness. The warehouse loomed ahead, three stories of concrete and steel. Most windows intact but filmed with decades of city grime. No light leaked through.

Training screamed ambush. Isolated location. Limited visibility. Unknown interior with multiple hiding spots. No backup. She should call it in, wait for uniforms.

Dempsey approached the fence. Found a spot where the chain-link sagged between posts. She hoisted herself up, movements economical. Her boots found purchase in the metal diamonds. At the top, she swung her legs over, dropped to the other side. The fence rattled but held.

Her feet hit broken asphalt. She crouched, waited. No response from inside the building. No new sounds. She drew her weapon and held it pointed down, finger alongside the trigger guard.

Twenty yards to the loading bay. She moved forward in a crouch, staying in the deepest shadows. Stopped every few steps to listen. Her breathing sounded loud to her own ears. The weight of her gun familiar in her hand.

The open bay door gaped ahead. She couldn't see beyond the threshold. Just darkness. She slowed her approach. No visible threat.

Ten yards out, she stopped again. The breeze shifted. The smell of old concrete and stagnant water drifted from the opening. No chemical smell that might indicate meth production. No copper tang of blood. Just emptiness and decay.

Five yards. She moved sideways now, presenting a smaller target. The opening was a standard loading bay, wide enough for pallets but not vehicles. The door was raised about four feet, enough to walk under without crawling. Rust flaked from its underside.

She reached the exterior wall. Pressed her back against it. Concrete cool and rough through her jacket. She listened again. Nothing but the distant city.

Dempsey took a deep breath. Steadied herself. She'd been a homicide detective for four years, beat cop for fifteen before that. She'd walked into worse places than this. Usually with backup, but still.

She angled her body toward the opening. One last check of the weapon. Safety off. Round chambered.

She stepped inside.

Darkness swallowed her. Complete. Dempsey froze just inside the entrance, letting her other senses work. The smell hit her first. Old concrete dust, stale air. She heard nothing beyond her own breathing and, somewhere distant, water dripping in steady rhythm.

She stepped forward. Her footsteps echoed softly despite her care. Years of tactical entries had taught her how to move quietly, but the emptiness of the warehouse amplified every sound. She stopped again. Listened harder.

Nothing.

Her eyes struggled to adjust. Shapes began to form. Darker shadows against dark. Support columns rose at regular intervals. The ceiling loomed high above, invisible. Her weapon stayed ready, pointed down, finger alongside the trigger guard.

She took another step. Then another. The concrete floor stretched before her, scarred from years of industrial use. She felt rather than saw the vastness of the space. The air hung cold against her face.

Her pulse quickened. Not fear. Anticipation. Something about this place felt wrong. Set up. She scanned what little she could see. No movement. No sound except the dripping water.

Her finger twitched near the trigger. Muscle memory from too many moments like this. Too many times when the darkness had held something waiting.

"Callisto."

The voice came from her left. Dempsey spun, weapon rising automatically. Her finger moved to the trigger.

"Let me turn on my light." A phone screen illuminated, then its flashlight activated. The beam caught a woman's face from below, casting strange shadows.

Mara Snowden stood fifteen yards away. Calm. Still. The phone light created a small circle of visibility around her, revealing nothing of the space between them.

Dempsey kept her weapon trained on Mara's chest. Her arms were steady. Her training held. But her heart hammered against her ribs. Mara was alive. Relief crashed through her, followed immediately by dread.

"Thank you for coming," Mara said. Her voice echoed in the empty space.

Dempsey didn't respond. She assessed quickly. Mara's hands visible, one holding the phone. No visible weapon. No visible injuries. No signs of duress.

"I wasn't sure you would," Mara continued. Her face remained unnaturally calm.

Dempsey lowered her weapon slowly. Kept it in her hand. "You could have called."

"No. Not for this."

Dempsey considered the risk, then holstered her gun. The snap of the retention strap sounded loud in the quiet space.

"Where have you been?" Dempsey took a step forward. "Five days. No contact."

Mara remained motionless, the light still illuminating her face from below. "I needed time. To think. To plan."

"Plan what?" Another step closer. Dempsey could make out more details now. Mara wore dark clothes, hair pulled back. Her expression revealed nothing. Not the Mara she knew from crime scenes, always quick with observations, sometimes a smile.

"It's complicated."

"Try me." Dempsey stopped ten feet away. Close enough to lunge if needed. Far enough to react if things went wrong.

"You came alone?" Mara asked.

"Of course." Dempsey studied Mara's face, looking for something familiar. Found nothing but this strange new composure.

"I wanted to see you," Mara said finally. "To explain."

"Explain what?" Dempsey's hand stayed near her holster.

"What I've done. What I'm going to do."

"I think I've figured out what you've done." Dempsey kept her voice neutral.

"Have you?" A smile ghosted across Mara's face.

"You killed Stefan Tapani." Dempsey watched for a reaction. Found none. "Behind The Dump. July 8th."

The smile on Mara's face widened. Not the reaction Dempsey expected. Not remorse. Not fear.

"Yes." Mara nodded once. "I did."

The simple admission hung between them. Dempsey had expected denial. Excuses. Not this calm declaration.

"Are you proud of that?" Dempsey asked.

"Yes." No hesitation. "Do you know what he did?"

Something tugged in Dempsey's chest. Protective. Uncomfortable. "I know."

"The whole story?"

"I saw the photos." Dempsey swallowed. "From your rape kit."

Mara nodded slowly. "Did you see the outcome?"

"Charges dropped."

Mara's face remained expressionless, but something flickered in her eyes. "Do you know why?"

Dempsey nodded. "He was a confidential informant."

The phone light trembled in Mara's hand. First sign of emotion. "How many women, Callisto? How many charges dropped because he was useful to someone?"

"At least one other sexual assault."

Mara's face hardened. "And they just let him walk. The cops—"

"I had no idea," Dempsey interrupted. "His record was locked. Confidential."

"But you found out." Mara's voice was flat.

"I'm good at my job." Dempsey maintained eye contact. "The fact that he was charged at all means the cops did their part."

Mara nodded slowly. "The DA then. The DA dropped the charges."

"Yes." Dempsey watched Mara's face. Couldn't read her expression in the strange lighting.

"The system." Mara's eyes seemed to calculate something. "Tell me about the records being locked."

"Standard procedure for CIs. Their criminal records are restricted access."

"Who can access them?"

Dempsey hesitated. "Department heads. Chief. District Attorney's office."

"Brandt." Mara's voice was suddenly sharp.

"Yes." Dempsey shifted her weight. "Your aunt's been worried about you. That's why she asked me to find you."

"Did she know? About Tapani?" Mara's light moved as her hand tensed.

"She knew some things." Dempsey chose her words carefully. "Not everything."

"How much do you know?" Mara's question came quickly.

Dempsey looked directly into Mara's eyes. "Almost everything." She paused. "Almost."

The warehouse fell silent except for their breathing and the distant drip of water. The phone light created a small island in the darkness where they stood, two women facing each other across an expanding gulf.

"I wanted to explain to you," Mara said. She lowered the phone, casting her face in deeper shadow. "That's why I left the note. Why I asked to see you."

"I think I've figured it out." Dempsey kept her voice neutral, professional. The way she spoke to suspects in interrogation rooms.

"Have you?" Mara's smile returned, wider now. Triumphant. "Then you know why I killed him."

"Revenge." Dempsey stated it as fact.

"Justice." Mara corrected. "Are you going to arrest me?"

"Yes."

"But can you?"

Dempsey didn't answer.

"Do you know what he did to me, Callisto?" Mara's voice hardened. "Beyond what you saw in those clinical photos?"

Dempsey felt something tug in her chest. Protective. Uncomfortable. "I know enough."

"He waited for me. Behind The Dump. I was taking photos of the city. Just having some fun."

"I read the report."

"Did the report mention he laughed?" Mara's voice remained steady. Too steady. "When he finished. When he zipped up and left me there."

Dempsey said nothing. There was nothing to say.

"I did everything right." Mara's phone light trembled. "Didn't shower. Went straight to the hospital. Rape kit. Statement. Identified him in a lineup. Physical evidence."

"I know."

"The system protected him." Mara nodded slowly. "So I removed him from the system."

"That's not how it works."

"It worked for me." Mara's voice was cold.

"My aunt knew." Mara's voice was flat.

Dempsey nodded once.

"She knew." Mara's statement hung between them. "She must have known what he did."

"She was concerned about you." Dempsey chose her words carefully. "That's why she asked me to find you."

Mara absorbed this. "Did she mention him? Tapani?"

"No."

"But you made the connection?"

"I'm a detective. It's my job."

"So you know I shot him." Mara's admission came easily. Too easily. "Three times. Heart. Head. Groin. With two different guns."

Dempsey tensed but kept her expression neutral. "Why two guns?"

"Confuse the crime scene. Make it look like two shooters."

"Multiple guns suggests multiple shooters. Keeps detectives looking."

"You're good at your job." Mara nodded.

"Why tell me this? You're confessing to first-degree murder."

"Because I trust you, Callisto. And because there's more."

"More what?"

"More to do." Mara's eyes glinted in the phone light. "More people responsible."

"No." Dempsey said it quietly.

"The DA, and the officers who knew Tapani was a predator but still used him as an informant."

"It doesn't work that way, Mara. The system—"

"Failed me." Mara cut her off. "Failed every woman he hurt because they decided his information was more valuable than our safety."

Dempsey took a step forward. "I can help you. We can do this the right way."

"This is the right way." Mara's voice hardened. "My way."

"People will get hurt."

"People already got hurt. I got hurt." Mara's control slipped for just a moment, her voice cracking. "Where were you then, Callisto? Where was your system?"

The question hit Dempsey like a physical blow. She had no answer.

"Do you know why I called you here?" Mara asked after a moment.

"To explain."

"To give you a choice."

"What choice?"

"Help me. Or stop me." Mara's face was deadly serious now. "But I don't think you'll stop me. I think you understand."

"This isn't justice, Mara."

"Isn't it?" Mara's smile returned, knowing. "You've spent your career watching guilty people walk free. Watching victims get ignored. How many times have you wanted to take matters into your own hands?"

Dempsey didn't respond.

Chapter 17

Dempsey looked at Mara's face in the phone's harsh light. Something about the woman's calm made her more dangerous than any perp Dempsey had faced in twenty years. She knew there was more. Had to be more. The pieces had been falling into place for days now.

"It wasn't just Tapani." Dempsey kept her voice flat, professional. "Deirdre Bonner. Barney Duke. Turner Pass."

Mara's face lit up. Not with fear or denial. With something like joy. "You figured it out."

"Yes."

"All of it?"

"Enough of it."

Mara's smile widened. "I knew you would. That's why I chose you."

The warehouse felt colder suddenly. The dripping somewhere in the darkness marked time between them.

"You arranged Bonner's car accident. Drugged Duke before staging his suicide. Made Pass's death look like a bicycle accident." Dempsey watched Mara's face for any crack in her composure. Found none. "All three witnessed Tapani assault you. All three did nothing."

Mara nodded slowly. Pride in her eyes. "The photo was the first clue. The spiral notebook was the second."

"Left in your apartment for me to find."

"Left for you specifically. I knew Brandt would ask you to look for me." Mara shifted the phone light. It cast her face in new shadows. "Did you enjoy the journal too?"

Heat crept up Dempsey's neck. Unexpected. Unwelcome. The black leather journal with its explicit photographs and writings had been something else entirely. Something not meant for police eyes. Something personal.

"How did you know I read it?" Dempsey asked.

Mara laughed, softly and intimately in the empty space. "You didn't just read it, Callisto. You took it."

Dempsey said nothing.

"I went back to my apartment after you'd been there. It was gone." Mara's eyes locked on hers. "I was hoping you'd take it."

"I assumed it was part of your plan." Dempsey kept her voice steady. "Another manipulation to bring me on your side."

Mara's smile faded. She shook her head slowly. "No. Not at all."

"Then what was it?"

"Truth." Mara's voice softened. "I've been in love with you since the first time we met. The Conway case. I watched you work, how you moved through that scene. How you saw everything."

Dempsey's mind flashed back. Three years ago. Double homicide in a suburban home. Mara had been the department photographer. They'd hardly spoken.

"You knew then?" Dempsey kept her tone neutral.

"I knew you were the woman for me." Mara's voice carried absolute certainty.

Something shifted in Dempsey's chest. Something she hadn't felt before. Wanted to believe it. That someone could want her that way. That anyone would look at her face, her body, her life, and desire it. Desire her.

But forty-eight years of evidence said otherwise. No one had ever wanted her before.

"If what you say is true, why kill them?" Dempsey changed the subject, moved to firmer ground. "Why not just reach out?"

"I tried."

"I'm talking about the witnesses. Bonner, Duke, Pass." Dempsey recalibrated. "If they were all there to see Tapani die, why not kill them then? Why wait?"

Mara tilted her head. The light shifted with her movement. "I'll tell you if you give me something first."

"What?"

"A kiss."

The word hung between them. Simple. Impossible.

"One kiss, and I'll tell you everything." Mara's voice was soft, but it filled the empty warehouse. "I promise."

Dempsey nodded quickly. Regretted it instantly as Mara stepped closer. The gap between them narrowing. Five feet. Four. Three.

The phone light bobbed with Mara's movement. Dempsey's hand twitched near her holster. Force of habit. She'd never kissed anyone. Never been this close to someone who knew the worst things she'd seen. The worst things she'd done.

Mara stopped two feet away. Close enough that Dempsey could smell her perfume now. Jasmine. Could see the slight rise and fall of her chest beneath her dark clothing. Could feel the heat radiating between them.

"Well?" Mara's voice was barely above a whisper.

"You're a murderer." Dempsey stated the fact plainly.

"Yes." No denial. No excuse.

"I should arrest you right now."

"You should." Mara nodded. "Will you?"

Dempsey didn't answer.

"I killed them because they watched him hurt me and did nothing." Mara's voice hardened for the first time. "Bonner looked right at me as he dragged me behind that dumpster. Duke laughed. Pass just walked away."

"That doesn't justify murder."

"Doesn't it?" Mara's eyes were steady on hers. "The system failed me, Callisto. Your system."

The statement hit like a physical blow. Dempsey had spent twenty years watching the system fail. Had spent twenty years collecting evidence that went nowhere, taking statements that judges dismissed, watching perps walk on technicalities or plea deals.

"Do you know what it feels like to be invisible?" Mara asked quietly. "To have something happen to you, something that breaks you apart, and everyone just looks away?"

Dempsey knew exactly what that felt like. Had felt invisible her entire life.

"Your kiss, Detective." Mara reminded her. "Then I'll tell you everything you want to know."

Dempsey hesitated. Trapped between duty and something else. Something that had been forming in her chest since she'd found that black leather journal with its photographs of her. With its descriptions of desire. With the knowledge that someone had seen her. Really seen her.

Mara was watching her face. Waiting.

Mara leaned in. Her lips found Dempsey's in the darkness. Soft at first, then urgent. Hungry. Dempsey's body responded before her mind caught up. Her hands found Mara's waist. Held on like she might fall.

The kiss deepened. Mara tasted like mint. Her hands moved to Dempsey's face, holding her there, fingers tracing her jawline. The phone in Mara's hand slid down, casting their shadows long against the warehouse wall.

Power surged through Dempsey. Not the power of her badge or her gun. Something else. Something she'd never felt before. The power of being wanted. Of being seen.

She would never tell Mara this was her first kiss. Forty-eight years on earth and no one had ever wanted to touch her like this. She filed the thought away, locked it down deep where no interrogation could reach it.

Mara pulled back first. Her breath came fast against Dempsey's face. "Now I'll tell you."

Dempsey stepped back. Put distance between them. Her lips still carried the pressure of the kiss. She touched her thumb to them, dropped her hand when she realized what she was doing.

"I'm listening." Her voice sounded strange to her own ears.

Mara moved away, began walking slowly around the empty space. Her phone light swept across broken concrete, empty corners. Dempsey followed, keeping a careful distance.

"I didn't kill the witnesses that night because it would have been obvious." Mara's voice was calm, as if discussing case details at a crime scene. "Three witnesses, all dead beside Tapani? Every detective in Homicide would have connected it to me immediately."

"So you waited."

"I planned." Mara corrected. "Made each death look natural or accidental. Spaced them apart. Gave each one its own investigation in different divisions."

The dripping water somewhere in the darkness kept steady rhythm. Their footsteps echoed as they walked the perimeter of the vast empty space.

"Deirdre's car accident. Duke's suicide. Pass's bike fall." Dempsey cataloged them. "Each one different. Each one ruled accidental or self-inflicted."

Dempsey moved forward as Mara backed up.

"I researched." Mara's voice carried a hint of pride. "Learned about commotio cordis for Pass. How to position Duke's body to make it look self-administered. The angle to strike Deirdre's head before the crash."

"Meticulous." Dempsey kept her tone neutral. Professional. She followed as Mara led her deeper.

"I had time." Mara swept her light across an empty loading dock. "I've been planning this since last Christmas. A gift to myself."

"Christmas?"

"Merry Christmas to me." Mara's voice hardened.

They reached a staircase leading to a mezzanine. Mara started up. Dempsey followed, hand again near her holster.

"It took me a while," Dempsey said, "but I put it together anyway."

"I knew you would."

"Which means I have to arrest you." Dempsey's voice echoed in the empty space.

Mara stopped at the top of the stairs. Turned. The light between them cast strange shadows on her face. "Do you?"

Before Dempsey could answer, Mara closed the distance. Kissed her again. This time harder, more desperate. Her hands found Dempsey's shoulders, pressed against them. The phone clattered to the floor, light spilling sideways across their feet.

Dempsey's mind went blank. Training and protocol dissolved against the heat of Mara's mouth on hers. She felt herself responding again. Felt her hands move to Mara's back, pulling her closer.

Then her training reasserted itself. She broke the kiss. Stepped back. Put a hand out to stop Mara from following.

"Why did you disappear?" Dempsey needed to regain control of the situation. "If you hadn't, your aunt would never have asked me to investigate."

Mara retrieved her phone from the floor. Checked that it still worked. The light caught the angles of her face as she looked up at Dempsey.

"That's exactly why."

"What?"

"It seemed the only way to get your attention." Mara's voice softened. "Everything else failed."

"Everything else?" Dempsey tried to recall any previous interactions with Mara beyond crime scene work.

"I didn't want to spend another Christmas alone."

The words hit Dempsey unexpectedly. Struck something raw inside her. How many Christmases had she spent alone? Every one she could remember. Always volunteering for the holiday shift so others could be with family.

"You could have just asked." Dempsey's voice came out rougher than intended.

"I did." Mara stepped closer again. Cautious this time. "Many times."

Dempsey frowned. Searched her memory. Found nothing.

"Every time I asked you for coffee. For dinner." Mara shook her head. "You always said you had to work."

Dempsey remembered now. Casual invitations she'd brushed off. Standard requests for after-work drinks she'd declined without a second thought. She never accepted those offers from anyone. Work was safer. Work made sense.

"So you decided murder was the best way to get my attention?" Dempsey kept her voice flat.

"They deserved what they got." No remorse in Mara's voice. "And yes, it got your attention."

They stood in silence for a moment, facing each other on the mezzanine. The vastness of the warehouse spread out below them, dark and empty. Their breath created small clouds in the cold air.

"You were always going to catch me." Mara's voice was quiet now. "I wanted you to."

Dempsey stared at her. Tried to make sense of it. "You wanted to get caught?"

"I wanted you to hunt me." Mara stepped closer. "Really hunt me."

The confession hung between them. Dempsey thought of the journal again. The photographs. The words. The naked want in them.

"I see you." Dempsey's voice was barely audible. "I see what you've done."

"I had to get creative," Mara said. She walked to the edge of the mezzanine, looked down at the warehouse floor. "You never noticed me otherwise."

"I noticed you at crime scenes." Dempsey stayed where she was. Kept distance between them.

"Professionally." Mara turned back to face her. "You noticed my photos. My evidence markers. Never me."

"That's not true."

"Isn't it?" Mara stepped closer. "Name one personal thing you know about me that isn't in my file."

Dempsey said nothing. There was nothing to say.

"You're such a workaholic." A hint of frustration crept into Mara's voice. "Asking you for drinks or dinner always got the same answer."

"Which was?"

"'I have to work.'" Mara mimicked Dempsey's flat tone perfectly. "'Maybe another time.'"

The imitation hit close enough to make Dempsey uncomfortable. She shifted her weight. Looked past Mara to the vast darkness of the warehouse beyond.

"I watched you." Mara's voice softened. "When you didn't know I was watching."

"That's—" Dempsey stopped herself from saying "creepy." Changed course. "That's invasive."

"It's observation." Mara's light caught her eyes, made them gleam. "For example, I'm the only person who knows your right eyebrow raises when you think a witness is lying to you."

Dempsey felt a chill. She did that. Had noticed it in a video playback of an interrogation.

"Your left hand taps your thigh twice when you're thinking. You order your case files by date, then reorganize them by suspect when you hit a wall." Mara took another step closer. "You eat lunch alone. Always reading files instead of talking to anyone."

Dempsey felt exposed. Stripped bare in a way that had nothing to do with the photos in the journal. Mara had seen her. Really seen her.

"You never meet anyone's eyes in the precinct bathroom." Mara continued. "Always look at the floor or the wall. But at crime scenes, you look at everyone. See everything."

"Stop." Dempsey's voice was sharper than she intended.

Mara fell silent. Her face unreadable in the phone's harsh light.

The observations were too precise. Too intimate. Professional surveillance grade. Dempsey had to respect the skill even as it violated her most private behaviors.

She remembered now. A few times Mara had caught her after a scene wrap, suggested coffee. Asked about getting dinner. Casual invitations that Dempsey had declined without thought. Work was always the excuse. Work was always the truth.

"Two guns. To look like multiple suspects?" Dempsey changed the subject. Moved back to firm ground. The case. The murders.

Mara allowed the shift. Nodded once, accepting the new direction.

"Misdirection." Mara's voice carried a hint of pride. "Two shooters suggests organization. Planning. Detectives would look for gang connections, drug involvement."

"Not a personal vendetta."

"Exactly."

Dempsey nodded. It was a smart play. The kind of detail that would have investigators chasing false leads for months.

"I thought it was clever, using both my left and right hands." Mara demonstrated, forming her hands into gun shapes. "Different heights, different trajectories."

"The shots to the head and heart came from your dominant hand." Dempsey recalled the M.E. report. "Right hand. Clean shots."

"Yes."

"The groin shot came from your left. Less steady. More personal."

"Very personal." Mara didn't deny it.

Dempsey watched her. Tried to reconcile the skilled crime scene photographer with the methodical killer standing before her. The woman who had photographed hundreds of victims now creating bodies for others to document.

"The crime scene told a story."

"All crime scenes tell stories." Mara's voice softened. "That's why I love photography. Finding the story in the evidence."

Dempsey thought of the journal again. The photographs of her. What story had Mara been telling there?

"Your aunt is worried about you." Dempsey tried another angle.

"Liar."

They faced each other across the mezzanine. The phone light between them caught dust motes hanging suspended in the cold air.

"What happens now?" Mara asked.

"You know what happens."

Dempsey's hand moved to her cuffs. Duty reasserting itself through muscle memory. But she didn't draw them.

"You have a choice." Mara was close enough now that Dempsey could feel her breath. "Help me finish this. Or take me in."

"There's nothing to finish." Dempsey's voice was firm. "Tapani and the witnesses are dead."

"There's more to do."

"You're not going to arrest me," Mara said. Her voice carried certainty. "You have no warrant. No imminent threat. Even my confession won't hold up."

Dempsey kept her hand near her cuffs but didn't draw them. "That's—"

"I'll confess properly if that's what you need." Mara lowered her phone. The light cast shadows upward on her face. "Face the consequences."

"That's the law." Dempsey's voice was flat.

"But before I do." Mara stepped closer. "Tell me what you want."

"What?"

"Not what the law requires." Mara's voice softened. "What you, Callisto Dempsey, want."

The question hung between them. The warehouse felt colder. The dripping somewhere in the darkness marked each second Dempsey didn't answer.

Twenty years of police work had trained her body to respond automatically. Draw the cuffs. Recite the Miranda. Call it in. The instinct was physical, embedded in her muscles and bones. But something else pulled against that training. Something new.

"What I want isn't as important as what I have to do." Dempsey's voice sounded distant to her own ears.

Mara closed the gap between them. Placed her hand over Dempsey's heart. The touch burned through her jacket, her shirt. "Would it hurt you to arrest me?"

Dempsey's pulse quickened under Mara's fingers. She nodded once. A small, tight movement.

"Would it be easier," Mara's voice was barely above a whisper now, "if I simply turned myself in? To my aunt?"

Mara's hand stayed on Dempsey's chest. Warm. Steady.

"Would that help you, Callisto?"

The sound of her first name from Mara's lips felt intimate. Dangerous. Something no one at the precinct ever used. Something separate from the badge and the gun and the case files.

"Yes." Dempsey's answer surprised her.

Mara's hand moved from Dempsey's chest to her face. Her fingers traced Dempsey's jawline. "Then that's what I'll do."

Dempsey didn't step back. Didn't pull away from the touch. She crossed a line. Knew it. Couldn't stop.

"When?" Dempsey's question was professional. Her body's response to Mara's touch was not.

"Today." Mara's thumb brushed Dempsey's lower lip. "I promise."

Dempsey was trapped. She has enough to *know* Mara was guilty, but not enough to *prove* it in court without destroying her own career. She couldn't get a warrant without admitting she broke the rules. She couldn't arrest Mara without evidence that won't be thrown out. And she couldn't go to the Chief without committing career suicide.

So here she stood. Not drawing her cuffs. Not calling it in.

The phone light between them flickered as the battery began to fade. Mara moved closer. Their bodies touched now. Dempsey could feel Mara's breath on her face.

"I knew you would understand." Mara's words were warm against her skin.

"I don't." Dempsey didn't move away. "I don't understand any of this."

"You will."

They stood facing each other. Something charged and dangerous filled the space between them. Something that smelled like jasmine and tasted like mint. Something Dempsey had never felt before.

Mara stepped back first. Her hand fell away from Dempsey's face. The absence felt cold.

"Goodbye, Callisto."

Mara turned. Walked toward the loading bay door they'd entered through. Her footsteps echoed in the vast empty space. Each one fading, carrying her further away.

Dempsey watched her go. Should have drawn her weapon. Should have called out. Should have given the standard command to stop.

Did none of those things.

Mara reached the loading bay door. Hesitated. Looked back at Dempsey, a silhouette against the dimly brightening sky beyond.

"I'll see you soon." Mara's voice carried in the empty warehouse.

Then she was gone. The sound of her footsteps continued outside, growing fainter until they disappeared altogether.

Silence filled the warehouse. The dripping water continued somewhere in the darkness. Tick. Tick. Tick. Like a clock counting down.

Dempsey stood motionless. Morning light began to filter through the high, grimy windows. Dust motes danced in the beams. The warehouse took shape around her as darkness receded. Concrete pillars. Metal stairs. Empty loading docks.

She'd just let a murderer walk away. Trusted her to turn herself in because she hadn't stuck to protocol.

Her detective's mind cataloged what she'd done. Failing to arrest a suspect after confession. Dereliction of duty. Obstruction of justice.

Fireable offenses. Criminal offenses.

She'd spent twenty years building her career. Four of those as detective. Had never broken a regulation. Never crossed a line. Her integrity had been the one thing she could count on. The one thing no one could take from her.

Until now.

Her legs felt weak. She moved to a concrete block nearby. Sat heavily. The stone was cold through her pants. Unyielding. Like the truth of what she'd done.

The weight of destroyed integrity settled over her like physical pressure. Pressed against her lungs. Made each breath shallow. This was how it happened, then. How good cops went bad. One compromise. One moment of weakness. One line crossed.

She thought of the journal again. The photographs. The words. The evidence of being seen, being wanted. That too felt like a weight now. A hook in her chest, pulling her toward something she couldn't name.

Dawn light strengthened. Gave definition to the emptiness around her. The warehouse stood silent, indifferent to what had transpired within its walls.

Chapter 18

Dempsey unlocked her apartment door at 7:18 AM. The familiar smell of old books did nothing to ease the tightness in her chest. She closed the door behind her. Stood with her back against it for three long breaths. Her badge weighed heavy on her hip.

She moved through her apartment without turning on lights. Muscle memory guided her past the kitchen table, around the worn armchair, down the hallway. She unbuckled her holster. Set it on the bathroom counter. Her gun and badge followed. The metal made a dull thud against the porcelain.

The mirror showed her a stranger. Hollow eyes. Tight mouth. Hair flattened on one side from leaning against the warehouse wall. She looked away.

Her clothes hit the floor in a pile. She didn't sort them for laundry like she always did. Just stepped out and over them. Turned the shower dial all the way to hot.

Steam filled the bathroom before she stepped in. The water hit her skin like judgment. Scalding. Cleansing. She turned her face up into it. Let it pound against her closed eyes, her forehead, her cheeks.

The soap bar slipped in her hands twice. She scrubbed her skin hard. Arms. Chest. Neck. Everywhere Mara had touched her. Everywhere that still carried the ghost of contact. Her lips burned under the hot water, still holding the memory of the kiss.

Twenty years. Twenty years of doing the job right. Of following procedure. Of being the one who got it done without breaking the rules.

Gone.

The water began to cool. She didn't adjust it. Kept standing under the stream as it went from hot to warm to cold. Her skin had long since turned red. Her fingertips wrinkled. The cold water kept coming. She kept standing.

Maybe if she stood here long enough, the evidence would wash away. The touch. The words. The compromised integrity. Maybe if she stood here long enough, she'd find a way to undo what she'd done.

But there was no undoing it.

The water ran ice cold now. Her body had gone numb. Just physical response to temperature. Not emotional response to shame. She told herself this as she finally reached for the dial. Turned it off.

The silence that followed was complete. Just the drip of the shower head and her own breathing. She pushed back the curtain. Reached for a towel. Her movements mechanical. Precise. The kind of movements that suggested control.

She had no control.

The towel was rough against her reddened skin. She dried methodically. Face. Arms. Torso. Legs. Feet last. The mirror had fogged completely. She didn't wipe it clear. Didn't need to see herself again.

Her clean clothes waited in the bedroom. She dressed with care. Fresh underwear and bra. Clean shirt. Pressed pants. Each item donned like armor. Protection against what was coming. What had to come.

Her hands trembled as she buttoned her shirt. The small plastic discs slipped between her fingers. One. Two. Three attempts at the third button before it went through. Four at the fourth. She tucked the shirt in with jerky movements.

The belt went through the loops unsteadily. The clasp clicked. She cinched it one notch tighter than usual. Felt the pressure against her stomach. A small discomfort to focus on. Better than the larger one expanding in her chest.

Her holster went on next. The weight of the gun settled against her hip. Familiar. Wrong now. She no longer deserved to carry it. The badge clipped to her belt. Another weight she had no right to.

She looked around her bedroom. The neatly made bed she hadn't slept in. The alarm clock showing 7:49 AM.

Back in the bathroom, she brushed her teeth. Combed her hair. Applied deodorant. No makeup. She never wore it anyway. The movements of normalcy when nothing was normal anymore.

The mirror had cleared enough now that she could see her face. The red blotches from the hot water. The pale lips. The eyes that wouldn't meet their own reflection.

She switched off the bathroom light. Walked back through the apartment. The kitchen clock read 7:58 AM. She'd been home forty minutes. It felt like seconds and hours simultaneously.

Her keys sat in the bowl by the door where she always left them. She picked them up. The metal was cool against her palm. She looked back at her apartment. The place that had always been her sanctuary from the job. Now the job had followed her home in the form of her own transgression.

Dempsey opened her front door. Stepped into the hallway. Locked up behind her. The routine motions of leaving for work. As if this were any other day. As if she were still the person she had been yesterday.

Her legs carried her down the stairs. Out the building's front door. Into the morning air that smelled of car exhaust and the bakery two doors down. Normal morning smells that belonged to a world that hadn't tilted on its axis.

She walked to her car. Got in. Started the engine. Her hands still shook on the steering wheel. She gripped it tighter until the shaking stopped.

The drive to the precinct would take eighteen minutes in morning traffic. Eighteen minutes to decide what to do. How to face what was waiting.

Dempsey entered the precinct at 8:32 AM. She nodded to the desk sergeant. Kept her face neutral. Badge visible on her hip. Shoulders square. The professional mask she'd worn for twenty years. No one could see the fracture lines underneath.

The elevator doors opened to the third floor. The bullpen spread before her. Desktop computers humming. Phones rang at irregular intervals. The smell of men's deodorant couldn't quite cover the sweat beneath.

She stepped out. Scanned the room automatically. Threat assessment ingrained after two decades. Exits. People. Movement patterns.

Then she saw her.

Mara Snowden stood by William Harris's desk. Coffee cup in hand. Camera bag slung over one shoulder. Laughing at something Harris said. Alive. Present. Not in custody.

Dempsey stopped mid-stride. Her lungs forgot how to pull in air. Mara shouldn't be here. Mara should be in an interrogation room. Or a holding cell. Not standing in the bullpen like any other Tuesday.

Mara glanced up. Her eyes found Dempsey's across the room. Her smile didn't falter. Just a small nod of acknowledgment. The slightest tilt of her head. Then back to her conversation with Harris. Smooth. Professional. As if they hadn't stood in an abandoned warehouse five hours ago. As if Mara hadn't confessed to four murders. As if they hadn't kissed.

Dempsey forced her feet to move. One step. Another. Her desk was twenty feet away. She needed to sit down before her legs betrayed her.

"Look who's back from the big city." Kevin Knight's voice came from behind her.

Dempsey turned. Knight's face held its usual smirk. Tie knotted carelessly. Coffee stain on his shirt collar. He gestured toward Mara with his coffee mug.

"What?" Dempsey's voice came out rough.

"Snowden." Knight nodded toward Mara. "Back from her fancy photography course in New York." He laughed. "Hope you feel like quite the investigator now."

Dempsey stared at him. The words made no sense. Photography course. New York. The floor seemed to tilt beneath her feet.

"What are you talking about?" She kept her voice flat.

Knight's smirk widened. "Chief's niece goes to New York for a few days. Chief panics when she can't reach her. Puts her best detective on the case." He made air quotes around "best detective." "And turns out she was just at some workshop the whole time. Administrative mix-up with her leave request."

Dempsey said nothing. The lie was so complete. So perfect. New York explained Mara's absence. Administrative error explained why no one knew where she was. The entire investigation rendered pointless. Her compromise for nothing.

"Some detective." Knight laughed again. Turned away.

Dempsey looked back at Mara. Still talking to Harris. Something about lighting techniques now. Harris nodding. Interested. Believing every word.

Mara's hand gestures were animated. Professional. Nothing like the woman who had stood in the warehouse darkness. Nothing like the woman who had confessed to murder with calm pride. Nothing like the woman who had pressed her mouth to Dempsey's.

Dempsey kept staring. Couldn't look away. Trying to reconcile the two versions of Mara Snowden. The skilled photographer explaining something technical to a colleague. The methodical killer explaining her perfect crimes.

"It's not polite to stare, Dempsey." R.B. Polla appeared at her elbow. Thick glasses. Thinning hair carefully arranged. Coffee breath.

Dempsey turned to him. "What?"

"You're staring at Snowden like she grew a second head." Polla adjusted his glasses. "She just got back from New York."

"So I hear." Dempsey's words came automatically.

"Some workshop on crime scene photography." Polla shrugged. "Cutting edge techniques. Chief approved it last month."

The lie had layers. Depth. Mara had built it carefully. Had people believing it before she'd even disappeared.

"Right." Dempsey nodded once.

"You okay?" Polla squinted at her. "You look like hell."

"Fine." She moved past him. Toward her desk. Away from this conversation.

"Did you even sleep last night?" Polla called after her.

She didn't answer. Couldn't. Sleep was for people whose professional integrity was intact. People who hadn't let killers walk away. People who hadn't crossed that line.

Her desk looked the same as yesterday. Files stacked neatly. Computer screen dark. Empty coffee mug waiting to be filled. The normalcy of it struck her as obscene. Nothing should look normal today.

She sat heavily in her chair. The familiar creak as it took her weight. She stared at her blank screen. Didn't move to turn it on. Just listened to the bullpen sounds around her. Phones. Conversations. Keyboards clicking. Life continuing as if nothing had happened.

This must be what it feels like the day after you find out your loved one is dead.

Across the room, Mara laughed again. The sound cut through everything else. Dempsey's head came up automatically. Mara was looking directly at her now. Still smiling. The smile didn't reach her eyes. Her eyes held something else. Knowledge. Power. Victory.

Dempsey couldn't breathe. The precinct walls seemed to close in. The air thickened. Her collar too tight. Her badge too heavy. The knowledge of her compromise too present.

She stood. Grabbed her keys from the desk. Needed air. Needed space. Needed to be somewhere Mara wasn't.

Knight watched her from his desk. Eyebrows raised. "Hot case, Dempsey?"

She didn't answer. Walked toward the elevator. Pushed the button. Waited with her back straight. Professional mask still in place. No one could see the turmoil underneath. No one except Mara, who watched her from across the room with those knowing eyes.

The elevator doors opened. Dempsey stepped in. Turned to face the bullpen as the doors closed. The last thing she saw was Mara's smile. Confident. Victorious. The smile of someone who had played a perfect game.

The doors closed. Dempsey was alone. She exhaled for what felt like the first time since entering the building.

Dempsey knocked once on Chief Brandt's door. Waited for the "come in" before entering. Standard procedure. Everything by the book now. Too late, but still. The office smelled of furniture polish and the Chief's signature perfume. Expensive. Subtle. Dempsey had always respected Brandt. Had trusted her judgment. Until now.

Chief Brandt looked up from her desk. Reading glasses perched on her nose. Case file open before her. Her blonde hair pulled back in its usual neat bun. Blue eyes sharp behind the lenses.

"Dempsey." She removed her glasses. Set them on the desk. "Come in."

Dempsey closed the door behind her. Stood with her hands at her sides. Not at attention, but close. Old habits.

Brandt shook her head. Shrugged slightly. "Well, this is embarrassing."

"Ma'am?" Dempsey kept her voice neutral. Professional. As if she hadn't let Brandt's niece walk away from a murder confession five hours ago.

"Mara." Brandt gestured to the chair across from her desk. "Sit."

Dempsey sat. Back straight. Hands on her knees. Waiting.

"She showed up this morning at six." Brandt leaned back in her chair. "Apparently she's been in New York since Thursday."

Dempsey said nothing. The lie had reached the highest level now. Complete. Perfect.

"Photography course at some institute." Brandt waved her hand dismissively. "Said she requested the time off weeks ago, but the email to HR never went through."

The betrayal. Mara had promised to confess. Had promised to turn herself in. Instead, she'd crafted this lie. Made Dempsey complicit in her freedom.

"I see." Dempsey's voice remained steady. Years of interrogation training. Never show what you're thinking.

"Administrative misunderstanding." Brandt sighed. "She had the course confirmation email. Hotel receipt. Everything."

Of course she did. Mara was meticulous. Had planned every detail of her murders. Why wouldn't she plan this too?

"She mentioned she tried calling me several times." Brandt continued. "But my phone was showing 'unknown caller' so I didn't pick up."

Another lie. Another carefully constructed detail to complete the picture. Dempsey wondered briefly if Mara had somehow blocked her own number from Brandt's phone. It wouldn't surprise her.

"That's what I get for being a doting aunt." Brandt's smile didn't reach her eyes. "Jumping to conclusions. Wasting department resources."

"Not wasted." Dempsey's response was automatic. The expected professional reassurance.

"Well." Brandt's hands smoothed an invisible wrinkle from her desk blotter. "I appreciate your time and effort, regardless. You were thorough."

Not thorough enough. Not by half. If she'd been thorough, she'd have recorded Mara's confession. Would have arrested her immediately. Would have followed procedure instead of listening to a murderer's justifications.

"Just doing my job." The words tasted bitter.

"Your report?" Brandt's question was casual.

Dempsey's mind raced. The report. Documentation of everything she'd found. The photos connecting Mara to the victims. The notebook from the first crime scene with spiral binding matching Mara's. The evidence she'd gathered without warrants. The journal she'd taken from Mara's apartment.

"I'll have it on your desk by end of day." Another lie to add to the collection. The report would never exist. Couldn't exist.

Brandt nodded. Picked up her glasses again. Put them on. The conversation was ending.

"Thank you, Dempsey." She looked back down at the file on her desk. "That will be all."

Dismissal. Clear. Final. The matter closed as far as Brandt was concerned.

Dempsey stood. Her legs felt wooden. Her movements mechanical. She turned toward the door. Each step precise. Controlled.

Her hand closed around the doorknob. Cool metal against her palm. She paused. Should say something. Should tell Brandt the truth. Your niece is a murderer. She killed four people. She confessed to me. I let her go.

The words didn't come. Couldn't come. Saying them would end her career. Would destroy the only life she knew. Twenty years of service reduced to a final act of failure.

"Dempsey?" Brandt's voice cut through her thoughts. "Was there something else?"

"No, ma'am." Dempsey opened the door. "Nothing else."

She stepped into the hallway. Closed the door behind her. Stood there for three breaths. In. Out. In. The corridor was empty. No witnesses to her silence. No witnesses to her complicity.

She walked away from Brandt's office. Each step echoing on the polished floor. The weight of what she knew. What she couldn't say. What she'd allowed to happen.

Mara had won. Had played everyone perfectly. Had turned Dempsey into an accessory after the fact. The perfect crime wasn't just the murders. It was this. The return. The lie. The trap she'd set for Dempsey without Dempsey even realizing until it was too late.

She reached the elevator. Pushed the button. Waited. Professional mask still in place. No one passing by would see anything wrong. No one would know she was coming apart inside.

The doors opened. She stepped in. Turned. Faced forward as the doors closed. Alone again with the knowledge of what she'd done. What she'd failed to do.

Dempsey stepped outside. The morning air hit her face. Cooler now. Traffic noise from the intersection. A siren in the distance. She walked ten paces from the entrance. Stopped. Turned. Walked back. Her body needed movement while her mind worked the problem. The impossible problem Mara had created for her.

She paced along the front of the building. Ten steps right. Turn. Ten steps left. Turn. The concrete beneath her feet solid. Dependable. Unlike everything else in her world right now.

Mara had confessed. Clear words in an abandoned warehouse. I killed Tapani. Shot him three times. Heart. Head. Groin. With two different guns.

She stopped. Leaned against the brick wall. The rough texture caught at her jacket. Grounded her in physical reality while her mind spun.

Even if she had recorded it, the confession might not hold up. She hadn't read Mara her rights. Hadn't formally arrested her. Any halfway decent lawyer would get it thrown out.

She pushed off the wall. Started pacing again. Her footsteps quicker now. The sidewalk filled with morning commuters. Men in suits. Women in professional attire. Normal people heading to normal jobs where they hadn't compromised everything they stood for.

The evidence she had gathered. All of it obtained without warrants. The journal taken from Mara's apartment without permission. The photograph she'd found at Tapani's crime scene. The spiral notebook. The connections she'd made. All useless in court.

Inadmissible. Every bit of it.

She stopped at the corner. Watched the traffic light cycle through red to yellow to green. Cars moved on command. People crossed when told. The world functioned on rules. On procedure. On doing things the right way.

She had done everything the wrong way.

Her hand moved to her pocket. Cell phone there. She could call her captain. Tell him everything. Confess her own violations. Hope that Mara's confession would be enough to start a proper investigation.

Her career would be over. Twenty years erased by one mistake. One compromise.

She pulled her hand away from the phone. Not yet. She needed to think this through. Find another angle. There had to be a way to bring Mara in without destroying herself in the process.

Dempsey resumed pacing. Her mind sorted through options like case files. Organized. Methodical. Professional. The way she'd approached every investigation for twenty years.

Option one: Full confession. Tell Brandt everything. About the warehouse. About Mara's confession. About her own failure to arrest Mara immediately. Result: Investigation opened into Mara. Investigation also opened into Dempsey's conduct. Best case: suspension. Worst case: termination. Criminal charges for obstruction.

Option two: Anonymous tip. Call in details only the killer would know. Force a new investigation. Result: New investigators would have the same problem. No evidence. Nothing admissible. Case closed again for lack of evidence.

Option three: Surveillance. Watch Mara. Wait for a mistake. Build a new case the right way. Result: Potentially years of waiting. No guarantee Mara would ever make a mistake. She was too careful. Too precise.

Option four: Death. If Mara died... No. Not that option.

None of the options worked. None of them led to justice for four victims without destroying Dempsey's career. Without revealing her own compromise.

She stopped pacing. Her back against the wall again. The brick cold through her jacket. She closed her eyes. Saw Mara's face in the phone light. Heard her voice. Felt her lips.

The kiss.

Her fingers moved to her lips. Traced where Mara's mouth had been. Hours ago now, but the sensation remained. The first kiss of her life. Given by a murderer. Taken by a compromised cop.

That was the real trap. Not just the evidence Dempsey couldn't use. Not just the confession she couldn't prove. The kiss. The connection. The way Mara had seen her. Really seen her. The photographs in that journal. The words describing Dempsey with desire no one had ever shown her before.

Dempsey opened her eyes. Stared at the people passing by. None of them looking at her. None of them seeing her. Just another cop outside the station. Invisible despite the badge. Unseen despite the gun.

Mara had seen her. Had known exactly how to get to her.

Dempsey pushed off from the wall. Stood straight. The professional mask back in place. She had been played perfectly. Had walked right into Mara's trap without seeing it until too late.

She touched her lips again. The last piece fell into place. Mara hadn't just outmaneuvered her professionally. She'd found Dempsey's blind spot. The loneliness. The isolation. The lifetime of feeling unwanted. And she'd exploited it masterfully.

Double-crossed. Not just as a cop. As a woman. As a human being who had, for the first time, felt seen.

Dempsey's hand fell away from her face. The weight of the realization settled over her. She had no move to make. No way forward that didn't end in her own destruction. Mara had won before the game even began.

She looked up at the precinct building. Somewhere inside, Mara was going about her day. Taking crime scene photos. Chatting with colleagues. Playing the role of the professional she'd always been. While four people lay dead by her hand. And the only detective who knew the truth could do nothing about it.

Dempsey stood motionless on the sidewalk. People flowed around her like water around a stone. The traffic light cycled through its colors again and again. The world continued as if nothing had changed. As if everything was as it should be.

Nothing was as it should be. Nothing would ever be right again.

Chapter 19

Dempsey ducked under the yellow tape. The victim lay twenty feet away, sprawled on the sidewalk. Blood pooled beneath him, soaking into concrete. A city worker on a cherry picker hung Christmas lights on the utility pole across the street. The white bulbs swung in the breeze. Festive decorations for a death scene.

Officer Mendez approached as she pulled on latex gloves. "Male victim, Erick Odom, age forty-two. Shot twice. Once in the chest, once in the head."

"Time of death?" Dempsey kept her eyes on the body.

"M.E. estimates between six and eight this morning. Mail carrier found him at noon."

Dempsey nodded. Scanned the surroundings. Suburban street. Mid-range homes with well-kept yards. No witnesses apparently. No one standing on porches or peering through windows. Neighborhood already processed what happened and retreated inside.

"Wallet still on him?" Dempsey asked.

"Yes. Cash and cards intact."

Not robbery then. She moved closer to the body. Odom wore khakis and a blue button-down. Business casual. No jacket despite the December chill. Left home in a hurry or died while taking out the trash.

The flash from a camera caught her attention. Mara Snowden crouched ten feet away, photographing blood spatter on the concrete. Her brown hair pulled back in a neat ponytail. Camera held steady in practiced hands. She didn't look up.

Dempsey's throat tightened. First time seeing Mara at a scene since the warehouse. Since the kiss. Since the betrayal. She forced her focus back to the victim.

Odom's face was pale. Exit wound visible at the back of his skull where it hit concrete. Shot in the face. Neat entry wound center forehead. Professional shot. The chest wound was messier. Close range. Looked like two different weapons.

Her mind flashed to Tapani. Heart. Head. Groin. Two different guns.

Harris appeared beside her. His tie today was burgundy. One of his three regulars. "Multiple weapons," he said without preamble. "Reminds me of that nightclub shooting last July."

"Tapani," Dempsey said automatically. Regretted it immediately.

Harris nodded. "Similar MO. Professional hit disguised as something else."

Dempsey kneeled beside the body. Studied Odom's hands. No defensive wounds. No skin under fingernails. He never saw it coming or never had a chance to fight.

"Neighbors?" she asked.

"Canvassing now. Nobody saw anything so far."

"Family?"

"Wife's at the station with a victim advocate. Says she left for work at 5:30. Normal routine."

Dempsey stood. Made a slow circle around the body. Blood pattern consistent with being shot where he lay. Not moved after death. Died here on his own sidewalk.

Mara shifted position. Moved to photograph the victim from a new angle. Her camera clicked steadily. She worked with precise efficiency. Professional. Detached. As if nothing had happened between them.

Dempsey counted five shell casings near the body. To be collected by crime scene techs, tagged, bagged. A sixth casing gleamed under a nearby hedge. Overlooked. She pointed it out to a tech who quickly catalogued it.

"Mara," she called. The name felt strange in her mouth. Professional distance only now. "Get the hedge too."

Mara looked up. Nodded once. "Absolutely." She moved to photograph the hedge where the casing had been found.

Their eyes didn't meet. Didn't need to. The tension between them was a third presence at the scene.

Harris watched them. His eyes narrowed. Detective's instincts picking up something off. Something not right between photographer and investigator.

Dempsey moved away. Walked the perimeter of the scene. Looked for footprints in the soft dirt of the flower beds. Found nothing. Checked the street for tire marks. Nothing unusual. Examined the mailbox where the carrier had stood when discovering the body. Gathered her thoughts.

"He was killed execution-style," she said when Harris joined her again. "One shot to incapacitate, one to finish."

Harris nodded. "Professional hit. Question is why. Odom was an accountant at Miller & Sons. No criminal record. No known enemies according to the wife."

"Everyone has enemies."

"True that." Harris pulled out his notebook. Old-school spiral bound. Jotted something down. "Wife says everything was normal. No threats, no strange behavior. Just a regular guy who ended up dead on his sidewalk."

Dempsey walked back to the body. Mara was photographing the victim's shoes now. Oxford brogues, well-polished. The kind of detail that mattered in reconstructing a victim's final moments.

Dempsey checked her watch. 2:43 PM. Six to eight hours since time of death. Killer had a significant head start.

She opened her notebook. Made preliminary notes. Victim. Time. Location. Witness status. The basics of any homicide. The foundation of finding justice for the dead.

Mara moved to photograph the street. Her back was to Dempsey now. The distance between them carefully maintained. Professional boundaries established by mutual, unspoken agreement.

Harris stepped closer to Dempsey. Lowered his voice. "Everything okay between you two?"

Dempsey didn't look up from her notebook. "Why wouldn't it be?"

"Just asking." Harris's voice was neutral. "Seemed like something changed."

"We're fine," Dempsey said. Closed her notebook. Put it away. "Just focused on the job."

Harris nodded. Didn't push. But his eyes remained thoughtful. Calculating.

Dempsey addressed a nearby officer. "I want the victim's phone records, bank statements, work computer. Full background. And I need to interview the wife."

The Christmas lights across the street were fully installed now. The worker descended in the cherry picker. Tested the switch. The white bulbs came to life despite the daylight. Cheerful, oblivious to death thirty feet away.

Dempsey took one final look at Odom's body. Shot twice with two different weapons. Executed on his own sidewalk. Professional job. The kind that rarely got solved.

She would solve it anyway.

Mara packed up her camera. Efficient movements. No wasted energy. She'd document everything. Would process the photos back at the station. Would be there when Dempsey returned.

Unavoidable. Like gravity. Like evidence. Like truth.

"I'll meet you at the station," Dempsey told Harris. "Need to interview the wife while the details are fresh."

Harris nodded. Turned to go. Stopped. Looked back at her. "Dempsey?"

"Yes?"

"You good?"

The question carried weight. Carried layers. Asked more than the words themselves.

"Always am," she answered.

The lie came easily now. Practiced. Just one more to add to the collection.

* * *

Interview over. The wife was no help. Dempsey stared at crime scene photos on her monitor. Erick Odom's body on suburban concrete. Blood pooled black in the digital images. She flipped through them methodically. Looking for something missed at the scene. The pattern of the blood. Position of the shell casings. Evidence of the killer's presence beyond the bullets left in the victim.

The bullpen hummed with the quiet efficiency of late afternoon. Most detectives gone for the day. Only three others remained at their desks. The cleaning crew moved through with their carts. The smell of industrial disinfectant mixed with stale coffee. A phone rang unanswered at an empty desk.

She clicked to the next photo. Shot of the hedge where they'd found the sixth casing. Mara's photograph. Perfect composition. Perfect focus. Professional work from someone who'd documented hundreds of crime scenes. And killed at least four people.

Harris's footsteps approached from behind. Distinctive cadence. Measured. Deliberate. He stopped at her desk. Dempsey didn't look up.

"Anything on Odom?" Harris asked.

"Nothing substantial yet." She kept scrolling through photos. "Financials show no unusual activity. Phone records clean. Wife says he had no enemies."

"Everyone has enemies."

"That's what I said." She clicked to another photo. Wide shot of the street. Cherry picker visible in the background. Christmas lights strung on the utility pole.

"Autopsy preliminary?" Harris leaned against her desk. His weight shifted a stack of files.

"Consistent with scene assessment. Two different weapons. Close range. Execution style." She closed the photo viewer. Looked up at him finally. "Why are you here this late?"

Harris straightened. Adjusted his burgundy tie. "Had a thought about an old case."

"Which one?"

"Tapani."

The name dropped between them like a stone. Dempsey kept her face neutral. Waited.

"You remember that witness? The one you couldn't identify." Harris pulled a small spiral notebook from his pocket. Flipped it open. "Erin Yes."

Dempsey's chest tightened. She swiveled her chair to face him fully. "What about her?"

"You never found her?"

"No." The lie came easily now. "Got pulled off the case."

Harris nodded. Made a note in his book. "Chief Brandt shut it down?"

"She did." Dempsey watched his face. Couldn't read his expression.

"But you told me all the witnesses were dead."

"Three were." She kept her voice flat. Professional. "The fourth, Erin Yes, I never identified."

The cleaning woman moved closer to their desks. Sprayed disinfectant on an empty workstation nearby. The sharp chemical smell cut through the air.

"If she was a witness to Tapani's murder," Harris said, "she might be in danger."

"Might be." Dempsey turned back to her computer. Clicked to another case file. Creating distance.

Harris tapped his pen against his notebook. Rhythmic. Thoughtful. "Seems odd that three witnesses end up dead, and the fourth vanishes."

Dempsey stared at her screen without seeing it. Her pulse quickened. "Coincidences happen."

"Not in homicide." Harris's voice hardened. "You know that."

She did know that. Twenty years on the job had taught her coincidences were usually connections not yet understood. Evidence not yet discovered. Truth not yet revealed.

"What's your interest in Tapani?" she asked. Careful to keep her tone casual. "That case is months old."

"Professional curiosity." Harris closed his notebook. Put it away. "Similar MO to Odom. Two different weapons. Professional-looking hit."

The cleaning woman moved away. The smell of chemicals lingered. The evening shift officer walked through the bullpen, checking empty desks, turning off forgotten desk lamps.

"Tapani was a drug user. Criminal record. Known associates in gang territory." Dempsey recited the facts mechanically. "Odom was an accountant with no record. Different victims. Different motives."

"Same execution style."

Dempsey shrugged. "Criminals copy each other. Read the same news articles we do."

Harris studied her face. His eyes narrowed. Looking for something. The same look he gave suspects who weren't telling the whole truth.

"You want to grab dinner?" he asked suddenly. "Discuss both cases. See if there's a connection we're missing."

"Can't." Dempsey closed the file on her computer. Started shutdown procedures. "Need to review Odom's work files tonight."

Harris nodded. Accepted the excuse without challenge. "Another time."

"Sure." She didn't look at him. Focused on her screen as it went black.

Harris walked back to his desk. Sat down. Opened a file. But his attention wasn't on the paperwork. Dempsey felt his eyes on her. Calculating. Assessing.

She gathered her things. Keys. Phone. Jacket from the back of her chair. Moved with practiced efficiency. Nothing rushed. Nothing that would suggest discomfort.

Harris was still watching when she headed for the elevator. She felt his gaze on her back. The weight of his suspicion.

The elevator doors opened. She stepped inside. Turned to face the bullpen. Harris had picked up his phone. Was dialing a number. Not looking at her anymore.

The doors closed. She was alone in the small space. Let out a breath. Leaned against the wall. The metal cool against her shoulder.

Harris was investigating the Tapani case. Looking into Erin Yes. Getting too close to Mara. Too close to the truth. Too close to Dempsey's compromise.

The elevator reached the ground floor. Doors opened. She stepped out. Walked through the lobby. Past the desk sergeant who nodded a greeting. Past the bulletin board with wanted posters. Through the glass doors to the outside world.

She needed air. Needed space. Needed to think through what Harris's interest meant. What he suspected. What he knew.

If he realized Erin Yes was Erinyes, he'd find Mara. If he found Mara, he'd find Dempsey's failure. Her compromise. Her fall.

Dempsey stepped outside the precinct. The evening air hit her face. Cold enough to sting. She closed her eyes. Took a deep breath. Her lungs filled with December chill. Clean compared to the chemical smell of the bullpen. She stood motionless. Counting breaths. One. Two. Three.

When she opened her eyes, Mara was walking toward her from the parking lot. Brown hair loose around her shoulders now. No camera. No professional distance. Just Mara, moving with purpose. Directly at her.

Dempsey looked away. Considered walking to her car. Leaving before Mara reached her. Avoiding whatever was about to happen. Her legs didn't move.

"Callisto!" Mara's voice carried across the concrete plaza. Intimate use of her first name. Public space. Anyone could hear.

Dempsey didn't respond. Didn't look back at her. Kept staring at the street beyond the precinct steps. Traffic lights changing. Cars stopping and going. Normal world continuing.

Mara reached her. No hesitation. Wrapped her arms around Dempsey in a tight embrace. The scent of jasmine filled Dempsey's senses. The warmth of another body pressed against hers. Unexpected. Unwelcome. And somehow still wanted.

Dempsey's arms stayed at her sides. Didn't return the hug. Her eyes scanned the precinct entrance. Two uniformed officers walked out. Stopped their conversation. Watched the embrace. Their faces registered surprise. Then something else. Something that looked like envy.

Mara stepped back. Kept her hands on Dempsey's shoulders. Smiled up at her. "I've been looking for you."

"Why?" Dempsey's voice came out harder than intended.

"We need to talk." Mara's eyes held hers. Direct. Unafraid.

"We don't."

The uniformed officers walked past them. Nodded to Dempsey. One of them grinned. A knowing look. The kind men gave each other when someone scored. Dempsey had seen it countless times in twenty years. Never directed at her. Until now.

"Five minutes," Mara said. "That's all I'm asking."

"I have work." Dempsey shifted her weight. Ready to leave. Not leaving.

"The Odom case can wait."

Dempsey's eyes narrowed. "How do you know about Odom?"

"I was there, Callisto." Mara's voice softened on the name. Private. Personal. "I took the photos."

A detective exited the building. Glanced their way. Did a double-take. Dempsey recognized him from Narcotics. He'd never looked at her twice before. Now his eyes lingered. Assessed. Reassessed.

"I don't want to hear it." Dempsey stepped back. Away from Mara's touch. Away from the jasmine scent that brought back the warehouse. The confession. The kiss.

"You need to hear it." Mara moved closer again. No touch this time. Just proximity. "You have questions. I have answers."

The glass doors opened again. Chief Brandt walked out. Saw them standing there. Her eyes flickered with something unreadable. She nodded once to Dempsey. Kept walking to her car.

People coming and going now. End of shift change. Each one noticing them standing there. Each one seeing something unexpected. Detective Dempsey and the Chief's niece. Crime scene photographer Mara Snowden and the bullpen's most isolated officer.

"Please." Mara's voice dropped lower. Urgent now. "For your own protection, you need to know."

"Know what?"

"Everything."

A patrol car pulled up. Three officers got out. Laughing about something. Their eyes found Dempsey and Mara. The laughter paused. Resumed with a different tone. One officer elbowed another. Whispered something. They looked back at Dempsey with new interest.

Being seen. Really seen. After decades of invisibility.

"Please, Callisto." Mara touched her arm lightly. "Ten minutes. That's all I need."

Dempsey watched the officers enter the building. Caught one looking back over his shoulder at them. Something shifted in her chest. A warmth that had nothing to do with integrity or procedure or doing the right thing.

Being wanted publicly. Being envied. Being the one others looked at and thought: how did she get someone like that?

"Tomorrow." Dempsey kept her voice professional. "I'm busy tonight."

"It can't wait." Mara's fingers tightened on her arm. "Harris is asking questions."

Dempsey's attention snapped back. "What questions?"

"About Erin Yes."

The evening air seemed colder suddenly. Another officer exited the building. Nodded to Dempsey. His eyes lingered on Mara. Moved between them. Made assumptions. Walked on.

Mara's eyes held hers. "He's getting close, Callisto. Too close."

More eyes on them now. A group of detectives leaving for the day. Some Dempsey knew. Some she didn't. All of them noticing. All of them seeing her with Mara. The whispers would start tomorrow. The questions. The speculation.

Let them talk. Let them wonder. Let them see her.

"Ten minutes," Dempsey said. "That's all."

Mara's smile returned. Relief and something else. Triumph maybe. "Thank you."

"Where?" Dempsey stepped back. Created professional distance between them. Too late. Everyone had already seen the proximity.

"The Brass Shield." Mara named a bar three blocks away. "I'll drive."

"I'll meet you." Dempsey wouldn't be trapped in a car with Mara. Wouldn't surrender that control.

"Fine." Mara nodded once. Understanding the boundaries. Respecting them. For now. "I'll get us a booth in the back."

Dempsey watched her walk away. The confident stride of someone who'd planned every move. Who knew exactly what she was doing. Who'd orchestrated this public meeting for maximum visibility.

Two more officers passed Dempsey on their way in. Both nodded to her. One smiled. The kind of smile men gave women they suddenly saw differently. The kind Dempsey had never received in twenty years on the job.

Until now. Until Mara.

She walked to her car. Unlocked it. Sat behind the wheel without starting the engine. Stared through the windshield at nothing.

Ten minutes to hear Mara out. Ten minutes that could destroy what little remained of her career if anyone knew what they'd really be discussing. What Mara had done. What Dempsey had covered up.

Ten minutes to be seen with someone who made others envious. Ten minutes to be the detective who somehow landed the attractive photographer. Ten minutes to be something other than invisible.

She started the engine. Pulled out of the parking space. Headed toward The Brass Shield.

Just ten minutes. What more could she possibly lose?

Chapter 20

The Brass Shield stood wedged between a dry cleaner and a pawn shop. Dempsey parked across the street. Killed the engine. Sat for thirty seconds watching the entrance. Mara waited under the faded wooden sign, collar turned up against the cold. No camera. No phone. Just watching the traffic as if expecting someone important.

Dempsey got out of her car. Locked it. Crossed between two parked cruisers. Mara spotted her, straightened. Her smile appeared genuine.

"You came." Mara's voice carried relief.

"Ten minutes." Dempsey checked her watch. Established the boundary.

Mara nodded. Pulled open the heavy wooden door. Dempsey followed her inside. The smell hit first. Old wood. Spilled beer. Fryer grease from the kitchen. The place wasn't crowded. Tuesday night. Four officers at a table near the jukebox. Two detectives at the bar. Booth in the back occupied by what looked like Vice.

Eyes found them immediately. Conversations paused. Heads turned. The two detectives at the bar – Shevchenko and DiMaggio – exchanged glances. The officers by the jukebox stopped their game of darts. One whispered something. The others laughed. The laughter carried meaning Dempsey didn't want to analyze.

Mara seemed not to notice. Or pretended not to. She moved toward the bar. "What would you like to drink?"

"I'll get them." Dempsey kept her voice neutral. "You grab us a booth."

"I invited you."

"I'll get them." Dempsey didn't frame it as a request. Couldn't let Mara handle her drink. Couldn't trust what might be in it.

"Espresso martini for me." Mara touched Dempsey's arm lightly. "I'll find us somewhere quiet."

Dempsey nodded. Watched Mara walk toward the back. The way the dark jeans fit her. The confident posture. The attention she commanded without effort. Conversation resumed around them, but now the subject had changed. Dempsey felt it in the glances. The new weight of being seen.

She approached the bar. Stood beside Shevchenko and DiMaggio. Nodded once to acknowledge them.

"Dempsey," Shevchenko said. "Didn't expect to see you here."

"Just meeting a colleague." She kept it professional.

The bartender approached. The same one who'd worked here for fifteen years. Towel over his shoulder. White shirt with the sleeves rolled up. "What can I get you?"

"White wine. And an espresso martini."

He nodded. Turned away to make the drinks.

"Espresso martini?" DiMaggio raised an eyebrow. "Fancy."

"It's not for me." Dempsey kept her eyes on the bartender. Watched him make the drinks. Didn't give DiMaggio the satisfaction of a reaction.

"The chief's niece, right?" Shevchenko's voice carried just enough innuendo. "The photographer."

"We're discussing a case." Dempsey didn't look at him. Kept watching the drinks being made.

"Is that what they're calling it now?" DiMaggio laughed.

The bartender returned with the drinks. Set them on the bar. "Twenty-two fifty."

Dempsey paid cash. Left a decent tip. Picked up the drinks. Walked away without responding to the detectives. Their laughter followed her.

Mara had found a booth in the back corner. Farthest from the jukebox. Away from the door. Good sightlines to the entire bar. Smart choice. Dempsey would have picked the same spot.

She set the drinks on the table. Slid into the booth opposite Mara. The vinyl seat was cracked. Patched with duct tape that caught at her pants. The espresso martini sat between them, dark and bitter. Like the truth.

"Thank you." Mara didn't reach for her drink immediately. Just watched Dempsey with those alert hazel eyes. The eyes that had seen too much. Done too much.

"Ten minutes." Dempsey reminded her. Checked her watch again.

Mara nodded. Then, instead of staying where she was, she slid out from her side of the booth. Dempsey tensed, thinking she was leaving. But Mara moved around the table. Slid in beside Dempsey on her side of the booth.

The move was smooth. Calculated. Dempsey found herself trapped between the wall and Mara's body. The smell of jasmine. The heat of another person pressed against her side. Thigh touching thigh. Shoulder touching shoulder.

"What are you doing?" Dempsey kept her voice low. Steady.

"It's easier to talk this way." Mara's eyes held hers. "Without shouting across the table."

The booth suddenly felt smaller. The air thicker. Dempsey resisted the urge to move away. To create distance. Her body had other ideas. Heat spread through her chest. Down her arms. Into her fingers. The kind of heat that had nothing to do with the temperature of the room.

"People are watching." Dempsey glanced toward the bar. Shevchenko and DiMaggio had turned on their stools to face the booth. The officers by the jukebox were whispering again.

"Good." Mara's smile was small. Satisfied. "Let them see."

"See what?" Dempsey fought to keep her voice level.

"Whatever they want to see." Mara lifted her espresso martini. Took a small sip. Left a lipstick mark on the glass. "They'll talk, regardless."

Dempsey reached for her wine. Needed something to do with her hands. The glass was cool against her fingers. A counterpoint to the heat radiating from Mara's body beside her.

"Your ten minutes started the moment we sat down." Dempsey took a sip. Set the glass down precisely. "What do you want?"

Mara turned. Her knee pressed against Dempsey's under the table. Intentional. "I want to know if you regret letting me go."

Dempsey didn't answer immediately. The question hung between them like crime scene tape marking a boundary already crossed. The bar noise receded. Just the two of them in this moment. This question. This reckoning.

Mara waited. Patient. Still. Her body radiating heat against Dempsey's side.

Dempsey took another sip of wine. Stared at the scarred tabletop. "I don't know what I feel."

"Honest." Mara nodded. Seemed to approve of the answer.

"I can't stop thinking about it." Dempsey kept her voice low. Below the level of the jukebox. Below the conversations at nearby tables. "About you. About my judgment."

"Questioning yourself?"

"Wouldn't you?" Dempsey looked at her directly. "In my position?"

Mara's smile faded. Her eyes remained steady on Dempsey's face. "I think you made the right call."

"I let a murderer walk." Dempsey's words were barely audible. "Four victims."

"Only four?" Mara asked. Corrected.

Dempsey's stomach tightened. "What?"

"Nothing." Mara took another sip of her martini. Calm as if discussing the weather.

Dempsey set down her glass too hard. Wine sloshed over the rim. Spread on the table like diluted blood. "You—"

"Not on my ten minutes." Mara put her hand on Dempsey's arm.

The bar seemed louder suddenly. Conversations. Laughter. The scrape of chairs on the floor. A glass breaking somewhere near the kitchen. The officers at the jukebox arguing about a song.

"Because I've been watching you." Mara's voice softened. "For a long time."

Something cold settled in Dempsey's stomach. "Explain."

Mara's hand slid down Dempsey's arm. Found her hand on the table. Covered it. "I know you, Callisto."

"You don't." Dempsey didn't pull her hand away. Couldn't.

"Six months ago, you changed your coffee order." Mara's eyes never left her face. "From black to cream and sugar. It was after the Langdon case. The little girl."

Dempsey stared at her. The Langdon case. Six-year-old drowned in the bathtub by her stepfather. Dempsey had gone home that night and vomited for an hour. Had stopped drinking her coffee black the next day. Too bitter. Too much like the world.

"When you're reviewing evidence and find something important, your left eyebrow moves." Mara continued. "Just a millimeter. Most people wouldn't notice."

Dempsey felt exposed. Like standing naked in a room of strangers. "Stop."

"You never smile at work." Mara's voice held something like tenderness. "Not at crime scenes. Not in the bullpen. Not in the elevator. I thought maybe you couldn't."

"I smile." Dempsey's protest sounded weak even to herself.

"Not where anyone can see." Mara's fingers intertwined with Dempsey's on the table. "I've counted three smiles in three years. All when you thought you were alone."

The bar fell away. The noise. The people. The music. Just Mara's eyes holding hers. Just Mara's hand on her hand. Just Mara's words peeling her open layer by layer.

"You shower at the precinct after bad cases." Mara continued. "Always bring a change of clothes on Wednesdays. Like you know something will happen. You carry your backup piece in an ankle holster, not standard issue. The right one, not the left."

"How—" Dempsey swallowed. "How do you know that?"

"I'm a photographer." Mara's smile returned. Small. Private. "I notice details."

"These aren't details. This is stalking." Dempsey felt her professional instincts kick in. The awareness of being watched. Cataloged. Studied.

"It's attention." Mara corrected. "The kind you deserve."

Dempsey pulled her hand away finally. Picked up her wine. Drained the glass. The alcohol did nothing to burn away the feeling of violation. Of intrusion.

And beneath that, something else. Something she didn't want to acknowledge. The thrill of being noticed. Being seen. The warmth that came with knowing someone had paid such careful attention.

"This isn't normal." Dempsey set the empty glass down. "What you're doing."

"Normal people didn't interest me." Mara leaned back. Created a small space between them. "You did."

"Since when?"

"The Conway case." Mara's answer came immediately. "Three years ago. The double homicide in Oakwood Heights."

Dempsey remembered. Husband and wife stabbed in their bed. Teenage son found the bodies. Dempsey had been the first detective on scene. Mara had been the department photographer.

"You walked in." Mara's voice took on a different quality now. Almost reverent. "Everyone else looked at the bodies. The blood. You looked at the spaces between things. The places where the killer had been."

Dempsey said nothing. Her breathing felt shallow.

"I watched you work that scene for six hours." Mara continued. "You never rushed. Never assumed. You saw patterns no one else did."

"That's my job." Dempsey kept her voice neutral. Professional.

"No." Mara shook her head. "Your job is collecting evidence. Making arrests. Closing cases. What you did was different. You communed with the dead. Spoke for them."

Dempsey looked away. Toward the bar where Shevchenko and DiMaggio still watched them. Their faces showed something between curiosity and envy. They couldn't hear this conversation. Couldn't know what Mara was revealing.

"I started volunteering for your cases after that." Mara admitted. "Requested the assignments specifically."

"The Chief—"

"My aunt didn't know why." Mara cut her off. "She just thought I was being ambitious. Taking more shifts. Building my portfolio."

Professional-grade surveillance. That's what this was. Systematic. Detailed. The kind that required planning. Patience. The same skills Mara had applied to her kills.

"You're scared now." Mara observed. "Your breathing changed. Pupils dilated. Fight or flight."

Dempsey met her eyes again. "Wouldn't you be? Learning someone's been watching you for years?"

"Depends on who was watching." Mara's hand found Dempsey's knee under the table. "And why."

The touch burned through Dempsey's pants. Direct. Intimate. Unwelcome. Wanted. The contradiction made her head spin. Or maybe that was the wine on an empty stomach.

"Ten minutes is up." Dempsey checked her watch. Needed an exit.

"Then let me buy you dinner." Mara's hand stayed on her knee. "You haven't eaten since breakfast."

Another observation. Another detail Mara shouldn't know. Dempsey hadn't told anyone about skipping lunch to review the Odom crime scene photos.

"How—" She stopped herself. Knew the answer already.

"I notice things." Mara squeezed her knee gently. "Important things."

The clock behind the bar read 11:17 PM. They'd been talking for nearly three hours. Dempsey's empty plate sat pushed aside, her second glass of wine half-finished. Mara nursed her third espresso martini, the previous glasses cleared away by a bartender whose patience was visibly thinning.

"The Pineda case still bothers me," Dempsey said. She traced the rim of her glass with one finger. "Husband reported his wife missing. We found her three days later in their basement freezer."

"Wrapped in shower curtains." Mara nodded. "I photographed the scene."

"He served her dinner every night at the table set for two." Dempsey's voice went flat. "While she was ten feet below him."

"People contain multitudes." Mara's shoulder pressed against Dempsey's. "Darkness and light."

The bar had emptied gradually. The officers by the jukebox were long gone. Shevchenko and DiMaggio had left an hour ago, but not before DiMaggio had given Dempsey a thumbs-up on his way out. Only three other patrons remained. A woman at the bar working on her laptop. Two men playing pool in the corner.

"The Reese stabbing," Mara said. "That was one of yours too, wasn't it?"

Dempsey nodded. "Seventeen-year-old killed his best friend over a video game. Thirty-seven stab wounds."

"He called 911 himself."

"Waited on the porch covered in blood." Dempsey remembered the boy's face. Blank. Empty. "Said he'd do it again if he could."

Mara's hand found Dempsey's knee under the table again. It had been there, off and on, throughout dinner. A gentle pressure. An anchor in the darkness of the conversation.

"The Garrett shooting was worse." Dempsey continued. "Store owner shot a shoplifter who died three blocks away."

"I remember." Mara's voice softened. "You testified at the grand jury."

"Store owner got eighteen months." Dempsey's mouth tightened. "For killing a fourteen-year-old who stole a candy bar."

The bartender approached their table. Wiped down a nonexistent spill nearby. His third passive-aggressive hint in twenty minutes. The bar closed at midnight on weeknights.

"We should go." Dempsey checked her watch. 11:28 PM.

Mara nodded but didn't move. Neither did Dempsey. The booth had become a bubble outside of time. Outside of reality. A space where a detective could sit with a murderer and discuss justice.

"One more drink?" Mara asked.

"I've had enough." Dempsey was careful to stay clearheaded. To maintain at least the illusion of professional distance.

The woman at the bar closed her laptop. Paid her tab. Left. The pool players racked their cues. Threw bills on the table. Followed her out. Just Dempsey and Mara now. And the increasingly impatient bartender.

"Tell me about the worst one." Mara's voice was barely audible. "The one that haunts you."

Dempsey looked at her. In this light, Mara's eyes appeared darker. Knowing. The eyes of someone who had seen the worst humanity offered and found it insufficient.

"Mason. 2018." Dempsey hadn't spoken this name in years. "Eight-year-old boy locked in a closet for three days."

Mara's hand tightened on her knee.

"We got there too late." Dempsey's voice remained flat. Professional. "Mother's boyfriend didn't feed him. Didn't give him water."

"That wasn't your fault."

The bartender approached again. No pretense this time. "Ladies, we're closing up."

Only the Brass Shield closed at midnight. Dempsey nodded. "Just settling the bill."

He placed the check on the table. "Take your time." His tone suggested the opposite.

Mara reached for it. Dempsey was faster.

"I've got it." She pulled out cash. Counted bills.

"You paid for the drinks." Mara protested. "Let me get dinner."

Dempsey shook her head. Left enough for the bill plus twenty percent.

The bartender collected the money. "Have a good night." He walked away, already counting down to closing time.

Mara slid out of the booth first. Dempsey followed. The space between them felt strange now after hours pressed together on the vinyl seat. Dempsey's side was cold where Mara's body had been.

They walked to the door. Dempsey held it open. Mara passed through. The night air hit them both. Cold. Clean after the stale beer smell of the bar. Dempsey breathed deeply. Tried to clear her head.

"My car's down the block." Mara pointed to the silver car parked under a streetlight. "Think I'll call a taxi."

"I'll wait with you." Dempsey fell into step beside her as Mara retrieved her phone and began to move.

The street was empty. Just parked cars and yellow pools of light from the streetlamps. Their footsteps echoed on the sidewalk. Synchronized somehow. Left foot. Right foot. The rhythm of people moving in tandem.

"Taxi's on its way." They reached Mara's car too quickly. Stood facing each other in the circle of light from the lamp above. The air smelled like snow and car exhaust. A combination that meant winter in the city. Dempsey's breath fogged between them.

"I'm glad you came tonight." Mara said. She leaned against her car.

"Ten minutes turned into three hours." Dempsey didn't smile. But something inside her did.

"You can't tell me you didn't enjoy it."

"I didn't say that." Dempsey looked past Mara to the empty street beyond. No witnesses to this moment. No colleagues watching from the bar. No one to see whatever happened next.

"Will you come again?" Mara asked. "Maybe without the professional pretense next time."

The question carried weight. Implications. Boundaries to be crossed. Lines to be redrawn. Dempsey had already compromised herself by letting Mara walk free. By keeping her confession secret. What was one more step over the line?

"I don't know if that's a good idea." She kept her voice steady. Professional.

"I didn't ask if it was good." Mara's smile was small. Knowing. "I asked if you'd come."

Dempsey's badge felt heavy on her hip. The weight of twenty years doing the right thing. Following procedure. Maintaining boundaries. Being the cop she'd always wanted to be.

But Mara had seen her. Really seen her. Beyond the badge. Beyond the gun. Had cataloged the smallest details of her existence when no one else bothered to look.

"Yes." The word slipped out before Dempsey could stop it. Another line crossed. Another boundary erased.

They stood there in the cold. Not touching. But close enough to feel the heat between them. Close enough that Dempsey could smell Mara's perfume. Jasmine. The same scent from the warehouse. From the kiss that had compromised everything.

Dempsey took a step back. Created distance. Tried to reclaim some semblance of the professional woman she'd been before all this started. Before Mara. Before the confession. Before the realization that she'd been watched for years without knowing.

The sound of The Brass Shield's deadbolt sliding into place echoed down the empty street. The lights in the bar went out one by one until just the neon OPEN sign remained. Then that too winked out.

Darkness settled deeper around them. Just the streetlight above and the distant glow of traffic signals down the block. Dempsey's car sat a hundred yards away. An easy walk. A difficult decision.

Her professional boundaries felt paper-thin now. Tissue separating duty from desire. The detective who followed procedure from the woman who wanted, for once, to be chosen. To be wanted. To be seen.

Mara smiled. The expression transformed her face. Made her look younger. Less dangerous. "Friday night date?"

"Friday." Dempsey nodded once. Committed to the path. Another choice that separated who she had been from who she was becoming.

They stood there in the pool of light. Neither moving. Neither willing to break the moment. A car passed on the distant avenue. Its headlights swept across the buildings, momentary illumination that emphasized the darkness when it passed.

"I should go." Dempsey said it again. Didn't move.

"You should." Mara stepped closer. Eliminated the careful distance Dempsey had created between them. "But you won't. Not yet."

Dempsey's breath caught. Mara was close enough now that their coats brushed. Close enough that the jasmine scent enveloped her. Close enough that she could see the flecks of gold in Mara's hazel eyes.

"What are you doing?" Dempsey's voice remained steady. A detective's voice. Professional. Controlled.

"What I want." Mara's hand came up. Touched Dempsey's face. Fingers cold against her cheek.

Dempsey should have stepped back. Should have maintained professional distance. Should have remembered that Mara had confessed to four murders. Had manipulated her. Had compromised her integrity.

She didn't move.

Mara leaned in. Her lips found Dempsey's. Soft at first. Questioning. Then more insistent when Dempsey didn't pull away. The kiss was different than in the warehouse. Not desperate. Not a bargain. Something else entirely.

Dempsey's hands came up automatically. Found Mara's waist. Held on. Her eyes closed. The street disappeared. The cold night air. The badge on her hip. Everything reduced to the point of contact. Lips on lips. The taste of espresso and vanilla.

Mara's hands moved from Dempsey's face to her hair. Fingers threading through the short strands. Holding her there. Deepening the kiss. Her body pressed closer. Eliminating any space between them.

Dempsey responded despite herself. Twenty years of isolation crumbled in the face of this connection. This desire. This moment of being wanted exactly as she was.

Mara broke the kiss first. Her breathing unsteady against Dempsey's lips. "I've imagined that so many times."

"Have you?" Dempsey's voice was rough. Unrecognizable.

"In every detail." Mara's hands moved down to Dempsey's shoulders. Her neck. The collar of her shirt. "The way you'd taste. The sound you'd make."

Dempsey hadn't realized she'd made a sound. Something between a sigh and a groan. Embarrassment flushed her face.

"Don't." Mara's fingers traced her jawline. "Don't hide from me."

"We're on a public street." Dempsey found her professional voice again. Barely.

"No one's watching." Mara's eyes held hers. "Just me."

Dempsey looked away. Down the empty street. The closed storefronts. The parked cars with frost beginning to form on windshields. No witnesses to this moment. No one to see her fall.

Mara's hand moved to her chin. Turned Dempsey's face back toward her. "Look at me."

Dempsey did. Saw something in Mara's eyes that frightened her more than the confession in the warehouse. More than the detailed surveillance. More than the murders. Saw desire. Genuine and uncalculated.

Mara kissed her again. Harder this time. One hand moving to Dempsey's hip. Pulling her closer. The other still on her face, holding her steady.

Dempsey's body responded without permission from her mind. Arms wrapping around Mara's waist. Mouth opening under the pressure of Mara's lips. Tongue meeting tongue. The kiss deepened, became something else. Something with intent behind it.

Mara pressed Dempsey back against the car. The metal cold through her jacket. A counterpoint to the heat building between them. Mara's hand slid under Dempsey's coat. Found the hem of her shirt. Warm fingers against bare skin.

The touch was electric. Shocking. Dempsey gasped into Mara's mouth. Felt rather than saw Mara's smile in response. The fingers moved higher. Tracing ribs. Finding the underwire of her bra.

"Stop." Dempsey broke the kiss. Caught Mara's wrist. "Not here."

Mara's eyes were dark in the streetlight. Pupils dilated. "Where then?"

The question carried implications. Invitations. Promises. Dempsey's apartment? Mara's? A hotel room somewhere anonymous? The possibilities spun out before her. All of them crossing lines that couldn't be uncrossed.

"I don't know." Dempsey's answer was honest. She didn't know what came next. Where this led. What it meant for her career. Her integrity. Her life.

Mara studied her face. Seemed to understand the internal struggle. Nodded once. "My taxi is here."

She stepped back. Created space between them. Cold air rushed in where her body had been. Dempsey felt the absence like a physical thing. A weight removed. A loss.

"I could love you, Callisto Dempsey." Mara's voice was soft. Matter-of-fact. "I could fall so easily."

The words hung between them. Impossible. Unbearable. Dempsey had no response. No frame of reference for this declaration. No protocol for a murderer's confession of a different kind.

Mara smiled at her silence. Understanding again. "I'll see you Friday." She stepped back, away. The sound of the taxi's engine was loud in the quiet street.

Dempsey watched as Mara opened the car door. Slid into the back seat. The interior light illuminated her face for a moment. Beautiful. Dangerous. Then the door closed. The light went out.

The taxi moved. Headlights swept across Dempsey as the car pulled away from the curb. She stood motionless. Watching the taillights recede down the block. Turn at the corner. Disappear.

Alone on the dark street. The taste of Mara still on her lips. The ghost of her touch still on Dempsey's skin. The weight of her words still in the air between them.

I could love you.

Dempsey touched her mouth. The lipstick wasn't hers. Evidence of what had happened. What she'd allowed to happen. Another line crossed. Another boundary erased. Another piece of her professional self compromised.

She turned. Began walking toward her car. Each step solid on the concrete. Each step taking her further from the detective she had been this morning. The woman who followed procedure. Who maintained boundaries. Who did things by the book.

That woman was gone now. Replaced by someone who let killers walk free. Who kissed them on dark streets. Who agreed to see them again, knowing what they had done. What they were capable of doing.

Dempsey reached her car. Unlocked it. Sat behind the wheel without starting the engine. The silence pressed against her ears. The darkness a blanket around the vehicle. She gripped the steering wheel. Tried to steady herself.

Another choice she couldn't take back. Another moment that changed everything. The taste of espresso and vanilla. The scent of jasmine. The words hanging in the cold night air.

I could love you.

The professional in her knew this was manipulation. Strategy. The woman in her wanted desperately to believe it was true. The contradiction tore at her. Left her raw. Exposed.

She started the car. Pulled away from the curb. Drove toward her empty apartment. Toward whatever came next. Toward whoever she was becoming.

Chapter 21

Dempsey wiped down her kitchen counter for the third time. The smell of bleach stung her nostrils. She checked her watch. Two hours until Mara arrived. The apartment already looked cleaner than it had in years. She moved to the living room. Straightened the books on the shelf. Adjusted the angle of the coffee table. Smoothed invisible wrinkles from the couch cushions.

She didn't recognize herself. Twenty years on the job and she'd never been nervous. Not when facing armed suspects. Not when testifying in court. But four days of waiting for Friday had hollowed her out.

The wine stood on the counter. A red she knew nothing about. The liquor store clerk had recommended it when she'd asked for "something nice." Forty-two dollars. More than she'd ever spent on alcohol for herself.

Dempsey opened her refrigerator. Ingredients for dinner sat organized on the middle shelf. Vegetables prepped in plastic containers. Meat already seasoned. She'd left work early to shop. Another first.

She closed the refrigerator door. Caught her reflection in the chrome. Distorted. Unrecognizable. She turned away.

Her bedroom closet stood open. Clothes pulled out and discarded on the bed. Three separate outfits she'd tried and rejected. She'd settled on dark jeans and a blue sweater the salesperson had once told her "brings out your eyes." She'd bought it three years ago. Still had the tags until this morning.

The clock on her nightstand read 6:17 PM. Mara wouldn't arrive until 8:00. More time to second-guess everything.

Dempsey gathered the rejected clothes. Hung them back up. Military corners and right angles. The habits of a solitary life. She smoothed her hands down the front of her sweater. The unfamiliar softness caught at her callouses.

"Friday the thirteenth," she said aloud to the empty room. "Figures."

Her voice sounded strange in the apartment. She rarely spoke here. No one to talk to but herself. She moved back to the bathroom. Stared at her reflection in the mirror.

The face that looked back was the same one she'd seen even before she became an adult. Deep-set brown eyes. Short steel-gray hair. Lines that came from squinting at crime scene evidence and bad fluorescent lighting. A mouth that rarely smiled.

Not ugly, she decided. Just… unused. A face that hadn't been needed for anything but the job.

But Mara had seen something else there. Something worth photographing. Worth writing about in that journal.

The journal. Dempsey had hidden it in her nightstand drawer. Had read it twice more since The Brass Shield. The photos of herself seen through Mara's eyes. The explicit descriptions of what Mara imagined. Things no one had ever thought about her before.

She turned away from the mirror. Walked to the kitchen. Opened drawers, checking that everything was where it should be. Forks. Knives. Spoons. All aligned with military precision.

Only two place settings. When was the last time she'd set the table for anyone else? She couldn't remember. Years. Maybe never. Her kitchen counter held the evidence of her solitary life. A single mug by the coffee maker. One bowl in the dish drainer. One set of utensils.

She picked up a water glass. Held it to the light. Checked for spots. Set it down precisely at the edge of the placemat.

This was insanity. Preparing dinner for a murderer. For a woman who had watched her for years. Who had manipulated her into this position.

And yet.

Dempsey moved to her living room window. Looked down at the street. Normal Friday evening traffic. People heading home. Heading out. Lives intersecting briefly before separating again.

She had spent twenty years watching other people's lives. Taking notes. Collecting evidence. Always the observer. Never the participant.

Until now.

Mara had changed that. Had pulled her from the edge of the crime scene into its center. Had made her a participant in something she still didn't fully understand.

Dempsey checked her watch again. 6:43 PM. Still too much time.

She walked back to her bedroom. The bed was made with hospital corners. The nightstand held only a lamp, a clock, and a book she hadn't opened in weeks. The walls were bare.

The silence of the apartment pressed against her ears. The familiar silence that waited for her every night. That followed her from room to room like a shadow.

She had lived with this silence for so long she had stopped noticing it. Until now. Until the prospect of someone else's voice filling these rooms made the silence unbearable.

If this ended—when this ended—the silence would return. Heavier for having been briefly lifted.

The thought terrified her more than Mara's confession in the warehouse. More than the knowledge of what Mara had done. More than the compromise of her own professional ethics.

Going back to this silence. To this emptiness. To eating dinner alone at her kitchen counter while reading case notes. To falling asleep with no one's breathing but her own.

She had been alone for forty-eight years. Had told herself it was by choice. That the job was enough. That she didn't need what other people needed.

Dempsey returned to the kitchen. Turned on the oven. The digital display blinked 7:15 PM. Forty-five minutes. She pulled the pot roast from the refrigerator. Placed it on the counter.

Her grandmother's recipe. The only thing she knew how to cook properly. The only food that felt like something more than fuel.

She opened the oven door. Placed the dutch oven inside. Set the timer. The mechanical movements steadied her. Gave her something to focus on besides the minutes ticking by.

7:27 PM. She straightened the dish towel hanging from the oven handle. Aligned it perfectly with the edge.

7:34 PM. She checked the wine again. Should it be opened to breathe? She didn't know the protocol. She opened it anyway. The cork came out with a soft pop that sounded too loud in the quiet apartment.

7:46 PM. She wiped down the counter again. Checked that the bathroom was clean. Straightened a hand towel that didn't need straightening.

7:58 PM. She stood in the center of her living room. Looked around. The apartment had never been this clean. This ready for another person.

The buzzer sounded. Dempsey's heart jumped in her chest. She moved to the intercom by the door.

"Yes?" Her voice steady. Professional. Betraying nothing of the chaos inside.

"It's Mara."

Dempsey pressed the button to unlock the building's front door. Listened to the click. Imagined Mara entering the building. Walking up the stairs. Getting closer with each step.

She opened her apartment door. Stood in the doorway. Waited. Counted heartbeats.

Mara appeared at the top of the stairs. Brown hair loose around her shoulders. Dark jeans. Green sweater that made her eyes look more hazel than brown. A bottle of wine in one hand. A small wrapped package in the other.

She smiled when she saw Dempsey. The kind of smile that transformed a face. That made the recipient feel like the only person in the world.

"Callisto." Mara said the name like it was something precious. Something rare.

Dempsey stepped back. Made space in the doorway. In her life.

"Come in." She held the door wider.

Mara crossed the threshold. The apartment wasn't silent anymore.

Mara stood in the center of Dempsey's kitchen. Dempsey took the wine bottle from her hand. Their fingers brushed. Barely a touch. Enough to make Dempsey's pulse quicken. She set the bottle on the counter. Reached for glasses. Filled them halfway. Handed one to Mara. They stood facing each other. Three feet of kitchen tile between them. Neither knowing what came next.

"Nice place." Mara's eyes moved around the room. Taking in details. Cataloging them.

"It's just an apartment." Dempsey sipped her wine. The taste was unfamiliar. Too sweet.

"It suits you." Mara didn't elaborate. Didn't need to.

The timer on the oven buzzed. Dempsey set her glass down. Opened the oven door. Heat rushed out. The smell of pot roast filled the kitchen. Familiar. Comforting.

"Smells amazing." Mara leaned against the counter. Watched Dempsey lift the dutch oven onto the stovetop.

"It's ready." Dempsey picked up her wine glass again. "We should sit."

They moved to the table. Dempsey served the pot roast. Meat. Carrots. Potatoes. The steam rose between them. Mara waited until Dempsey sat before lifting her fork.

"This is incredible." Mara took another bite. "You've been holding out on me."

"It's my grandmother's recipe." Dempsey cut a piece of meat. "The only thing I can make properly."

"Well, it's perfect." Mara reached for her wine. "My grandmother taught me to cook too. But I never mastered her pot roast."

"What did you master?"

"Bread." Mara smiled. "Sourdough, specifically. During lockdown."

"COVID baker." Dempsey nodded. Remembered the empty grocery shelves. The flour shortage.

"Everyone needs a pandemic hobby." Mara shrugged. "Mine was watching bread rise."

They ate in silence for a moment. The clink of forks against plates. The soft sound of chewing. Wine glasses lifted and set down. The mundane choreography of a shared meal.

"I'll make you bread sometime," Mara said. "Fair exchange for this pot roast."

The promise of future meals hung between them. Dempsey didn't acknowledge it. Took another bite instead.

"Have you ever cried at a TV commercial?" Mara asked suddenly.

The question was so unexpected Dempsey almost laughed. "What?"

"TV commercial. Made you cry. Yes or no?"

Dempsey considered denying it. Considered lying. Found herself answering honestly instead. "The phone company one. With the guy dressed like an egg."

Mara's eyebrows rose. "The egg? Really?"

"It's stupid." Dempsey shook her head. Embarrassed now.

"It's not." Mara's voice softened. "Mine's the soldier coming home to his dog."

"That one gets everyone."

"Not the tough homicide detective, apparently." Mara smiled. "She needs a man in an egg costume."

It wasn't that funny. But Dempsey found herself smiling anyway. A small break in the professional mask she'd worn for decades.

The wine bottle emptied as they ate and talked. Dempsey opened the one Mara had brought. The conversation moved easily now. The initial awkwardness fading with each glass.

"Why'd you become a cop?" Mara asked.

The question was predictable. Everyone asked it eventually. Dempsey gave her standard answer. "Wanted to help people. Solve puzzles. Make a difference."

"The real reason." Mara's eyes held hers.

Dempsey set down her fork. "My father was killed when I was fifteen. The case is still open."

The truth. One she rarely shared. It sat on the table between them like another dish.

"I'm sorry." Mara's voice was soft. Sincere.

"It was a long time ago."

"Not to you."

Dempsey didn't respond. Took another sip of wine instead. Changed the subject. "Why photography?"

"Control." Mara answered immediately. "I decide what's in the frame. What matters. What stories get told."

The honesty surprised Dempsey. She'd expected something about artistic expression. About capturing beauty.

"Same reason I became a detective." She admitted. "Control. Order. Making sense of chaos."

Mara nodded. Understanding. "We both document the worst days of people's lives."

"And you create some of those worst days." Dempsey hadn't meant to say it. The words slipped out before she could stop them.

The air between them changed. Thickened. Mara didn't look away. Didn't flinch.

"Yes," she said simply. "I do."

They stared at each other across the table. Across the moral chasm that separated them. A detective and a killer. Sharing pot roast and wine.

"Does it bother you?" Mara asked. "Being here with me?"

Dempsey considered lying. Considered getting up and ending this entire evening. Did neither. "Yes. And no."

"Explain."

"I can't." Dempsey set down her wine glass. "I don't understand it myself."

Mara nodded. Accepted this. "The food was amazing."

The shift in conversation felt like relief. Like oxygen returning to the room. Dempsey stood. Started clearing plates. Mara rose too. Gathered silverware. Followed Dempsey to the sink.

"You don't have to help." Dempsey turned on the water. Hot steam rose between them.

"I want to." Mara stood beside her at the sink. Their shoulders touched. "You cook, I clean. That's the rule."

"Whose rule?"

"Everyone's rule." Mara took a plate from Dempsey's hand. Their fingers brushed again. Lingered this time.

Dempsey washed. Mara dried. The domesticity of it struck Dempsey as absurd. As impossible. As something that couldn't be happening in her apartment on a Friday night.

And yet it was.

Mara handled Dempsey's dishes with care. Found the correct cabinets for each item without being told. As if she'd been here before. As if she belonged here.

"You're watching me," Mara said without turning. Her back to Dempsey as she placed a glass in the cabinet.

"Yes." No point denying it.

"Professional observation or personal interest?" Mara closed the cabinet. Turned to face her.

"Both."

Mara smiled. The kind of smile that transformed her face. That made her eyes brighter. That pulled an answering response from somewhere deep in Dempsey's chest.

"I like both," Mara said.

They finished the dishes in silence. The comfortable silence of people who don't need to fill every moment with words. Dempsey wiped down the counter. Mara hung the dish towel on the oven handle. Aligned it perfectly with the edge. The same way Dempsey did.

Dempsey noticed. Said nothing.

"Living room?" Mara asked.

Dempsey nodded. Led the way. The remnants of dinner put away. The kitchen clean. The evening stretching ahead of them with possibilities she couldn't name.

Mara sat on the couch. Not in the center. Off to one side. Making room for Dempsey beside her. Dempsey hesitated. Chose the armchair instead. Distance. Safety.

Disappointment flashed across Mara's face. Quick. Almost imperceptible. She covered it with another smile.

"Thank you for dinner." Mara's voice was soft. Sincere.

"It was just pot roast."

"It was more than that." Mara's eyes held hers. "It was an invitation."

Dempsey didn't respond. Didn't know how to respond. The wine had loosened something in her chest. Made it harder to maintain the professional distance she relied on.

Mara looked around the living room. At the books on the shelves. The absence of personal mementos. "Your home is exactly like you. Precise. Orderly. Nothing wasted."

"Is that a compliment or an insult?" Dempsey's voice was steady despite the wine.

"Observation." Mara leaned back against the couch cushions. Comfortable. At ease. "Neither good nor bad. Just true."

The intimacy of having Mara in her space struck Dempsey again. The strangeness of it. The rightness of it. The contradiction made her head spin. Or maybe that was the wine.

"I've never been good at this," Dempsey said. She gestured vaguely at the space between them. The wine made her honest. Made her reckless. "Personal connections. The job was always enough."

"Until it wasn't." Mara's observation wasn't a question.

"Until recently." Dempsey looked down at her hands. The small scars from twenty years of police work. The callouses from her service weapon.

Mara watched her from the couch. Patient. Still. Her posture relaxed but attentive. The way she looked at crime scenes. Missing nothing.

"When did it change?" Mara asked.

Dempsey considered lying. Found herself answering honestly instead. "The Holloway case. Last year. Eight-year-old girl. Strangled by her mother's boyfriend."

"I remember." Mara nodded. "I photographed her."

"We did everything right. Evidence. Witness statements. Arrest. But the mother changed her story. Said he wasn't there that night. Said she'd been mistaken. Gave him an alibi. The case fell apart."

Mara's eyes never left Dempsey's face. "You went home that night."

"I went home." Dempsey nodded. "To this apartment. These empty rooms. No one to talk to about what I'd seen. What I'd heard. No one who understood."

"Isolation." Mara's voice was soft.

"Professional distance." Dempsey corrected. "That's what they teach us. Maintain perspective. Don't get emotionally involved."

"And you believed that."

"I lived that." Dempsey stood. Walked to the window. Looked down at the street. "For twenty years."

Behind her, Mara rose from the couch. Dempsey heard her soft footsteps crossing the room. Felt her presence at her back. Not touching. Close enough to feel her warmth.

"What's changed?" Mara asked.

Dempsey kept looking out the window. At the people passing below. Lives intersecting briefly before continuing on separate paths. "I've changed."

Mara didn't speak. Waited. The silence between them was comfortable now. Patient.

"Or maybe I'm just tired." Dempsey turned. Found Mara closer than expected. "Tired of going home to empty rooms. Tired of professional distance. Tired of being no one outside the job."

"You've always been someone." Mara's voice was firm. "I saw that years ago."

The statement hung between them. Simple. Direct. A confession of its own kind.

"No one's ever really seen me before." Dempsey admitted. "Not as a person. Just as a function. Detective. Investigator. Witness. Never just... me."

"I've seen you." Mara's eyes held hers. Steady. Certain. "Everything you are."

The journal. The photographs. The words. Evidence of being seen. Of being wanted. Of existing beyond the badge and the gun and the case files.

"The journal." Dempsey said the words aloud. Couldn't help herself.

"Did you enjoy it?" Mara stepped closer. The distance between them narrowing to inches.

Heat flushed Dempsey's face. The wine made it impossible to lie. "Yes."

Mara smiled. The kind of smile that held secrets. Promises. "I'm not embarrassed about what I wrote. What I imagined."

"I would be." Dempsey's voice was rough.

"Why?" Mara's head tilted. Curious. "Because you're a professional? Because detectives don't have desires?"

"Because it's private."

"Not anymore." Mara reached out. Her fingers touched Dempsey's wrist. Barely a touch. Enough to make Dempsey's pulse jump. "You know what I want now. What I've wanted for years."

The touch burned through Dempsey's skin. Direct. Electric. She didn't pull away.

"Did any of it frighten you?" Mara's question was soft. Direct. Her eyes never leaving Dempsey's face. "What I wrote. What I photographed."

"Yes." Honesty again. Dangerous.

"What part?"

"The attention." Dempsey swallowed. "Nobody looks at me that way."

"I do." Mara's fingers moved up Dempsey's wrist. Traced the veins there. The bones. "I always have."

Dempsey stood motionless. Trapped between wanting to step back and needing to step forward. Between professional distance and personal desire.

"Do you want me to stop?" Mara's fingers stilled on her wrist. Waiting for permission. For rejection.

The question hung between them. Simple. Direct. The kind Dempsey asked suspects. The kind that demanded truth.

"No." The word escaped before Dempsey could stop it.

Mara stepped closer. No space between them now. Her body against Dempsey's. Warm. Solid. Real.

"I'm going to kiss you now." Mara's voice was barely above a whisper. "Unless you tell me not to."

Dempsey said nothing. Her heart hammered against her ribs. Her breath caught in her throat. Twenty years of isolation crystallized in this moment. This choice. This line she couldn't uncross.

Mara moved carefully. Deliberately. She took Dempsey's face in her hands. Drew her down. Pressed their lips together.

The kiss was different than the one outside the bar. Softer. More tentative. A question rather than a demand.

Dempsey's hands came up automatically. Found Mara's hip. Held on like she might fall. Might drown. Might disappear.

Mara pulled back first. Her eyes searching Dempsey's face. Looking for regret. For hesitation. Finding neither.

"Okay?" Mara's breath was warm against Dempsey's lips.

Instead of answering, Dempsey kissed her again. Harder this time. Hunger replacing hesitation. Her arms tightened around Mara's waist. Pulled her closer. The feel of another body against hers after so long made her dizzy. Made her reckless. Made her brave.

Mara responded immediately. Her hands moved from Dempsey's face to her hair. Fingers threading through the short gray strands. Holding her in place. The kiss deepened. Became something more than a question. More than an answer.

They broke apart, breathless. Mara's eyes were darker now. Pupils dilated. Her lipstick smudged.

"I've thought about this for years," Mara said. Her voice low. Intimate.

Dempsey didn't respond. Couldn't find words for what she was feeling. The contradiction of wanting this woman who had killed. Who had confessed to murder. Who had manipulated her way into Dempsey's life.

And yet.

Mara stepped back. Created space between them. Dempsey felt the absence like physical pain. Like withdrawal. Like loss.

"Too much?" Mara asked. Her eyes still on Dempsey's face. Still missing nothing.

"No." Dempsey's voice was rough. Unrecognizable.

Mara smiled. Reached for Dempsey's hand. Led her back to the armchair. Pushed her down gently. Then, with a grace that seemed impossible, Mara sat on Dempsey's lap.

Dempsey's hands found Mara's waist again. Steadied her. The weight of another person against her thighs was unfamiliar. Intoxicating. Terrifying.

"Is this okay?" Mara's voice was soft against Dempsey's ear.

Dempsey nodded. Couldn't speak. Couldn't think past the sensation of Mara's body against hers. The warmth. The weight. The reality of what was happening.

Mara kissed her again. Deeper this time. More insistent. Her hands cupped Dempsey's face. Held her there. No escape. No retreat. Just this moment. This connection. This reality.

Dempsey's mind emptied of everything except sensation. The taste of wine on Mara's lips. The scent of jasmine from her skin. The sound of their breathing in the quiet apartment.

For the first time in twenty years, she wasn't thinking about the job. About case files or evidence or procedure. Wasn't thinking about professional distance or ethical boundaries. Wasn't thinking about the lives she couldn't save or the justice she couldn't deliver.

Just this. Just now. Just the feeling of Mara's mouth on hers. Mara's body against hers. Mara's hands in her hair.

Dempsey's pulse raced under Mara's fingers. Her heart hammered in her chest. Her hands moved up Mara's back. Pulled her closer. Eliminated any space between them.

The kiss deepened. Mara made a small sound in the back of her throat. A sound of pleasure. Of want. Of need. The sound broke something open in Dempsey's chest. Something that had been locked away for decades. Something she'd convinced herself she didn't need. Didn't want. Couldn't have.

Connection. Desire. The simple human need to be touched. To be seen. To be wanted.

Mara's lips left hers. Trailed across her jaw. Found the sensitive spot just below her ear. Dempsey gasped. Her hands tightened on Mara's back. Her head fell back against the chair.

"Callisto." Mara whispered the name against her skin. Like a prayer. Like a confession. Like a promise.

The use of her first name cracked something open inside her chest. Something frozen. Something isolated. Something she'd protected for so long she'd forgotten it existed.

Forty-eight years of being untouched. Unwanted. Invisible.

Ended by this moment. This woman. This impossible, dangerous connection that made no sense and perfect sense simultaneously.

Mara's lips found hers again. Hungry now. Demanding. Her hands moved from Dempsey's hair to her shoulders. Her chest. The zipper of her sweater.

Dempsey felt decades of isolation crack open. Fall away. Leave her exposed and vulnerable and more alive than she could remember being.

Mara tasted of wine and something darker. Something Dempsey couldn't name but recognized on some primal level. The taste of danger. Of falling. Of surrender.

She let everything except this moment go.

Chapter 22

Dempsey woke at 5:17 AM. Her bedroom was gray with pre-dawn light. The weight of another body in her bed felt foreign after a lifetime alone. Mara slept facing away from her, brown hair spread across the pillow. Dempsey's gun and badge sat on the nightstand where she'd left them. Within reach. Always within reach.

She didn't move. Just watched the steady rise and fall of Mara's breathing under the sheet. A car drove past outside, headlights briefly illuminating the ceiling before disappearing. The building's early riser in 2B left for their morning run, door closing with a familiar click.

Three feet away, a murderer slept in her bed.

Dempsey's analytical mind cataloged evidence of last night. Wine glasses in the sink. Clothes scattered across the floor. The unfamiliar ache in muscles long unused. Her body carried the physical memory of Mara's touch. Her neck held a mark just below her ear where Mara's teeth had been.

She should regret it. Should feel horror at what she'd done. Should already be reaching for her cuffs.

Didn't. Couldn't.

Mara's back was smooth. A constellation of small freckles marked her left shoulder blade. Dempsey resisted the urge to trace them with her finger. To verify their pattern like evidence at a crime scene. She had touched that skin hours ago. Had mapped every inch of Mara's body with her hands. Her mouth.

Twenty years of police work. Of procedure. Of maintaining professional distance. Undone in a single night.

The woman had shot a man three times. Heart. Head. Groin. Had arranged three other deaths with meticulous care. Had confessed these things to Dempsey in an abandoned warehouse while Dempsey's gun stayed holstered. Had manipulated Dempsey into this position with calculated precision.

And yet.

Mara shifted in her sleep. The sheet slipped lower, revealing more skin. The curve of her waist. The outline of her hip. Dempsey's eyes followed the line of her body. Memorized it with the same attention she'd give a crime scene. The same focus she used to reconstruct a victim's final moments.

Only Mara was no victim. Was a killer instead. Was alive and warm and real in Dempsey's bed.

For twenty years, Dempsey had gone home to empty rooms. Had eaten dinner alone at her kitchen counter while reading case files. Had fallen asleep to the sound of her own breathing. Had convinced herself it was enough. That the job filled the spaces where other people had relationships. Connections. Lives beyond work.

She hadn't known how empty those rooms were until now. Until they weren't.

Mara stirred. Her breathing changed rhythm. She turned, eyes still closed, and reached toward Dempsey. Found her arm. Fingers gentle against skin.

"Morning." Mara's voice was rough with sleep.

"Morning." Dempsey's came out steadier than she felt.

Mara's eyes opened. Hazel in the gray light. Alert instantly. She smiled. The kind that transformed her face. That made her look like someone who hadn't killed four people with methodical precision.

"You're watching me." Mara's fingers traced up Dempsey's arm.

"Yes."

"Professional observation or personal interest?" The same question from last night.

"Both."

Mara's smile widened. "I dreamed about you."

"About what?" Dempsey's voice remained neutral. Detached despite the heat blooming under Mara's touch.

"About this." Mara moved closer. Pressed her lips to Dempsey's. Morning breath and wine residue. Real. Human. Dempsey's hands found Mara's waist automatically. Held on.

The kiss deepened. Became something more urgent. Mara pulled back first. Her eyes darker now. Hungry.

"You were amazing last night, Callisto." The use of her first name still felt intimate. Dangerous. "I knew you would be."

"You didn't know anything about me." Dempsey kept her voice flat. Professional.

"I knew everything about you." Mara's fingers found the mark she'd left on Dempsey's neck. Traced it gently. "I knew how you'd taste. How you'd sound. How you'd feel against me."

Heat flushed Dempsey's face. The memory of those sounds. Those tastes. Those feelings. Her professional mask slipped. Cracked. Revealed something underneath that had no name.

"I didn't know." Dempsey admitted. Hated the vulnerability in her voice. "I didn't know it could be like that."

Mara's expression softened. Understanding dawned in her eyes. "You've never been with anyone before."

Dempsey looked away. At the ceiling. The wall. Anywhere but Mara's face. Forty-eight years of isolation exposed in a single sentence.

"Hey." Mara's hand found her chin. Turned her face back. "That makes it more special. That you chose me."

"Did I choose?" The question escaped before Dempsey could stop it. "Or was I manipulated?"

Mara didn't flinch. Didn't look away. "Both. I arranged for us to meet. To talk. But what happened after was your choice. Your desire."

Dempsey considered this. Found truth in it she didn't want to acknowledge. Her desire. Her choice. Her fall.

"I never planned past getting your attention." Mara's thumb traced Dempsey's lower lip. "Everything after that surprised me too."

Dempsey caught Mara's wrist. Held it away from her face. Needed space to think. To breathe. "This can't work."

"It already is." Mara didn't fight the grip. Just waited. Patient. Still. The same stillness she'd shown in the warehouse. The stillness of someone who knew how to wait for exactly the right moment.

Dempsey released her wrist. Mara's hand fell to the sheet between them. The space of a breath. The distance between duty and desire.

"I should arrest you." Dempsey's voice was rough.

"You won't."

"How can you be so sure?"

Mara's smile returned. Soft now. Private. "Because you understand why I did it. What they deserved."

The statement hung between them. Simple. Direct. True in ways Dempsey couldn't deny. Couldn't admit. Couldn't reconcile with the oath she'd taken twenty years ago.

"And because you want me." Mara's hand found Dempsey's hip under the sheet. "As much as I want you."

The touch burned through Dempsey's skin. Electric. Alive. Her body responded before her mind could object. Heat pooled low in her stomach. Her pulse quickened under Mara's fingers.

Mara leaned in. Kissed her again. Deeper this time. More insistent. Dempsey's arms circled Mara's waist. Pulled her closer. The sheet between them an unwanted barrier. Mara's body pressed against hers. Warm. Solid. Real.

The kiss broke. Mara's breath quick against Dempsey's face. "Tell me to stop and I will."

Dempsey said nothing. Couldn't find words for the contradiction inside her. The detective who followed procedure. The woman who had been alone too long. The professional who knew right from wrong. The human who wanted, just once, to be chosen. To be wanted. To be seen.

Her silence was answer enough.

Mara moved over her. Straddled her hips. The sheet fell away. Morning light touched Mara's skin. Traced the curves Dempsey had memorized in darkness hours before. Mara's hands found Dempsey's. Fingers intertwined. Pinned them gently beside her head.

"Callisto." Just her name. Just that. Enough.

Dempsey stopped thinking altogether.

* * *

Dempsey stood at the kitchen counter. Made coffee with mechanical precision. Two mugs set out. Not one. The digital clock on the microwave read 6:42 AM. Too early for a Saturday. Too late to undo last night. She measured grounds into the filter. Poured water. Hit the switch. The machine gurgled to life. Familiar sound in an unfamiliar context. Nothing familiar about any of this.

She leaned against the counter. Bare feet on the cold tile. She wore sweatpants and a tank top. Her hair stood up in places where Mara's fingers had gripped it. Her neck still carried marks. Evidence of what had happened. Proof that couldn't be erased.

The coffee maker hissed. Steam rose from the pot as it filled. The smell filled the kitchen. Normal morning ritual in a life suddenly not normal at all.

Footsteps from the hallway. Soft. Deliberate. Dempsey didn't turn. Just watched the coffee drip. Listened to Mara approach. Her breath caught when Mara appeared in her peripheral vision.

Mara wore Dempsey's shirt. The white button-down from yesterday. Nothing else. The shirt hung to mid-thigh. Collar open. Sleeves rolled up. Her legs bare. Hair loose around her shoulders. She looked nothing like the crime scene photographer Dempsey knew from work. Nothing like the methodical killer from the warehouse.

She looked like someone's lover. Dempsey's lover.

"Morning." Mara's voice was warm. "Again."

"Coffee's almost ready." Dempsey kept her voice neutral. Professional distance impossible with Mara wearing her clothes. With the memories of last night still fresh in her body.

Mara moved to the counter. Stood beside Dempsey. Close enough that their arms touched. "Smells amazing."

"It's just coffee."

"It's more than that." Mara's smile was small. Private. "It's coffee in your kitchen. With you."

Dempsey didn't respond. Watched the last drops fall into the pot. The mundane task anchoring her in reality while everything else tilted. Shifted. Transformed.

She poured two cups. Handed one to Mara. Their fingers brushed during the exchange. Dempsey's skin remembered those fingers elsewhere. Remembered their precise movements. Their deliberate touch.

Mara took a sip. Closed her eyes. "Perfect."

Dempsey watched her over the rim of her own mug. Cataloged details with a detective's precision. The small scar on Mara's left temple. The freckle just below her collarbone. The chipped nail polish on her right thumb. Human details that didn't fit with calculated murder. With methodical revenge.

They stood in silence. Drinking coffee. The domesticity struck Dempsey again. The sheer normalcy. As if they were any other couple on a Saturday morning. As if Mara hadn't killed four people. As if Dempsey hadn't let her walk away.

Dempsey's kitchen had never held this kind of quiet intimacy before. Had never contained another person's breathing. Another person's presence. The space felt different with Mara in it. Warmer. Lived in. Real in a way it hadn't been before.

The clock on the microwave changed to 6:47. Five minutes of standing together. Saying nothing. The moment stretched between them. Comfortable in a way that made Dempsey uneasy. That made her question everything she thought she knew about herself.

Mara set her mug down on the counter. Moved closer to Dempsey. Slipped her arms around Dempsey's waist from behind. Pressed her body against Dempsey's back. Her chin rested on Dempsey's shoulder. The position intimate. Familiar. As if they'd stood this way a hundred mornings. Not just their first.

Dempsey didn't pull away. Her body recognized Mara's touch now. Responded to it. Relaxed into it despite everything her mind knew. Everything her training told her.

"What are you thinking?" Mara's breath was warm against Dempsey's ear.

"Too many things." Dempsey's voice came out rough.

"Tell me one." Mara's arms tightened around Dempsey's waist. Not restraining. Anchoring.

"This feels too normal." Dempsey kept her gaze on the window above the sink. At the gray morning light. The building across the street. The ordinary world continuing as if nothing had changed.

Mara was silent for a moment. Her breathing steady against Dempsey's back. "Is that bad?"

"I don't know." The honesty came easier now. After last night. After everything they'd shared. "It should be."

"But it's not."

Dempsey set her mug down. Covered Mara's hands with her own where they rested on her stomach. "No. It's not."

They stood that way for several breaths. Connected. Still. The coffee cooled in their abandoned mugs. Traffic sounds filtered in from outside. The city waking up around them while they remained in this bubble of impossible intimacy.

"I have feelings for you, Callisto." Mara's voice was soft against Dempsey's ear. "Strong feelings."

The statement hung in the air between them. Simple. Direct. The kind of declaration Dempsey had never heard before. Had never expected to hear.

"I have them too." Dempsey's admission felt like stepping off a ledge. Like falling. Like flying. "But I'm confused."

"About what?"

"About everything." Dempsey turned in Mara's arms. Faced her directly. Needed to see her eyes. "About you. About me. About what we're doing."

Mara's hands stayed on Dempsey's waist. Her expression open. Unguarded. "That's understandable."

"Is it?"

"Of course." Mara's eyes held Dempsey's. Steady. Sure. "Nothing about this is simple."

Dempsey studied her face. The face of a woman who had killed without remorse. Who had manipulated her way into Dempsey's life. Who now stood in Dempsey's kitchen wearing Dempsey's shirt as if she belonged there.

And somehow, impossibly, she did.

"I love your honesty." Mara's hands moved up Dempsey's arms. Came to rest on her shoulders. "You don't pretend. Don't hide. Even when it would be easier."

The word "love" caught in Dempsey's chest. Expanded there like something physical. Something with weight and substance. Something she couldn't ignore or dismiss or explain away.

Love.

One syllable that changed everything. That shifted the ground beneath her feet. That made the world simultaneously more clear and more complex than it had been moments before.

Dempsey's heart responded before her mind could intercede. Before her training could assert itself. Before her professional ethics could remind her of all the reasons this was wrong. Impossible. Forbidden.

Her heart soared at that single word. Love.

Even knowing it wasn't directed at her fully. Even knowing it referred only to her honesty. Still, her body responded. Her pulse quickened. Her breath caught. Her hands tightened on Mara's waist.

Love.

She'd never said it. Never heard it said. Had convinced herself it was a concept that applied to other people. Normal people. People who hadn't seen what she'd seen. Done what she'd done. Been what she'd been.

The detective who followed procedure. Who maintained professional distance. Who did things by the book.

That woman was gone now. Replaced by someone who let killers walk free. Who kissed them in dark streets. Who took them to bed knowing what they had done. What they were capable of doing.

Replaced by someone who felt her heart lift at the word "love" spoken in her kitchen on a gray Saturday morning.

"What are you thinking now?" Mara's question pulled her back to the present moment. To the kitchen. To the woman in her arms.

"That I'm not who I thought I was." Dempsey's voice was steady despite the chaos inside her. "That maybe I never was."

Mara smiled. The kind that transformed her face. That made her eyes brighter. That pulled an answering response from somewhere deep in Dempsey's chest.

"I know exactly who you are, Callisto Dempsey." Mara's hands framed Dempsey's face. "I always have."

Dempsey believed her. She stepped back from Mara's touch. Created distance. Not rejection. Space to think. The kitchen suddenly felt too small. Too intimate. The coffee had gone cold in their mugs. Outside, traffic sounds increased as the city fully woke. She ran her hand through her hair. The strands still tangled from Mara's fingers hours earlier.

"I'm not sure what I should do." Dempsey's voice was steady despite the uncertainty of her words. "About this. About us."

Mara leaned against the counter. Her posture relaxed. The white shirt—Dempsey's shirt—rode up on her thighs when she crossed her legs at the ankle. Dempsey looked away. Focused on the refrigerator. The microwave. The ordinary kitchen objects that had existed before this moment. That would exist after.

"Do what your heart tells you, Callisto." Mara's voice held no pressure. No demand. Just certainty.

"My heart and my job are in conflict."

"They don't have to be."

Dempsey looked back at her. Studied her face. The face of a woman who had calculated four deaths with precision. Who had enacted perfect justice where the system had failed. Who now stood in Dempsey's kitchen as if she belonged there.

"If I had my way," Mara continued, "we would be lovers."

The word hung between them. Simple. Direct. Loaded with meaning and consequence. Lovers. Not a one-night transgression. Not a mistake to be forgotten. Something ongoing. Intentional. Chosen.

Dempsey nodded once. A small, tight movement. Said nothing. Her silence neither acceptance nor rejection. Just acknowledgment of the possibility. Of the reality already forming between them.

"We'd need rules." Mara picked up her coffee mug. Set it in the sink. Professional efficiency in the mundane task.

"Rules," Dempsey echoed. She liked rules. Lived by rules.

"Professional distance at work," Mara said.

"Obviously." Dempsey's detective mind engaged automatically. Problem-solving. Tactical thinking. The familiar ground of logistics rather than the unknown territory of emotion.

"We'll need to be careful about scheduling." Mara turned back to face Dempsey. "When we can see each other."

"My schedule is unpredictable." Dempsey's hand went to her neck. To the mark Mara had left there. Evidence that needed to be hidden. Concealed. "Homicide doesn't keep regular hours."

"Neither does crime scene photography." Mara smiled. "We're called to the same scenes, after all."

The practical conversation felt surreal. Scheduling details. Professional boundaries. The ordinary concerns of a relationship discussed by a detective and a killer in a kitchen on a Saturday morning. As if this were normal. As if they were normal.

"This won't be easy." Dempsey moved to the sink. Stood beside Mara. Not touching. Close enough to feel her warmth.

"Nothing worth having is."

Dempsey washed her mug, squeezed water from the dish cloth. Set it in the drain board. The mundane task anchoring her in reality while everything else shifted. Transformed. Became something she couldn't have imagined forty-eight hours ago.

"There's risk." Dempsey kept her voice neutral. Professional. "For both of us."

"I know." Mara's voice carried no hesitation. No doubt.

"More for me." Dempsey turned. Faced her directly. "Professionally speaking."

Mara didn't argue. Didn't disagree. Just nodded once. "Yes."

The honesty was refreshing. No pretense between them. No false reassurance. Just the stark reality of what they were doing. What they were considering. What they had already begun.

Outside, a siren wailed in the distance. Someone honked three times in quick succession. The city's soundtrack continued uninterrupted. Oblivious to the conversation happening in Dempsey's kitchen. The lines being crossed. The boundaries being erased.

"We exist in a dangerous space now." Mara's observation was precise. Clinical almost. "Where professional and personal have collapsed."

"Yes." Dempsey recognized the photographer's eye in Mara's assessment. The ability to capture the essence of a moment. To define it with perfect clarity.

They stood facing each other in the kitchen. The intimate domesticity of earlier replaced by something more careful. More deliberate. The weight of their situation settling between them like physical pressure.

"Do you think I'm evil?" Mara's question came suddenly. Direct. Unadorned.

Dempsey didn't answer immediately. The question deserved consideration. Real thought. Not a reflexive response. The traffic sounds outside grew louder. A truck rumbled past. Someone shouted a greeting to a neighbor. Life continued its ordinary rhythm while Dempsey contemplated a question that was anything but ordinary.

Was Mara evil? The woman who had shot Stefan Tapani three times. Who had arranged three other deaths with meticulous care. Maybe a fourth. Who had manipulated her way into Dempsey's life with calculated precision.

The woman who had also been violently assaulted. Whose case had been dismissed because her attacker was useful to the system. Who had watched the same system fail other victims. Who had taken justice into her own hands when no one else would deliver it.

Evil was too simple a word. Too absolute for the complex reality of what Mara had done. What she was. What existed between them now.

"No." Dempsey's answer came finally. Firm. Certain. The certainty surprised her. Settled in her chest with unexpected weight. "I think you were justified."

The words hung between them. Impossible to take back. Impossible to unhear. The final line crossed. The final boundary erased. A homicide detective declaring vigilante killings justified. Not just any killings. Mara's killings. The woman who now wore her shirt. Who had slept in her bed. Who had touched her in ways no one ever had before.

Mara didn't smile. Didn't look triumphant. Just nodded once. Acceptance rather than victory. "Thank you for that."

They stood in silence. The kitchen clock ticked off seconds. The refrigerator hummed. Ordinary sounds in a moment that was anything but ordinary.

Dempsey had just compromised everything she believed about justice. About the law. About her own moral code. Had declared herself on the side of someone who had killed four people without legal sanction. Without due process. Without the system's approval.

And yet she felt no regret. No doubt. No uncertainty about her declaration. Just a strange, unexpected peace. The peace of truth finally spoken aloud. Of conviction finally acknowledged. Of a choice finally made.

The choice had been forming since that night in the warehouse. Since Mara's confession. Since the kiss that had compromised everything. Had been growing with each moment between them. Each touch. Each word. Each revelation.

She had chosen Mara. Had chosen this. Had chosen them. Whatever "them" would become in the dangerous space they now occupied together.

"What happens now?" Not fear in her voice. Not doubt. Just pragmatic inquiry about next steps. About the path forward.

Mara moved closer. Took Dempsey's hands in hers. The touch gentle. Certain. Connected. "Now we begin."

The words felt like both promise and sentence. Like gift and burden. Like everything Dempsey had never known she wanted until it stood before her wearing her shirt on a Saturday morning in a kitchen that had never held this kind of truth before.

Begin. Such a simple word for such a complex reality.

Dempsey nodded once. Accepted the word. Accepted what came with it. Accepted Mara and all she had done. All she was. All they might be together.

Now we begin.

Chapter 23

Dempsey sat at her desk. The date in the corner of her computer screen read Monday. Just Monday. She'd never hated Mondays before. Mondays meant cases to solve. Work to do. But this Monday meant leaving Mara at dawn. Meant professional distance after a weekend of anything but.

She clicked through case files. Forced her mind back to the job. The Odom murder sat open on her screen. Execution-style. Professional hit. Two different weapons. Like Tapani. Like the killings she now knew Mara had committed.

The precinct buzzed around her. Phones ringing. Keyboards clicking. The sounds she'd filtered out for twenty years now grated on her nerves. Made concentration impossible. Made her aware of every door opening. Every set of footsteps. Every possibility that Mara might walk through the bullpen.

Dempsey checked her watch. 2:17 PM. Mara would be in the lab. Processing photos from a morning scene. Professional. Efficient. The same Mara who had left marks on Dempsey's neck that her high-collared shirt now covered.

Her desk phone rang. Dempsey grabbed it before the second ring.

"Dempsey."

"Detective, dispatch. Body found at Ward and Larsen. Patrol on scene requesting Homicide."

She wrote down the address. Hung up without saying goodbye. Grabbed her jacket from the back of her chair. Her movements precise. Automatic. The detective who followed procedure reasserting herself through muscle memory.

Harris looked up from his desk as she passed. "Catching?"

"Ward and Larsen."

"Want company?"

"I've got it."

The elevator doors closed before he could say more. Dempsey leaned against the wall. Closed her eyes. Three deep breaths. Professional distance. The job. Focus on the job.

Her car was cold. The heater blew icy air for the first mile. She drove with both hands on the wheel. Radio off. Mind cataloging what she knew about the area. Ward and Larsen. Empty lot on the corner. Abandoned buildings. High crime. Low witness cooperation.

The scene came into view two blocks out. Patrol cars with lights flashing. Yellow tape stretching between light poles. A small crowd of onlookers kept back by a uniform. Dempsey parked behind the coroner's van. Killed the engine. Sat for five seconds. Detective mode. Only detective mode now.

She stepped out. The cold hit her face. The sky threatened snow. She tugged her gloves on as she approached the tape. Badge already out. The uniform—Morton by his nameplate—lifted the tape for her.

"What have we got?" Dempsey ducked under.

"Female victim. Partially clothed. Blunt force trauma to the head." Morton fell into step beside her. "Found by a guy looking for scrap metal. He's over there."

Morton pointed to a man sitting in the back of a patrol car. Thin jacket. Worn boots. Dempsey nodded. "I'll talk to him after I see the scene."

"We did a canvass already." Morton flipped open his notepad. "No one saw anything. No one heard anything. You know how it is around here."

Dempsey did know. Areas like this had their own code. Don't see. Don't tell. Don't get involved. You won't be next. She walked toward the center of the lot where a white sheet covered a form on the ground. The M.E. crouched nearby, writing notes.

"Time of death?" Dempsey asked without preamble.

The M.E.—Dyer, new to the department—looked up. "Impossible to know right now. I have to check the overnight temperature, how much snow fell. I'll know more after autopsy."

Dempsey nodded. Circled the body. The ground around it told its own story. Footprints in the fresh snow. Multiple sets. Different sizes. Some deep, as if carrying weight. Others light. Moving quickly. And the drag marks. Clear lines through the snow leading from the street to where the body now lay.

"She wasn't killed here." Dempsey pointed to the drag marks. "Brought here after."

Dyer nodded. "Minimal blood at the scene supports that."

Dempsey crouched. Lifted the edge of the sheet. Young woman. Early twenties maybe. Blonde. Pretty once. Not anymore. Her face was purple on one side where the blow had landed. Her eyes open. Empty. Her shirt torn open. Bra intact. Jeans pulled down to her ankles.

Dempsey let the sheet fall back. Stood. Surveyed the lot again. The footprints told of at least three people. The drag marks of a body moved after death. Brought here to be found. To hide the true murder scene.

"Any ID?" she asked Morton who hovered nearby.

"Nothing on the body. No purse. No wallet. No phone."

"Tattoo on her wrist though." Dyer pulled the sheet back to reveal a small design. "Might help with identification."

Dempsey studied it. Simple black lines forming what looked like a bird in flight. Not distinctive enough to be immediate help. She'd need missing persons reports. Dental records. The usual process.

"What about this?" Morton pointed to a brick lying a few feet from the body. Dark stains on one side. "Found it when we secured the scene."

Dempsey bent over. The stains looked like blood. Old blood. Dried.

"Bag it." She told the nearest tech. "Could be the murder weapon."

She stood. Made a slow circle around the scene. Taking in details. Memorizing the layout. The footprints. The drag marks. The brick. The partially clothed victim.

Dempsey pulled out her notebook. Wrote down her observations. The footprints in the snow. Three distinct sets. The drag marks from street to center of lot. The brick with blood. The tattoo. The clothing. All of it pointing to a scene created rather than a crime discovered.

"Get photos of all the footprints before they melt or get contaminated." She told the nearest tech. "And I want those drag marks documented from every angle."

The tech nodded. "Photographer's late. He'll be here soon." The tech began setting up markers. Preparing to document everything before the scene changed. Before the snow melted. Before evidence disappeared.

Dempsey looked back at the patrol car where the witness waited. Time to get his statement. Time to build the case. Time to find out who this woman was. Who had killed her. Who had created this scene.

Time to speak to the man who found her.

* * *

Dempsey closed her notebook. The witness had seen nothing useful. Just a body already on the ground when he arrived looking for copper wire to strip. She tucked the notebook into her pocket. Turned back toward the crime scene. Stopped. Mara was ducking under the yellow tape, camera bag over her shoulder, face composed in professional concentration. Nothing in her expression revealed what they'd been doing twelve hours earlier.

Dempsey's pulse quickened. She forced her breathing steady. Kept her face neutral. Detective face. Professional face. The face she'd worn for twenty years before this weekend changed everything.

"Mara Snowden," she said to Morton as she checked into the scene. "Frank couldn't make it. Flat tire."

Mara moved toward the body. Set down her camera bag. Kneeled to speak with Dyer about the scene. Her movements were efficient. The same movements Dempsey had watched at dozens of crime scenes before. Different now that she knew how those hands felt on her skin.

Dempsey walked back to the center of the scene. Stood with hands in her pockets. "Snowden," she said. Professional acknowledgment. Nothing more.

"Detective." Mara nodded once. Her eyes met Dempsey's briefly. Held something only they understood. "What am I documenting?"

"Everything." Dempsey gestured to the scene. "Footprints in the snow. Drag marks from the street. The brick over there might be the murder weapon. And the victim's tattoo."

"Got it." Mara unzipped her camera bag. Pulled out her camera. Checked the settings. The same fingers that had traced patterns on Dempsey's back at 3 AM.

Dempsey turned away. Walked the perimeter of the scene again. Created distance. Physical space that did nothing to diminish the awareness between them. She could feel Mara's presence like heat on her back. Like a second pulse beneath her skin.

The shutter clicked. Rhythmic. Professional. Mara photographed the drag marks first. Moving in a pattern Dempsey had never paid attention to before. Concentric circles. Moving inward. Creating a complete record of the evidence before it could change or disappear.

Dempsey hadn't noticed before how Mara angled her body when taking low shots. The precise tilt of her head. The way she braced one hand on the ground. The small adjustments she made between frames. Details that hadn't mattered before this weekend. Before knowing Mara's body as intimately as her own.

"Detective?" Morton appeared at her elbow. "M.E.'s ready to transport the body."

Dempsey nodded. "Make sure Snowden gets the photos she needs first."

Morton moved away. Spoke to Dyer. Dempsey watched them talk. Focused on them instead of Mara. Tried to pull her mind back to the case. The victim. The evidence. The job.

Mara was photographing the footprints now. Placing markers beside each one. Documenting size. Direction. Depth in the snow. Her methodical precision was the same precision she'd applied to her kills. To her revenge. Dempsey knew that now. Recognized the careful attention to detail that had made Mara's crimes perfect.

And she'd let her walk away.

"I need close-ups of the victim." Mara's voice came from behind her. Professional. Detached. Nothing like the voice that had whispered in Dempsey's ear this weekend.

"Dyer's waiting for you." Dempsey didn't turn. Kept her eyes on the drag marks in the snow. The story they told of a body moved after death.

Mara moved past her. Close enough that their sleeves brushed. The contact barely perceptible through winter coats. Enough to make Dempsey's skin tighten. To make her aware of the marks still hidden beneath her collar.

Dempsey watched as Mara kneeled beside the body. As Dyer pulled back the sheet. As Mara's camera documented death with professional detachment. The same hands that had touched Dempsey with such care now cataloged violence with clinical precision.

The contradiction made Dempsey's head spin. The professional photographer. The methodical killer. The woman who had slept in her bed. All the same person. All Mara.

Dempsey walked toward the street. Looked up at the buildings surrounding the vacant lot. Counted windows. Doorways. Possible vantage points. Places where someone might have seen something.

"Any security cameras in the area?" She asked Morton who had followed her.

"One on the corner store two blocks up." He pointed north. "And a traffic cam at the intersection. We're pulling the footage now."

Dempsey nodded. "I'll check it when I get back to the precinct."

She needed to leave. Needed space from this scene. From Mara. From the professional distance that felt like a lie now. That was a lie now.

Mara had finished with the body. Was photographing the brick now. Her camera angled to capture the blood stains. The potential murder weapon preserved in digital detail before being bagged and tagged. Her face showed nothing but professional focus.

As if she'd never killed. As if she'd never held Dempsey against her kitchen counter and whispered things no one had ever said to her before.

Dempsey turned away. Found Morton by the patrol car. "I'm going to check those cameras. Head back to the office."

Morton nodded. Pulled out his clipboard. "Sign you out?"

Dempsey scribbled her name and time on the checkout sheet. Standard procedure. One of the rules she still followed. Still respected. Unlike all the others she'd broken since meeting Mara.

She walked to her car without looking back at the scene. Without acknowledging Mara again. Professional distance maintained in public view. The private connection humming beneath her skin like electricity.

The drive back to the precinct would take fifteen minutes in afternoon traffic. Fifteen minutes to rebuild the walls between Detective Dempsey and the woman who had spent the weekend in her bed. To separate the professional from the personal. To become the detective who followed procedure again.

She started the engine. Pulled away from the curb. Didn't look in the rearview mirror. Couldn't bear to see Mara still working the scene. Still playing her role perfectly while Dempsey struggled to remember hers.

Dempsey walked into the bullpen. Early evening quiet had settled over the precinct. Just a few detectives at their desks. The overhead lights hummed. Coffee maker gurgled its last cycle. She headed for her desk, mind still at the crime scene. Still with Mara's camera documenting death with the same hands that had touched her hours earlier.

"Well, look who's back." Knight's voice carried across the room. Too loud. Intentionally public. "Heard you caught a half-naked dead girl at Ward and Larsen."

Dempsey ignored him. Hung her jacket on the back of her chair. Sat down. Reached for her keyboard.

Knight stood. Walked toward her desk. Stopped too close. His aftershave was cheap. Overpowering. "That's probably the only way you'll ever see a woman naked, right, Dempsey?"

The bullpen went silent. Three other detectives looked up. Waiting for Dempsey's usual non-response. The tight smile. The turned back. The professional deflection she'd used for twenty years.

Something snapped inside her chest. Hard. Final. Like bone.

"You better stop your shit right now." Her voice was ice. Low at first. Then rising. "Or I'll have your fucking badge."

The word hung in the air. Fucking. A grenade rolled across the polished floor of her professional restraint. Dempsey never swore. Never raised her voice. Never engaged.

Until now.

Knight's mouth opened. Closed. Opened again. "Jesus, Dempsey. It was just a joke."

"A joke?" She stood. Her chair rolled back. Hit the desk behind her. "You think sexual assault is funny? You think a dead woman deserves that kind of disrespect?"

Knight's face flushed. He glanced around the bullpen. At the other detectives now watching openly. No allies there. Just witnesses to his humiliation. To Dempsey's unprecedented reaction.

"Come on, I didn't mean anything by it." He tried to smile. Failed. "Just giving you a hard time."

"I wonder what Chief Brandt would make of that kind of joke." Dempsey stepped closer. Into his space now. "I wonder how it would sound repeated to her. To Internal Affairs. To the union."

Knight's face went pale. His promotion was up next month. His record already had two complaints. A third would end his career. "I didn't—I was just—"

"Just what?" Dempsey's voice was steel now. Cold. Hard. "Just harassing a colleague? Just disrespecting a victim? Just being the same miserable excuse for a detective you've always been?"

The bullpen was cemetery quiet now. No one typed. No one moved. Just breathing and the distant ring of a phone at the front desk. Knight stood frozen. Caught between retreat and retaliation. Dempsey saw the calculation in his eyes. The weighing of options. The decision.

"I didn't mean any harm." His voice dropped. Placating now. "It was a bad joke. I'm sorry."

"Not good enough." Dempsey stepped closer. Six inches between them now. She'd never stood this close to Knight before. Had never wanted to. Had always kept her distance from his toxic presence.

Not anymore.

"You ever treat me like that again." She spoke quietly now. Just for him. Just between them. "I go to the Chief. To IA. To the union. You understand me?"

Knight's jaw tightened. A muscle jumped in his cheek. His eyes darted around the room again. Seeking support. Finding none. "Yeah. I understand."

"Say it back to me." Dempsey didn't move. Didn't give him the space to retreat with dignity. "What happens if you ever speak to me like that again?"

Knight swallowed. His Adam's apple bobbed once. "You go to the Chief."

"And?"

"IA. The union."

"Good." Dempsey stepped back. Created distance. "Now keep your damn mouth shut unless you have something professional to say."

Knight stared at her. Something like hate in his eyes. Something like fear too. He turned without another word. Walked back to his desk. His shoulders rigid. His steps too careful. A man retreating from a battlefield he'd expected to dominate.

Dempsey became aware of the silence around her. The stares of the other detectives. The weight of what had just happened. She'd broken the unwritten rule. Don't fight back. Don't make waves. Don't call out bad behavior.

She'd done all three in thirty seconds.

Her hands trembled. Adrenaline aftershocks. Her face burned. Not with embarrassment. With something else. Something that felt like triumph. Like relief. Like twenty years of silence finally broken.

She picked up her coffee mug. Walked toward the break room. Needed water. Needed space. Needed a moment to process what she'd just done. Who she'd just become.

The women's washroom was closer. She changed course. Pushed through the door. Let it swing shut behind her. The fluorescent lights buzzed overhead. The faucet in the second sink dripped steadily. Tick. Tick. Tick. Counting down seconds in a life suddenly, irrevocably changed.

Dempsey turned on the faucet. Cold water rushed over her hands. She cupped them. Brought water to her face. The shock of cold against her flushed skin grounded her in the moment. In what she'd just done. In who she'd just become. Water dripped from her chin. Splashed on the countertop. She did it again. And again. As if she could wash away twenty years of silence with tap water and institutional soap.

She reached for a paper towel. The rough brown paper scraped against her skin as she dried her face. Her hands still trembled. Adrenaline aftermath. Fight response slowly receding.

Knight had been making those comments for years. Four years, two months to be exact. Since the day she made detective. Small cuts delivered with surgical precision. Designed to remind her she didn't belong. Wasn't one of them. Would never be accepted.

Four years of taking it. Of professional distance. Of telling herself it didn't matter. That responding would only make it worse.

Until today.

She dropped the paper towel in the trash. Gripped the edge of the sink. The porcelain was cold under her fingers. Solid. Anchoring. She looked up. Met her own eyes in the mirror.

Same face she'd seen this morning. Deep-set brown eyes. Short steel-gray hair. Lines that came from squinting at crime scene evidence and bad fluorescent lighting. But something had changed. Something in the set of her mouth. The angle of her jaw. The steadiness of her gaze.

Three days with Mara had done this. Had changed how she saw harassment. Had connected her to the damage done by sexual violence in a way twenty years of investigating it hadn't. Made it personal. Made it something she couldn't ignore or deflect or professionally distance herself from.

The victim at Ward and Larsen deserved respect. Even in death. Especially from a detective. The clothing. The assault. These weren't jokes. Weren't punchlines. Were violations that continued beyond the grave.

Dempsey straightened. Her reflection did the same. Water still dripped from her hairline. Ran down her temple. Along her jaw. She didn't wipe it away. Just watched its path like evidence at a crime scene. Trace evidence of her transformation.

She pictured Knight's face when she stood up to him. The shock. The calculation. The fear when he realized she meant it. That this wasn't the Dempsey he'd known. The one who took it. Who walked away. Who maintained professional distance at all costs.

This Dempsey fought back.

She hadn't planned it. Hadn't scripted her response. The words had erupted from a place she hadn't known existed inside her. A place of anger. Of righteous indignation. Of pride.

Pride.

The realization settled in her chest. Warm. Unfamiliar. She was proud of what she'd done. Proud of standing up. Proud of finding her voice after twenty years of silence.

Her face in the mirror flushed again. Not with embarrassment. With something else. Something that looked like power. Like agency. Like the woman Mara had seen when no one else had bothered to look.

The woman who had spent a lifetime being professional. Being correct. Being ignored. Had just made herself impossible to ignore.

She reached for another paper towel. Dried her face completely this time. Straightened her collar. Smoothed her hair where water had disrupted it. Professional appearance restored. But the woman beneath the professional mask had changed. Had found something she'd been missing.

Her own voice.

Knight wouldn't report the incident. His pride wouldn't allow it. The other detectives wouldn't talk about it directly. But word would spread. Through the precinct. Through the department. Detective Dempsey stood up to Knight. Detective Dempsey wasn't taking it anymore. Detective Dempsey had teeth.

Good.

Let them talk. Let them wonder. Let them see her.

Dempsey dropped the paper towel in the trash. Squared her shoulders. Her reflection did the same. They regarded each other across the small space. The woman she had been. The woman she was becoming. Not so different on the surface. Transformed underneath.

She turned from the mirror. Walked to the door. Her steps steady now. Her hands no longer trembling. Her purpose clear.

The same cop who had followed procedure for twenty years. Who had maintained professional distance. Who had done things by the book.

And also someone new. Someone who stood up. Who fought back. Who had found her voice after decades of silence.

Both versions of herself now. Integrated. Whole in a way she hadn't been before Mara. Before the warehouse. Before the kiss that had compromised everything.

Before standing up to Knight.

Dempsey pushed open the washroom door. Stepped back into the precinct. Back into her life. Changed.

Chapter 24

Hussain's desk was orderly. Case files stacked in precise alignment. Pens in a black metal holder. Family photo turned at an exact forty-five-degree angle. He motioned Dempsey to the empty chair across from him. She sat, back straight. Professional distance maintained despite the tension coiling in her stomach.

It had been two days since her blowup with Knight, and everyone was treating her differently now. They nodded hello. Said goodnight. Stopped the cruel jokes. They almost respected her.

And now here was Hussain, asking for her help.

"Thanks for making time." Hussain pushed three folders across the desk. Manila. Worn edges. Department-standard file labels with dates and case numbers typed in precise block letters. "Need a fresh set of eyes on these."

Dempsey lifted the top folder. Didn't open it yet. "Cold cases?"

"Not exactly." Hussain leaned back in his chair. The leather creaked softly. "Closed cases. Accidental deaths and a suicide. Harris asked me to review them."

"Harris?" Dempsey kept her voice neutral. Maintained eye contact.

Hussain nodded. "Said something felt off. Asked me to take a look." He tapped the stack with his index finger. "When I went to interview witnesses from a different case, realized most were dead."

Dempsey opened the top folder. Barney Duke stared up at her. Male, 34. Suicide. The photo showed him slumped in a car seat. Face discolored. Eyes half-open. Died in his garage from carbon monoxide poisoning.

Her stomach dropped. She recognized him immediately. The bar witness from the Tapani case. One of Mara's victims.

The second folder contained Turner Pass. Age 41. Accidental death. Fell while working on his bicycle. Grip hit his chest. Commotio cordis. Heart stopped instantly. Another witness. Another victim.

The third folder. Teagan Tapia. Female, 29. Accidental death. The name wasn't familiar. But the pattern was unmistakable.

"Interesting cases." Dempsey kept her voice flat. Maintained the mask of professional detachment while her pulse raced under her skin. "Any particular reason Harris flagged these?"

"Said they connected to something he was working. Didn't elaborate." Hussain watched her face. His eyes missed nothing.

Dempsey focused on Duke's toxicology report. Noted what she'd observed before when investigating Mara. "Duke had no prescription for Zolpidem." She turned the page. "Could've gotten it elsewhere. Black market. Friend. The usual sources."

Hussain nodded. Made a note in his small spiral notebook. "Anything else?"

Dempsey moved to Pass's file. Turner Pass. Bicycle accident in his front yard. She remembered the case. Remembered the M.E.'s photos. The scratch on his palm. The evidence of Mara's knife before she'd struck him in the chest. Precise. Fatal.

"Pass has a cut on his palm." Dempsey pointed to the notation in the autopsy report. "Consistent with falling against the bicycle. Metal parts could cause that kind of injury."

Hussain wrote something else. His handwriting small. Precise. "M.E. mentioned it could have occurred right before death."

"That fits the accident scenario." Dempsey closed the file. Moved to Tapia's. A woman she didn't know. Fallen down basement stairs. Broken neck. Clean scene. No witnesses. Just another accident.

Not one of Mara's. Her name never came up.

She felt Hussain's eyes on her face. His attention focused like a laser. Watching for reactions. For tells. For anything that would reveal she knew more than she was saying.

Dempsey kept her expression neutral. The face she'd worn in interrogation rooms for twenty years. The professional mask that revealed nothing.

"These inconsistencies aren't unusual." She closed Tapia's file. Stacked all three neatly in front of her. "Toxicology report shows Duke was heavily sedated. Might explain why he didn't simply exit the car when he realized what was happening. Pass's hand injury is consistent with the accident. Nothing in Tapia's file jumps out."

Hussain took the files back. His movements deliberate. Controlled. "Not enough to reopen any of them."

"No." Dempsey made it a statement. Definitive. Professional. "All three have clear findings from the M.E. Accidental deaths happen. Suicides happen. People make mistakes. Take too many pills. Fall down stairs. Trip down stairs."

Hussain studied her face. "Three witnesses from the same case dying within two months doesn't strike you as odd?"

Dempsey blinked. "Same case? Which case?"

"Stefan Tapani homicide." Hussain's voice stopped her breath for a moment. She inhaled by force, kept her face neutral, waited.

"Teagan Tapia." Hussain tapped the third file with his index finger. "You know who she was?"

"No." The truth made this answer simple. Dempsey had never heard the name before today. Her hands remained still at her sides. No fidgeting. No tells.

"I think she might be Harris's mystery witness."

Dempsey opened the file again, looked at the DMV photo. Young woman. Dark hair pulled back. Serious expression.

"The one from the Tapani case. Erin Yes." Hussain sounded certain.

Relief flooded Dempsey's system. Cool and sudden as summer rain. Hussain had made a connection, but the wrong one. Erin Yes was Mara. Not this woman. Not Teagan Tapia.

She kept her face impassive. Didn't react to the photo. Didn't smile at Hussain's mistake. Didn't give away the knowledge that Erin Yes was actually standing in the crime lab right now, processing photos from some homicide.

"I wasn't able to identify that witness." Dempsey kept her voice neutral. Professional. "Canvass produced the name. Nothing more."

Hussain watched her face. Detective's eyes. Missing nothing. "Take another look at Tapia's report."

Dempsey took the file. Opened it. Scanned the details as if seeing them for the first time. Teagan Tapia. Age 29. Found at the bottom of basement stairs in her home. Broken neck. Death instantaneous according to the M.E. No signs of forced entry. Nothing missing. No suspects.

"Accident." She read the conclusion aloud. "Appears she tripped and fell."

"That's what the report says." Hussain took a small notebook from his pocket. Different from the one he'd been writing in earlier. Flipped to a marked page. "But her phone records put her within two blocks of the alley where Tapani was shot. Night of July 8th. Between 11 PM and 1 AM."

"Same time frame as the murder." Dempsey nodded. Kept her expression professional. Interested but not overly so. Just another detective discussing case details.

"Exactly." Hussain closed the notebook. Put it away. "Makes me think Harris is right. These witnesses are connected."

"Good work tracking that down." Dempsey handed the file back. Her fingers steady. No trembling. No hesitation. Nothing to suggest this information affected her personally. "Phone records can break cases wide open."

She turned away. Started walking toward her desk. Each step measured. Not too fast. Not too slow. The pace of a detective with work to do. Not a woman retreating from danger.

"Dempsey." Hussain's voice carried across the bullpen. Stopped her again. "Don't you think it's odd? All these witnesses dying?"

She turned. Looked back at him. Met his eyes directly. Calculated her response in the fraction of a second between heartbeats.

"Yes." One word. No elaboration. No theories offered. Just acknowledgment of the obvious pattern without engaging further.

She continued walking to her desk. Felt his eyes on her back the entire way. The weight of his suspicion following her across the bullpen like a shadow.

At her desk, Dempsey sat. Pulled a case file from her inbox. Opened it. Stared at the pages without seeing them. Her mind raced despite her calm exterior.

Hussain was connecting the deaths. Had already tied two of them to the Tapani case. Had misidentified Tapia as Erin Yes, but that mistake wouldn't protect Mara for long. A good detective would keep digging. Would find more connections. Would eventually discover the truth.

What would happen when he did?

She forced herself to focus on the file in front of her. To read the words. To process the information. The professional mask remaining in place while beneath it, everything shifted. Transformed. Became more complicated with each passing hour.

Hussain still watched her from across the bullpen. She felt his attention like heat on the back of her neck. Didn't look up. Didn't acknowledge it. Just kept reading. Kept pretending this was a normal day. That everything was fine.

Nothing was fine.

The clock on the wall ticked forward. Each second bringing them closer to a reckoning she couldn't prevent. Couldn't control. Could only delay through careful performance of normalcy. Through professional distance maintained despite the intimacy of her knowledge.

Through lies told by omission and commission.

She turned a page in the file. Made a note in the margin. The actions of Detective Dempsey. The professional. The by-the-book investigator who had spent twenty years following procedure.

Not the woman who had compromised everything for Mara. Who continued to compromise with each passing day. Each decision made. Each truth concealed.

Hussain eventually looked away. Turned his attention back to his own desk. His own work. The moment of direct observation passed.

But the investigation continued. She knew that as surely as she knew her own name. He wouldn't stop now. The pattern was too clear. The coincidences too numerous. The detective instinct too strong.

It was only a matter of time.

The bullpen was quiet. Afternoon lull. Most detectives out following leads. Taking statements. Attending court. Only Hussain and Greene remained at their desks across the room. The overhead lights hummed. A phone rang three times, stopped. No one answered.

Dempsey opened her drawer. Second one down. Right side of her desk. The drawer where she kept personal items. A spare phone charger. Breath mints. Extra pens. Now it held lunch. The lunch Mara had made for her that morning in Dempsey's kitchen.

Tuna sandwich. Multigrain bread. The way Mara had stood at the counter, spreading mayonnaise with the back of a spoon instead of a knife. Precise movements. The same precision she applied to everything. Crime scene photography. Murder. Making lunch for her lover.

The sandwich was wrapped in wax paper. Folded neatly at the ends. Tucked in on itself. Dempsey lifted it from the drawer. Set it on her desk. The clock on the wall read 1:37 PM. Later than she usually ate. The morning had been consumed with reports. Follow-ups on the Ward and Larsen homicide.

She unwrapped the sandwich. The wax paper crinkled. Released the smell of tuna and lettuce. She didn't hear Hussain approach. Didn't notice him until he was standing at the edge of her desk. A book in his hand.

"Found this at the bookstore on Maple." Hussain held up the book. Hardcover. Arabic title. English subtitle: "The Silent Witnesses." The cover showed a shadowy figure standing over what appeared to be a grave.

Dempsey looked up. Kept her expression neutral. "New novel?"

"Non-fiction, actually." Hussain turned the book over. Read from the back cover. "About a man in Algeria who killed his wife in public. In front of twelve witnesses."

"Non-fiction? Sounds interesting." Dempsey took a bite of her sandwich. Chewed. Swallowed. The motions of normalcy while her mind sharpened to a point of focus. Analyzed Hussain's unexpected approach. The book in his hand. The casual conversation that felt anything but casual.

"The interesting part comes after." Hussain opened the book. Flipped through pages covered in Arabic script. "He decided to eliminate all the witnesses. One by one. Made each death look accidental."

Dempsey took another bite. Said nothing. Waited. The tuna tasted like ash in her mouth.

"First witness fell from a balcony. Second drowned in his bathtub. Third had a kitchen fire." Hussain closed the book. "Each death seemed unconnected to the others. No evidence tying the killer to the scenes."

"Sounds almost Russian." Dempsey kept her voice neutral. Professional interest only. Nothing more.

Hussain held her gaze for a moment. "The detective who worked the case noticed the pattern." Hussain tapped the book cover. "That's what this is about. Written by the detective himself. He realized all the victims had one thing in common. They'd witnessed the original murder."

Dempsey nodded. Took another bite of her sandwich. Her appetite gone. The food necessary cover for this conversation. For the normalcy she needed to project. "Good detective work."

"The killer almost got away with it." Hussain leaned against her desk. Casual posture. Eyes not casual at all. "Murdered five witnesses before he was caught."

A cold weight settled in Dempsey's stomach. The implication clear. The parallel unmistakable. Hussain wasn't simply making conversation. Wasn't sharing an interesting book. Was sending a message: *I know what's happening. I'm connecting the dots.*

"Thought I might get a few pointers from a successful detective." Hussain's smile was almost crocodilian. "Always looking to improve my technique."

The threat hung between them. Veiled but unmistakable. Wrapped in professional courtesy the way the sandwich had been wrapped in wax paper. Neat. Precise.

"I'd double-check the Tapia and Duke cases. They were inside. Contained. Look through what's already there. I found misidentified evidence in the Zamora case, just sitting there." Dempsey kept her breath steady. Then nodded once.

"Let me know what you learn." Dempsey maintained eye contact. Her hands still. Nothing in her demeanor betraying the ice spreading through her veins. The fear crystallizing in her chest.

Hussain pushed off from her desk. Tucked the book under his arm. "Will do." He turned. Walked back to his own desk. Sat down. Opened the book. Began reading as if the conversation had been nothing more than a casual exchange between colleagues.

It hadn't been.

Dempsey looked down at her sandwich. Half-eaten now. The wax paper crinkled beneath it. Mara's sandwich. Made in her kitchen with Mara's hands. The hands that had killed at least four people. Maybe more. The hands that had touched Dempsey with tenderness.

She took another bite. Made herself chew. Swallow. The motions of normalcy while her mind raced through implications. Through consequences. Through the narrowing paths available to her now.

Hussain was building a case. Methodically. Carefully. The way detectives were trained to build cases. The way Dempsey herself had built cases.

Before everything changed.

The overhead lights continued to hum. The clock on the wall ticked forward. The bullpen remained quiet. Just three detectives at their desks. Each focused on their own work. Their own cases. Their own priorities.

One building evidence against a killer.

One protecting that same killer.

One oblivious to the silent battle unfolding between colleagues.

Dempsey finished her sandwich. Crumpled the wax paper. The sound too loud in the quiet room. She stood. Walked to the trash can. Dropped the paper inside. Returned to her desk.

Hussain didn't look up from his book. Didn't need to. His message had been delivered. His position established. The next move was hers.

Dempsey waited fifteen minutes. Completed a report form. Answered an email. Professional routine maintained. Nothing to suggest urgency. Nothing to indicate the conversation with Hussain had affected her. She stood, grabbed her jacket from the back of her chair. Casual movements. Unhurried. "Going to interview a witness on the Larsen case," she told Greene as she passed his desk. He nodded without looking up from his computer.

The elevator doors closed behind her. She exhaled. The first full breath since Hussain had shown her the book. Her hands remained steady. Her face composed. The professional mask held firm while beneath it, everything tilted off-axis.

The parking lot was half-empty. Afternoon sun glinted off windshields. A police cruiser pulled in as she walked toward her car. She nodded to the uniform behind the wheel. Kept walking. Keys already in hand. The weight of them familiar. Grounding.

Her car stood three rows back. She unlocked it. Got in. Closed the door. The silence inside felt like sanctuary after the charged atmosphere of the bullpen. She started the engine but didn't put the car in drive. Instead, she pulled her phone from her pocket. Dialed Mara's number.

One ring. Two. Three.

"Hey, you." Mara's voice came through the speaker. Warm. Intimate. The voice of a lover, not a killer. "Missing me already?"

"We need to talk." Dempsey kept her voice low despite being alone in her car. Precaution born of twenty years in law enforcement. Walls had ears. Parking lots had cameras. She hovered her hand over her mouth. "Private."

"Hold on." Mara's voice changed. Professional now. The sound of movement came through the phone. A door closing. "There. I'm alone in the supply closet. What's wrong?"

"Hussain knows." Dempsey watched the parking lot through her windshield. Checked her mirrors. No one nearby. No one watching. Just habit. Professional paranoia. "He's connected Pass and Duke. Knows they were both witnesses in the Tapani case. Both dead under suspicious circumstances."

"I see." Mara's voice remained calm. Untroubled. As if Dempsey had mentioned a change in the weather. Nothing more significant.

"He showed me a book. About a detective who caught a killer targeting witnesses." Dempsey's free hand gripped the steering wheel. Knuckles white against black leather. "He's sending a message. Building a case."

"A book?" Mara laughed. The sound unexpected. Incongruous with the gravity of the situation. "That's his move? Literary parallels?"

"This isn't funny." Dempsey's voice sharpened. "He's a good detective. Methodical. Thorough. He'll keep digging."

"Let him dig." Mara sounded unconcerned. Almost amused. "He won't find anything connecting me to those deaths. I was careful. You know that."

The confidence in Mara's voice should have been reassuring. Instead, it sent a chill down Dempsey's spine. The calm certainty of someone who had planned everything perfectly. Who had accounted for every possibility. Who had killed at least four people and left no evidence.

"Connecting them as witnesses isn't the same as finding evidence of murder." Mara's voice softened. "Don't worry about Hussain. He's good, but he's not that good."

"He's that good." Dempsey checked her mirrors again. Still no one nearby. Still safe to speak. For now. "And he's focused now. Won't stop until he finds something."

"Callisto." The use of her first name shifted the conversation. Made it personal again. Intimate. "I care about you too much to let Hussain become a problem for us."

"What does that mean?" Dempsey's grip tightened on the steering wheel. The implication in Mara's words clear. Dangerous. Impossible to ignore.

"It means I love you." Mara said it casually. As if it were something she'd said a thousand times before. Not the first declaration of those words between them. "It means I'll handle this."

"No." The word came out sharper than Dempsey intended. Almost a command. "No more handling. No more accidents."

Mara laughed again. The sound light. Musical almost. Completely disconnected from the weight of their conversation. From the implications. From the danger. "Whatever you say, Detective."

The tension in Dempsey's chest tightened. Pressed against her ribs like physical pressure. The contradiction between Mara's tone and their situation made her head spin. Made her question her own grasp on reality. On consequences. On what should happen next.

"What would you like for dinner tonight?" Mara changed the subject abruptly. Completely. As if they'd been discussing weekend plans. Not murder. Not investigation. Not the walls closing in around them. "I'm thinking pasta. That penne with vodka sauce you like."

"How can you be so calm?" Dempsey's voice dropped lower. The question torn from somewhere deep. Raw. Honest in a way professional distance never allowed. "Hussain is building a case against you. He knows what happened to the witnesses."

"He suspects." Mara corrected. "He has no proof. No evidence. Just a pattern that suggests something worth investigating."

"Patterns break cases." Dempsey echoed Hussain's words from earlier. "He won't stop now."

"Keep your heart, Callisto." Mara's voice softened. Became something almost tender. Almost sad. "It's more powerful than you dare."

The statement hung between them. Cryptic. Poetic. Completely unlike Mara's usual precise communication. Unlike anything Dempsey had expected to hear in this moment of crisis.

"What does that mean?" She asked. Needed clarification. Direction. Something concrete to hold onto while everything else shifted beneath her feet.

"It means I'll see you at home." Mara's voice returned to normal. The intimate tone of a lover making plans. "Pasta at seven. Bring wine if you want."

The call disconnected before Dempsey could respond. Before she could press for answers. Before she could make sense of Mara's strange calm in the face of imminent danger.

She lowered the phone. Stared at the blank screen. The conversation replayed in her mind. Each word. Each tone shift. Each implication beneath the surface.

Keep your heart, Callisto. It's more powerful than you dare.

Her own heart beat against her ribs. Steady. Strong. The organ that had been professional first for twenty years. That had been guarded. Protected. Isolated.

Until Mara.

Dempsey put the car in drive. Pulled out of the parking space. Whatever came next, she would face it with her heart intact. Whatever that meant.

Chapter 25

Dempsey arrived at the precinct at 7:15 AM. The squad room was half-empty. Most detectives wouldn't show for another hour. Across the bullpen, Hussain sat hunched over his desk, tie loosened, coffee untouched. The intensity of his focus made her stomach tighten. He hadn't gone home.

She hung her coat on the rack. Moved toward her desk without looking his way. Hussain didn't acknowledge her. Didn't look up. Just turned a page in the file and made a note on his legal pad.

Dempsey set her bag on her chair. Opened her desk drawer. Placed Mara's sandwich inside. Whole grain chicken salad wrapped in wax paper. Mara had pressed the edges with her fingers this morning. Made the corners sharp. The lunch sat beside Dempsey's favorite pen. Personal and professional life sharing the same drawer.

Her computer screen glowed to life. Password, two clicks. The Charlie Soto case folder opened. The victim's face stared back from the DMV photo. Alive then. Dead now. Bludgeoned at Purple Seal Ironworks where he'd worked for eight years.

She scanned the witness statements again. Leonard Friedman, co-worker. Said he heard shouting that suddenly stopped. Didn't see anyone leave. Otto Summers, also co-worker. Heard shouting but dismissed it. Factory got loud. People often yelled to be heard over machinery. Alberto Clarke, the boss. Said all employees were present and remained at the factory when police arrived. Said everyone hated Soto. Was planning on firing him at the end of the month. Clarke found the body himself.

The statements lined up too neatly. Too tidy. Everyone at work. Nobody missing. Nobody saw anything. Just a dead man with his head caved in.

Dempsey pulled up the crime scene photos. Clicked through them methodically. Body lying between two work stations. Blood spatter on the concrete floor. The murder weapon hadn't been found. Soto's blood on the floor where he fell. A trail of droplets leading to the body. He staggered before he died.

She checked the autopsy report again. Blunt force trauma. Three blows. First to the back of the head. Not immediately fatal. Second and third to the face. Crushing blows. Delivered after he was down. Overkill. Personal.

A sharp sound from across the bullpen. Hussain had slapped his desk. He stared at his monitor, grinning. Hit it with his palm again. Softer this time. Celebration, not frustration.

Dempsey kept her eyes on her screen. The knot in her stomach tightened. Hussain had found something. Something that made him happy. Something related to the witness deaths. To Mara.

She looked up when Hussain stood. Watched him walk to the printer. Wait for pages to emerge. His back was straight now. Shoulders relaxed. The stance of a detective with a breakthrough.

Dempsey closed the Soto file. Stood. Stretched as if stiff from sitting. Casual. Unconcerned. Moved toward the coffee pot near Hussain's desk.

"Good morning." She poured a cup. Black. No cream. No sugar. Not since Mara. "You look happy."

Hussain glanced up. Folded the papers he'd printed. Slipped them into his jacket pocket. "Just clearing up some details on an old case."

"Anything interesting?" She took a sip. The coffee burned her tongue. She didn't react.

"Nothing important." His smile was professional. Close-lipped. The smile he used with suspects. "Just tying up loose ends."

Lie. The set of his shoulders. The way he'd tucked the papers away instead of showing her. The careful neutrality of his expression. All told her he'd found something significant. Something he wasn't sharing.

"Let me know if you need another set of eyes." She kept her voice casual. Collegial. The voice of someone with nothing to hide. Someone who hadn't spent the night with a killer.

"Will do." Hussain returned to his desk. Sat down. Turned his attention back to his computer.

Dempsey walked to her desk. Set down the coffee cup she didn't want. Sat. Reopened the Soto file. The victim's face filled the screen again. Dead man who couldn't tell her who killed him. Who couldn't help her understand what Hussain had found.

The knot in her stomach had become a stone. Hard. Heavy. She forced her attention back to the case. To Leonard Friedman's statement. To the dropped charges against the victim three months ago. To the blood spatter pattern that suggested he'd been standing when first struck.

Professional distance. The job. Focus on the job.

But her eyes kept drifting to Hussain. To his face as he typed. To the pocket where he'd put those papers. To the satisfaction in his posture that told her he'd found a connection. A thread that would lead to Mara.

Her phone buzzed on the desk. A text from Mara. "Thinking of you. Dinner tonight?"

Dempsey didn't reply immediately. Hussain might be watching. Might be noting who she texted. Might be cataloging her reactions the way she cataloged evidence. The way she built cases.

She picked up her pen. Made a note about Charlie Soto's previous assault charge. About the co-worker who'd filed it. About the way it had been dropped when the witness stopped cooperating.

Her phone buzzed again. "Say yes. I have something special planned."

She typed back. One word. "Yes." Put the phone down. Returned to the case file. To blood spatter and defensive wounds. To the trajectory of the blow that killed a man with too many enemies.

The same trajectory that had brought her to this moment. To this desk. To this compromise that would destroy everything if Hussain had found what she feared he had found.

The first blow from behind. Unexpected. Devastating.

Like Mara walking into her life.

* * *

Dempsey parked in her usual spot outside the brownstone. Killed the engine. Spotted Mara's silver sedan two cars down. Her pulse quickened despite the day's tension. Despite Hussain's discovery. Whatever it was. She grabbed her bag from the passenger seat. Locked the car without looking back.

The steps to her building had been cleared of snow. Salt crunched under her boots. White residue on black concrete. She took the stairs two at a time. Key already in hand. The weight of the precinct falling away with each step.

Third floor. Her door. She unlocked it quickly. Stepped inside. The apartment smelled of tomato sauce and garlic. Of home in a way it never had before Mara. She dropped her keys in the bowl by the door. Set her bag on the side table. Hung her coat on the rack.

"In here." Mara's voice came from the kitchen. Warm. Intimate.

Dempsey moved through the living room. Rounded the corner. Found Mara at the stove, stirring a pot of red sauce. Bath towel wrapped around her torso. Hair damp against her neck. Water droplets on her shoulders. She turned. Smiled. The kind that transformed her face.

"You're early." Mara tapped the wooden spoon on the pot's edge. Set it in the spoon rest Dempsey hadn't owned before last week. "I was going to be dressed before you got home."

"Got lucky with traffic." Dempsey moved closer. Breathed in the smell of Mara's shampoo beneath the tomato and garlic. "Smells good."

"Spaghetti with meat sauce." Mara gestured at the pot. "Simple but satisfying. Hope you're hungry."

"Starving." Dempsey realized it was true. She hadn't eaten lunch. The sandwich had stayed in her drawer. Forgotten when Hussain made his discovery.

"Ten minutes." Mara touched Dempsey's arm lightly. "Let me get dressed."

She moved past Dempsey. Down the hallway to the bedroom. Water droplets marked her path on the hardwood floor. Would evaporate before dinner was over. Leave no trace.

"Tough day?" Mara's voice carried from the bedroom. Casual. Conversational.

"Long." Dempsey checked the sauce. Bubbling gently. She stirred it once. "Lot of case work."

"Anything interesting?" The sound of dresser drawers opening. Closing. Mara choosing clothes from the space Dempsey had cleared for her two days ago. Second drawer. Right side.

"Working the Charlie Soto case." Dempsey moved to the cabinet. Took down two plates. Set them on the counter. "The ironworks murder."

"I remember." Mara's voice closer now. In the hallway. "Messy scene. Blood spatter on three different work stations."

"That's the one." Dempsey got glasses from another cabinet. Filled them with water. "Having a hell of a time finding the murder weapon. Some piece of iron from the shop, we think."

"Missing?" Mara appeared in the doorway. Jeans. Dempsey's NYPD sweatshirt. Hair still damp but combed. Bare feet on the hardwood. "Criminals of opportunity don't typically hide evidence."

"We're thinking it wasn't opportunity." Dempsey set the glasses on the table. "More deliberate." Dempsey moved back to the stove. Stirred the sauce again. "Three blows. First from behind. Not immediately fatal. Last two delivered face to face. Personal."

Mara crossed to the other pot. Lifted the lid. Steam escaped. Pasta nearly ready. "Everyone accounted for at the scene?"

"That's the problem. All employees present when the body was found. Nobody missing. Everyone with obvious motive."

"Unusual." Mara turned off the burner beneath the pasta. "Most workplace homicides are gunshots. Well, most *murders* are gunshots."

"Exactly." Dempsey stepped back as Mara moved to the sink with the pasta pot. "Makes me think we're missing something."

Mara drained the pasta into a colander. Steam rose around her face. Made her features momentarily ghostlike. Then solid again. "If I'd killed someone at Purple Seal Ironworks, I would have thrown the weapon into the forge."

The statement hung in the kitchen. Matter-of-fact. Professional observation. The perspective of someone who thought about the mechanics of murder. Who had committed it.

"High temperature would destroy evidence." Mara continued. Transferred the pasta to a serving bowl. Added the sauce. Stirred. "Metal recycled. No trace left."

Dempsey watched her work. The efficient movements. The practical consideration of evidence destruction. The casual way she discussed murder while making dinner. The contradiction made Dempsey's head spin. Made her heart race. Made her question everything except the simple fact of wanting Mara here. In her kitchen. In her life.

"I'll check if they used the forge that day." She kept her voice neutral. Professional. Detective speaking to a consultant. Not a lover who had killed at least four people. Maybe more.

"Worth looking into." Mara brought the pasta bowl to the table. Set it down. "Shall we eat?"

Dempsey nodded. Pulled out Mara's chair. An old-fashioned gesture she'd never made before. Never thought to make. Mara smiled. Sat. Waited for Dempsey to take her own seat.

"This looks amazing." Dempsey said. Meant it. The simple meal more appealing than anything she'd eaten alone in this apartment. More satisfying than the expensive restaurants she'd visited for work dinners.

"It's just spaghetti." Mara served them both. Pasta on plates. Sauce spread evenly. Precise. Deliberate.

"It's more than that." Dempsey took her first bite. The sauce was perfect. Rich. Flavorful. "It's dinner with you."

Mara's smile softened. Her eyes held Dempsey's for a moment. Something passed between them. Something that transcended the tension of the day. The danger of Hussain's discovery. The impossibility of their situation.

"Is there something you want to ask me?" Mara took a sip of water. Direct. Unafraid. "You've been tense since you walked in."

"Was it you?" Dempsey set her fork down. Met Mara's eyes directly. "Charlie Soto. Did you kill him?"

Mara didn't flinch. Didn't look away. "No."

"You sure?" Dempsey studied her face. Looked for tells. For the micro-expressions she'd been trained to spot in interrogation rooms.

"I'm sure." Mara took another bite. Chewed. Swallowed. "I don't kill indiscriminately, Callisto."

"What about Teagan Tapia?" Dempsey kept her voice level. "Did you kill her?"

"Who?" Mara reached for her water glass.

"Teagan Tapia." Dempsey watched Mara's hand. Steady. No tremor. "Found dead at the bottom of her basement stairs. Neck broken."

"Never heard of her." Mara set the glass down precisely. No condensation ring on the table. "Why are you asking?"

"Hussain thinks she was Erin Yes." Dempsey kept her eyes on Mara's face. "From the Tapani scene."

Mara's expression didn't change. Nothing to read there. Nothing to interpret. Just calm attention. Interest without concern.

"That's quite a leap." She twirled pasta around her fork. "Based on what?"

"Phone records put her near the alley when Tapani was killed."

"Near isn't in." Mara took another bite. "Maybe she was in a taxi, driving by."

"Her death fits the pattern." Dempsey didn't touch her food. "Witnesses from the Tapani case dying in accidents and suicides."

"Phone records and coincidence." Mara shrugged. "Not evidence."

"It's enough to keep Hussain digging." Dempsey pushed her plate away. "He found something today. Something that made him happy."

"He won't find anything concrete." Mara reached across the table. Touched Dempsey's hand. "You didn't, and you're a better detective."

The compliment warmed her despite everything. Despite knowing it might be manipulation. Might be Mara playing her like a witness. Like a mark.

"I found plenty." Dempsey didn't pull her hand away. "Just nothing I could use legally."

"Exactly." Mara's thumb stroked the inside of Dempsey's wrist. The spot where pulse met skin. "You found me because I wanted to be found. By you specifically."

The touch lingered. Soft. Deliberate. A reminder of control. Of choice. Of the connection that had formed between them despite everything.

"What if Hussain connects you to Erin Yes?" Dempsey's voice lowered. "What if he finds evidence you were at the alley that night?"

"He won't." Mara's confidence was absolute. Unshakeable. "I was careful."

"You can't know that."

"I can." Mara released Dempsey's hand. Returned to her pasta.

The statement hung between them. Simple. Direct. Terrifying in its implications. In its admission. In the casual way Mara acknowledged her history of murder.

Dempsey picked up her fork again. Tried to eat. The food tasted like ash now. Like doubt. Like the compromise she'd made and continued to make with every moment she didn't arrest Mara. Didn't report what she knew.

"You're overthinking." Mara's voice softened. "Hussain has suspicions. Not evidence. There's a vast difference."

"Suspicions become evidence with enough digging."

"Not if there's nothing to find."

Dempsey wanted to believe her. Wanted to trust Mara's confidence. Wanted to believe they could continue this impossible relationship without consequences. Without discovery. Without the walls closing in around them both.

Mara's phone dinged. On the counter where she'd left it. She glanced at it. Something flickered across her face. Too quick to read. Gone before Dempsey could interpret it.

"Everything okay?" Dempsey watched as Mara rose. Moved to the counter. Picked up the phone.

"Fine." Mara checked the message. Typed a quick response. Put the phone face down. "Just work stuff."

"At eight p.m.?"

"Says the detective who gets called out at two in the morning." Mara returned to the table. Sat down. Her shoulders were tighter now. Tension where there had been none before. "Had a difficult shoot today."

"What kind of difficult?" Dempsey recognized deflection. Used it herself with witnesses. With suspects. With colleagues who got too close to personal matters.

"The kind I don't want to talk about." Mara's voice was firm. Final. "Not over dinner."

Dempsey nodded. Didn't push. Professional courtesy extended to personal space. The boundary between work and home maintained despite the impossibility of truly separating them. Not in their situation. Not with what existed between them.

"I was thinking." Mara's voice shifted. Lighter now. Deliberate change of subject. "We should go away for a few days. After Christmas. Before New Year's."

"Away?" The word felt foreign in Dempsey's mouth. She hadn't taken a vacation in three years. Hadn't seen the point. Hadn't had anyone to go with.

"Upstate. Rent a cabin. Build fires. Drink wine." Mara smiled. The kind that transformed her face. That made her eyes brighter. "Ring in the new year away from all this."

The suggestion opened something in Dempsey's chest. A possibility she hadn't considered. A future that extended beyond the immediate danger. Beyond Hussain's investigation. Beyond the next day. The next hour.

"I'd have to request time off." She said it like an objection. Meant it like acceptance.

"So request it." Mara's hand found hers again on the table. "We both deserve a break."

A break from murder. From investigation. From the constant performance of normalcy while everything shifted beneath their feet. A break that felt impossible and necessary simultaneously.

"I'll see what I can do." Dempsey turned her hand over. Let their palms meet. Let their fingers intertwine. The connection physical. Real despite everything else. Despite the danger. Despite the lies. Despite the bodies buried behind them.

"Three days." Mara squeezed her hand gently. "Just us. No precinct. No cameras. No dead bodies."

The promise hung between them. Simple. Appealing. Almost normal. The kind of plan couples made every day without thought. Without the weight of murder and justice complicating every moment.

"Sounds nice." Dempsey meant it. Found herself wanting it more than she'd expected. More than made sense given their situation. Given Hussain's discovery. Given everything still unresolved between them.

Mara stood. Still holding Dempsey's hand. Tugged her gently to her feet. "Leave the dishes. They can wait."

Dempsey followed her from the kitchen. Through the living room. Down the hall to the bedroom that had been just hers a week ago. That now held Mara's clothes in the second drawer. Mara's toothbrush in the bathroom. Mara's book on the nightstand.

The dangers of the day receded. Not gone. Never gone. Just distant for now. Pushed back by the simple reality of this moment. This connection. This impossible, dangerous thing that had grown between them despite everything.

For tonight at least, they had this. Tomorrow would bring Hussain's discovery. Would bring questions. Would bring danger closer.

But tonight was theirs.

Chapter 26

Dempsey pulled up to the curb three houses down from the crime scene. Morning light cut across the quiet residential street. Yellow tape marked the boundary between ordinary life and violent death. A patrol officer logged arrivals at the perimeter. Dempsey showed her badge without speaking.

Birds chirped from nearby trees. The sound felt wrong against the backdrop of flashing lights and the coroner's van. A cold wind gusted, lifting the crime scene tape, then letting it fall. Dempsey ducked under it.

Officer Quinn stood at the edge of the driveway, clipboard in hand, uniform crisp despite the early hour. She nodded as Dempsey approached.

"Morning, Detective."

"What have we got?" Dempsey's eyes moved past Quinn to the body on the concrete.

"Victim is Alfred Li, fifty-six. Shot once in the back of the head." Quinn flipped a page on her clipboard. "Neighbor found him around five-thirty when he came out to mow his lawn."

"Neighbor hear anything?"

"Says no. Name's Patterson. Lives next door." Quinn pointed to a gray-haired man sitting in a patrol car. "Claims he didn't know Li well. Said he was quiet, kept to himself."

Dempsey surveyed the scene. Residential neighborhood. Upper middle class. Houses set back from the street. Privacy fences. Mature trees. Not the kind of place where gunshots went unnoticed.

"No shell casings found," Quinn continued. "But we did get doorbell footage from across the street. Doesn't show much—just a shadow walking by, disappearing for a moment, then running down the street."

"The shooting itself?"

"Not on camera. Angle's wrong." Quinn tucked the clipboard under her arm. "Li's wife was contacted at work. Another officer drove her to headquarters. She's waiting to be interviewed."

"Time of death?"

"M.E. hasn't confirmed yet. Been dead for hours though."

Dempsey nodded. Moved closer to the body. Alfred Li lay face down on his driveway, a dark stain spread from beneath his head. One arm stretched forward, the other tucked beneath his body. His legs were straight, feet pointing outward. He wore a puffy winter jacket, slacks, dress shoes. Dressed for work. Never made it to his car.

A silver sedan pulled up behind the coroner's van. Mara stepped out, camera bag over her shoulder. She signed in at the perimeter, ducked under the tape. Her face showed nothing when she saw Dempsey. Professional distance. Just as they'd agreed.

"Snowden," Quinn greeted her. "M.E.'s almost done. You can start with the perimeter shots."

Mara nodded. Unzipped her bag. Pulled out her camera. Her movements economical, practiced. She adjusted settings without looking at the controls. Muscle memory. Dempsey watched her hands.

Mara began working the scene. She photographed the driveway first. The body's position. The blood pattern. The victim's clothing. The neighborhood backdrop. Creating a complete visual record of death's intrusion into suburban quiet.

Dempsey turned back to Quinn. "Doorbell footage. How clear?"

"Not great. Shadow's pretty indistinct." Quinn checked her notes. "Tech unit will do their best."

"Send it to me when it's ready." Dempsey walked a slow circle around the body. Looked for shell casings, footprints, anything the first responders might have missed.

The M.E. finished his preliminary examination. Stood, back cracking audibly. "Ready for transport when your photographer's done."

Dempsey nodded. Watched as Mara approached the body. Camera raised. Face composed in professional concentration.

Mara's shutter clicked rhythmically. She changed position. Crouched lower. Got the angle that would show the wound clearly. The evidence of violence captured in pixels. Documented. Preserved.

Dempsey studied the position of the body. The lack of defensive wounds. The single shot to the back of the head. Someone Li never saw coming. Or turned away from.

"No signs of robbery," Quinn said, following Dempsey's gaze. "Wallet still in his pocket. Watch still on his wrist."

"This wasn't random." Dempsey circled back to the street. Looked in both directions. Low traffic area. No pedestrians. No witnesses except doorbell cameras that caught shadows, not faces.

Mara finished with the body. Moved to the lawn adjacent to the driveway. Her brow furrowed. She crouched, camera aimed at something in the grass. Clicked three shots. Lowered the camera. Looked across the scene at the crime techs working the perimeter.

"Franco," she called. Her voice harsh, cut off. It caught Dempsey's attention.

The tech looked up from collecting soil samples near the street. Crossed to where Mara crouched by the lawn.

Dempsey watched their interaction. Saw Mara point to something on the ground. Franco kneeled beside her. Their heads close together. Conferring about something that had caught Mara's professional eye.

Dempsey walked over to where Franco kneeled beside the shoe print. Mara stood a few feet back, adjusting her camera lens. The morning sun caught on the metal casing. Franco looked up as Dempsey approached, his gloved hands hovering over the impression in the soft soil.

"What have we got?" Dempsey kept her voice professional. Detached.

Franco sat back on his heels. "False alarm on this one, Detective." He gestured to the shoe print. "Snowden was just explaining she accidentally stepped on the grass while getting an angle on the body."

Dempsey looked at the impression. Soft edges. Tracing of snow. Deep heel mark. Distinct tread pattern. Not fresh.

Not fresh at all.

Mara raised her camera. Clicked three shots of the print from different angles. Her movements jerky. Unusual for Mara. "I'm documenting it before anyone else disturbs the area," she explained. Her voice was louder now. Back to professional.

"Great," Franco agreed. He placed a small yellow marker beside the print. "We'll log it as exclusionary evidence. Rule it out since it belongs to Snowden."

Dempsey studied Mara's face. Nothing there. No guilt. No concern. Just the focused expression of a crime scene photographer doing her job.

"Which shoes are you wearing?" Dempsey asked. Kept her tone casual. Conversational.

Mara glanced down at her boots. Black. Heavy tread. "These. I stepped backward without looking. Rookie mistake." She shrugged. "Sorry for the confusion."

Franco stood. Brushed snow from his knees. "No harm done. Better to document everything than miss something important."

Dempsey nodded. Watched as Franco took his own photos of the print. Placed a ruler beside it for scale. Followed procedure exactly as he would for actual evidence.

Evidence that would never be processed further. That would be labeled and filed away. That would never connect to any suspect. Because it belonged to Mara.

Mara finished her shots. Lowered her camera. Met Dempsey's eyes directly for the first time since arriving at the scene. "Sorry about the sloppy work, Detective." Her voice carried just enough contrition to sound genuine to anyone listening. "Won't happen again."

Then she winked. Quick. Almost imperceptible. Gone before anyone but Dempsey could have noticed.

The wink changed everything. Made the "accidental step" deliberate. Made Mara not just a photographer who'd made a mistake, but something else entirely.

Dempsey's stomach tightened. The wink confirmed what she'd suspected immediately. Mara had called attention to it on purpose. Had ensured it would be documented and then dismissed. On purpose.

Franco stood, evidence kit in hand. "I'll get this logged. Anything else you need from this area, Detective?"

Dempsey shook her head. "I'm good. Thanks." Her voice remained steady despite the realization forming in her mind. The implications of what Mara had just done. Of what that wink meant.

Mara had been here before. Not just at this crime scene this morning. But earlier. Before the police arrived. Before the body was discovered.

The print wasn't from photographing the scene. It was from when she'd killed Alfred Li.

Dempsey turned away. Needed space to process this. To think through the implications. Mara had just manipulated evidence at an active crime scene. Had just ensured that any matching shoe prints found elsewhere would be attributed to her official visit, not to an earlier presence.

And she'd done it with such confidence. Such ease. Right under the noses of a dozen law enforcement professionals. Including Dempsey.

Dempsey looked back at the scene. The body was being loaded into the coroner's van. Techs still worked the perimeter, collecting samples, measuring distances, documenting everything. Quinn stood by her patrol car, radio to her mouth, coordinating with headquarters.

And Mara moved through it all like a ghost. Camera raised. Face composed. Professional. Efficient. Nothing in her demeanor suggesting she was anything but the crime scene photographer doing her job.

Except that wink.

A shiver ran down Dempsey's spine that had nothing to do with the morning chill. Part horror at what Mara had done. Part admiration for how perfectly she'd done it.

Twenty years in law enforcement had taught Dempsey to recognize the techniques criminals used to cover their tracks. To hide evidence. To mislead investigators. She'd seen it all. Had caught perpetrators who thought they were clever. Who thought they'd outsmarted the system.

None had been as elegant as Mara. As precise. As confident.

She should arrest her. Right now. Should call Quinn over. Should explain what she suspected. Should do her job the way she'd been trained to do it for twenty years.

But she didn't move. Couldn't. The weight of everything between them held her in place. The weight of the other deaths Mara had admitted to. The weight of Dempsey's own complicity in keeping those secrets.

And something else. Something she didn't want to acknowledge even to herself. Pride. Approval almost. At how skillfully Mara had ensured she wouldn't be officially connected to this crime. At how completely she'd manipulated the system that had failed her.

Dempsey shook her head. Partly in disbelief at Mara's boldness. Partly in disgust at her own reaction to it. She turned away from the scene. From Mara. From the evidence being collected that would never lead to the real killer.

She headed back to her car. Called over her shoulder to Quinn as she passed. "I'm heading to the office. Sign me out."

Quinn nodded. Made a note on her clipboard.

Dempsey didn't look back to see if Mara watched her go. Didn't need to. Could feel the weight of those hazel eyes on her back as surely as she could feel the badge on her hip. The gun at her side. The responsibility she'd abandoned the moment she'd seen that wink and understood its meaning.

She got into her car. Started the engine. Pulled away from the curb without looking at the crime scene again. The morning sun glinted off her windshield. The birds continued their chorus from nearby trees. The world continued as if nothing had changed.

But everything had.

* * *

Dempsey sat at her desk, computer screen glowing in the fluorescent light of the bullpen. The afternoon shift brought a steady hum of activity. Phones rang. Keyboards clicked. Officers passed back and forth with coffee mugs and case files. She typed Alfred Li's name into the database. Waited for the system to respond.

The record appeared. DOB, address, driver's license number. She clicked deeper. Found what she was looking for in the court records. Case number, filing date, charges: Sexual Assault in the First Degree.

Her finger hovered over the mouse. Clicked again.

Case Status: Closed - Acquittal.

Dempsey leaned back in her chair. The springs creaked beneath her weight. The database wouldn't have details. Just the bare facts of the legal outcome. Not the story behind it. Not the reason a sexual assault case had ended in acquittal rather than conviction.

She opened a browser window. Typed "Alfred Li sexual assault" into the search bar. The first results were local news articles from eight months ago. She clicked the top link.

The headline filled her screen: "Assault Survivor 'Devastated' as Case Thrown Out on Technicality."

Dempsey scrolled down. Read quickly. Efficiently. The way she'd been trained to extract information.

"Sexual assault charges against Alfred Li were dismissed yesterday in county court after procedural errors by prosecutors led to the suppression of critical evidence. The alleged victim, speaking through her attorney, called the outcome 'a complete failure of the system.' Li, 56, walked free despite what prosecutors called 'compelling evidence' that was ultimately deemed inadmissible due to the mishandling of the case."

She continued reading. The details were sparse. The victim's name withheld. Standard practice for sexual assault cases. The evidence that had been suppressed involved Li's cell phone. The defense had successfully argued that the search warrant had been improperly executed. The judge had agreed. Everything from the phone had been thrown out.

Including text messages that, according to the prosecutor quoted in the article, "clearly demonstrated predatory intent."

Dempsey clicked back to the search results. Found another article. More details emerged. Li had been a manager at a local accounting firm. The victim had been an employee. Twenty-four years old. First job out of college. The assault had occurred during a work trip. Hotel room. After-hours drinks.

The prosecutor had gone forward. Until the evidence suppression. Then nothing. Case dismissed. Li went free. Returned to his job. His life. His freedom.

While his victim spoke through attorneys about devastation. About failure. About a system that had promised justice and delivered none.

Dempsey closed the browser window. Stared at her desktop screen. The pieces assembled themselves in her mind with the precision of years of detective work.

Alfred Li. Sexual assault case dismissed on a technicality. Shot in the back of the head in his driveway. Professional. Efficient. No witnesses except doorbell cameras that caught only shadows.

And Mara. At the scene with her camera. Documenting the evidence. Correcting her own sloppy mistake. Clever.

Dempsey wiped her face with her hand. Felt the dampness of sweat on her palm. Leaned her head back and stared at the ceiling tiles. The fluorescent light made her eyes ache.

Mara had done it again. Had become judge, jury, and executioner for someone who had escaped the legal system's justice.

And had manipulated the crime scene afterward. Had realized she'd left evidence behind. Her footprint in the soft soil beside the driveway. Evidence that could connect her to the scene before police arrived. Before she returned in her official capacity as crime scene photographer.

So she'd created a cover story. Had "accidentally" stepped in the exact same spot during the official documentation. Had ensured her print would be cataloged, documented, and then dismissed as belonging to the photographer, not the killer.

Had winked at Dempsey afterward. Confident. Unafraid. Certain of her lover's complicity.

And Dempsey had let her walk away. Again. Had said nothing to Quinn. Nothing to Franco. Nothing to any of the professionals working the scene who might have questioned why a crime scene photographer had stepped onto the grass when standard procedure required staying on paved surfaces precisely to avoid contaminating potential evidence.

Dempsey's phone buzzed on her desk. Text message. She didn't need to look to know who it was from. Knew it would be Mara. Asking about dinner. About plans for the evening. About whether Dempsey wanted wine or beer with whatever meal was being prepared in the kitchen that had become their shared space.

She let the phone buzz. Didn't pick it up. Couldn't bring herself to read the message. To respond as if nothing had changed. As if she hadn't just confirmed that the woman she was sleeping with, the woman who had said "I love you," had executed another person that morning.

A person who, by all evidence, had committed a terrible crime and escaped punishment. A person who had hurt someone vulnerable and walked away free.

The kind of person Dempsey had spent her career trying to put behind bars. The kind of case that had always left her frustrated when the system failed. When technicalities outweighed justice. When procedure protected the guilty.

The kind of case that had made her doubt the system she'd sworn to uphold. That had made her wonder if there wasn't another way. A more direct path to justice when the official channels failed.

The path Mara had chosen.

Dempsey looked back at her computer screen. At Alfred Li's record. At the case that had ended in acquittal rather than justice. At the evidence of a system that sometimes protected the wrong people for the right reasons.

And knew with absolute certainty that Mara had killed him. Had put a bullet in his head for his crimes. Had manipulated the crime scene afterward to hide her involvement.

And knew with equal certainty that she, Detective Callisto Dempsey, twenty-year veteran of the police force, upholder of law and order, would do nothing about it.

Nothing at all.

Chapter 27

Dempsey sat in the living room. One lamp on. The rest of the apartment in shadow. She held a glass of wine she hadn't sipped. Just waited. Her service weapon lay on the coffee table. Not a threat. Just a reminder of who she was. Who she had been.

The key turned in the lock at 10:37 PM. The door opened. Closed. Soft footsteps in the entryway. Mara's voice called out, "Callisto?"

Dempsey didn't answer. Kept her eyes on the glass in her hand.

Mara appeared in the doorway. Coat still on. Purse over her shoulder. Her smile dropped when she saw Dempsey's face. Saw the gun on the table. The untouched wine. The single lamp.

"What's wrong?" Mara didn't move further into the room.

"Are you kidding me?" Dempsey looked up. Met Mara's eyes directly.

"Did something happen at work?" Mara took a step forward. Stopped when Dempsey's expression hardened.

"You killed him, didn't you?" Dempsey set the glass down beside her weapon. The sound seemed louder than it should have been.

"Killed who?" Mara's head tilted. Playful. Almost amused.

"Alfred Li."

Mara stood still for three long seconds. Then she removed her coat. Hung it on the back of a chair. Set her purse on the side table. Ordinary movements performed with deliberate care. She turned back to Dempsey.

"You'll never be able to prove it." Not a denial. Not an admission either.

Dempsey stood. Hands at her sides. "This can't go on."

"Of course it can." Mara moved to refrigerator. Poured a tall glass of orange juice. No pulp. She took a sip. Didn't flinch at the burn. "It will."

"No." Dempsey shook her head once. "I can't keep doing this. Can't keep looking the other way."

"Looking the other way?" Mara smiled over the rim of her glass. "Is that what you've been doing?"

"You know what I mean."

"I'm not saying I killed anyone." Mara took another sip. Her eyes never left Dempsey's face. "But Li's case was dismissed on a technicality. We both know he was guilty."

"That's not the point."

"It's exactly the point." Mara walked to the couch. Sat down where Dempsey had been. Crossed her legs. Comfortable. At home. "The system failed. Again."

"This is a country of laws." Dempsey remained standing. Created distance between them. Needed it to think clearly. "The rule of law matters."

Mara laughed. A short, sharp sound without humor. "Ask the President about that."

"What's that supposed to mean?"

"It means powerful men break laws every day and walk free." Mara set her glass down beside Dempsey's abandoned wine. "While their victims watch them go on with their lives."

"So you appoint yourself judge and executioner?" Dempsey's voice sharpened. "Decide who deserves to live or die based on what? Your moral compass?"

"Someone has to." Mara's voice softened. "When the system fails repeatedly."

"That's not how this works."

"Isn't it?" Mara leaned forward. Elbows on knees. "Callisto, when a guilty man walks free because of paperwork errors, what message does that send? That justice is a game of procedures, not morality."

Dempsey said nothing. Had no ready answer.

"When people see the system fail them repeatedly, they stop believing in it." Mara continued. Her voice steady. Reasonable. "The legal system loses its moral authority to punish anyone."

She gestured to herself, an open-handed movement that encompassed her body, her presence, her existence in Dempsey's living room. "That's when we find other solutions."

The words hung between them. Plain. Direct. Unavoidable. We.

Mara watched her face. Missed nothing. "You know I'm right."

"No." Dempsey shook her head again. Harder this time. "I know you're dangerous."

"To who?" Mara smiled. The kind that transformed her face. That made her look like someone who hadn't killed at least five people. "Not to you. Never to you."

"To the law." Dempsey took a step back. Put more distance between them. "To everything I've spent my life upholding."

"The same law that let Li walk free?" Mara's voice hardened. "That let Tapani continue to attack women? That failed me when I was raped in that alley?"

Dempsey flinched. They rarely spoke directly about Mara's assault. About the night that had started all of this. About the justice system's failure that had set Mara on her current path.

"The system isn't perfect." Dempsey's voice was quieter now. "But it's all we have."

"No." Mara shook her head. "It's all you have. I found another way."

They stared at each other across the room. Across the moral chasm that separated them. A detective and a vigilante. Lover and killer. The contradiction that had become Dempsey's life.

"What if you get it wrong?" Dempsey asked. The question that had haunted her for weeks. "What if one of your victims is innocent?"

"I don't get it wrong." Mara's certainty was absolute. Terrifying in its conviction. "I'm more thorough than any court. More careful than any jury."

"You can't know that." Dempsey's hand went to her face. Rubbed her eyes. Suddenly exhausted. "Nobody can be that sure."

"I am." Mara stood. Moved toward Dempsey slowly. Giving her time to retreat if she wanted to. She didn't. "I've never been more sure of anything in my life."

She stopped a foot away. Close enough that Dempsey could smell her perfume. The jasmine scent that now permeated their shared bedroom. That lingered on pillowcases and towels. That had become as familiar as Dempsey's own soap.

"Think about it, Callisto." Mara's voice softened. Almost tender now. "How many case files have you read where the killer had prior charges? Where the system had a chance to stop them and failed?"

The question hit with precision. With accuracy. With the same care Mara took with her camera. With her murders.

Dempsey had no answer. Had read hundreds of those files. Had thought those exact thoughts. Had wondered how many lives might have been saved if someone had acted sooner. Had intervened before the violence escalated. Before more victims fell.

"You're trying to justify murder." Dempsey's voice was barely above a whisper.

"I'm explaining necessity." Mara reached out. Her fingers touched Dempsey's wrist. Barely a touch. Enough to make her pulse jump. "I'm not asking you to help me. Just to understand."

Dempsey pulled her wrist away. Needed distance from Mara's touch. From the electric connection that still sparked between them despite everything. Despite the bodies. Despite the lies. Despite the moral compromise that threatened to swallow Dempsey whole.

"What you're doing is wrong." She said it firmly. Definitively. The way she'd say it to any other killer.

Mara just smiled. Sad now. Almost pitying. "Then why haven't you arrested me yet?"

The "why" landed like a fist to Dempsey's sternum. She couldn't breathe for a moment. Why. Mara had pulled her into it. No, that wasn't right. She'd walked into it herself, eyes open. The moment she'd seen that wink at Li's crime scene and said nothing. The moment she'd let Mara leave the warehouse after confessing to Tapani's murder. She was already part of it. Complicit.

"You don't have to say anything." Mara's voice was soft. Understanding. "I know it's complicated."

Complicated. Such a small word for such a massive ethical collapse. For twenty years of certainty crumbling in weeks.

Dempsey moved to the window. Looked down at the street below. A couple walked arm in arm under the streetlight. Normal people living normal lives. Not harboring killers in their beds. Not weighing the lives of rapists against the sanctity of the law.

How many case files had she read where the killer had prior charges? Almost always escalating into murder. The familiar pattern. The predictable trajectory. Domestic abuser becomes murderer. Sexual predator becomes killer. Each step documented in court records. In police reports. In the system that was supposed to protect people.

How many times had she thought, if only someone had stopped him the first time?

"He didn't deserve to die." Dempsey said it without turning around. Said it to the window glass. To her own reflection there. To the detective she'd once been.

"Neither did his victim deserve what he did to her." Mara hadn't moved closer. Gave Dempsey the space she needed. "What he would have done to others."

Dempsey closed her eyes. Saw case files spread across her desk. Photographs of bodies. Transcripts of testimony. Evidence of patterns that repeated because intervention came too late. Or not at all.

She'd always believed the system worked if you worked hard enough. If you gathered enough evidence. If you interviewed enough witnesses. If you built an airtight case that no defense attorney could dismantle.

But Alfred Li proved it didn't. His case had been solid. The evidence compelling. The victim credible. And still he'd walked free because someone executed a search warrant incorrectly. Because procedure mattered more than truth.

Because the system protected its own rules at the expense of those it was designed to serve.

"Callisto." Mara's voice was closer now. She'd moved a few steps toward the window. Not touching. Still giving space. "I know what you're thinking."

"No, you don't." Dempsey opened her eyes. Watched a car pass on the street below. Headlights illuminating the empty sidewalk.

"You're thinking about all the cases that went wrong." Mara took another step closer. "All the guilty who walked free. All the victims who never got justice."

Dempsey didn't respond. Didn't need to. The accuracy of Mara's assessment made words unnecessary.

"You're thinking I might be right." Mara was close enough now that Dempsey could feel her warmth. "That sometimes the system needs help."

Dempsey turned from the window. Faced Mara directly. Saw the certainty in her eyes. The absolute conviction that what she was doing was necessary. Was right. Was justified.

"What you're doing is murder." Dempsey kept her voice steady. Professional. "Not justice."

"This is justice. This just isn't the law." Mara hadn't flinched from the accusation.

Dempsey had no response. She moved past Mara. Walked to the coffee table where her untouched wine still sat. Picked it up. The glass was room temperature now. Like evidence left too long at a scene.

"I can't be part of this." Dempsey walked to the kitchen. Poured the wine down the drain. Watched the red liquid swirl away. Like blood at a scene. Like evidence being destroyed. "I can't keep looking the other way."

Mara followed her to the kitchen doorway. Leaned against the frame. "What are you going to do?"

The question hung between them. Simple. Direct. The kind Dempsey had asked hundreds of suspects. The kind that demanded truth as an answer.

"I don't know." Dempsey set the empty glass in the sink. The admission cost her. Made her voice rough. "I don't know what I'm going to do."

Mara nodded. Accepted this. The uncertainty. The possibility. The danger.

"Whatever you decide," she said, "I love you. That hasn't changed."

The words twisted in Dempsey's chest. Made it hard to breathe again. Made her want to cross the kitchen. To take Mara in her arms. To pretend none of this was happening. That they were just two women in love. Not a detective and a vigilante. Not law and outlaw.

But they couldn't go back. Couldn't untangle what they'd become.

"I need some air." Dempsey moved past Mara in the doorway. Their arms brushed. The contact burned through her jacket sleeve. "I'm going for a walk."

"I'll come with you." Mara turned, ready to follow.

"No." Dempsey's voice was sharper than she'd intended. She softened it. "I need to be alone. To think."

Mara stopped. Nodded once. Understanding in her eyes. Acceptance. "Be careful out there."

Such an ordinary caution. The kind lovers exchanged every day. As if they were normal. As if one of them hadn't killed at least five people. As if the other wasn't sworn to uphold the law that had been broken.

Dempsey didn't respond. Grabbed her coat from the rack by the door. Didn't look back as she left the apartment. As she closed the door behind her. As she walked to the stairwell instead of waiting for the elevator.

Needed movement. Needed distance. Needed space to think beyond the pull of Mara's presence. Beyond the certainty in Mara's eyes. Beyond the love that had compromised everything Dempsey had once believed.

She took the stairs two at a time. Like leaving a crime scene. Like pursuing a suspect. Like running from something she couldn't outpace.

Herself.

Dempsey walked under yellow streetlights. Light, dark, light, dark. A rhythm that matched nothing inside her. Cold air burned her lungs. She hadn't grabbed gloves. Hadn't thought about anything except getting out. Getting away from Mara's certainty. From her own doubt. From the apartment that held both their lives now, tangled beyond separation.

The street was quiet. A few cars passed. Their headlights swept over her, then disappeared. A couple emerged from an apartment building ahead, laughing. They turned the opposite direction. Didn't see her.

Just three days until Christmas. Store windows held displays of fake snow and red ribbons. A wreath hung on nearly every door she passed. The holiday decorations seemed obscene against her thoughts. Against the knowledge that Alfred Li lay in the morgue with a bullet in his skull. That Mara had put it there. That Dempsey had seen the evidence and Mara had explained it away.

She passed a coffee shop closed for the night. Her reflection appeared briefly in the dark window. A stranger looked back. Not the detective who had built a career on procedure and evidence. Not the woman who had gone home to empty rooms for twenty years. Someone new. Someone unrecognizable.

A homicide cop who lived with a murderer. Who loved a murderer.

The contradiction made her head pound. Made her steps falter momentarily. She kept walking. One foot in front of the other. The simple mechanics of movement when nothing else made sense.

Mara would not stop. Dempsey knew this with absolute certainty. The conviction in Mara's eyes. The righteous anger beneath her calm demeanor. The precision of her kills. All pointed to someone who believed completely in what she was doing. Who saw it as necessary. As justified. As right.

But Dempsey had to stop her. Somehow. Had to find a way to end this before more bodies appeared. Before more evidence pointed to Mara. Before Hussain or someone else put the pieces together and did what Dempsey couldn't bring herself to do.

A dog barked in the distance. Sharp. Urgent. Then quiet again. Dempsey tucked her hands into her pockets. The night air had turned her fingers numb. Like the rest of her. Numb to what she'd become. To what she was allowing to continue.

She turned at the next corner. No destination in mind. Just movement. Just distance.

How would she ever explain this to Chief Brandt? The thought appeared from nowhere. Made her almost laugh at the absurdity. As if she could walk into Brandt's office and explain that her beloved niece was a serial killer. That the chief's sister's daughter had murdered at least five people. That Dempsey had known for weeks and said nothing.

It sounded insane even in the silence of her own mind. Would sound worse said aloud. Would destroy more than just Mara if the truth came out. Would destroy Brandt too.

Would tear apart the department. Would expose the chief's own blind spot for the niece she'd helped get hired as a crime scene photographer.

The very position that gave Mara access to crime scenes. To evidence. To the tools she needed to hide her tracks.

Ahead, a traffic light turned green. No cars were in sight to respond to its permission. Just an automated system continuing its cycle. Giving direction that no one needed. Following procedure that served no immediate purpose.

Like the justice system that had failed Li's victim. That had failed Mara. That had failed all the women whose attackers walked free on technicalities. On procedural errors. On the fine points of law that had nothing to do with guilt or innocence.

Solving homicides had been Dempsey's life. The thing that kept her breathing when nothing else seemed worth the effort. The purpose that got her out of bed each morning. That made the empty apartment bearable. That gave meaning to years of solitude.

And yet she now had a case that would tear her in two if she gathered enough evidence to arrest Mara. If she did the job she'd sworn to do. The job that had defined her for two decades.

She stopped at a crosswalk. Waited for the signal though no traffic approached from either direction. Habit. Training. Procedure. The things she'd built her life around before Mara had broken all the rules.

No one had loved her before Mara. The truth of it sat in her chest like stone. Cold. Heavy. Undeniable.

No one would love her after.

The crosswalk signal changed. Dempsey didn't move. Stood at the corner while the white walking figure blinked. Turned to a flashing hand. Counted down the seconds. Ten. Nine. Eight.

Like the countdown to her own decision. To what she would do with what she knew. With who Mara was. With what they had become together.

The signal turned red again. Still she didn't move. Just stood on the corner. Looked around at the empty streets. The dark windows. The spaces between streetlights where shadows pooled.

No one was there. No one saw her. No one waited for her to return to the apartment. To Mara. To the impossible choice between love and duty.

She was completely alone.

Chapter 28

Dempsey stepped off the elevator at 8:17 AM. Her shoulders ached. She hadn't slept. The walk last night had taken her six miles through empty streets before she'd returned to find Mara asleep on the couch. They hadn't spoken. Just existed in the same space like strangers. Morning came too soon.

The bullpen hummed with Monday energy. Phones ringing. Keyboards clicking. Conversations overlapping into white noise. She headed for the break room instead of her desk. Small act of delay. Small rebellion against routine.

The refrigerator was packed. Tupperware containers stacked like evidence boxes. Yogurts lined up for identification. She shoved aside a soda can labeled "Polla" and made space for her lunch. Corned beef on rye wrapped in wax paper. Not Mara's careful folds. Her own clumsy attempt this morning while Mara showered.

Dempsey reached for a clean mug. Department-issue. White ceramic with a chip on the rim. She poured coffee that had been sitting too long. The liquid steamed but smelled burned. She took a sip. Tasted like crap. Didn't matter.

She walked back through the bullpen. Coffee in hand. Lunch stored away. Small steps toward normalcy when nothing felt normal.

Knight looked up as she passed his desk. Nodded once. No comment. No joke. The new boundary between them holding firm. She nodded back. Kept walking.

Her desk was as she liked it. Case files stacked in her locked drawer. Computer screen dark. Service weapon locked in the top drawer. She sat down. Pressed the power button. Waited for the machine to boot. Pulled out her files.

The Li case file sat on top of her stack. She opened it. Crime scene photos spilled out. Alfred Li face down on his driveway. Blood pooled beneath his head. The exit wound visible in the back of his skull. Professional. Clean. Mara's work.

She flipped through witness statements. The neighbor who found the body. The wife who wasn't home. The coworkers who spoke of a quiet man who kept to himself. Nothing useful. Nothing that would lead to Mara.

Nothing except Dempsey's determination.

The bullpen fell silent suddenly. Conversations stopped mid-sentence. Phones still rang but no one answered. Dempsey looked up.

Chief Brandt stood in the doorway. Uniform pressed. Back straight. Face composed in professional neutrality. The room's attention fixed on her like a spotlight.

"Morning." Brandt's voice carried without shouting. Authority in every syllable. "I have an announcement."

Chairs creaked as detectives shifted. Paper rustled as reports were set down. Screens glowed abandoned as all eyes turned to the chief.

"Detective Hussain has been transferred to Property Crimes Unit." Brandt's voice remained steady. "Effective immediately."

The silence deepened. Became something physical. Something with weight and presence. Dempsey's hand tightened on her pen. Her breath caught for a moment before she forced it steady.

Hussain transferred. The detective who had been connecting victims. Who had shown Dempsey the book about witnesses. Who had found something significant yesterday that made him smile. Gone now. Relegated to stolen bicycles and shoplifting cases.

"His open cases will be transferred across the squad." Brandt continued. "You'll receive assignments shortly." She looked around the room. Missed nothing. "Any questions?"

No one spoke. No one moved. The chief nodded once. Turned. Left. The sound of her heels on the tile floor faded down the hallway.

The room exhaled. Conversations resumed. Hushed at first. Then louder. Theories blossomed in every corner. Disciplinary action. Personal request. Major screw-up. Each more unlikely than the last.

"Bet he pissed off someone important." Greene's voice carried from two desks over. "Dude always thought he was smarter than everyone else."

Knight shrugged. Kept typing. "Not our business."

Computers dinged across the room. Email notifications arriving simultaneously like digital dominoes. Assignment spreadsheets. Case transfers. The redistribution of Hussain's work among those who remained.

Dempsey's computer chimed with the others. She clicked the notification. Scanned the attachment. One case assigned to her. Jane Doe found in the East River. Female. Young. No identification. Hussain had been working it for a week. Now it was hers.

She closed the email. Returned to Li's file. To blood spatter analysis and trajectory reports. To witness statements that led nowhere. To evidence that would never point to Mara.

Hussain had been Dempsey's problem. The detective connecting dots. Building a case. Finding patterns that led to Mara. Now he was gone. Transferred without warning or explanation. The threat neutralized without Dempsey lifting a finger. Without bloodshed.

She turned a page in Li's file. Studied the autopsy report. Caliber of the bullet. Angle of entry. Exit wound dimensions. All consistent with a professional hit.

But Hussain wouldn't see that connection now. Wouldn't build that case. Wouldn't threaten what Dempsey and Mara had become. The relief of this realization settled in her chest. She had become her only threat now. Unwelcome. Uncomfortable. Undeniable.

The next page held Li's court records. The sexual assault case. The dismissed charges. The technicality that had set him free. The failure of justice that Mara had corrected with a single bullet.

Dempsey closed the file. Pushed it aside. Pulled the Jane Doe case from her inbox instead. New victim. New evidence. New direction for her thoughts.

Away from Mara. Away from Li. Away from Hussain's sudden transfer that felt too convenient. Too perfectly timed. Too much like Mara's other careful manipulations.

She opened the Jane Doe file. Started reading. Forced her mind to focus on this victim. This case. This job that had defined her for twenty years before Mara had redefined everything.

The bullpen noise faded to background. Just Dempsey and the file now. Just evidence and procedure. Just the familiar rhythm of investigation that had carried her through two decades of emptiness.

That wasn't empty anymore. That held Mara now. For better or worse.

* * *

Dempsey unlocked her apartment at 7:03 PM. Soft piano notes drifted through the apartment. Not her music. Mara's. The smell of jasmine lingered in the entryway. The scent that now marked home.

Mara sat on the couch. Book open in her lap. Reading lamp casting a circle of light that caught in her hair. She looked up. Smiled. The kind that transformed her face. The kind that still made Dempsey's breath catch despite everything she knew.

"You're home." Mara closed her book. Set it on the coffee table. Stood in one fluid movement.

She crossed the room. Wrapped her arms around Dempsey's neck. Pressed her lips to Dempsey's. The kiss was soft. Familiar now. The taste of mint toothpaste. The pressure of bodies fitting together like puzzle pieces.

"Long day?" Mara stepped back. Hands still on Dempsey's shoulders.

Dempsey nodded. Shrugged out of her coat. Hung it on the rack by the door. Normal movements. Ordinary routine. Nothing to suggest she'd spent last night walking six miles trying to reconcile her duty with her heart. To suggest Hussain was demoted and his open cases, ignored cases, reassigned.

"Wine?" Mara moved toward the kitchen.

"Please."

Dempsey kicked off her shoes. Left them by the door. Followed Mara into the kitchen where a bottle was already open. Two glasses waiting.

Mara poured. The liquid caught the light. Deep red. Almost black. She handed a glass to Dempsey. Their fingers brushed during the exchange. The contact still electric after everything. Still real.

"Merlot." Dempsey took a sip. Let the tannins coat her tongue. Swallowed. "Good choice."

Mara smiled again. Softer this time. Private. "Thought you might need it today."

Dempsey didn't answer. Just took another sip. Let the wine warm her from inside. Chase away the chill that had settled in her bones since seeing the evidence of what Mara had done. Since Hussain's transfer that felt too convenient. Too neat. Like one of Mara's crime scenes.

"Hungry?" Mara leaned against the counter. Wine glass in hand. Casual. At ease.

"Starving." Dempsey sat at the kitchen table. Let her body collapse into the chair. Realized it was true. Hadn't eaten since morning. The sandwich in the breakroom fridge forgotten during the day's chaos.

"Burgers or steak?" Mara opened the refrigerator. Light spilled across the tile floor. Illuminated her legs in soft glow. "I have both."

Dempsey raised her wine glass. Studied the color through the light. "Steak would go great with this."

"Steak it is." Mara pulled a package from the refrigerator. Set it on the counter. Moved with the efficient precision she brought to everything. Crime scenes. Murder. Dinner preparation.

Dempsey watched her work. The deliberate movements. The careful attention. The routine they'd established in the weeks since Mara had entered her life. Since everything had changed.

Mara pulled a cast iron pan from the cupboard. Set it on the stove. Turned the burner to high. The blue flame licked the bottom of the pan. She unwrapped the steaks. Season them with salt. Pepper. Nothing else.

"So." Mara's voice was casual. Conversational. "Anything interesting happen at work today?"

Dempsey's hand tightened on the wine glass.

"Hussain was transferred." Dempsey kept her voice neutral. Watched Mara's face for reaction. For the tell that would reveal foreknowledge. Involvement.

"Really?" Mara glanced up from the pan. Eyebrows raised. "Where to?"

"Property Crimes Unit."

"That's a downgrade, right?" Mara turned back to the steaks. Laid them in the hot pan. The sizzle filled the kitchen. The smell of cooking meat replaced the jasmine scent.

"Significant one." Dempsey took another sip of wine. Studied Mara over the rim of her glass. "Effective immediately."

Mara nodded. Didn't look up from the pan. "What happens to his cases?"

"Reassigned." Dempsey set down her glass. Watched the ripples settle in the wine. "Email notifications throughout the office. He had a lot open."

"Which ones did you get?" Mara flipped the steaks. The fresh side sizzled against hot iron. She moved to the refrigerator again. Pulled out potatoes. A head of cauliflower. Set them on the cutting board.

"Just one. A Jane Doe." Dempsey's eyes followed Mara's movements. The precise knife work as she cut the cauliflower into florets. The efficient peeling of potatoes. "Found in the East River last week."

"That's good." Mara smiled. The knife moved in her hand with practiced ease. "Hussain's real cases need to be solved."

Dempsey's hand froze halfway to her wine glass.

"What do you mean?" The question came out sharper than she intended. The detective voice. The interrogation voice. Not the lover asking for clarification.

Mara looked up from the cutting board. Her knife stilled mid-slice. Her eyes met Dempsey's across the kitchen. Nothing in her expression changed. No guilt. No concern. Just calm assessment of the question and what lay beneath it.

The moment stretched between them. Seconds marked by the sizzle of steaks. The soft piano notes from the living room. The sound of their breathing in the quiet apartment.

"What do you mean?" Dempsey repeated. Softer this time. Less accusation. More invitation to explain. To justify. To reveal what she knew about Hussain's sudden departure from Homicide.

Mara set down the knife. Wiped her hands on a dish towel. Reached for her own wine glass. Took a sip before answering.

"I just meant dead bodies shouldn't stay unclaimed." Her voice was steady. Reasonable. "Jane Does deserve names."

The explanation hung in the air. Plausible. Innocent. Nothing in it to suggest deeper knowledge.

And yet.

Dempsey saw something in Mara's eyes. A flicker. There and gone. The kind of micro-expression she'd been trained to spot in interrogation rooms. The tell that said there was more beneath the surface. More that wasn't being said.

Dempsey set her wine glass down hard. Red liquid sloshed over the rim. Stained the tablecloth. She ignored it. "Did you have something to do with Hussain's transfer?" The question landed between them like a thrown gauntlet.

Mara looked up from the cutting board. Her knife paused mid-slice through cauliflower. "What makes you ask that?"

"'Real cases.'" Dempsey quoted the words back. "You knew what he was working on. What he was connecting."

Mara laughed. The sound light. Dismissive. She resumed chopping. "I have no influence over my aunt's staffing decisions."

"That's not an answer."

"If Brandt transferred Hussain, it was on Brandt." Mara scraped cauliflower florets into a bowl. Started on the potatoes. The knife moved with practiced precision. "Not me."

"So it's just coincidence?" Dempsey stood. Took a step toward the counter. "The detective building a case against you gets transferred the day after he finds something significant?"

"You don't know what he found, or which case it was about. Neither do I. Coincidences happen." Mara's eyes remained on the cutting board. "Even to detectives."

Dempsey watched her work. The sure hands. The steady movements. Nothing in her posture suggesting guilt or concern. Just the calm efficiency she brought to everything. Cooking. Photography. Murder.

"I don't believe in coincidences." Dempsey's voice hardened. "Not like this one."

Mara looked up. Met her eyes directly. "You sound like you wish he was still investigating me."

"I want the truth." Dempsey held her gaze. "Did you do something to make this happen?"

Mara set down the knife. Wiped her hands on a dish towel. Something shifted in her expression. A calculation made. A decision reached.

"I'm sure the photos of the trunk of Hussain's car helped." She said it casually. Like commenting on the weather. On traffic. On any ordinary fact.

Dempsey's shoulders had begun to relax at Mara's initial denial. Now they tensed again. The muscles in her neck tightened. "What photos?"

"The ones I took last Friday night." Mara turned to check the steaks. Flipped them. Adjusted the heat. "I followed him home."

"You followed him?" The words came out sharp. Edged with disbelief.

"He opened the trunk to get his briefcase." Mara continued as if Dempsey hadn't spoken. "I was across the street with my telephoto lens. Just curious what he was working on."

The image formed in Dempsey's mind. Mara in shadows. Camera raised. Doing what she did best. Documenting. Observing. Creating evidence.

"When I checked the images later, I noticed something interesting." Mara moved to the refrigerator. Took out butter. Herbs. "A police evidence box in his trunk."

Dempsey's breath caught. Evidence removed from the precinct. A clear violation of the chain of custody. Of department policy. Of the procedures that protected cases against tampering claims.

"You're sure?" Her detective mind engaged automatically. Looking for confirmation. For certainty before judgment.

"Hard to mistake those boxes." Mara melted butter in a small pan. Added herbs. The smell mixed with the cooking steak. "White cardboard. Evidence tape. Case number on the side."

Dempsey moved to the counter. Leaned against it. Let it support her weight while her mind processed the implications. "He took evidence home?"

"Appears that way." Mara nodded. Stirred the butter sauce. "I sent the image anonymously to Brandt that night."

"You what?" The question came out too loud. Too sharp.

"Online complaint form." Mara didn't flinch at Dempsey's tone. "From a library computer across town. The photo was clear enough to read the case number on the box."

Dempsey pushed off from the counter. Paced three steps. Turned. Paced back. "You had Brandt ambush him."

"I didn't have Brandt do anything." Mara's voice remained calm. Reasonable. "I just provided information. What she did with it was her choice."

"She must have checked the evidence log." Dempsey's detective mind continued piecing it together. "Confronted him when he came in this morning."

"And caught him red-handed with evidence that should have been secured." Mara finished for her. "Yes. That would be my guess."

The scenario played out in Dempsey's mind. Brandt waiting for Hussain. The evidence box still in his car. The confrontation. The immediate transfer that removed him from Homicide. From the witness deaths. From Mara's trail.

"Jesus Christ." Dempsey ran a hand through her hair. The weight of what Mara had done settled on her shoulders. In her chest. "Do you understand what you've done?"

"Exposed a detective who violated procedure? One whose damned cases would be tossed on a technicality?" Mara raised an eyebrow. "I thought that was a good thing in your world."

"You manipulated the system." Dempsey's voice hardened again. "Again. To protect yourself."

"To protect us." Mara corrected. She drained the potatoes. Added them to a serving dish. "Hussain was getting too close."

"So you got him fired?"

"Transferred." Mara's distinction was precise. "Not fired. He still has a job. Still has a pension. Still has his reputation."

"For now." Dempsey's hands curled into fists at her sides. "Until Brandt decides to file formal charges for evidence tampering."

"That's between them." Mara shrugged. Added the herb butter to the potatoes. Stirred them gently. "Nothing to do with me. But if she does, *everything* he was working on gets called into question."

"Everything to do with you." Dempsey's voice rose again. "You orchestrated this whole thing."

"He brought it on himself." Mara looked up. Her eyes steady on Dempsey's face. "He broke the rules. Not me."

The statement hung between them. The contradiction at its core exposed in the kitchen's bright light. Mara who had killed at least five people claiming moral high ground over rule-breaking. Mara who had manipulated crime scenes judging a detective for evidence tampering.

Mara who had created justice by breaking laws criticizing Hussain for procedural violations.

"This has to stop." Dempsey's voice was quieter now. Almost a whisper. "The killings. The manipulation. The lies."

"You want to go back to the way it was before?" Mara asked. Her voice soft. Almost sad. "When the system failed victims and monsters walked free? When cops took evidence and thought it wouldn't affect the trial? When you were alone every night in this apartment? When no one loved you?"

Each question hit like a physical blow. Precise. Targeted. Dempsey had no answer for any of them. Couldn't find words for the contradiction that had become her life. The compromise that had become her moral center.

Mara turned back to the stove. Removed the steaks from the pan. Set them on a plate to rest. Added the cauliflower to boiling water.

"Dinner will be ready in five minutes." She said it without looking back at Dempsey. Without acknowledging the weight of what had just passed between them. The line that had been crossed. "Table's already set."

The normality of the statement after everything that had been revealed made Dempsey's head spin. Made her question her own reality. Made her wonder which was the dream: the detective who had followed procedure for twenty years, or the woman who now stood in a kitchen with a killer she couldn't bring herself to arrest.

Mara moved around the kitchen. Plated the steaks. Arranged the potatoes beside them. Drained the cauliflower and added it to the plates. The domestic routine continued as if they hadn't just discussed evidence tampering. Career destruction. Manipulation of the justice system.

As if everything was normal.

Nothing would ever be normal again.

Chapter 29

Dempsey squinted at her monitor. The unicorn tattoo on Jane Doe's forearm was distinctive. Purple and blue ink. Celtic knot work in the mane. She clicked through another tattoo shop's online gallery. Nothing matched. She rubbed her eyes. Four hours and twenty-six websites in, she was no closer to identifying the body pulled from the East River last week.

Outside, wind rattled the precinct windows. The storm had rolled in around noon. Heavy snow piling up against glass and concrete. Lightning flashed, illuminating the bullpen in brief, stark bursts. Snow and lightning was not as rare as everyone pretended it was. The weather had driven most detectives indoors. Bodies at desks instead of out on cases. The room hummed with voices and ringing phones. The constant percussion of keyboards.

Dempsey clicked to the next website. Another gallery of tattoo designs. Another dead end.

The door to the bullpen swung open. Cool hallway air rushed in. Harris shook snow from his coat. Drops spattered across the floor. He nodded to a uniform near the door, headed to his desk. His shoes squeaked against the tile.

Dempsey watched him settle in. He hung his wet coat on his chair back. Pulled a handkerchief from his pocket. Dried his face. His hair. The back of his neck. Routine movements performed with military precision. The detective who never seemed affected by anything, not even a storm that had half the department complaining.

She looked back at her monitor. The Jane Doe case file sat open beside her keyboard. Thin. Almost empty. Basic facts but no real investigation. Time of death estimated between 72-96 hours before discovery. No ID. No fingerprint match in the system. No missing persons report matching her description. Just the body of a young woman. Early twenties. Brown hair. The unicorn tattoo her only distinctive feature.

The wind howled louder.

Dempsey closed the browser window. Stood. Walked to Harris's desk. He looked up as she approached.

"Harris." She stopped at the edge of his desk. Kept her voice professional. Neutral.

"Dempsey." He leaned back in his chair. The springs creaked beneath his weight. "Need something?"

"Did you get one of Hussain's cases?" She kept her hands at her sides. Forced them to stay relaxed.

"Yeah." He nodded. "Drug dealer shot execution-style. Found in a field out by the county line." He pulled a thin file from his desk drawer. Held it up. "Bare bones. Not much here."

"Same with mine." Dempsey gestured back toward her desk. "Jane Doe found in the East River. Almost no investigative work done."

"Not surprised." Harris set the file down. Tapped it once with his index finger. "Hussain seemed distracted lately. Like he was only focused on one case."

"The Tapani murder." Dempsey said it without inflection. Just a statement of fact. Her heart beat a fraction faster beneath her blouse.

"Yeah." Harris nodded again. "Got obsessed with it. Forgot to do his job properly on everything else."

Thunder cracked outside. Close enough to rattle the windows. The overhead lights flickered once.

"That case." Dempsey kept her voice casual. Uninterested. Just shop talk between colleagues.

Harris leaned forward. Dropped his voice lower. "He really lost it on that one. Came to me with some wild theory." He glanced around the bullpen. No one paying attention. Everyone focused on their own work. Their own conversations. "Said he thought the chief's niece might have done it."

"Mara?" Dempsey's eyes widened before she could control her reaction. Felt blood drain from her face. The floor seemed to tilt beneath her feet. She sat.

Harris nodded. Watched her face too closely. "Crazy, right? Said he had a theory connecting her to witnesses who died after the shooting."

Dempsey's hand went to the edge of Harris's desk. Steadied herself. The room's noise receded behind the sudden roaring in her ears. Her mind raced ahead. If Hussain had told Harris, who else knew? How far had his theory spread before his transfer?

"You okay?" Harris's eyes narrowed. "You look like you've seen a ghost."

"Did he have any proof?" The question slipped out before Dempsey could stop herself. She pulled her hand from Harris's desk. Straightened her spine. "No, forget I asked. You shouldn't tell me any of this."

Harris waved her concern away. "Look, Dempsey. Everyone knows you and Mara have something going on."

The statement hit her like a physical blow. She kept her face neutral through sheer force of will. The precinct suddenly felt too loud. Too exposed. Too many eyes potentially watching this conversation.

"But I can tell you," Harris continued, "there was nothing to his theory. Nothing solid. You've got nothing to worry about."

Dempsey didn't feel reassured. Her mouth had gone dry. She swallowed hard. "What made him suspect her?"

Harris leaned closer. Lowered his voice further. "Everyone knows Mara was one of Tapani's victims. Rape case went nowhere because he was a CI. Protected by the DA's office."

"I didn't know that was common knowledge." The truth felt hollow in her mouth. "Not at the time."

"That's because you never talk to anybody." Harris's eyes softened. Almost pitying. "Just sit at your desk and work work work. You miss all the department scuttlebutt."

Wind roared outside. Another detective cursed as his coffee sloshed over the rim of his mug. The storm's rage had the room on edge. Made everything feel more intense. More immediate.

"I still don't understand." Dempsey leaned back. Needed distance from the conversation. From Harris's knowing gaze. From the implications of what he was saying.

Harris glanced around the room again. The bullpen's noise provided cover for their conversation. He motioned her closer. "Mara's a sweet girl. Everyone likes her. She's worked with hundreds of cops over the years. Maybe thousands. Not a single person has a bad word to say about her."

Dempsey nodded. Waited for him to continue. Her heart still hammered against her ribs.

"My opinion?" Harris's voice dropped to where Dempsey could barely hear him over the hum of conversation and the storm's assault on the windows. "When the charges against Tapani were dropped, there wasn't a cop in the entire department who didn't want that man dead for what he did to our little Mara."

The realization hit Dempsey with the force of the storm that seethed outside. The department didn't suspect Mara. They suspected one of their own.

"I think a cop killed Tapani." Harris said it plainly. Directly. No hint of shock or outrage in his voice. Just cold assessment. "Would explain why none of the witnesses would talk. They knew."

Dempsey stood perfectly still. The noise of the bullpen receded again. The storm outside faded to background. The floor beneath her feet stabilized. Harris's words replayed in her mind. A cop killed Tapani. Not Mara. A cop.

She had no response. No words. The theory—wrong as it was—offered a layer of protection she hadn't anticipated. Hadn't considered. The department's attention directed away from Mara. Toward their own ranks. A blue wall of silence protecting the wrong killer.

"Look, I know you're pretty naïve, Dempsey." Harris's voice held no judgment. Just statement of fact. "But sometimes cops do bad things."

The storm outside intensified. Sleet now, clawing at the windows like it wanted in. The lights flickered again. Longer this time. For three seconds, the bullpen dimmed before power stabilized.

Harris leaned closer. Dropped his voice to barely above a whisper. "I could name the four cops who beat the crap out of DA Franklin."

Dempsey blinked. District Attorney Franklin had been hospitalized six months ago. Mugging outside a restaurant. Random street crime according to the official report. She'd never questioned it. Had no reason to.

"Why would they attack Franklin?" She matched Harris's volume. Found herself leaning toward him. Their heads now inches apart across his desk.

"Because Franklin arranged Tapani's status as a CI." Harris's eyes never left her face. Watching for reactions. Reading her understanding. "He kept the case from going to prosecution. Everyone blamed him for what happened to Mara."

The implications piled up in Dempsey's mind. Cops beating a district attorney. A department conspiracy of silence. A murdered confidential informant whose case would never be solved. All connected to Mara.

To her Mara.

"I'll deny everything if Internal Affairs asks." Harris's eyes hardened. The warning unmistakable beneath his casual tone. "Just like everyone else will."

Dempsey understood suddenly. This wasn't just conversation. Wasn't just department gossip. Harris was warning her. The unwritten boundaries she shouldn't cross.

She drew her finger across her lips. The universal sign for silence. For understanding. For compliance.

Harris nodded. Satisfied. "The Tapani murder case will stay cold. That's how it needs to be."

"What about the witnesses who died?" The question escaped before she could reconsider. She needed to know how much Harris knew. How much the department suspected.

Harris straightened. Put another inch between them. His posture shifted from conspirator to superior. "None of those deaths were declared homicides. So leave it at that."

It wasn't an answer. Was instruction. Was boundary-setting.

"Hussain thought he was smarter than that." Harris continued. "Went digging where he shouldn't. But if it was a cop who killed Tapani—" He paused. Emphasized his next words carefully. "And I'm not saying it was for sure. But if it was, any investigation is going to stir up shit that should be left undisturbed."

The rain beat a staccato rhythm against the windows. The bullpen noise continued unabated around them. Detectives talking. Phones ringing. Keyboards clicking. Life continuing while Dempsey's understanding of her world realigned.

"Just a theory, of course." Harris picked up a pen. Clicked it once. The conversation over. The warning delivered.

Dempsey nodded. Stood straighter. Stepped back from Harris's desk. "Of course."

She walked back to her workstation. Each step measured. Deliberate. Her mind racing with the implications of what Harris had told her. What he believed. What the department believed. What she believed.

They thought a cop had killed Tapani in vigilante justice for Mara. They'd created a blue wall of silence to protect that unknown officer. Had even attacked a district attorney for enabling Tapani's crimes.

And all of it—every assumption, every action, every conspiracy—unknowingly protected Mara. Protected the real killer. Protected Dempsey's lover.

She sat at her desk. Pulled the Jane Doe file closer. Stared at the crime scene photos without seeing them. The unicorn tattoo blurred before her eyes.

The storm outside continued its assault, tearing through the sky, throwing itself against the windows. The precinct's power flickered once more but held.

Dempsey picked up her pen. Made a note in the margin of the file. The ordinary action of a detective doing her job. No outward sign of the revelation echoing through her mind.

No cop had killed Tapani. But the entire department was prepared to protect whoever had. Were already protecting them without knowing it. Were already protecting Mara. And by extension, protecting Dempsey herself.

A system built on procedure and evidence and rules had created its own shadow justice. Had drawn a circle of protection around exactly the wrong person for exactly the right reasons.

She turned the page in the Jane Doe file. Started reviewing the autopsy report again. Back to work. Back to routine. The detective who followed procedure. Who solved cases. Who now understood far more about the department she'd worked in for twenty years than she had yesterday.

The irony wasn't lost on her. Mara had been right all along. Sometimes the system failed. And sometimes, without meaning to, it created its own justice in the shadows.

Chapter 30

Dempsey stepped into her apartment. Water dripped from her hair, her clothes, her skin. A puddle formed around her boots. The sleet outside had turned vicious, hurling itself sideways at anything in its path. She pushed the door closed against the wind. The lock clicked. The storm outside continued to rage.

"Jesus, Callisto." Mara appeared in the hallway. Her eyes widened at the sight. "You're soaked through."

"Storm's worse than they said." Dempsey stood motionless. Didn't want to track water further into the apartment. "Much worse."

Mara disappeared down the hall. Returned with a large bath towel. "Hold still." She draped it over Dempsey's head, began gently patting her face dry. "Ever heard of an umbrella?"

"Wouldn't have helped." Dempsey let Mara work the towel through her short hair. "It's coming from every direction."

Mara's hands were gentle against her scalp. Methodical. The same precision she brought to everything. Dempsey closed her eyes. Let herself be cared for. Something still unfamiliar after decades of self-reliance.

"You look like you swam home." Mara moved the towel to Dempsey's shoulders, neck.

Dempsey shrugged out of her jacket. Water had soaked through to her shirt. The fabric clung to her skin. Cold. Heavy. Her pants were wet to mid-thigh. Her socks squelched inside her boots.

"This is going to take forever to dry." Mara held the jacket at arm's length. Water dripped from the sleeve onto the floor. "You need to get out of these clothes before you catch pneumonia."

"I've been wet before." Dempsey stood still as Mara set the jacket aside. Felt Mara's fingers at her collar. Unbuttoning her shirt with care. One button. Then the next. Exacting. Loving.

Mara slid the wet shirt from Dempsey's shoulders. "Arms." Dempsey lifted them. Let Mara pull the fabric away from her skin. Shivered as the apartment air hit damp flesh.

"Belt." Mara's voice was soft. Not quite a command. Not quite a question. Dempsey unfastened it herself. Let Mara's fingers take over at the button of her pants. The zipper. Felt the wet fabric slide down her legs. Stepped out of the puddle they made on the floor.

"Boots." Mara crouched. Untied the laces. Held each boot steady as Dempsey lifted her feet. One. Then the other.

"Socks too." Mara peeled them off. "Panties. Bra. They are soaked."

She gathered the wet clothes. Kissed Dempsey's belly. Stood. "I'll hang these in the bathroom." She moved past Dempsey, down the hall. The apartment was warm against Dempsey's damp skin. The contrast almost painful after hours in the storm.

"There's a robe in the bedroom." Mara called back.

Dempsey moved down the hallway in her underwear. Cold against her skin now. No longer part of her. Something to be discarded like the rest of the wet clothes. She entered the bedroom. Found the white robe on the back of the door. Soft terry cloth. The texture almost shocking against her sensitized skin.

She passed the mirror. Stopped. Stared. The woman who looked back was someone she barely recognized. Same deep-set brown eyes. Same steel-gray hair. Same angular face that had spent decades in fluorescent-lit precinct rooms.

But something had changed. The set of her shoulders. The angle of her jaw. The steadiness in her eyes. This wasn't the detective who had followed procedure for twenty years without questioning. Who had maintained professional distance at all costs.

This was someone new.

She tied the robe around her waist. Turned away from the mirror. Away from the questions in her own eyes. Away from the woman she was still becoming. Still learning to recognize.

In the kitchen, Mara stood, pouring two glasses of red wine. The bottle's label caught the light. Something expensive. Something Dempsey wouldn't have bought for herself before Mara. Before all of this.

"Feel better?" Mara handed her a glass. The wine was deep red. Almost black in the lamp light.

"Much." Dempsey took a sip. Let the warmth spread through her chest. Chased away the lingering chill. "Thanks."

"How was work?" Mara settled onto the couch. Tucked one leg beneath her. The casual pose of someone completely at home. In this apartment. In this relationship. In this impossible situation.

"Good, actually." Dempsey sat beside her. The cushion dipped under their combined weight. "Identified my Jane Doe."

"The one from the river?" Mara's interest seemed genuine. Professional curiosity about a case she hadn't worked. "The girl with the unicorn tattoo?"

Dempsey nodded. "Ellen Martinez. Twenty-four." She took another sip of wine. "Realized she had some dental work. I called every dentist within twenty miles of her last known address. Found one who remembered the tattoo. Got the production warrant for her dental records."

"That's fantastic." Mara's smile was warm. Genuine. Her free hand found Dempsey's shoulder. Squeezed gently. "Of course you did. That's what you do."

"What I try to do." Dempsey felt pride uncurl in her chest. The simple satisfaction of giving a victim back her name. Her identity. The first step toward justice.

"No." Mara's voice was firm. Her eyes held Dempsey's. "It's what you do. You find people who others have forgotten. You speak for those who can't speak for themselves." Her fingers traced a pattern on Dempsey's shoulder. Through the robe. "It's who you are."

The praise settled in Dempsey's chest. Warm. Unfamiliar. She'd gone decades without hearing it from anyone. Without believing it herself.

Dempsey swirled the wine in her glass. The silence between them had stretched comfortable, easy. But something else pressed against her thoughts. The conversation with Harris. The department's misunderstanding about Tapani. She needed to tell Mara.

"I talked to Harris today." Dempsey kept her voice neutral. Professional. "About the Tapani murder case."

Mara's body tensed against hers. Subtle but unmistakable. The muscles in her shoulders went rigid. Her breathing paused for a fraction of a second. Her fingers tightened on the stem of her wine glass.

Dempsey waited. Watched. Felt Mara's silent calculation through the slight shift in her posture.

"What about it?" Mara's voice remained casual. Only someone who knew her body as intimately as Dempsey would have detected the tension.

"Harris thinks a cop killed Tapani." Dempsey delivered the words matter-of-factly. Watched Mara's face for reaction.

The change was immediate. Mara laughed. A genuine sound that started deep in her chest. Her body relaxed against Dempsey's side. The tension dissolved from her shoulders, her neck, her fingers.

"A cop?" Mara shook her head. Still smiling. "That's his big theory?"

"He's convinced of it." Dempsey took another sip of wine. "Said Hussain was building that case before his transfer. That's why Hussain was looking into all those accidental deaths."

Mara settled deeper into the couch. Her weight pressed comfortable against Dempsey's side. "So much for Hussain's brilliant detective work."

"There's more." Dempsey set her glass on the coffee table. Turned to face Mara directly. "Apparently Harris thinks everyone loves you so much that any one of a couple thousand cops would have killed Tapani for what he did to you."

Mara's smile faltered. Her eyes widened. "Everyone loves me?"

"His words, not mine." Dempsey watched the surprise register on Mara's face. "He called you 'our little Mara.' Said there wasn't a cop in the department who didn't want Tapani dead after what he did to you."

"I had no idea." Mara's voice was softer now. Almost wondering.

Dempsey reached for her wine again. "And cops protect their own. You're family to them. Chief's niece. Department photographer. The girl who gives great testimony in court. Photos that gets convictions."

Mara's lips curved upward. Pride mixed with something else. Something Dempsey couldn't quite name.

"There's even a rumor that the D.A. who withdrew the charges against Tapani was beaten up by cops." Dempsey watched Mara's face carefully. "Remember District Attorney Franklin? That 'mugging' six months ago?"

"Franklin?" Mara's eyebrows rose. "The one who ended up in the hospital?"

Dempsey nodded. "Harris claims he knows the four cops who did it. Said Franklin arranged Tapani's status as a CI. Protected him from prosecution."

"Jesus." Mara leaned forward. Picked up her wine glass. "They beat up a district attorney?"

"Apparently." Dempsey shrugged. "Harris seemed proud of it. Said he'd deny everything if Internal Affairs asked. Like everyone else would."

Mara stared at her wine for a long moment. Then her lips curved into a smile. She raised her glass in a toast. "Here's to me. Untouchable."

The smugness in her voice made Dempsey's jaw tighten. Made something cold settle in her chest.

"The Fates will have something to say about your hubris." Dempsey didn't touch her glass to Mara's. "The minute you think you're untouchable, you're vulnerable. You'll become prone to leaving tracks."

Mara's smile faded. The wine glass hovered in the air between them. Her eyes met Dempsey's. Something passed between them. A challenge. A warning. A reminder of what they both knew but rarely spoke aloud.

Then Mara's smile returned. Softer now. Less certainty in her eyes.

"You're right." She lowered her glass. Recalibrated. Raised it again with a different light in her eyes. "Here's to being seen only by those who matter."

This time Dempsey lifted her glass. Let it touch Mara's with a soft clink. The sound seemed loud in the quiet apartment. Outside, the storm continued to batter the windows. Inside, another kind of storm brewed between them. Unspoken. Dangerous.

They drank. Eyes locked over the rims of their glasses. Dempsey saw the calculation in Mara's gaze. The recalibration. The adjustment to this new information. Saw her processing what it meant that an entire police department thought they were protecting her without knowing what she'd actually done.

Mara set her glass down first. Her fingers trailed along Dempsey's knee. Up her thigh. Stopped at the tie of her robe. A diversion. A return to the physical connection that sometimes allowed them to forget the moral chasm between them.

Dempsey caught her wrist. Held it gently but firmly. "Don't."

Mara's eyes widened. Question in them. Challenge.

"We need to talk about what this means." Dempsey released Mara's wrist. "The department thinks they're protecting a cop who killed Tapani. What happens when they realize there's no cop to protect? That it was you all along?"

"They won't." Mara's confidence remained unshaken. "They've already decided what happened. People see what they expect to see."

"Until they don't." Dempsey leaned back. Created a few inches of space between them. "Until someone looks harder. Connects different dots."

"Like you did." Mara nodded. Acknowledgment without fear. "But you're different, Callisto. You see things others miss. It's why I love you."

The declaration sat between them. Simple. Direct. Dangerous in its truth. In what it revealed about both of them.

Dempsey reached for her wine again. Took a long swallow. Said nothing. Let the storm outside fill the silence between them.

The storm settled into softer rhythms. No longer battering the windows with sleet, just steady rain that pattered against glass. The wind had died down. Occasional thunder rumbled in the distance, moving away. They'd been quiet for a long time, just sitting, just drinking, just existing in the space between confessions.

Dempsey set her empty glass on the coffee table. The wine had left her tongue slightly numb. Her thoughts clear but heavy.

"I need you to understand something." She turned to face Mara fully. Needed her to see the truth in her face. "For as much as I care about you. Love you. Worship you." Each phrase dropped like a stone between them. "If...when one of your cases came across my desk, I will work to solve it. Work to arrest you and put you away forever."

She said it without anger. Without judgment. Just fact, laid bare between them like evidence.

Mara placed her glass beside Dempsey's. Turned her body until they faced each other completely. Her expression remained calm. Untroubled by the declaration.

"I would expect nothing less from you, Callisto." Her voice carried no fear. No surprise. "After all, you are a huntress."

Callisto, the nymph-turned-bear, the hunter, the constellation that guided travelers north. Deliberate. Meaningful.

Dempsey laughed. The sound surprised her. Genuine amusement cutting through the weight of the moment. "Be careful or I will end up hunting you." She reached out. Tucked a strand of hair behind Mara's ear. "And you know how the hunt will end."

"Do I?" Mara's eyes held hers. Something like challenge in them. Something like invitation.

Dempsey's attention shifted to the window. The change outside registered suddenly. "Look. The storm is finally breaking." She nodded toward the glass, where rain still fell, but lighter now. Sporadic. "The stars are coming out."

Through breaks in the clouds, pinpricks of light emerged. Distant. Cold. Eternal witnesses to everything that happened below.

Mara followed her gaze for a moment. Then shifted her attention back to Dempsey. In one fluid movement, she rose from her spot on the couch. Stepped forward. Lowered herself onto Dempsey's lap, knees on either side of Dempsey's thighs.

Her weight settled solid. Real. Her hands framed Dempsey's face. Held her there. Forced eye contact that neither could escape.

Mara leaned forward. Pressed her lips to Dempsey's with deliberate intent. Not gentle. Not asking. Taking. Claiming. Her mouth tasted of wine and certainty.

Dempsey's hands went to Mara's waist automatically. Held her there. Responded to the kiss with equal force. Equal intent. Their bodies knew this dance now. Had memorized the steps. The rhythm. The pressure that turned thoughts to static.

Then Dempsey pulled back. Broke the connection. Needed to see more than feel.

She looked at Mara. Really looked. Tried to memorize this: Mara's face in lamplight, wine-flushed and fearless, still believing she could outrun the sky itself. The confident curve of her mouth. The certainty in her eyes. The arch of her brow that revealed intelligence not even murder had dimmed. Beautiful. Dangerous. Ephemeral in ways Mara herself couldn't yet see.

Dempsey knew how this story ended. Had read enough case files, tracked enough killers, seen enough patterns to recognize the inevitable conclusion. No one escaped forever. Not even someone as careful as Mara. Not even someone protected by an entire police department that didn't know what they were protecting.

"I will catch you," Dempsey said. Not a threat. A promise. A prophecy she saw written in the air between them.

Mara's expression didn't change. No fear. No anger. Just that same absolute conviction that had carried her through multiple murders without remorse. Without hesitation. Without detection.

Her thumb traced along Callisto's jawline. Slow. Deliberate. Memorizing in her own way. "If it's going to be anyone, it should be you."

The question wasn't just about capture. About arrest. About the inevitable end of what they'd built together. It was deeper. About seeing. About knowing. About the recognition that had existed between them from the first moment.

Outside, the clouds continued to part. Stars emerged in greater numbers now. The ancient patterns taking shape above the city. Above their heads. Above this room where hunter and hunted sat entwined.

Callisto. The bear. The huntress. The one who never failed to find her target.

Mara. The photographer. The killer. The one who believed she would never be caught.

Their story was already written in the stars now appearing through the breaking storm. Had been written long before either of them were born. Would continue long after both were gone.

Hunter and prey. Locked in eternal chase across the night sky.

The rain stopped completely. The storm passed. The stars watched in silent witness.

Dempsey's hands remained at Mara's waist. Mara's thumb still traced the line of Dempsey's jaw.

Neither looked away.

Neither surrendered.

Neither moved to end what had only just begun.

www.ingramcontent.com/pod-product-compliance
Lightning Source LLC
Chambersburg PA
CBHW070936010826
48976CB00028B/2098